Praise for Ma...

TIME R

featuring psycholog...

"*Time Release* sizzles, cooks and singes! It's a whipcord thriller full of deftly drawn characters, intrigue and taut action . . . This is a spellbindingly accomplished first novel. Martin J. Smith may well become a thriller force to be reckoned with."

—JAMES ELLROY, author of
American Tabloid and *My Dark Places*

"A good creepy debut thriller."

—PUBLISHERS WEEKLY

"[Proves] that fear isn't a tamper-resistant emotion."

—LOS ANGELES TIMES

"Unexpected plot twists and breathless tension combine for a suspenseful ride that doesn't let up."

—KANSAS CITY STAR

"*Time Release* is a fast, smart read and one fine thriller."

—ROBERT FERRIGNO, author of *Horse Latitudes*,
Dead Man's Dance and *Dead Silent*

"*Time Release* delivers a powerful dose of suspense as memory expert Jim Christensen confronts the guarded secrets of the mind and darkest corners of the soul . . ."

—Pulitzer Prize–winner MARY PAT FLAHERTY,
The Washington Post

"Smith's first novel has an intoxicating quality . . . Like the works of John Grisham . . . the plot drives relentlessly forward."

—OC METRO (Orange County, CA)

continued . . .

"A rapid-fire thriller . . . As *Time Release* barrels toward its conclusion, its message is clear: The world is not a safe place, and neither is the mind."

—CHRISTOPHER WEIR,
Metro Newspapers (San Jose, CA)

"A thunderbolt read . . . a good rip-roaring scare . . . hard to put down."

—*PITTSBURGH* magazine

"Tense, well-crafted."

—*SEATTLE* magazine

"It's got a breakneck pace, a truly unsettling atmosphere and some very clever turns of story. What I liked best, though, were the fully realized characters, each with his or her own urgent plans. A terrific first novel from a writer with loads of promise."

—T. JEFFERSON PARKER, author of *Laguna Heat*,
Little Saigon and *The Triggerman's Dance*

"Intense . . . a compulsive page-turner you won't want to put down."

—*BIRMINGHAM NEWS*

"*Time Release* is a taut, enthralling thriller that will keep you guessing to the end. In Jim Christensen, Martin Smith has created a smart and sensitive hero for the Nineties."

—Pulitzer Prize–winner EDWARD HUMES, author of
Mississippi Mud and *No Matter How Loud I Shout*

"Former reporter Martin J. Smith makes a thrilling fiction debut . . . *Time Release* is earning high marks for its plausibility and finesse."

—*THE ORANGE COUNTY REGISTER*

SHADOW IMAGE

MARTIN J. SMITH

JOVE BOOKS, NEW YORK

SHADOW IMAGE

A Jove Book / published by arrangement with
the author

PRINTING HISTORY
Jove edition / June 1998

The Penguin Putnam Inc. World Wide Web site address is
http://www.penguinputnam.com

ISBN: 0-515-12286-6

A JOVE BOOK®
Jove Books are published by The Berkley Publishing Group,
a member of Penguin Putnam Inc.,
200 Madison Avenue, New York, New York 10016.
JOVE and the "J" design are trademarks belonging to
Jove Publications, Inc.

PRINTED IN THE UNITED STATES OF AMERICA

10 9 8 7 6 5 4 3 2 1

for JUDY

Acknowledgments

There is much I don't understand about the artistic expression of emotions and memories in Alzheimer's patients, but what I do know I owe mostly to Selly Jenny of the Alzheimer's Association of Orange County, California, and her remarkable "Memories in the Making" project.

Tricia Winklosky of the John Douglas French Center for Alzheimer's Disease in Los Alamitos, California, was kind enough to let me impose on her art class and patiently answered all my questions. Other staff members at the French Center provided me with useful background on the nature of the disease and its predictable stages.

Pamela L. Hess, a clinical evaluator at the Harmarville Rehabilitation Center near Pittsburgh, shared her time and expertise about that wonderful facility. Her assistance was critical in helping me imagine the fictional Harmony Brain Research Center.

Many other people helped in less specific but critically important ways.

Susan Ginsburg of Writers House is more than just my agent; she is my mentor. The value of her contributions to this book, and to my education in general, is immeasurable.

I'll forever be grateful to Berkley Senior Editor Hillary Cige for her early faith in my stories and her insights into their execution, as well as to the many enthusiastic booksellers who have put my work into the hands of readers. Copyeditor Amy J. Schneider was remarkably thorough, and her work is much appreciated.

The members of my monthly writing groups have been typically generous with their time, support, and advice.

Sherley Uhl taught me much about western Pennsylvania politics during my years as a reporter there, and he did it with unparalleled style. Patrick J. Kiger, another original, first showed me how much fun it can be to break the rules imposed by journalism professors and newspaper editors. I salute them both.

Publisher Ruth Ko and the staff of *Orange Coast* magazine tolerated my constant fatigue as I wrote this book and its predecessor, and I suspect that, at times, my dual careers may have increased their burden. If that's the case, they have my sincere apologies. And if the climactic scenes of this book succeed, they do so thanks to the early suggestions of former *Orange Coast* managing editor Allison Joyce.

As grateful as I am to those people, none of them bore the additional burden of hearing my alarm clock go off each day at 4 A.M. or, two hours later, finding me dazed at the computer in my smelly blue bathrobe. That grim duty fell to my beloved wife, Judy, to whom I dedicate this book, and to our children, Lanie and Parker. They are my strength.

M. J. S.

The gentle curve of faded denim ended at the base of Brenna's spine, leaving a wedge of ivory skin between the waistband of her jeans and the bottom of her ragged white oxford shirt. She'd tied her shirttail Elly May Clampett–style in front for practical reasons, to keep it from falling over her hands as she worked, but the effect was driving Christensen insane. She was all business there on her knees with her coppery hair pulled into a long ponytail, bent deep into the gap where their upstairs toilet had once stood. But if he leaned just so against the bathroom counter, he could follow the glistening trail left by the single bead of sweat that disappeared into the enticing valley just above her backmost belt loop. It was a late-April Sunday and the sap was rising. He felt nineteen.

"Smell the rot?" She sat up suddenly, caught him staring. "God knows how long the seal's been bad. I just can't figure why it didn't come through to the dining-room ceiling."

"Nice plumber's butt."

A playful smile. "Hand me the work light."

She took the light, tested it, waved it into the damp and

mysterious place. "The water's going somewhere, that's the problem. Follow it and we'll find the next big nightmare."

The house was a money pit; the inspector told them so even before they closed. "It's a hundred and twenty years old and been vacant all winter," he'd said. "You're a long way from wallpapering." But they both loved Shadyside, not for its too-chic Walnut Street trendoids or lively club scene or white-wine liberals, but because its public schools were among Pittsburgh's best. When after five years they'd decided to merge their households and families, they agreed without a second thought on where to do it, though Brenna discouraged his impulse to sanction the union with a marriage certificate. And, with some work, the house at 732 Howe could be a stunner—three stories of whitewashed clapboard, hardwood floors, and leaded-glass windows. They were fully aware of the rotted subfloors, clanging radiators, and Rube Goldberg–style basement furnace that frightened him beyond words.

"Did we buy too fast?" He nudged a piece of peeled linoleum with a toe of his Nikes. "There was that other place in Squirrel Hill."

"Wrong ward. I'll need a Shadyside pedigree to get serious about city politics." She grabbed a hammer and brought it down on one of the floor's crossbeams, crushing it like brittle cardboard. "Relax."

He spied himself in the bathroom mirror. Behind the rimless eyeglasses, close-cropped gray beard, and smug detachment of a tenured 45-year-old academician, he saw the reflection of a classic beta male emasculated by an alpha mate. Brenna handled home repairs and power tools with aplomb. Relaxed? Definitely not.

"Where'd you learn how to do this stuff?" he said.

"I'm going to have to carve all this out and reinforce the floor before we can even think about replacing the toilet seal," she said. "The kids'll just have to use our bathroom for a while. That's the least of it, though. That water's going somewhere."

"What you can't see won't hurt you. I truly believe that."

She sat back on her heels. "Odd opinion for a psychologist, Jim. Malpractice insurance paid up?" She plugged her saber saw into an extension cord, tested it, then offered a sly smile. "Maybe you can expand that little home-repair theory into a self-help book: *Embracing Denial* or *Chickenshit for the Soul.* Something like that. You're on sabbatical. You've got time."

The saw's blade chewed through the crossbeam with a chattering howl. A plume of sawdust rose from the gap in the floor. "That other one has to come out, too," Brenna said, pausing just long enough to extract the rotted two-by-four. The saw howled again. "Oh baby," she shouted, "we've got big problems."

A matter of perspective, he thought. If they had survived the last five years together, they could survive a rotted subfloor and a renegade water leak. He wasn't naïve enough to think all their problems were behind them—he didn't consider himself capable of naïveté after watching his late wife, Molly, wither—but he was buoyed these days by a genuine sense of renewal, a well-placed hope for their reconstituted family. His older daughter, Melissa, was finally okay, lonely during her second month in France as an American Field Service scholar, but past the corrosive anger that had followed Molly's death. At eighteen, Melissa was calling him Daddy again, which could be jarring. With her soft, round face, almond eyes, and loose curtain of black hair, she was a photocopy of Molly at the age he first met her. His younger daughter, Annie, on the other hand, had inherited his face, a face that even at eight was all angles and boyish vitality. Put the beard and glasses on her and she could probably counsel his clients without them noticing his absence. Much to his relief, Annie still tolerated Brenna's seven-year-old son, Taylor, who remained appropriately worshipful and did everything she said.

Brenna stood up and brushed off the front of her shirt.

She caught him staring again, but this time he didn't retreat. He gathered her into his arms and kissed her damp forehead. She smelled of sweat and sawdust and Eternity, and the combination was irresistible. She pushed him away, gently.

"We need to properly christen the new house," he said. "It's in the mortgage agreement. It's the law."

She smiled. "That afternoon before the final walk-through doesn't count?"

They'd hung their clothes on a back bedroom doorknob and sent their real-estate agent out for coffee. He smiled, too. "We hadn't officially closed."

Christensen knew a hair-trigger place on her neck just below her left ear where her pulse was warm and every nerve in her flawless body seemed to converge, so he kissed her there. She started to push him away, then melted against him, saying, "Mmmm." It sounded like victory.

"Your whiskers scratch," she said. "I'm a mess."

"Absolutely." He ran a finger down her spine to her tailbone, traced a circle around each dimple there.

"We have too much to do."

"What time do the kids get back from Simone's birthday party?"

She said, "Two-thirty," but her eyes were closed, offering no resistance as he untied the knotted front of her shirt. He worked the buttons from the bottom up. "The bed's not set up yet," she said, even as she maneuvered him through the bathroom door, down the hall and toward the mattress on the hardwood floor of their new bedroom. "It's not proper."

"We'll just keep trying until we get it right, then."

She pulled him down into a long, slow kiss. Her hips started to move with his, a gentle exchange of pressure at first but about as erotic as he could stand. She worked a hand down his back, leading him in their dance. She usually did, and it didn't intimidate him like it used to. He laid open her shirt and fumbled with the front clasp of her cream-colored bra until she intervened. She shrugged out of the clothes and he lost himself in her scent and softness until they could no longer ignore the ringing telephone on the floor.

"The machine'll pick up," she whispered, her lips against his ear.

His electronic greeting began after the third ring. At the tinny beep, Terry Flaherty's rich baritone filled the room. "Brenna? I know you're there."

Christensen kissed her eyelids, but he could tell that her attention had shifted to her law partner's voice.

"Call me as soon as you get this," Flaherty said, his voice without any trace of his puckish Irish humor. "I'm at the office."

Christensen tried the spot on her neck again, but Brenna was rigid. "Sorry," she said, looking him in the eye, briefly, before rolling away and reaching for the phone.

"Wait, Terry," she said, over the answering-machine feedback. "I'm here."

Brenna's devotion to work no longer surprised him. She was talented, obsessive, and ambitious, perfect for Pittsburgh politics, and her reputation these days as Pittsburgh's best criminal-defense attorney went unchallenged by even the most predatory of the Grant Street crowd. Building that reputation had cost her a marriage, and she struggled with that. But not often, and never for very long. She slid her bra back on as she listened and buttoned her shirt all the way up, probably not even aware she was doing so.

"He asked specifically for me?" She listened a while longer, shaking her head from time to time, once raising an eyebrow at him. "When did it happen?"

He'd heard variations of her end of the conversation a dozen times, whenever she took on a new case. She reached for her purse on the floor near the bedroom window and rummaged until she found her trusty Mont Blanc. With nothing to write on, she grabbed one of the kids' abandoned coloring books and tore out a page.

"How badly injured?" Scribbling now. "Has anyone talked to the investigators?" She listened for a full minute, motionless. "Well, what kind of evidence are we talking about? Who's the witness?"

Brenna looked at her watch. "Fox Chapel's not far, but it'll take me an hour by the time I get cleaned up." She scratched an address beside Cinderella's pumpkin coach and folded the coloring book page in half. "Good thing you were in the office, Terry. Thanks."

Brenna was out of her shirt again in seconds, tossing it onto the mattress with a gesture as sharp as it was preoccupied. Then she was headed into the functional bathroom, her only comment a muttered "Unbelievable." Christensen heard the pipes groan as she turned on the water in the shower. He followed, less disappointed now than amused by her intensity.

"So I should make other plans for the next hour, then?" he said over the shower's unsteady roar. He traced the lines of her body on the plastic shower curtain. Brenna suddenly peeled it back, catching him with his finger on the shadow of her breast. Her hair was already soaked.

"Oh baby, I'm sorry," she said. "I'm going to need a rain check."

"Hey, no problem," he said. "Maybe we can use these testicles for bookends."

Brenna laughed, but then closed the curtain and lathered her head.

"What's so unbelievable?"

"Three guesses who called the office looking for me this morning," she said.

"Harrison Ford?"

"Nope."

"The Nobel committee?"

"One more."

"Bill Gates?"

She laughed again. "Close."

He waited while she rinsed her hair. "Bill Clinton?"

"Closer." She peeked out. "Ford Underhill."

His jaw actually dropped.

Brenna nodded. "He told Terry I came highly recommended."

"The state's next governor needs a criminal-defense attorney?"

"I doubt it. It's complicated. Just between us, all right?"

"Of course." Christensen adjusted the bottom of the curtain to redirect a stream of water back into the tub as Brenna soaped her shoulders and arms.

"His mother tried to commit suicide yesterday."

"Floss? You're kidding."

Brenna stopped her furious lathering and peeked around the curtain again. "You sound like you know her."

"I do, sort of. From Harmony. She's been a day patient there off and on since she was diagnosed."

"Alzheimer's?"

"About six years ago. The Underhills are the center's biggest benefactor, and she's the signature patient. They named the new auditorium after her."

"Don't tell me she's one of the people in your memory study."

"I've been following an art class. She's one of about fourteen people in it." He shook his head. "Suicide? Really?"

"Why do you say it like that?"

Floss Underhill was seventy, maybe more, the wife of former two-term Pennsylvania governor Vincent Underhill II. Vincent was the third-generation heir to Andrew Underhill's vast industrial fortune, as well as to the family reputation as great liberal champions. Christensen knew her as the feisty and unpretentious scourge of the Harmony art room, but he also knew she was, before Alzheimer's, the grande dame of Pittsburgh's charity fundraising scene.

"At her age, suicide tends to be a pretty rational decision," he said. "She's demented, unpredictable. Demented people aren't usually able to think through a choice like that.''

Brenna turned off the shower. He passed a towel into the cloud. She wrapped it around herself and stepped out, heading for a cardboard carton of clothes in a corner of the bedroom. She pulled out a pair of lacy white panties and stepped into them. They disappeared beneath the towel hiding hips that, at forty-six, gave only the slightest hint that she'd borne a child. He stepped in front of the window and closed the miniblind.

"You still didn't answer," he said. "Why does Ford Underhill want to talk to a criminal-defense attorney?"

He knew from The Look that some things stay between an attorney and her client. All she said was, "It's complicated."

Brenna set her briefcase on the Legend's black leather seat and slammed the rear door. Christensen waved from the porch, but he knew she was gone long before she dropped behind the wheel and bounced out of the driveway, her cellular phone already to her ear. He noticed only then that she'd managed to get his belt unbuckled. It hung limp against his leg as he opened the front door and stepped inside.

Empty houses still scared him. An irrational fear, he knew, but it had lingered now for five years. After Molly's accident, as she faded into the black hole her doctors called a "persistent vegetative state," he found he couldn't easily stay by himself in their old Highland Park house. It was Molly's house, infused with her spirit, a three-story monument to a life cut short. His memories of life there after Molly weren't good. Melissa had hated him then, hated that he'd made the decision to quietly disconnect her mother's respirator without letting her daughters be part of the decision. What he'd intended as a simple gesture of love and mercy had exploded like a grenade, and not just inside their house on Bryant Street. After J. D.

Dagnolo, the county's overbearing district attorney, floated the possibility of prosecuting him for the mercy killing, it was all over the local TV news. The issue was a guaranteed ratings boost for Dagnolo among the city's mostly Catholic electorate, and the D.A. would have milked it for years if Brenna and Grady Downing, the homicide detective assigned to the case, hadn't shut Dagnolo down. But if Melissa had resented him for ending Molly's life, she'd resented him even more once Brenna's role as his defense attorney evolved into something more personal.

When the girls were there, at least the Bryant Street house had been a burble of homework, phone calls, and dinners cobbled together from raw carrots and cottage cheese and whatever was in the cupboard; at least he wasn't alone with his thoughts about the drunken little prick who'd weaved across the center line and met Molly's car head-on; at least the report of her heart monitor didn't echo in his memory like a crow's call. But when the house was empty . . .

The front hallway of the Shadyside house was a riot of moving cartons, Brenna's stacked dining-room chairs, and the scattered pieces of a forsaken Candy Land game that had ended badly two hours earlier with Annie accusing Taylor of planting the Queen Frostine card to his advantage. The conflict was annoying at the time, but as he swept the cards into a pile and tracked the far-flung game pieces, it made him smile. Kids weren't nearly as entertaining in the moment as they could be with a few hours' distance.

The phone rang again. Christensen checked his watch. Still thirty minutes until Simone's birthday party ended.

"Hey Jim, me again." With his basso profundo voice and trace of Dublin lilt, there was never a need for Terry Flaherty to be more specific.

"Ford Underhill?"

"Wh-what?" Flaherty said.

"Brenna filled me in." Christensen waited through a long pause.

"Loose lips sink ships."

"You ethical titan. Relax. She told me who, but that's it. What's the deal?"

"We still don't know what the hell is going on, but it's so bizarre. She still around? I found some background she may need."

"Just left. You have the cell phone number." Christensen folded the Candy Land board in half and put it on the kitchen counter. "Brenna didn't tell me anything. about what happened. Really."

Flaherty laughed. "I'll leave that up to her, then. Ford Fucking Underhill. You think he pays his bills?"

It was hard not to notice the Underhill name in Pittsburgh. The family's generosity over the past century had left it on dozens of Downtown buildings, a sprawling public park in Oakland, and an urban plaza near the old Grant Hotel. In the past decade alone, thanks apparently to the generosity of former governor Vincent Underhill, the family's controlling heir, the Underhills had helped underwrite the neo-natal wing at Mount Mercy Hospital, the Harmony Brain Research Center, an overly splendid Downtown ballet theater, and one of the most convenient concourses at the city's massive new airport. Florence, Italy, had the Medicis, Pittsburgh, the Renaissance City, had the Underhills.

"The old man's kind of disappeared the last couple of years, hasn't he?" Christensen asked. "I mean, compared to Ford."

"Ford's the family's front guy now, yeah. Vincent's playing Joe Kennedy to Ford's John. But Vincent's still a player."

"Meaning?"

"That's his rep, anyway. He's out of the spotlight for decades, since he left Harrisburg, but he didn't exactly retire. Took what was left of the family fortune and diversified into retail and office development, public-works construction, all that. The family's companies built a lot of what got built in Pennsylvania during the last twenty years. Christ, they get a chunk of practically every major public contract that's awarded, so he still had a lot of friends in politics when he left office.''

Christensen absently opened the refrigerator. They'd moved a few staples from Brenna's house before unplugging her fridge the day before, but nothing snackable. And even if he felt like warming Thai takeout leftovers from last night, where was the microwave? ''What does any of that have to do with them needing a criminal-defense attorney?''

Christensen let the remark hang, hoping its weight would pull Flaherty into an explanation of what had happened to Floss Underhill.

''The Underhills are just big power brokers, is all.''

''There's a news flash. Come on, Terry. I've dealt with the wife, Floss, out at Harmony. She's a second-stage Alzheimer's patient. I'm just curious.''

The phone rustled in Christensen's ear. He imagined Flaherty shifting his bulk in his plush leather execu-chair, trying to squirm out of the conversation. ''She wandered away from her keepers and jumped into a ravine. There. Happy?''

Christensen waited until he couldn't wait anymore. ''On purpose?''

''People don't jump into ravines by accident. That's all I'll say.''

''Don't be a stiff. What else?''

''That's it. Really. There's one witness who heard something and saw something strange—enough for the cops to take him seriously. It's probably nothing, but Underhill wanted Brenna on board to help clear up the confusion. They don't want rumors floating around ten days before the primary. You know how things get crazy in politics. And at this point, the Rosemond people are desperate for anything they can use against Ford Underhill . . .'' Flaherty mumbled something and said he'd try Brenna's cell phone, then hung up.

"Later," Christensen said to the dial tone.

He checked his watch. Fifteen minutes until Annie and Taylor would be home. He wanted them home now. The house felt as big as a hangar. If he picked them up early, though, there'd be a battle about being the first to leave. Just stay busy, he thought. Find something to do. It's only fifteen minutes or so.

He and Brenna had decided the downstairs bedroom would be the office, so he moved quickly down the hall to do some unpacking. His oak desk—the one Molly had found at an auction, the one the seller claimed came from the Frick family warehouse—was shoved against one wall, its matching chair trapped in the corner by a stack of cartons containing his PC and Brenna's Power Mac. Brenna's chrome-and-glass workstation was against another, a black leather office chair overturned on top, wheels to the sky. It looked like a jet fighter's cockpit seat after an ejection. The rest of the room was strewn with boxes—files, books, some boxes inscribed MISC OFFICE in black marker. He chose one of those, peeled the packing tape from its lid, and folded back the top flaps.

One of Molly's favorite photographs stared up at him from inside, a black-and-white shot she'd taken of a tuxedoed opera fan after a Heinz Hall performance. The man was reacting to a homeless woman on Liberty Avenue. He leaned away from her outstretched hand as if she were handing him a piece of dog shit. The picture had hung for years on the wall opposite his desk in the Bryant Street house, and he'd memorized its every detail. When he had packed up the house the week before, he'd taken it down and put it into the carton with the few others that Molly had deemed worthy of display. Annie had found him sitting on the floor that day, pondering the sad squares of discolored paint where each had hung.

He flipped through the images. Molly'd worshipped Cartier-Bresson, and her own photographs showed it.

Their common thread was a sense of humor, cutting at times but always driven by compassion. Molly had loved life's everyday ironies, the little dramas played out at bus stops and on fire escapes where the subjects were unguarded and their emotions were open to anyone who cared to see. He'd watched her work once, from a distance. She moved like a hummingbird, pausing only briefly to raise her tiny Leica, capturing moments before moving again. He was certain that the opera fan and the homeless woman never knew.

Empty walls surrounded him, as did the promise of a new life with Brenna. He'd reached a crossroads, and he thought a few long moments about his choice. Then he closed the carton's flaps. A black marker and packing tape were where he'd left them in his desk's bottom left drawer. He sealed the box of photographs and uncapped the marker, writing MELISSA/ANNIE MISC on the side before taking it to the attic.

3

Fox Chapel was changing. Two generations ago, it was the kind of place where Brenna's mother had always imagined herself living, a leafy, private oasis that Pittsburgh's landed gentry called home. Before developers carved it up into buildable lots and mansions sprouted like mushrooms, it sheltered some of western Pennsylvania's grandest estates. She remembered her mother scouring each monthly issue of *Architectural Digest* for spreads or back-of-the-book ads featuring one of the original Fox Chapel homes. The magazine didn't come here to photograph faux rustic ranch houses or angular contemporaries. It came for the heavy woods and rich tapestries and unapologetic excess of people who got their money the really old-fashioned way—through inheritance.

She steered into the cool embrace of two-lane Fox Chapel Road, which bisected the community like an oaken green tunnel. The pavement was still dry despite the drizzling rain. From the main road, small side lanes led past some of the world's most carefully barbered real estate. Her mother had deserved this. Maybe it was just a surviving daughter's guilt; maybe it was the inevitable result of their bond at the end after three cruel years of finally getting to know each other. But if there was a God who kept track of dignified, stoic suffering—and God knows Claire Kennedy suffered as the cancer devoured her—surely her mother would have in the afterlife one of the original Fox Chapel estates that had eluded her in life. Brenna scanned the newer Tudor fantasies flashing past the Legend's side windows until the ringing cell phone punctured the moment.

"Me again," her partner boomed. Road noise was never a problem with Terry Flaherty. "I did an online search and made a call to get more background. You want it now?"

Brenna glanced at her watch. "I'm probably three minutes away, so give me the short version. I also just got off the phone with Ernie Cohnfelder at the *Press*. He owes me some favors, so he read me headlines from the clip file and said he'd photocopy everything they had in the paper's library. The library finally went electronic three years ago, so everything later is on a database. But it's a start."

"Anything useful?"

"At this stage everything's useful, Terry. The more recent stuff was from the society pages, mostly fundraising stuff for various charities. Through the late eighties it was the airport and Mount Mercy Hospital projects. In the early eighties it was Downtown redevelopment stuff. Everything before that is thirty-year-old coverage out of Harrisburg, and there's a ton of that, most of it positive, Ernie said. He said Vincent is tight with the whole Koberlein family, especially the cranky one who first bought the paper. Leo, I think."

Almost too late, Brenna spotted the sign for Silver Spur Road. She braked hard and turned the wheel, barely missing the abutment of an old stone bridge. As if she needed more adrenaline.

"Anything on Ford in what you've got, Ter?"

"Everything on Ford. The guy's got a publicity machine like you wouldn't believe, and I wasn't about to wade into that. Mostly just election-year crap. Some personal stuff.''

''I'd almost forgot he lost a son, a three-year-old. Ernie said there was a horseback-riding accident about three years ago. The story's in the database, not the clips, but he remembered it.''

''Jesus, Brenna, how could you forget? It's the whole subtext of that goofy Underhill campaign slogan: 'Tolerant, true, tested and ready.' ''

She imagined Flaherty, a wickedly cynical Irishman, rolling his eyes. ''That's how you tell the real pros in politics,'' she said. ''They can package any personal tragedy for public consumption. Anything else?''

''Talked to my mole down at the sheriff's department, too. Wouldn't say much, but she let slip something you should know. The crime lab's apparently involved. They showed up at the hospital to do fingernail scrapings on the old lady.''

''And?''

''No idea what they found, but they must be taking this witness or the physical evidence pretty seriously.''

Brenna slowed the car outside a wrought-iron gate, behind which a driveway curved up into the woods and disappeared. The entire front of the property was surrounded by an ancient, ivy-covered red-brick wall. She searched the pillars on each side of the gate for an address. No mailbox, either. ''I think I'm here,'' she said. ''Don't these people believe in house numbers?''

''Want me to call them back and make sure you're in the right place?''

''No, there's a buzzer and intercom thingy. If this isn't it, I'll call you. But I should get on in there. We don't want to lose this one.''

''Speak for yourself, Kennedy. We're swamped as it is. Besides, I've got no aspirations, politics-wise.''

''What's that supposed to mean?''

"I can hear the wheels turning in that ambitious head of yours."

"Right now they're just another client, Ter."

Flaherty laughed. "And Microsoft is just another software company."

"Gimme a break."

"No sucking up now."

The man waved her into a parking area to the right of the house's main entrance. With his tailored silk sports coat and white linen shirt open at the collar, he was too well dressed for hired help. Brenna took a closer look as she wheeled past him into a spot between a Range Rover and a black Thunderbird. It was the state's probable next governor, a telegenic creature with broad shoulders and a too-large head topped by TV-anchorman hair. Ford Underhill waited a respectful distance from the car as she gathered her briefcase.

"Ms. Kennedy, thank you for coming," he said as she stepped out. The somber concern in his eyes didn't stop them from straying to her legs. "May I call you Brenna?"

"Please." She extended a hand, felt a chill as he took it. He held it a beat longer than necessary.

"Very sorry about the short notice," he said. "Phil Raskin brought your name up right after all this happened late yesterday—he's a big fan, apparently—and I'm afraid it couldn't wait until Monday."

She got a lot of referrals from civil attorneys, but never from one as high-profile as Raskin. They'd met only once, and she knew little about him beyond his top rank at Raskin, Hartman, & Bailey, the city's leading civil-law firm, and his longtime role as the Underhill family's political consultant. By reputation, Raskin still approached politics as an art, not tracking-poll science, and didn't hesitate to use artistic license when needed. If that involved poll money in certain districts or an occasional hooker for a reluctant ward chairman, in more than thirty years no one had ever ratted him out. He was *that* good.

"I'll make sure to thank Mr. Raskin the next time I see him," she said.

Underhill gestured to the front door. "He's inside."

For the first time, Brenna focused on the house, a great gabled meringue of stone and timber, hardly the granite mausoleum she'd pictured as home to the bluest of western Pennsylvania's bluebloods. She imagined the *AD* headline: "Rustic elegance from the time of tycoons." But of course, these weren't the kind of people who opened their homes to shelter magazines, no matter how prestigious. Their name alone conferred position; at this level, there was no one to impress.

Brenna followed Underhill across the circular drive, stepping as he directed around an enormous pile of fresh horse shit. "My wife's bay left us a little gift," he said, smiling. "Johnnie just walked it down to the stables."

The flagstone steps were flanked by barrel-sized cast-iron pots bursting with red geraniums. The front doors were open—walnut, Brenna guessed—and they stepped onto what seemed like an acre of earth-colored paving stones that made the massive front hall seem almost intimate. When Underhill closed the doors behind them, Brenna noticed a pair of soiled paddock boots, an English saddle, and a saddle pad in a neat pile on a delicate antique chair to her right. These were true horse people, she thought, the inspiration for Ralph Lauren's mass-marketed images of the rugged rich.

"Excuse the mess," Underhill said, nodding toward the chair. "It's been a little chaotic around here since Mother's fall."

He led her across the entry toward a wall of French doors that opened onto a covered patio, where Brenna counted four people seated stiffly around a sturdy plank table. They were framed by a brilliant green lawn. It was bordered by the kind of gardens reserved only for those with a staff of full-time gardeners. The smell of spring rain was overpowering. As they stepped through the patio doors, everyone stood. The only ones Brenna recognized were Raskin and Ford Underhill's wife.

The wife was the first to reach for Brenna's hand. Her grip was strong, and from her clothes Brenna assumed she was the one who'd been out riding. She was about forty, Brenna figured, but looked years younger with her blond hair pulled back into a ponytail. When she smiled a perfect Candidate's Wife smile and cocked her head to one side, Brenna thought of Nancy Reagan. "I'm Leigh Underhill," she said, wrinkling her nose ever so slightly. She gently deflected Brenna's attention to the man to her left. "This is my father-in-law, Vincent."

The family patriarch seemed to force a smile as he extended a hand. His intense blue eyes were filled with sadness, maybe fatigue, but even at seventy-two Vincent Underhill was a striking presence. Well over six feet tall, he radiated an aura of entitlement and privilege. He was lean and in shape, with hair the color of fresh snow. It swept back off his forehead in gentle waves, and gold-framed reading glasses were perched on the end of his long, thin nose—how Jim might look in thirty years if fate was kind. His face was deeply tanned, and its lines did nothing to diminish the overall effect. They enhanced it, suggesting the wisdom of age.

"My pleasure," she said.

"No, mine." His hand was soft and warm.

"Brenna, I think you know Phil," Ford said. Raskin set down his drink. Brenna caught a whiff of good bourbon as she shook his cold, damp hand.

"We met at the Pitt law symposium last year," she said.

"Of course I remember. Thanks for coming on such short notice. Something like this, we needed someone with your background."

"Appreciate you thinking of me," she said.

"Raskin, Hartman prides itself on its breadth of civil-law experience, but something like this—"

"We wanted everybody to sit in on the meeting this

afternoon, Brenna," Ford broke in. "We want you to have all the necessary background and context to what happened with Mother. I hope you don't mind us taking that liberty."

Ford suddenly gestured to the man to Brenna's immediate right, whose hands remained clasped behind his back. "I'm sorry, I've forgotten Mr. Staggers. He handles security at my parents' house here and can fill you in on the sheriff's department activity last night and earlier today."

The man extended his hand. He wore a pinkie ring the size of a pecan, but everything else about him—from his tailored suit coat to the silk handkerchief in his breast pocket to the perfect Windsor knot of his rep tie—suggested elegance and good taste. He smiled. "Call me Alton."

As if on cue, everyone except Ford Underhill and Brenna sat down again. Ford offered Brenna one of the empty wrought-iron chairs, then took the only remaining one for himself. Before anyone could speak, an ancient black maid appeared with a crystal pitcher of iced tea and six empty glasses.

"Thank you, Lottie," Ford said. No one spoke again until she'd set the tray on the table and retreated silently through the French doors into the house. Ford poured a glass of tea and set it in front of Brenna, then poured one for his wife. Leigh ignored the china sugar bowl and opened a wallet-sized Hermés leather pouch, where she apparently carried sugar cubes for her horse. She dropped a cube into her glass and crushed it on the bottom with a long-handled spoon.

"Help yourselves," Ford said to the others, offering the pitcher. "Why don't I just start with an update on Mother?"

Ford reached across his wife's lap and patted his father's arm. "Dad just came from Mount Mercy, so this is as of two hours ago," he said. "But it's pretty good news."

Vincent Underhill's eyes shifted, focusing somewhere beneath the table.

"Mother is conscious but heavily sedated because of the injuries," Ford said. "The X-rays show a spinal fracture, but she's regained feeling in her toes. So we think we've cleared that hurdle."

Nods and smiles all around.

"Her left arm is broken just above the elbow. At her age, that's a wait-and-see. She's tough as an old shoe, so we expect it to heal okay." Ford shifted in his chair. "Brain imaging tests show no damage there other than what we know is the result of her condition. She told the sheriff's people she doesn't remember anything about what happened, but that's not surprising."

Vincent Underhill leaned forward with a sad smile. "Last night she didn't know how she ended up in the ravine," he said. "By this morning, she was talking about how Brindle balked at a seven-foot jump and threw her."

Ford seemed to sense Brenna's confusion. "Alzheimer's," he said. "Brindle was a big mare, a champion show-jumper Mother rode when she was younger. She's been dead for, what, thirty-five years, Dad?" He paused for his father's nod. "Bottom line, Brenna, we still have no idea why she did this."

Brenna scanned the faces at the table. Leigh Underhill was listening to her husband with rapt attention, the time-honored pose of a woman who has adopted her husband's ambitions as her own. The others, too, seemed attentive and concerned. Only Vincent Underhill reacted to his son's report. He twisted off his reading glasses and drew a sharp breath, then fixed his eyes on the timbered patio roof above his head.

"Forgive my lack of background," Brenna said, "but I'm not really up to speed either on what happened yesterday or on Mrs. Underhill."

Ford stared. "No, please forgive me. I wasn't sure how much information Mr.—"

"Flaherty."

"—your partner, had passed on. Yes, Mother's a late Stage Two Alzheimer's patient, more unpredictable than usual in the past few months."

"Stage Two?" Brenna said.

"There are only three stages," he said, letting the implications settle. "At this point, her short-term memory is a disaster; long-term is unreliable, at best. She still recognizes us, sometimes, but beyond that she struggles. What memories she has are sort of free-floating, without context. Nothing seems connected."

His words reminded Brenna how easily a patient's family learns the terminology of disease. Within days of her mother's ovarian cancer diagnosis, Brenna could speak with authority about cell migration and colon blockage percentages.

"At any rate, Mother had a terrible fall yesterday afternoon, into the ravine out past the back gardens. We're still trying to sort out what happened. Dad says she was with him in the house one minute, and then gone the next. He didn't think she'd go outside because of the rain, but she'd been very agitated—''

Vincent Underhill stood up suddenly. "I'm sorry. If you'll excuse me—'' He turned to go, then turned back. "Very sorry."

Ford didn't continue until his father was well into the house and out of sight. "We, ah, this thing has sort of kicked us all in the ass. We just can't figure it. Never a hint that she was considering suicide. And the timing couldn't have been worse for me—''

"Ten days before the goddamned spring primary," Raskin said.

"Phil, please," Ford said. "I'd started to say how insignificant that is compared to what Dad's going through. He's blaming himself for losing track of her, and it's really tormenting him. He's just been—'' His voice trailed off.

"You were saying about your mother?" Brenna prompted, waiting for someone to bring up the witness, or the crime lab's apparent interest.

"Yes, she gets that way. Agitated. So many things upset her and there's just no way to predict it." Ford pointed toward the gardens, which covered at least two acres behind the house. "It drops off pretty abruptly out there near the gazebo."

Brenna squinted into the distance. The gardens ended in a clean line at the edge of the property. The ravine, she figured. A large filigreed gazebo sat on its edge like the top of some enormous wedding cake. Beyond the drop-off, she saw nothing but the gentle chop of forested western Pennsylvania hills rolling like a green ocean to the horizon.

"As I said, we're still trying to understand what happened out there. But the short version is that Mother ended up at the bottom of a pretty sheer twenty-foot drop."

"She's how old again?" Brenna asked.

"Seventy," Ford said. "It's remarkable she's alive."

Leigh Underhill leaned forward. "A miracle, really."

Ford nodded. "Not surprising, in some ways. Before she was diagnosed six years ago, Mother used to talk about how she intended to die in the show ring at a hundred and five. So this little episode simply won't do. Mother hates script changes."

Brenna pulled a legal pad from her briefcase and laid it on the table, then uncapped her Mont Blanc, a gift from Jim. This might be the one place she wouldn't feel self-conscious using a $400 pen. She needed specific information, sooner rather than later. "What law-enforcement agency did you say is involved?"

Ford reached for the pitcher of tea and poured himself a glass before answering. "Allegheny County Sheriff."

"Did you or anyone in the family speak to the investigators?" Brenna felt herself tense, anticipating the answer.

"They took statements from everyone who was on the property at the time," he said. "Mother, too, down at the hospital. Like I said, she wasn't much help. Everyone else answered their questions as best they could. We have nothing to hide."

Probably nothing to worry about either, she thought. Despite the crime lab's interest in Floss's fingernails, Sheriff Sherman Mercer wasn't called "Sherm the Worm" without reason. The man's whole career was made possible by the thick Pittsburgh accent that made him a favorite with the electorate and his willingness to serve as an obliging toady to Allegheny County's entrenched powers. Her favorite image of Mercer came to mind: On the advice of his television consultants before his last election, the 400-pound sheriff had permed his thinning hair into a sorry mass of dyed-brown curls. The effort was the video-age equivalent of draping earrings on a pig. Brenna stifled a smile.

"Who spoke with them?" she said.

"Leigh and I were hosting a small fund-raiser at our

home in Sewickley Heights when we got the call,'' Ford said. ''We were just back from a rally in Erie, I think, or was it Williamsport? At any rate, they questioned my father even though he was terribly distraught. Lottie, of course. Mr. Staggers. And Enrique and Selena.''

''The groundskeeper and his wife,'' Staggers interrupted. He turned to Brenna. ''Says he heard some commotion on the gazebo deck, but he was, like, way the hell out by the greenhouses. A hundred yards, maybe. I mean, from there, how much could he have perceived auditorily?''

The table went silent. Staggers's odd turn of phrase hovered like a garish piñata. No one bothered to take a swing.

''What's Enrique's last name?'' Brenna asked.

Ford and his wife shrugged. Staggers pulled a small black notebook from inside his suit jacket and riffled its pages. ''Chembergo,'' he said.

Brenna wrote the couple's names beneath Vincent Underhill's. ''And Lottie's?''

Staggers flipped his pages again, then shrugged.

''We'll get that for you,'' Ford said.

She added Lottie the maid and Alton Staggers, then counted the names of the five people on the property at the time Floss Underhill fell. Thinking like a cop always helped. ''Now, let me go back a second,'' she said. ''You said the investigators were just taking statements. But you also said they were asking specific questions.''

Raskin sucked an ice cube from his highball glass, then spit it back in. ''Ah, the *complication*,'' he said.

Leigh Underhill sipped her tea. Raskin and Staggers exchanged an indecipherable glance.

''They had some specific questions,'' Ford said. ''Is that a problem?''

''Cops don't ask specific questions unless they're after specific information,'' she said, thinking: Sherm the Worm would never authorize his people to ask uncomfortable questions of one of the state's most powerful families unless the investigators found serious inconsistencies in the Underhills' version of events. If Mercer loosed his guys to find out what happened to Floss Underhill, he must have been damned sure there was more to the story.

"We understand there's some concern about the groundskeeper's statement," Ford said, as though he'd been reading her mind. "That's one of the reasons we contacted you, Brenna. As I said, we've nothing to hide here. But we're told there are some unexplained inconsistencies that raised suspicions, apparently, and that's why the police took so many pictures out at the gazebo, why they're talking to some of our neighbors and friends about my parents. Never mind that my parents have reprimanded Mr. Chembergo at least twice for his drinking. We don't blame the investigators for following up."

"They're thinking faultily," Staggers said, adjusting his ring.

Brenna said, "Explain 'inconsistencies.' Those have a nasty way of coming back to bite you."

"It's just Dagnolo's usual bullshit," Raskin interrupted. "We all know where this is coming from. Our goddamned district attorney."

The Underhills' political consultant stepped to center stage without hesitation. Ford tried to interject, but Raskin ignored him. "I'm sorry, but the guy's just a whore. Ford jumped into the Democratic primary six months ago and blew Dagnolo's doomed little plan to run for governor right out of the water, and ever since he's been looking for a way to fuck us. So now, nine days before the election, he's got that slug of a sheriff stomping around and making noise about all this so Dagnolo can come off like some man-of-the-people giant-killer. I mean, there's no mystery to all this, folks."

Brenna scribbled some notes and set down her pen. "Okay, slow down. Let's deal with what happened here first."

"Look, Phil," Ford said, "we're all pretty much on edge here. Let's let Brenna get the information she needs right now and save the editorializing for some other time." He ran a finger around the lip of his glass, creating the unmistakable song of fine crystal, then took a deep breath.

"My parents have been married for forty-eight years, Brenna. Married right out there in that gazebo, as a matter of fact, and they'd be the first to tell you it wasn't a perfect union. You probably know Mother didn't go with him to Harrisburg when he was governor."

"I remember the big media fuss," she said.

"Mother said she wouldn't live in that, quote, city without a soul, unquote, and she didn't mind talking about it to any reporter who asked."

Brenna smiled, remembering Floss Underhill's reputation for plain-spoken independence at a time when politicians' wives were expected to behave like Jackie Kennedy.

"But if you watch them long enough, Brenna, even since Mother got sick, you'll still catch them holding hands, walking together arm in arm, sharing some private laugh at the dinner table. We should all be so lucky."

Ford reached for his wife's hand just as she reached for her tea glass. She offered him a vague smile instead. "I tell you all that not to create some fantasy love story, but to give you some context," he said. The maid stepped quietly onto the patio, and Ford seemed to sense her presence behind him. "We're fine, Lottie, thank you," he said, waving her away.

"When this disease began stealing my mother's mind—and you could see it, bit by bit, over those first couple of years—my father reacted in a way I'm told is quite typical of Alzheimer's spouses. Since he couldn't control what was happening to her mind, he decided to control her body as best he could. He took the lead role in her care then, and that hasn't changed."

Brenna was lost. "The point being?"

"We're not ruling out any possibilities, that's all. I'm convinced that Mother had a rare moment of clarity and realized what was happening to her. Believe me, if that was the case, suicide might seem pretty appealing. But I think we're all familiar with the term 'caregiver burnout.' ''

Brenna spoke without thinking. ''Your father?''

''A possibility, that's all,'' Ford said. ''Mother hasn't been sleeping. She's been up at all hours. He's been exhausted. He was there day and night—bathing, feeding, dressing, everything. Sometimes people in those situations just—'' He snapped his fingers. ''Of course, there's no evidence to suggest that happened here. But I'm just trying to reconcile Mr. Chembergo's statement with what we know happened. Dad was the last one with her.''

Brenna swallowed hard. She knew the caregiver's dilemma. Her mother was diagnosed the same week Brenna started work in the public defender's office. During the next year, as she struggled to launch her career, she and her mother fell into a wounded silence. Brenna knew that her touch, once so tender, grew rougher as her mother's condition eroded. Eventually, she couldn't insert the catheter or roll her mother's wasted body off the soiled bedclothes fast enough. Claire Kennedy knew that her disease was derailing her daughter's powerful ambitions, knew that Brenna resented it. And Brenna knew the exact moment when her reason had been lost to rage. Her mother's gaunt face took shape in Brenna's mind. Before she could will the memory away, she saw her own hand sweep across it, hard, an involuntary open-handed slap. Her mother's face crumpled into tears, just as it had that horrible, frustrating day more than a decade ago.

''Brenna?'' Ford said.

She blinked. ''Sorry.'' She cleared her throat. ''Do you think your father is capable of hurting her?''

Ford shook his head. ''Never, at least not consciously. We're just trying to be open with you. I know the last two months she's been especially difficult. And I've been so busy with the campaign, I could have overlooked any warning signs. Dad's so damned stoic—the Underhill way, you know. But like I said, except for Mr. Chembergo's strange statement, there's no evidence we know of that suggests she did anything but jump.''

"So," she baited, "no signs of a struggle or anything?''

"Nothing we're aware of.''

Brenna looked around the table. Everyone shrugged at the same time. "Any reason to think the groundskeeper is lying to cover up his own involvement?'' she asked.

Ford Underhill leaned back in his chair and folded his hands in his lap, apparently considering the idea. Finally, he shook his head. "Why would he hurt Mother? He's treated well here.''

"Okay, then," Brenna said. "Let's get back to what we know happened yesterday.''

"Of course, sorry," Ford said. "I don't mean to get ahead of you. We're still just sorting this out.''

"What time did it happen?''

"Shortly after four. It was still light. The groundskeeper says he heard something in the gazebo, a thumping he said, and came out of the greenhouse to see what it was. He told the sheriff's people he saw something, a form, maybe a man, walking away from the gazebo. That's when he heard Mother down in the ravine. She was crying.''

Brenna held up her hand to slow the story. "Didn't you say before that the groundskeeper just heard something?''

"He called 911 immediately.'' Leigh shook her head. "His coming along right then probably saved her life. If she'd been unconscious, she could have laid down there for days.''

Four nodding heads. "And that's it," Ford said. "They got her back up and helicoptered her out. She was on her way to Mount Mercy when we got the call.''

Ford glanced at his watch. Raskin checked his as well.

"We've got the Hill District ministers and ward leaders in forty minutes," Raskin reminded. "Reverend Pratt and company hate to wait.'' He turned to Brenna. "The black vote in Pittsburgh and Philly is gonna be critical."

She waited through an uncomfortable silence until Ford stood up. "Brenna, again, thank you for coming on short notice," he said. "I really think we needed someone with a clear head on this. Is there anything else you need from us right now?"

Brenna studied the faces around her. They seemed to be waiting for her response. She scratched a few notes, collecting her thoughts, then peeked at her watch. Jim had planned their first dinner together in the new house as a family, but it might have to wait until tomorrow. She reached into her purse, pulled one of her business cards from its leather holder, and wrote her home number on the back.

"This has all my numbers," she said, pushing it across the table to Ford Underhill. "Office, home, cell phone."

He looked it over and handed it to Staggers, then shifted from foot to foot. Brenna studied the man, so powerful, but at the moment apparently looking for reassurance she wasn't in a position to give.

"I'd like to speak privately with your father," she said.

Ford's eyes shifted to the floor, then back to hers. "Of course," he said. "Can you give us a few minutes? I'd like to make sure he's up to it right now."

Brenna's eyes fixed on the gazebo. A drizzle continued to fall from the slate-gray sky. "I'll need to see where it happened," she said.

Ford seemed to notice the rain for the first time. "Of course." He looked down at his watch, then at his gleaming Ferragamos. "The garden path's a bit boggy this time of year. I'm afraid we're running very late."

"Let me give her the tour," Staggers said, standing up suddenly. "I watched the sheriff's people do their thing. I can fill her in, if Ms. Kennedy has no objections."

Staggers moved with casual elegance through the French doors and into the house. Brenna left her briefcase and followed, assuming that was his intention. Staggers noticed her behind him as he opened the front door, headed for the driveway. "Oh, no, sorry," he said. "I was just getting a golf umbrella from my car. I may have a pair of Totes in there, too."

"That'd be great," she said. "I left home in such a hurry—"

"Wait here." Without apparent concern for his loafers or the hems of his tailored pants, Staggers stepped through a half-dozen puddles between the front door and the trunk of his Thunderbird. He returned with the red-and-white Ping umbrella already open and offered her an oversized pair of slip-on rubber boots. Raindrops clung to the stiff strands of his too-black hair and sparkled like diamonds on the silken shoulders of his suit jacket. She looked down at her favorite flats, $90 even at the Joan & David outlet where she'd found them. "Chivalry lives," she said. "Thanks."

Staggers hoisted the umbrella. "Shall we egress?"

5

Christensen probably wouldn't have noticed the stain, except that he'd propped an unshaded lamp on a moving carton to light the dim office while he unpacked. Its harsh light flooded that corner of the white ceiling, which was discolored by an off-white patch the size and shape of a kidney. His every instinct told him to ignore it, but he couldn't forget how the toilet-seal leak worried Brenna.

He shoved his desk across the floor until it was just underneath the stain, then took off his shoes and climbed onto the desktop. The patch didn't feel wet, but then the toilet hadn't been flushed much in the past year. He pressed hard with his fingertip.

Solid enough to overlook for now.

The doorbell rang. At least that works, he thought as he checked his watch. Probably Simone's mom dropping the kids off after the birthday party. He smoothed his hair and beard and picked his way across the front-hall clutter toward the door. Annie burst in as soon as he unlocked it.

"Chuck E. Cheese swore at me," she said.

Taylor was right behind her. "A really bad word," he

added. "She didn't hardly do anything, either."

Christensen looked up. Pamm D'Orio, Simone's mom, forced a smile. He'd treated people for post-traumatic stress who looked more collected. Her dark hair, bound so neatly into a bun when she'd picked the kids up three hours earlier, had erupted and hung in undisciplined strands over her ears and forehead. She brushed a particularly unruly one off her face. A smear of tomato sauce marred her left shoulder, and on the thigh of her faded jeans was a cola-colored shoeprint. Two other children were waiting among a thicket of helium balloons in a minivan at the curb.

"I brought it to the manager's attention, but—" She waited until Annie and Taylor moved deeper into the house. "It wasn't entirely unprovoked. He'll be okay."

"Who?"

"Chuck E. Cheese. The guy in the mouse suit. The manager said it's not the first time the tail caused problems."

"Oh shit, Pamm."

"It's fine, really. They have one of those little spaceship rides that lifts the kids about six feet off the ground, and the tail somehow got wrapped around the joystick. In a perfect half hitch."

Christensen swallowed hard. "Like the one she just learned in Indian Princesses?"

She nodded. "His back was turned, and when it went up it sort of dumped him."

"Oh, Jesus."

"It's fine. The mouse head is padded—it's like a helmet, the manager said—so the guy's fine." Finally, she smiled. "It was a *really* bad word, though."

He drew a deep breath. How to handle this? "I'll talk to them."

"Taylor's clean, I think. He was playing Skee-Ball when it happened." She nodded toward the minivan. "Better run."

"We had a problem there once before. They're going

to have her picture posted at the door, like at the post office."

"Say hi to Brenna," she said over her shoulder.

"Pamm, I'm sorry," he called, but she didn't turn around.

He caught Annie by the arm as she blew past him, headed upstairs. Taylor passed them both, didn't even slow down. "I think we need to talk about what happened, don't you?"

She sat on the bottom step and looked up at him. Her victim face. "He swore at me. I was scared."

"I'm sorry you were scared. Why do you think he used bad language?"

She cupped her chin in her hand and pouted. "He's not really a mouse."

"Annie—"

"He's a rat."

He stooped to look her in the eye. "How would you feel now if he'd gotten hurt?"

Her lower lip trembled. She bit it to keep from crying, and he knew he'd said enough. When he hugged her, she smelled like ketchup.

A flagstone path ran along the south side of the massive house, past an industrial-sized air-conditioning unit. It was raining harder now, but Staggers showed no interest in joining her beneath the umbrella as he led the way. An overhanging willow branch drenched him as he brushed past, but if the soaking caused him any discomfort it didn't show.

"Are you sure you don't want to share this?" she asked. "It's really coming down."

"I'm copacetic, thanks." He didn't turn around.

The path split at the rear corner of the house. To the left, the flagstones led between the barbered shrubs along the back wall toward the patio and the six-foot hedgerow that bordered the gardens and central lawn. She couldn't see over it, but she could smell the roses blooming on the other side.

"Spring comes earlier in Fox Chapel than where I live," she said, savoring their perfume. "It must be a zoning thing."

Staggers stopped and turned around. "How's that?" Strands of damp black hair clung to his forehead, revealing the bald spot beneath his artful comb-over. She could tell by his eyes her humor hadn't connected.

"The roses. They bloom early here."

"They do?" He shrugged. "Mrs. Underhill loves the gardens."

"So she walks out here a lot?"

His dark eyes narrowed. "She does?"

"No, I'm asking. Does she?"

Staggers seemed to weigh the question far more carefully than she intended. "Why do you want to know?"

Brenna let it pass. He was either really dense or really paranoid, characteristics not uncommon in the private-security trade, but neither lent itself to casual conversation. Or maybe he was just playing dumb. "So what do you do exactly?" she tested.

"This and that."

"I mean, how long have you worked for the Underhills?"

"You ask a lot of questions." His eyes narrowed again, but suddenly his face was split by a relaxed smile. "But of course, that's your meatier. You're on our side."

Métier?

"Sorry if I seem a little overprotective," he said. "I've been dealing with cops for the last twenty-four hours. They have a propensity to twist things."

Brenna shifted the umbrella to her other hand. "You have an excellent vocabulary."

Staggers apparently took it as a compliment. "I'm taking a course. We're supposed to practice. I'm a believer in self-improvement."

Dense, she decided.

" 'The power to change is within us. Plug in!' " he said. "Know who says that? William DeForce. I've got the whole *Summon Your Creative Potential* audiotape series—that's the one with the *Word Power Plus* tape—plus the *Burning Path* fire-walking primer. I personally think the man's a genius."

"A genius," Brenna repeated.

"Damn straight. You read his first book?"

Brenna shook her head.

"Brilliant."

"Really?"

"*Get Behind Me and Stay There*. Changed my life, I'll be the first to tell you." Staggers offered a conspiratorial wink. "Next paycheck, I'm going for the gusto: the whole ten-tape *Ten Days to More Effective Decision-Making*. Then look out world."

There was an odd charm to him that Brenna couldn't quite define. She thought of the chubby, hopeless dork in Taylor's class with the thick glasses and the billowing shorts that were forever bunched up his crack. Life wouldn't be easy for him, she knew, but it was hard not to root for him.

"You don't seem overprotective," she said. "You just seem really dedicated to the Underhills, that's all."

"They've been so good to me. Gave me a job, a place to live. Treat me like their own. And they've been through hell these last few years. Can't go through that with people and not feel some sort of, you know, affination."

"That's nice. So you're on staff here?"

"Special projects and things. Troubleshooting. Very utilitarian." He turned and started walking again. "Between you and me, I think the cops made them pretty uneasy. I'm just trying to help them understand what's going on at that end."

"So you have a law-enforcement background?"

Staggers seemed to take the question seriously, wrinkling his brow and bringing his hand to his chin, but all that thinking just produced a vague "No."

The path curved gently around the outside of the garden, and Staggers turned left into the first gap in the hedge. Suddenly they were surrounded by an orderly march of color—red, pink, yellow, white—perfect rows of rosebushes in early bloom stretching away from them like a thorny carpet. The gardens were even more impressive from here than they were from the covered veranda.

"Unbelievable," she said.

The flagstones led through the roses and into a central lawn, then curved back toward the bordering roses. Beyond that was the gazebo. From ground level it was far bigger and farther away than Brenna had first thought. What she'd imagined from above as a little place to sit and enjoy the view looked more like a rotunda with open walls. If Vincent and Floss Underhill were married there, they probably could have put a couple hundred guests under the roof without much effort.

Staggers stepped around a pile of clippings. While most of the bushes were perfectly trimmed, the section just ahead was overgrown. "Watch yourself through here," he said. "Enrique's been clearing." He pushed back an overhanging branch and held it while she passed. As he again took the lead, she noticed blood dripping from the hand that had held the branch.

"That rose must have got you," she said.

Staggers examined his hand. It was only a trickle, but mixed with the rain the blood ran in a steady red stream across his palm, making it look far worse than it probably was. A dark thorn was still deep in the flesh just below his ring. He didn't flinch as he yanked it out.

They climbed the five steps to the gazebo floor. Brenna turned back to look at the house. "Those are the greenhouses up at that end?"

Staggers nodded.

"And where did Mrs. Underhill—" She searched for the right word. "—fall?"

Staggers pointed first toward a railing at the rear of the gazebo, then led her to it. She checked the location first, to see if sound traveling from where Floss must have stood would flow unimpeded to the greenhouses.

"You clog?" she asked.

Staggers seemed puzzled as he wrapped his silk handkerchief around his bleeding hand.

"The dance, clogging?" she said. She stomped her feet, faking her way through a noisy dance step. The hollow thump of her shoes on the wooden floor resounded in the afternoon rain despite the borrowed rubber Totes. "Like that."

Staggers shook his head.

"Is there a storage space or something under the gazebo, Alton?"

He nodded. "Why?"

"Just wondering."

Brenna approached the railing and ran her hand along it, sweeping raindrops into the chasm below. The gazebo deck was built out over the rim of the ravine, so that the initial drop was sheer and unobstructed. "Right here?"

Brenna hated heights, but she looked down. There was a muddy divot ten feet below, where Floss Underhill must have first crashed against the ravine wall. She imagined the terror of falling, falling, seeing the rocky inevitable streaking up to crush you like a bug; the hopeless scrabbling as you tumbled, clutching at roots, tree trunks, outcroppings, anything; or, as seemed quite possibly the case, the mute horror of falling like a rag doll after the spine went numb and the brain lost contact with the nerves.

"Big drop," she said, leaning against the railing, catching herself when the top rail gave slightly against her weight. Clutching the rail tighter, she backed off and nudged it with her hip, this time with more weight. Wood splintered.

"Alton, how long has this been broken?"

"The cops were asking about that, too," he said. "I don't know."

Brenna looked to her right. Staggers was about ten feet away, watching her little experiment. She moved away from him, to the next section of railing. She turned and leaned casually against it. It didn't give at all. She wandered to the center of the gazebo floor, very casual, then back to the section of railing to the right of where Floss

Underhill went over. Again she leaned heavily against the top rail. Solid as a rock.

"Ready to head back up?" Staggers said.

"Another minute."

Back to the broken section. Brenna scanned the hillsides. "Wonderful view," she said, filling her lungs with the cool, moist air. "Don't you think?" She ran her fingers along the back side of the top rail, feeling for the connecting bolts. The wood was smooth the entire length. She leaned out, her stomach clenching as she did, and glanced down at the back sides of the supporting posts. Halfway down the one on the left, the wood around the bolt was splintered. Something heavy had been shoved against it from the deck side.

Staggers hadn't taken his eyes off her. "We should get back up to the house," he said.

Brenna tried to imagine all the possible scenarios, beginning with Ford's own theory. Floss Underhill, unusually coherent, suddenly recognizing the hopelessness of her condition, slips away from her vigilant husband and heads straight for the gazebo to throw herself to her death.

Negligence? Endangerment? Dagnolo wouldn't dare. She could defend against charges like those in her sleep.

She tried again. The groundskeeper, a disgruntled employee, sees the old woman wandering alone in the gardens. He coaxes her into the gazebo to get out of the rain. Then what? Decides to kill her? The railing splinters as they struggle? Maybe, but why? Right now, Brenna just couldn't see any logic in it.

She tried again: In a moment of unthinking rage after years of devoted care to his demented wife, Vincent Underhill snaps. He shoves Floss and she stumbles backward. Her momentum carries her over the railing, splintering it, and into the ravine. Then, according to the groundskeeper, he leaves? Knowing she'd probably die down there? A jury might sympathize with Vincent Underhill. They'd find a way to acquit.

She tried, finally, to imagine the worst case, as Dagnolo

no doubt would: The overwrought Vincent finally snaps, picks his wife up off her feet, carries her to the railing, and drops her into the ravine, his forward motion carrying him into the railing and splintering it. Then, the deed already done, convinced it's for the best, he leaves. That wouldn't seem impulsive, and certainly not accidental. It had a brutality, a coldness that was missing from the other possibilities—something Dagnolo would love. That's just the sort of thing that bugs a jury. If it ever came to that, the groundskeeper's version and the physical evidence were going to be critical. She thought of the crime lab's interest in Floss Underhill's fingernails.

"Alton, do you know if the police found any scratches or marks on Mrs. Underhill? Or anyone else?"

Staggers shrugged. "They're waiting for you up at the house. We should go."

"No idea?"

Staggers walked away without looking up. They retraced the path to the house without talking, with only the sound of their shoes on wet stone and the rain's monotonous rhythm on her umbrella.

Vincent Underhill met them at the front door after having watched their approach from the rear veranda. Brenna twirled the golf umbrella to dislodge the raindrops clinging to its dome, folded it, and handed it to Staggers. She peeled the Totes off her feet and handed those over, too. "Thanks so much," she said, expecting him to set them to dry beside the front door. Instead, he headed back out into the downpour with the umbrella and boots tucked under his arm.

"He's a good man. Loyal to a fault," Vincent said as they watched Staggers slog to his car and return the rain gear to the trunk. Brenna felt the former governor's eyes on her even before she turned to meet them. "Loyalty is something this family cherishes, Ms. Kennedy. We expect it, but we also reward it."

Brenna smiled, flustered by his unexpected intensity. She looked across the house's grand foyer and through the French doors. Everyone else was gone. She recognized the silhouette of Lottie the maid in the overcast light as she gathered the iced-tea glasses onto a tray. "The others left?"

Vincent turned around, as if he were double-checking. "Ford and Phil needed to get going. Leigh wasn't feeling well, so she went on back to their house. Look, I'm sorry about earlier."

Staggers brushed past them and into the house. With each step, his shoes made the squishing sound of sodden leather. Then, as if he'd forgotten something, he headed back out into the spring shower.

"Perfectly understandable. It's a difficult time. Mind talking about it for a few minutes now?"

The former governor led her down a short hall and into a sumptuous paneled study. A fire was lit in the stone fireplace, which stood between two windows overlooking the driveway and front entrance. Brenna wasn't cold or wet, but the pull of the flames was irresistible. Vincent Underhill was staring out one of the floor-length windows, his back to her, when he began to speak.

"There are terms we use sometimes, 'we' being families affected by Alzheimer's," he said, his eyes fixed on something outside. "You either 'know,' or you 'can't know.' Which are you, Ms. Kennedy?"

A cherry log crackled and hissed behind her. "My grandmother on my father's side, but I was little, and it was before it had a name, I think. So which am I?"

He turned and looked at her, but didn't answer. "I'm going to tell you something that might seem callous. But I'm going to tell you anyway, because I want you to understand. Last night, Ms. Kennedy, with my wife out of the house for the first night in six years, I slept like a baby."

Was he waiting for her reaction? "I understand from your son—"

"It's not like I didn't have things to think about. My God, trying to make sense of what happened yesterday, trying to understand what I could have done differently, I should have been wide-eyed from the moment I got back from the hospital at eleven. But I wasn't. I slept. Straight through. First night in years when I wasn't up five or six times with her. She'd launch these projects, just vital nonsense that couldn't wait, day or night. It's like her brain's on a timer that clicks on at random times. One night, maybe two years ago, she got out of the house before I woke up. She was sitting in the Benz, naked, trying to find the ignition. Said she was heading for Heinz Hall, late for the symphony.''

He crossed the room and leaned against the mantel at the opposite end of the fireplace. ''Scared the hell out of me. After that, I never slept too deeply.''

''That's understandable,'' Brenna said.

''No, it's not,'' he said, smiling. ''You can't know.''

Their eyes locked. Another pop and hiss from a fireplace log. ''Point taken,'' she said. ''So tell me something I can understand. What was she like? Before, I mean.''

Vincent Underhill's face transformed. Suddenly, he laughed—deep, genuine, affectionate. He seemed to search for a word. ''Unique,'' he said.

Brenna took advantage of his sudden mood shift. ''Help me get to know her a little. Let's try this: If Floss Underhill were one of the seven dwarfs, which one would she be?''

He thought a moment, then laughed again. ''Is there a Cranky?''

''There's a Grumpy.''

Vincent Underhill shook his head. ''No, that's different. Cranky is more like it. Didn't give a good goddamn, pardon my French, what anybody thought.''

''She smoked cigars, didn't she? I remember that from somewhere.''

''Yes! *Everybody* remembers that. *Fortune* magazine sent a reporter and photographer out to the house about thirty years ago. We must have talked for two days about things going on around the state, economic development stuff. And what do you think made it into the lead? What do you think everyone remembers about that story? My wife firing up a Macanudo in front of the photographer! We'd managed to keep her little vice a secret for so long, not that *she* gives a damn, of course.''

''She still smokes them?''

Underhill's smile dimmed. ''We can't let her have matches.''

''Of course,'' Brenna said. ''I'm sorry. I'm just trying to imagine her on the social circuit around here.''

''Oh, Christ, don't get me started,'' Underhill said, his mood buoyed again. ''She was an absolute scourge. Had no patience, none whatsoever, for those women—'the ladies who lunch,' she called them. Not that they didn't fall into line when she told them to, when she needed money or volunteers for one cause or another. But she was much more comfortable in filthy horse clothes than in anything Bob Mackie ever made for her.''

''I knew I liked her,'' Brenna said. ''So that I-gotta-be-me thing wasn't all just charming political image-making?''

''Floss?'' He laughed out loud. ''Is a tornado concerned about its image, Ms. Kennedy? No. It's all about energy and unpredictability and free will.''

''Tornadoes are dangerous, though,'' she said.

''Not if you get out of their way, or know how to duck and cover at the right time,'' he said with a wink. ''I'll say this: made for a damned interesting marriage.''

The flames were too warm, so Brenna edged away from the fireplace toward one of the long windows. It overlooked the estate's carport, where Alton Staggers was down on one knee in the rain beside her Legend, peering underneath as if he'd dropped something.

''Would you like to sit down?'' Underhill motioned her toward a massive wing chair.

She shook her head. ''No, I won't keep you. I just wanted to hear your version of what happened yesterday. Would that be all right?''

"Ford didn't tell you?"

"He did. I just had a couple questions."

Underhill sat down on a couch across from the wing chair. Brenna stayed standing.

"What were you doing when you realized your wife had wandered away?"

Underhill folded his hands, his index fingers forming a spire beneath his nose. "I'd told Selena—she's our home nurse—to take a couple of hours off. She'd been watching Floss most of the day while I made some fundraising calls for Ford." He closed his eyes. "At about three, Floss decided to paint. She has this paint set she's always fooling around with. So I set it up for her in the study, and I sat down to read."

"So you were both in the study? For how long?"

"I don't know. A while."

"Then at some point she left?"

He nodded. "At some point, yes. The paints were still there when I—"

"Was it still light outside when she left?"

"I don't know. I'm sure it was."

"Because Ford said she apparently was at the gazebo at about four." Brenna leaned on the back of the wing chair.

"I believe that's correct."

"So, sometime between three and four, she got up and left. Did she say where she was going?"

"I don't remember, Ms. Kennedy. You're on our side, right?"

Brenna wouldn't, couldn't back down. "The district attorney isn't, and he's going to want these same answers. Please bear with me. Did she seem upset, or distraught?"

Underhill stood up suddenly. "I'm sorry, I don't—"

"Because—"

"Ms. Kennedy," he said, drawing a deep breath, "I fell asleep. On the couch, when I was supposed to be watching her. The next thing I know, there's a goddamned medevac operation going on out by our gazebo. She got hurt on my watch. It's my fault, and I'm trying to deal with that, and I trust you'll never repeat this conversation to anyone outside this family. I think you know how a mistake like that would be twisted into a mortal sin by a man like Dagnolo. Does that clear everything up for you, Ms. Kennedy? Now do you understand?''

Bewildered by the change in tone, her voice suddenly caught in her throat, Brenna nodded. ''You can't blame yourself.''

''Do you understand?''

She nodded again.

''No,'' he said, still edgy. ''No. That's the thing. You *can't know*.''

7

Light poured into the dark bedroom as their bathroom door swung open. Brenna stood for a moment in its frame as she brushed her hair, a dancer's silhouette in a thin T-shirt. It was nearly midnight before she got the toilet in the other bathroom reconnected, but she didn't want to come to bed without a shower. He'd waited patiently while she dried her hair.

"The stain's where again?" she said.

"The office. Toward the back, not right below the kids' bathroom, though."

She flipped off the bathroom light and slid between the sheets. "That doesn't mean anything. Water can follow a crossbeam or duct and wind up pooling in a space three rooms away. I'd check it tomorrow, but I've got to work early."

"Earlier than usual?" He pulled her to him. She reached across his bare chest and set the alarm for five-thirty, then rolled back onto her side of the bed.

"It's going to be like this for a while. What'll we do?"

"I can handle things. The sabbatical leaves me pretty flexible." Her shampoo smelled like watermelon.

"So you can drop them at school *and* pick them up?" she said. "You sure? We can get some help."

"Don't sweat it." He tried again. She jumped up, crossed the room to her briefcase and, in the pale glow of a bright moon outside their window, scribbled something in her Day Runner. The omens weren't good. The ebb and flow of their lovemaking was determined almost entirely by the level of her anxiety about work. "There'll be times when I'm busy, too. It'll even out. What are you so worried about?"

Brenna stopped writing and looked out the window. Two blocks south, the Walnut Street bars were alive with reckless youth. On clear nights, the sound carried. Tonight, they both listened to a silence broken only by a motorcycle easing down the narrow channel between cars parked along Howe.

"I want this to work," she said. "Us." She pointed to the hall that led to the bedrooms where Annie and Taylor were sleeping. "Them."

Her first marriage had collapsed because of her zealous work habits, unable to survive the forward thrust of her ambition in the first years after her mother died. Still, the answer surprised him.

"Nice try," he said. "It's this Underhill thing, isn't it?"

"That, too."

He patted the bed. She put her Day Runner back in the briefcase, glided across the room and slid in beside him. He could see her more clearly now that his eyes had adjusted to the moonlight. "After all you've told me about Sherman Mercer, Bren, you're actually taking his investigation seriously?"

She pulled her knees to her chest and put her chin on her forearms. "The name of an old friend of yours name came up today: J. D. Dagnolo."

"Mr. Congeniality?"

"Him," she said. "Someone wondered if maybe the D.A.'s office was pulling the strings on this. There's no love lost between Dagnolo and the Underhills right now.''

Christensen shrank back in mock alarm. ''You mean our district attorney is *political*?''

Brenna didn't react, not even with an exasperated roll of those perfect green eyes.

''What?'' he said.

''I don't know if Dagnolo's behind it or not. It wouldn't surprise me. I think the guy'd do pretty much anything to chop the Underhills.''

''They really stuffed him when Ford got into the governor's race, huh?''

''He figured the job was his, and it probably was. I know he's a snake, you know he's a snake, but his rep statewide is pretty good—Mr. Fearless Crime Buster. And, what the hell, the questions Mercer's guys are asking aren't altogether unreasonable.''

Christensen sat up and turned to face her. This was a twist.

''You're not going to ruin my image of the Underhills now, are you?'' he said. ''I know they've had their minor scandals. Hell, the family lives in a fishbowl. But I've always liked their priorities. Forget all the Renaissance stuff, the commercial stuff. Jesus, they practically underwrote Harmony's whole adult day-care facility. I can almost overlook the fact that they're obscenely rich.''

''And if I really want to pursue the city council seat, a kind word from them would pretty much do it for me in the Seventh Ward,'' she said. ''It's just—''

''What?''

''—not cut and dried, that's all.''

''How much can you say?''

She bit her lower lip. ''A hypothetical, okay? Let's say there was some physical evidence that might support an eyewitness's story. Nothing conclusive, but something that might intrigue the cops, something that makes the witness's story seem at least plausible. If there was a struggle or something on the gazebo deck, even a short one, and this witness was standing at the greenhouses, I'm sure he could have heard it.''

"That's the hypothetical gazebo and greenhouse?" he said.

"You know I can't talk about a specific case."

He kissed her. "Love that."

"Okay, so there's a big storage room underneath the gazebo. It's pretty loud even when you walk across the floor. Stomp your feet and it sounds like a bass drum. The witness hears the sounds and comes out to look, sees somebody, a man, leaving the gazebo."

Christensen nodded. "Logical. But a little thin, theory-wise, don't you think?"

"By itself, sure."

"Then?"

"The deck has a railing, about waist-high. Right where she jumped, or fell, it's broken. Not like somebody stood on top and jumped outward. It's splintered around one of the bolts on the back, like something heavy fell against it from the deck side. The splintering looks pretty recent."

"Lot of assumptions there," he said. "Somebody moving heavy furniture or equipment around anytime in the last few weeks could have bumped against it. They use the gazebo for parties and fund-raisers and stuff, right?"

"That'd be easy enough to check," she said.

"And you said the railing's waist-high. What if Floss stumbled against it and fell over? It was raining, probably slippery."

Far-fetched, he knew, but no more than any other scenario she'd brought up.

Brenna made a face. "All I'm saying is there's enough that the investigators probably had to follow up. Sherm's up for election, too. Funny things happen during elections. What if the media got hold of a tape of the grounds-keeper's 911 call? If he said something about a struggle on the phone, it'd look pretty bad if Sherm's people didn't at least ask questions."

"Cover-your-ass time."

"Maybe," Brenna said.

"And Dagnolo would drag himself over a hundred yards of broken glass for a chance to take them down, right? So he's probably pushing like hell."

"Believe me, Sherm's squirming. The Underhills are a force of nature around here, politically. There's just no upside for him in this, so you'd think the whole thing would be over with by now. But it isn't."

Christensen leaned close and kissed both of her knees, a reminder of his less conversational interests.

"No upside at all," she said.

He gave up. "Finish what you said earlier about Vincent, the thing about the paints."

"He says she wanted to paint, so he set it up for her," she said. "Then he fell asleep. That's when she wandered off."

"You believe him?"

"I think so. I mean, it's one thing when the body deteriorates, Jim, but at least my mother stayed in bed. He says Floss gets up five or six times a night and wanders around. He gets up with her to make sure she doesn't get hurt. How long can a person handle that?"

Her eyes shifted to the window, to the moon. "I can read people's eyes. I think the guy's an open wound—" Her voice trailed off. "Sorry. It's just the way he talked about it, it hit close to home."

Christensen didn't know her when she was nursing her mother, knew only the scars left by the experience. He'd heard her sob in her sleep and wake in a funk; watched her fall apart the day Taylor threw up in the backseat of her beloved Saab. She'd had the car detailed the same day, and traded it for the Legend by the end of the week. Something about the smell, an overreaction hard-wired straight into her guilt. Brenna wasn't a weak woman, far from it. But nursing her mother that final year had drained and devastated her with its isolating treadmill of bed changes, laundry, bathing, feeding, medication, and doctor visits. Twice since then, in cases that made statewide headlines, she'd passionately defended caregivers who were accused of assault. She'd won both times.

Christensen tried to think of the last time he saw Floss Underhill, just three days ago. "I told you Floss is one of the fourteen people in Maura Pearson's art class, right? The one I'm observing at Harmony."

Brenna nodded.

"Any idea what she was painting?"

She shook her head. "Why?"

"You just never know with Alzheimer's, that's all. That's what I'm finding with this representational art study. Sometimes the images that surface in their work are incredibly telling."

Brenna sat up, pulled off her T-shirt and crossed her legs. Naked, they sat facing each other in the center of their bed like two yogis, holding hands. Her eyes strayed down.

"At ease, soldier."

"Sorry. Been that way since this afternoon."

Brenna shrugged. "I should find out what she was painting."

"Don't get your hopes up, Bren. It could mean absolutely nothing."

"Explain it to me," she said. "You never talk much about what you're working on, anyway."

Christensen smiled, recalling her earlier hesitation to reveal professional secrets. "It's complicated."

"Grow up," she said, smacking his arm. "I filled you in on my day."

True enough. "Okay," he said. "The way I explained it in my grant proposal was pretty simple. Language is the brain's most highly evolved form of communication. But with Alzheimer's patients, especially advanced-stagers like Floss Underhill, the brain stops processing the information they need in order to talk about things like you or I might, like they did before the disease. Alzheimer's leaves their brains this weird jumble of disconnected wires and phantom thoughts. It devastates their short-term memory—that's why she can't remember how to button buttons or what she had for breakfast—and they have no context for a lot of their long-term memories. She might remember things, but she won't know what they mean.''

Brenna was listening as intently as he'd ever seen her. "Blink," he said.

"I just want to understand."

"Representational art is a different kind of communication, much simpler," he said. "Images bubble up randomly and find their way onto the canvas. Sometimes they have deep meaning, sometimes they don't mean anything. The artist usually doesn't even know where they came from."

"Wait." Brenna held up her hand for him to stop. "So how do you tell what the images mean, if they're significant or not?"

Her mind was quick, intimidatingly so, and she had a chess master's vision. Watching it all work fascinated him. "That's what makes this study so tricky, see. I can't rely on the artist to articulate it, or even understand it. So that leaves two options. The first is my own research into the patient's life. When I get to the point where I'm ready to do case studies, I'll try to learn as much as I can about how they lived, their family, what they did professionally, their hobbies."

The moonlight accented the delicate curve of her breasts. "And the other?"

"Hmm?"

She lifted his chin. "The other option?"

"Oh, um, their family." He found her eyes again. "*Their* memories still work, so if it goes the way I hope, family members will be a great resource for interpreting the images."

He hugged her, awkwardly but tight. She ran her hand up the side of his head, pulling his face to her warm neck. He tried the spot, and suddenly her hand was on the inside of his thigh.

"Your opinion," she whispered.

"Hmm?"

She bit his earlobe, held it with her teeth, and pulled him down as she lay back on the pillows. Their eyes met as he kneeled over her. "So someday Floss might just, you know, out of the blue, paint a picture of what happened on the deck," she said.

"Maybe. You never know. Depends."

"On?"

"Someone would have to work with her. Even then, it'd be a total crapshoot."

She ran a hand down his ribs to his hip, ready to guide him. It rested there lightly until he started to move, but then her elbow locked, holding him away.

"Hey, wait a minute—"

She leaned up and kissed him, but on her terms. "I need a favor."

The ancient gas stove was days away from working, but at least the refrigerator was humming away. The day before, Christensen had found two vital appliances in a misplaced carton—the toaster and the coffeemaker. He'd unpacked enough bowls and silverware to make cereal an option, but they were already dirty. He was thinking frozen waffles. Why not be a hero with the kids?

"Where's my mom?" Startled, he turned and found Taylor standing unsteadily in the kitchen doorway. The pants and shirt of his soccer pajamas were on backward. Annie pushed past him in her oversized Penguins T-shirt and took her place at the table.

"Morning, Mr. T! Your mom had to go to work a little early today." He knelt down and gathered the boy into his arms, but not before dealing four Eggos into the four-slice toaster and pushing the handle down. "And she told me to give you that."

Taylor seemed to enjoy his affection. Any affection. Christensen tried to hug Annie, too, but she pushed him away and complained about his morning breath.

"Who was on the phone?" Taylor asked.

What was the name? Rankin? Raskin? "Somebody for your mom," he said, thinking, *Some arrogant prick who felt perfectly free to call without apology at six-thirty on a Monday morning: somebody who dismissed me like I was the directory-assistance operator.* The Underhills' anxious political strategist, Brenna had explained after she hung up. The sheriff's investigators were asking neighbors about the relationships between Underhill family members. They'd also heard from a contact Downtown that other deputies were pursuing trust documents that might show who, if anyone, might benefit from Floss Underhill's death.

Brenna was already dressed and heading out the door to her office when she got the call. "Mercer's people aren't letting up," she said. "They just want me to stay on top of it. I may be late." She blew him a kiss as he sipped French roast from the first mug he'd found in the first kitchen box he opened. It read "World's Greatest Mom."

He flipped on the countertop television and made school lunches as the kids ate, swabbing peanut butter onto whole-grain bread, studding it with banana wheels, and drizzling honey over the top. When he looked up, Annie and Taylor were licking the syrup from their paper plates. Tomorrow, he'd start watching their sugar intake more closely.

The jolly banter of *G'Morning Pittsburgh!* filled the cluttered kitchen. "Coming up, news headlines at seven!" said the impossibly dimpled co-host. "We've got the morning traffic hot spots, and our own Tim Mausteller will be along with his umbrella index." She wrinkled her nose at the camera. "So don't go away!"

Christensen muted the commercials with a confident wave of the remote. No one was predicting rain today. "If you're done, guys, I want you both upstairs to get dressed and do your teeth. It's supposed to be warm today, so you can wear shorts if you want to. Annie, bring me the hairbrush when you come down, okay?"

"More syrup," she said, pointing to a place on her spotless plate. "Just a little pile right there."

"You've had plenty," he said. "Upstairs. Don't forget the hairbrush."

His eight-year-old stared coolly over the edge of her plate. "The magic word?"

"Sorry. *Please* bring me the hairbrush."

"Okay," she said. "Let's watch that."

She would rule the world someday, he knew, possibly with an iron fist. Annie was a formidable intellect even now, with the unshakable confidence of a Zen master and the mood stability of a Texas thunderstorm. Her logic was always flawless, her arguments airtight. He suspected that even her most vulnerable moments were simply ways to manipulate him to mysterious ends that he could never fully appreciate. She allowed him a role in her life, but it wasn't a lead, and she never let him forget *she* was directing. For now, Annie regarded the occupants of 732 Howe Street, as well as her entire third-grade classroom, more like subjects than peers. She considered herself supremely benevolent in dealing with their shortcomings.

"My momph!"

Taylor sprayed waffle mulch as he pointed at the TV, trying to swallow an Eggo wad and talk. "Lowda! Lowda!" He reached across the kitchen table for the remote and got the mute button after changing channels twice. When he found the right station again, Brenna's face filled the screen. For a moment, Christensen had the unsettling feeling that she'd simply come back after forgetting her car keys or her Starbucks travel cup.

"—on the injuries to Mr. Underhill's mother?" someone asked from off-camera. A microphone topped by a stylized 2 hovered near Brenna's face.

"Turn it up, Taylor," he said.

Taylor changed channels again, then in a panic began pushing buttons randomly. The set blinked off. Christensen snatched the remote from the boy's hands too quickly. "You're doing a good job, T, but maybe it's not working.

Mind if I check it?'' He found the right channel on the second try.

''—sustained some injuries during the fall, none permanent or in any way life-threatening.'' Brenna was wearing her Professional Face. ''The Underhills look forward to having her home in a few days.''

The camera panned back. Christensen recognized the ground-level view of Grant Street, the metal-and-glass entrance of One Oxford Centre. The reporter and camera crew must have caught her on the way up to the sixteenth-floor offices of Kennedy & Flaherty. He recognized the reporter, too, but he couldn't remember his name. The word ''Live'' flashed over and over at the bottom of the screen.

''We understand the Allegheny County sheriff is investigating the possibility that Mrs. Underhill's fall was suspicious in nature. Any comment on that?''

Professional Face. ''I'm not aware of details of any investigation, if there is one, into this difficult situation,'' Brenna said. ''The family is just relieved that she's going to be okay.''

The reporter waited. Brenna waited. She knew how to play the game.

''Is she in trouble?'' Annie asked. Christensen shook his head, held an index finger to his lips.

''They're telling us, quote, the investigation is continuing, unquote,'' the reporter persisted, ''which obviously suggests that there is some concern on their part about how Mrs. Underhill was injured.''

Brenna smiled. ''Obviously, Mr. Underhill is concerned about how his mother fell, too, as we all are. We'd certainly hope the sheriff shares that concern as well.''

''Any evidence this was anything other than a suicide attempt?'' the reporter asked. Christensen could tell he was getting frustrated.

''Not that we're aware of,'' she said.

''But you're a criminal-defense attorney. You've also been involved in several high-profile cases that bear striking similarities to this one, all of which involved disabled elderly people. Why did Ford Underhill's campaign office refer us to you?"

"I can't speak to that. I'm not involved in Mr. Underhill's campaign."

"That's our point—"

"The family's main focus right now is getting Mrs. Underhill back home, and we're cooperating fully with the sheriff's office to clear up questions about the fall. Any speculation beyond that right now would be inappropriate. Thank you for your concern, though."

She smiled when she said it. The reporter surrendered as Brenna turned and walked into the office tower. The camera shifted from Brenna's back to the bulldog face of Channel 2's Myron Levin, whose name appeared suddenly at the bottom of the screen. "Again, Kelly, that's Underhill family spokesperson Brenna Kennedy with the latest on the—" Levin cocked an eyebrow—"*perplexing* fall on Saturday that injured the mother of Democratic gubernatorial front-runner Ford Underhill. Back to you."

Kelly looked worried. "We'll certainly keep Mrs. Underhill in our thoughts."

"We certainly will," offered co-anchor Rob. He looked worried, too. "Thanks, Myron."

Taylor's fork hung halfway between his plate and his mouth, as it had since his mother's face first appeared on the screen. He'd seen his mom interviewed on television before, each time with the same dumbfounded amazement. "Awesome," he said.

Christensen patted him on the back. "You know that lady?"

"Brenna looks fat on TV," Annie said.

Christensen noticed the stove clock and checked it against his watch. "Whoa guys, it's ten to eight. Finish up, get your clothes, brush your teeth, and let's get out the door. Hate to rush you, but the bell rings in ten minutes."

"She should tell them just to show her face," Annie said. "She has a pretty nice face."

"Upstairs," he said.

New living arrangement aside, the morning was building to a familiar crescendo. Christensen collected the paper plates and put away the syrup and margarine. He turned off the coffeemaker, rinsed the silverware, and dropped it into the kitchen's ancient dishwasher, which was half full of plates and bowls unpacked at random in moments of need. He poured Cascade into the soap holder, shut the door, and clicked the dial to normal cycle. The machine groaned once and stopped with an unhealthy noise. He spun the dial again. *Kachunk,* it said. He tried again but it made no noise at all.

Even if he had time to tinker with it, he didn't have the slightest idea what might be wrong. He scribbled a Post-it note for Brenna—"Bren: It went kachunk and stopped. Help!"—and stuck it on the dishwasher door. "Everybody ready?" he shouted.

The kids rumbled down the stairs looking like a Disney mule train, Taylor beneath an overstuffed and weighty *Hercules* backpack, one of Annie's discards, and carrying a lunchbox that looked like the disembodied head of Mickey Mouse. He'd insisted on it over Christensen's objections. Annie was strapped into her silver *Action Rangers* backpack with matching lunchbox.

Christensen tested the weight of Taylor's pack. "What's *in* there, buddy?"

"Rocks."

The phone rang. "Let the machine pick up," Christensen said, but too late.

"This is Annie speaking," she said. His daughter nodded, shrugged, and handed him the phone with a scowl. "It's not for me."

Christensen jammed the phone between his shoulder and his ear. "Hello?"

"Yes, uh, I—geez, I was expecting just to leave a message on Brenna's home answering machine."

Christensen paused, struck by the odd sensation of *déjà vu*. He recognized the man's voice, so familiar, so recent, but couldn't match it to a face. "She's not in right now," he said, "but you can probably reach her at her office."

"No, I know that. I just—" The caller hesitated.

"Or I can take a message," Christensen said. He grabbed the Post-its from the table.

"This is, uh, a reporter friend of hers." Bingo. Myron Levin. "I need to talk to her as soon as possible."

Nothing made sense. This was the same toad who'd just ambushed Brenna outside her office five minutes earlier, no question. Why was he calling here? "Like I said," Christensen said, "if you call her office—"

"I left a message there, too, but, uh, just tell her I really need to talk to her."

Christensen could see the kids through the open front door, waiting for him by the Explorer. "May I say who's calling?" he baited.

"Myron. She'll know. Tell her it's about an interview with Enrique Chembergo."

Christensen scribbled quickly, but stalled at the name. "You're going to have to spell that one for me."

Levin spelled the name, then said, "Just say the gardener. She'll know."

"And you want to line up an interview with this person?"

"No, no," Levin said. "I already talked to him. So just tell her that. Tell her he knows what happened, but not why. Actually, since I've got you on the line, any chance you could get that message to her, like, now? Her secretary just took my name and number, but I've got some information I really think she might need."

"I'll do my best," Christensen said. "Where can she reach you?" He wrote down Levin's cell phone and pager numbers, then read them back to make sure he had them right. Through the front door, he could see the kids drawing faces in the accumulated dirt on his car.

"Appreciate the help," Levin said.

''Listen, is there a problem—'' The line clicked and went silent, leaving Christensen with his mouth open and, for some reason, the hair on his arms standing on end. ''Hello?''

Despite the rush, he listened until the dial tone returned. He wasn't sure why.

Christensen steered the Explorer through the flock of minivans gathered in front of the Westminster-Stanton School and wheeled into an open spot near the first-grade classrooms. He kissed a hugely embarrassed Annie good-bye in front of a swarm of fellow third-graders and walked Taylor to room 14, where his second-grade teacher, Mrs. Gehrls, seemed to think it perfectly reasonable for a 48-pound transfer student to arrive with a backpack of apparently equal weight. They watched the boy struggle out of the straps and hang the load in the cupboard.

"Rocks," Christensen said.

The teacher nodded sagely. "I see."

He expected tears, or at least trembling hesitation. Taylor could be fragile. When they told him they intended to become a family, Brenna said the prospect brought on three days of relentless anxiety and nausea. He was doing well in his school in Mount Lebanon, even had a few friends, and the idea of changing homes and schools at the same time really threw him. But now, as Taylor walked down the aisle of his classroom, he seemed almost calm. He rearranged the clump of red hair on top of his head and took an empty seat at a cluster of four small desks. He folded his hands on the desktop and seemed to wait patiently for class to begin. Christensen didn't fully appreciate the depth of his anxiety until, trying to get a good-bye hug, he had to pry the boy's locked fingers apart.

"I'll be okay," Taylor said. His lower lip trembled. "I've got rocks."

"Of course you will. What's with that, anyway?"

Taylor's eyes shifted nervously to the classroom's cupboard. "You think I could bring my pack up here? What if it happens and my rocks are all back there?"

Christensen tried to read the boy's eyes. They registered real fear. "What if *what* happens?"

Taylor leaned close and whispered. "Third-graders. What if they attack?"

Annie.

Christensen bit his lip as soon as he realized, imagining his daughter's lurid description of the violence new students must face from the entrenched Westminster-Stanton elementary-school marauders. "Do you really think that will happen, Mr. T? Or do you think Annie might have been trying to scare you?"

The boy shrugged.

"Do you think any of the teachers or grown-ups here would let you get hurt?"

Taylor shook his head.

"You'll be fine, I promise."

Outside, Christensen spotted a break in the parking-lot snarl and made his move. The Explorer squeaked between a Volvo wagon and a Dodge Caravan into daylight, its dashboard clock reading 8:04. He'd have a session with Annie when they got home, but he already had other things on his mind. He snatched the car phone from its holder and poked the programmed number for Brenna's office.

"Kennedy & Flaherty. How may I direct your call?" The receptionist, Liisa, spoke with a dignified air that betrayed nothing about her multiple tattoos or her years as a Liberty Avenue hooker. When Brenna was a public defender, she represented the then-teenager a half-dozen times, and knew she wanted a fresh start. All Liisa needed was a job, and she was the first one Brenna called when she and Flaherty opened their practice.

"It's Jim, Liis. Brenna around?"

"Hey," she said, dropping her professional voice. "How'd day one go for the little skipper?"

"I think he's okay. Little rough and I just wanted to fill Brenna in. Is she swamped?"

"Who knows?" she said. "I just screen her calls, remember? Haven't seen her since she came in."

"Are *you* busy?"

"Like a one-armed paperhanger."

He steered onto Fifth Avenue, headed toward the Allegheny River and the Harmony Brain Research Center. "Tell her it's important, okay?"

The morning's odd phone call replayed in his head as he waited at the Negley light. In Levin's voice he'd heard a troubling mix of anxiety and concern, in addition to the smarmy I-know-something-you-don't tone that had come across on TV. Christensen paid close attention to people like that. He remembered, too, the newspaper and magazine clippings and printouts that Brenna and Flaherty had found while doing background research on the Underhills. She'd picked up the fat Nexis printout at her office after meeting the Underhills in Fox Chapel, and he'd scanned it while she worked on the bathroom.

Flaherty had searched only by the family name, not by Allecorp, the name of the family's main development company, so the computer had ignored much of the Underhill-related Renaissance development during the 1970s and 1980s. Still, the printout was as thick as a phone book. Practically everything the family did made news. He'd found references to a nasty probate dispute among grandfather Andrew Underhill's siblings in the mid-1950s, to the family's embarrassed attempt to explain

a drunken indiscretion by young Ford as a Princeton senior, to a single, brief account of the accidental horseback-
riding death three years earlier of Ford's only child—an
unblinking chronicle of life in the fishbowl of wealth and
celebrity. Only a few of the stories were negative. He
could have gorged himself on tales of philanthropy. The
last quarter-inch of the chronological printout was nothing
but stories about the Underhills' heroic role at Harmony.

Brenna picked up suddenly. "So how'd he do?"

The driver behind him leaned on the horn. The Explorer
lurched as he stomped the gas. "Stiff upper lip. I think
Annie told him some horror story about what happens to
new kids, so he started in a hole. I'll talk to her."

"But he was okay when you left?"

"Fine. He was pretty excited, actually, after seeing you
on TV."

"You saw that?" she said. "Myron's such a jerk. He
knows I'll talk to him if I can, but the visuals aren't as
good unless it looks like he stalked me."

Christensen shifted the phone to his other ear and
moved with the morning traffic. "So the sheriff's people
are still nosing around?"

"It's weird. Nobody Downtown's talking."

Christensen pulled a folded Post-it from his shirt pocket
and unfolded it. "Somebody is. Levin called you at home
right after the live report."

"He called the house, too? It's a brand-new number.
Myron's such a pain in the ass." Brenna waited.

"Said he'd interviewed—" Reading from the Post-it
now. "Enrique Chembergo."

The line was silent, but only for a moment. "The gardener," Brenna said. "*Shit*. He talked to Myron?"

"That's the guy who heard something or saw something when Floss fell, right?"

"*Hell*. He and his wife both work for the Underhills.
She does home-care stuff with Floss, actually. Both from
Central America somewhere. I read his statement to the
cops. Seems pretty sure what he saw. I'm sure Myron'll

make the most of that. He say anything else?''

"He wants to talk to you ASAP. Said this guy knows what happened, but not why, and that he had information you might need.''

No response.

"Bren? He's just blowing smoke, right?''

"Maybe. Hard to say. I've known Myron a long time.''

"Then call him, okay?'' he said. "I'd feel better.''

"How's your schedule today?''

"Open,'' he said. "Just doing some screening out at Harmony, still trying to find case-study candidates. I want to be back by three to get the kids.''

"You can let them go to Kids' Korner after school, you know. No need to pick them up until six.''

"Just for today. I'll feel better.''

"Where are you now?'' Brenna said. Her voice had changed.

He looked around. A state police headquarters flashed past on his left. "Washington Boulevard. Almost to Allegheny River Boulevard.''

"Still on this side of the river?''

He slowed as he approached the intersection. Directly in front of him, across the busy boulevard, the Allegheny River ran high and muddy. He watched a battered tug churn its way east.

"What?'' he said.

"You're not *that* far from Mount Mercy, that's all. It'd sure be nice to know if Floss remembers anything about what happened. You could be there in ten minutes.''

"Bren—''

"She has some megasuite on the fourteenth floor, which is no big surprise. You knew the family built the new wing, right?''

He knew, just as he knew every corridor of Mount Mercy Hospital, every ICU nurse on every shift, every sad-eyed priest who roamed its halls dispensing platitudes like aspirin. Today was Monday. If nothing had changed during the past five years, the Mount Mercy cafeteria dinner special would be a gelatinous Swiss steak. Tomorrow: Overcooked lemon chicken. He'd tried them all during the tortured months that he and the girls waited through Molly's coma, never wanted to walk back into the place again, wasn't even sure they'd let him in again after he'd barred the ICU door, disconnected Molly's respirator, and let his wife die with the dignity her doctors seemed so intent on denying her. The last time he'd left there, he was in handcuffs.

"Right?" Brenna said.

"Huh?"

"The Underhills helped build the new wing."

"Two wings, actually. Look, Bren, it's not like I know the woman well enough to just drop by. Other people at Harmony are much more involved with her." He waited. "I mean, don't you think that would look odd?"

"You know you want to talk to her, Jim. You have as much right as anybody else out there. You're a researcher, for God's sake. You have every reason to ask questions. And I need your help."

He *was* curious, and not just in an academic sense. Levin's cryptic message was troubling enough, but it was the reporter's tone, that unexpected undercurrent of sincerity and concern, that stuck with him. Still, the idea of returning to Mount Mercy . . .

"Floss'll probably be back at Harmony in a few days," he said. "I can wait."

"I'm not sure *I* can, Jim. There's so many people I need to talk to today just to get a handle on this thing. And from what it sounds like, with the Alzheimer's and everything, I'd need you along to help me interpret what she says anyway. Come on, baby, do it for science."

"Bren?"

"Yes."

"It'd be my first time back there."

"I know. You'll be fine."

"Bren—" he protested again, but she was right. It was as good a time as any to face it down. He eased the Explorer to the inside lane and slowed down, looking around for cops. This was going to be a risky U-turn.

10

The automatic doors opened with a familiar hiss, welcoming Christensen back to a place he'd been trying to forget for five years. He didn't stop walking. Better not to until he'd crossed the psychological threshold of Mount Mercy's ground-floor entrance, but even as he cleared that point he wondered if the place and the grim chapter it represented in his life might stop him midstride in a flood of fresh grief. In the lobby reception area, he forced himself to look up.

The place was cheery enough, but still too familiar. Flat-leafed indoor plants flourished beneath the Plexiglas skylights. The lobby furniture was an inviting blend of deep cushions and soothing colors. Along the left wall, a thousand brass rectangles remembered each of the hospital's $10,000 contributors. Above them, maybe a hundred larger silver rectangles acknowledged the $25,000 donors. A dozen gold-on-walnut Million-Dollar-Plus Club plaques hung above those, and surely at least one generation of Underhills was among them. Topping that shameless philanthropic pyramid was an oil portrait of the Pope.

He recognized the front-desk receptionist, a dignified

woman of maybe sixty. He remembered her mostly because of the forelock of silver on her head of otherwise
impossibly black hair. Melissa, being a malevolent thir-
teen at the time Molly was here, nicknamed the woman
"The Bride," with Frankenstein understood. As the
months wore on and Molly showed no signs of recovering
from the damage done by the drunk who hit her head-on,
they'd all begun using the nickname. The receptionist
seemed just as aggressively professional and humorless as
he remembered.

Christensen kept moving. The elevator door opened
onto the fourteenth floor with an upbeat *ping*! An unfamiliar face was peering into a computer monitor in the
nurse's station—thank goodness for small favors. The
man, maybe thirty-five, wearing scrubs and the arrogance
of a surgeon, didn't even look up as Christensen approached the counter.

"Room 1436?" Christensen asked.

He noticed the man's hospital badge, which identified
him as an R.N. The nurse glanced away from the monitor
only long enough to locate a box of disposable anti-
infection masks on a nearby shelf. He pushed one of the
plastic-wrapped masks across the counter, then returned
to the screen. "Wear that. Doctors don't want her sick on
top of everything else."

Christensen nodded. "The room?"

"To the left. You're family, right?"

"No."

The nurse looked up, apparently annoyed, and considered Christensen over the rims of his painfully hip eyeglasses. "What, then?"

"I work with Mrs. Underhill at the Harmony Center. I
do Alzheimer's research there."

After a long moment, the nurse shrugged. "End of the
hall."

The fourteenth-floor corridor was windowless and artificially bright, and Christensen unwrapped the mask as
he weaved his way between carts filled with the remains

of the morning meal. About halfway down, he stopped to drop the mask's plastic wrapper into the trash receptacle on a cleaning cart. The door to Room 1416 opened suddenly, and a sturdy woman wearing the light-blue uniform of the hospital's cleaning staff strode out with a load of damp, wadded white towels. Her forearms looked like oak logs. Christensen remembered her from a hundred linen changes five years ago, even if he couldn't recall her name. He remembered, too, her habit of talking to Molly as she worked, asking her how she was feeling, what she thought about the day's fine weather, trying to overcome the devastation of his comatose wife's brain and make her feel somehow still a part of life. Christensen often wondered if the woman hated him for doing what he did.

"Morning," she said. Her smile was polite and weary, not one of recognition, as she dumped the towels into the waiting hamper and trundled it and the cleaning cart on down the hall.

Christensen turned the other way and covered his nose and mouth with the mask, snugging the elastic band around the back of his head and adjusting the fit so it didn't pull at his beard. Anonymity felt safer. He had no illusions about this visit, even if Brenna did. Floss Underhill was deep into the second stage of Alzheimer's, the cruelest stage, a few years from terminal with just enough left of the person who once was to define the differences between then and now.

In Floss's case, Christensen knew she sometimes didn't recognize family members and close friends. Since he started monitoring Maura Pearson's art class two months earlier, he'd also seen her repeat the same speech to Maura at the start of each class. After two years meeting five times a week in the same room, Floss still introduced herself as a new student before taking her seat. The chances of her connecting with a coherent memory about what had happened two days earlier were probably about the same as the chances of a sudden electoral upset of her only son—nil. Brenna was right about one thing, though.

He *was* curious. How capable would a second-stage Alzheimer's patient be of attempting suicide? Or if something else happened on that gazebo deck, how much of that trauma might she remember? Even a casual conversation might give him a clue. At worst, he figured he could wish her a speedy recovery, introduce himself to a family member or two and explain his research at Harmony. If they were curious, he'd explain more.

The door to Room 1436 was slightly ajar, dead-center at the end of the hall, different from most of the other halls in Mount Mercy. Most of the hallways ended with a cramped row of three doors, each leading into a separate double room. Here, a single door led into what he assumed was a three-room suite reserved, no doubt, for the hospital's big donors and wait-listed transplant patients with Saudi bloodlines.

The corridor was oddly quiet. He'd seen patients in most of the rooms he passed, heard the tinny murmur of their remote-controlled overhead televisions, so he knew the bed count was high. But it was quiet. His light knock on Floss Underhill's door sounded like a battering ram. He knocked again more softly when no one answered.

"Warren?"

He knew the voice, knew it was hers, but it still created sudden and unshakable images for him: A three-pack-a-day frog. A shovel edge slicing into gravel. Janis Joplin fresh from sleep.

"Get in here, you cussed old bastard," she said.

"Uh, no," Christensen said as he eased open the door. "Mrs. Underhill, I'm Jim Christensen from the Harmony Research Center. We've met in Maura Pearson's art classes."

She was silhouetted against the harsh glare from the room's wide window, seated in a wheelchair. He could tell she was turned toward him, but everything else about her was blown out by the morning sun streaming through the window. "You're not Warren," she croaked.

He stepped a few feet farther into the room, which was

more hotel than hospital. The furniture wasn't the grim, uncomfortable institutional stuff found everywhere else at Mount Mercy. It was real wood and fabric. The bed was fairly standard, but made with nice linens and a thick down comforter. Needlepoint throw pillows and hand-made quilts gave it the look of an elderly aunt's bedroom, though on his second look Christensen noticed the words "Mount Mercy" spelled out in stitches across one of the pillows. Floss was alone, which flustered him.

"I heard about your injuries, Mrs. Underhill. I wanted to come by and say hello," Christensen said. "Is that all right?"

As he edged closer, Floss sharpened into view. She was wearing a royal-blue robe, plush, with the lived-in quality of something personal. Her reading glasses were low on her nose, but even so he could see that the skin below her eyes was the color of a plum, probably the result of a concussion. A patchwork of scratches scarred the left side of her face, and her left arm was in a heavy cast from her wrist to her shoulder. She rested it on the arm of the motorized wheelchair. There was an indefinable strength to her. A drawing pad lay on a tray affixed to the chair's arms. On the small table to her right, just beside the right hand in which she held a pencil-thick paintbrush, was a bowl of inky blue water and an open Disney-character watercolor paint set just like the set Annie had. Her hand didn't waver as it moved from the pad to the paint and back again.

She studied him. "You're not Warren," she repeated.

"No, ma'am, I'm not."

Floss Underhill turned back to the pad on her tray, seemed to notice it for the first time. Its surface was washed with patches of dark color, but his eyes were still adjusting and he couldn't make out the images. Her gaze shifted to the paintbrush. She leaned forward and plunged it into the bowl of water, then swirled the tip into a pale yellow. Her brush tip found the pad, and the images came clearer as she worked a splash of yellow into what looked like a fading sun in a deep blue and threatening sky. The rest was a landscape of dark hills, typical of many Alzheimer's patients, but everything was blurred by the imprecision of watercolors. The one bright image at the center of the 2-by-3-foot pad was that of an indistinct dapple-gray horse, riderless, with wings.

"Pegasus," he said.

Her hand stopped moving, but only for a moment, then she daubed her brush tip back into the water bowl. She dipped it then into the purple. "Gray," she said.

Christensen waited, hoping his reverent communion might build trust. A full minute of silence passed. "You paint very well, Mrs. Underhill," he prompted. "Can you tell me about this picture?"

"These paints won't stay where I put 'em," she said. "Run all over the damned page." Her hand moved toward her sun without so much as a tremor. She sat forward in her wheelchair and put her right elbow on the wheelchair's arm. Across the bleached sun, she sketched a pattern that left a pale trail of diluted purple. The resulting image looked like a melted hood ornament.

"Are those letters in the circle, or numbers?" he asked.

She turned slightly toward him, grimacing from the effort. Despite the injuries, despite her years, Floss Underhill was a beautiful woman. Her white hair was pulled into a tight French twist, and he wondered briefly if that or cosmetic surgery might explain the girlish smoothness around her clear blue eyes.

"You're Spencer Crean's boy, Parker," she said. "Take off that mask."

"They told me not to, Mrs. Underhill. Sorry."

"You grew a beard, I can tell. For the life of me I can't see why. They just look like hell, beards. Women don't like 'em." Her face suddenly was full of mischief. "You know why, don't you?"

Christensen shook his head. She reached out with her right hand, hooked a finger in his shirt pocket and pulled him closer. He caught a whiff of good tobacco.

"They scratch our thighs," she said.

He pulled away, a startled reflex. She winked, then laughed out loud, a deep throaty thing that was part Bette Davis, part Harley-Davidson. She dipped her brush in the purple again and retraced the lines she had sketched earlier across the face of the sun. The shapes were letters, two apparently, but blended in a way that they shared an upright leg.

"Your parents still have that mare, Sophie, the chestnut with the one white foreleg?" she said. "God, she was something. Took Warren a month just to get her to take a bit."

"No, I'm Jim Christensen, Mrs. Underhill, from the Harmony Center. We met in Maura Pearson's art class. I came by to visit you here at Mount Mercy."

"She nearly broke Warren, that one did. Cranky old fart deserved it, too. I don't care if he is the best god-damned trainer on earth. If I had a dime for every time I caught him cheating at gin rummy—" Her voice trailed off.

"You'd be rich?" he prompted.

"I am rich."

Christensen laughed. "No, ma'am, you were talking about someone named Warren."

She thought about that. "Know how to tell if a man's a good stable manager?" she said suddenly. "Take a comb, see. Show up at the stables without calling, middle of the day maybe. Don't let him know you're coming. Then try to run that comb through your horse's tail. It's real simple: The comb snags, you need a new stable manager. The good ones use conditioner. Every day."

"Warren was a good one?"

"The man knew horses like I don't know what." Another wink. "Women, too."

"Really?" Christensen stifled a smile. This was a side of Floss Underhill he never expected to see, or even imagined.

"Really."

She turned back to her drawing pad, fixing her eyes for a long time on the winged horse at its center. "Warren took Gray away," she said. "Still can't figure it. He wasn't even out that day."

Christensen reached an index finger toward the center of the drawing pad. "Gray, that's the horse with the wings?"

"Gray could fly," she said. "Me, too."

Christensen caught another whiff of tobacco. The smell seemed especially intense here, in a hospital room where smoking was presumably not allowed. "Mrs. Underhill, have you been smoking?"

She worked her hand into a pocket of her robe and pulled out something dark and foul. The remains of a cigar as thick as his thumb. As quickly as she pulled it out, though, she thrust it back in. "Macanudo Jamaica," she said. "Almost Cuban, but don't tell that man."

"What man?"

She pointed her paintbrush over Christensen's left shoulder. "*That* man," she said. "Old bastard won't let me smoke."

Christensen whirled around, startled to see that they were not alone. Vincent Underhill filled the room's doorway, his face instantly recognizable even thirty years after he left public office. The hair was whiter, the jawline less chiseled than before, but the former governor was an indelible part of Christensen's memory, though not, apparently, a part of his demented wife's. Flustered, Christensen stood up and extended a hand. He pulled it back when it went unshaken.

"We told you people no paints," Underhill said.

Christensen still felt a need to introduce himself. "I'm—"

"We were very clear on that, as well as on the cigars." The former governor was fully in the room now. He turned away from Christensen for the moment and patted his wife's good arm. "Good morning, Miss Florence. Sleep well?"

Floss seemed to appraise him. "I slept fine. You a doctor?"

Vincent Underhill offered a tight smile, gave his wife's arm a little squeeze. With his other hand, he gently plucked the paintbrush from her. He snapped the metal lid of the paint set closed and handed the box and the brush to Christensen.

"Hey," Floss protested.

Underhill studied the watercolor image on his wife's drawing pad, then took the pad, too. He closed it, but that he kept. He tossed it onto the bed, away from Christensen, who wondered if, because of his mask, he'd been mistaken for a hospital staffer. He caught Underhill's eyes searching his chest for a name tag.

"Actually, the art work is very therapeutic," he said. "It'll help with her fine motor skills, and some people think it's a way for her to connect with some of her lost memories."

Christensen couldn't interpret Underhill's impassive face, so he continued. "And you probably know about the nicotine studies, how even one cigarette can improve communication between the neurons and the hippocampus. That's the learning and memory part of the brain." Still no reaction. Christensen, nervous, rushed to fill the silence. "So, actually, in terms of recall, she may be one of the few people who actually *should* smoke. No one's quite sure why it works that way, just that it does. So—"

"Let me be very clear about this," Underhill interrupted. His voice was stern but not hostile, a teacher talking to a misguided student. "From now on, please see to it that our family's wishes are followed. No paints. No cigars."

"But the cigars might—"

Underhill turned away, busying himself with the remains of his wife's last meal. Christensen surrendered. He still had his anonymity, at least. If he left now, there'd be no awkward explanation of why a marginally involved memory researcher from the Harmony Center was in the private hospital suite of a woman he barely knew.

"Sorry for the oversight," he said.

Vincent Underhill nodded his absolution. "Now if you'll excuse us, I'd like to spend some time alone with my wife."

"You're not a doctor, then?" Floss said to her husband. "I'm confused."

Christensen found the hall a welcome relief. A different nurse, a woman, was at the nurse's station, but she was on the phone. He set the paint set and brush on the counter without a word or even a wave, and headed for the elevator. He didn't take off the mask until he got to the parking-lot exit, and then only because the nervous attendant put his hands in the air.

The Harmony Brain Research Center was an unappreciated marvel of futuristic architecture hidden like some roosting alien craft in the hills of O'Hara township, just northeast of the city. In miles, it wasn't far from their new house in Shadyside, but it was, as Pittsburgh natives said, "across the river." In this case, it was just on the north side of the Allegheny River, removed from the cities and townships crowded into the irregular wedge of land between the Allegheny to the north and the Monongahela River to the south. But in parochial Pittsburgh, the phrase "across the river" was much more than a geographic truism. It suggested some far-off and exotic destination, someplace other than where you belonged.

Even if you were in the vicinity, Harmony wasn't the kind of place you visited without a reason. You came only if Alzheimer's had flared somewhere in your family. In the two months he'd spent doing research there, Christensen had begun regarding the center as the pleasant but inevitable terminus of a thousand slow-motion tragedies.

He nosed the Explorer up the serpentine drive, rapping out a rhythm on the steering wheel. A nervous habit. He'd willed himself to stop twice already, but he started again each time he thought about Vincent Underhill. What was *that* about? He tried again to think of reasons why the man would object to his wife's painting, or to having an occasional cigar that could only goose her faulty synapses and improve her memory function, but Underhill's genteel hostility had him curious. He knew the family was sensitive to the plight of Alzheimer's victims—its generous support of Harmony and deep involvement in Floss's care demonstrated that. Maybe since Christensen was relatively new at Harmony, he didn't yet have a good grasp of the family dynamics of Alzheimer's. Or maybe, while monitoring Maura Pearson's art classes, he'd just overlooked the Underhill family's resistance to certain activities.

Still.

He'd been assigned a temporary spot in the staff parking lot about as far from the entrance as was possible, and he wheeled the Explorer into it at full speed. The front tires bounced off the concrete wheel-stop. He turned off the engine and drew a deep breath. After five more, he opened the driver's-side door for the long walk. By the time the automated lobby door swished open, he'd decided his first stop was going to be Pearson's office. She'd dealt with the Underhills for at least two years. She could help him understand what had happened back there.

"Got a minute?" he said, poking his head around the edge of her open door.

The art therapist was hunched over her desk in an office that reminded him of a landfill. She looked a lot like Janet Reno after Waco—large and ungainly, desperately preoccupied, a woman who, unlike the Clinton administration's attorney general, was seemingly anchored to the planet by the ridiculously overstyled Air Jordan basketball shoes she insisted on wearing with the laces undone. At the moment, she was peering through her black horn-rimmed glasses at the palm of her hand, where something brown was squirming.

"Take the shade off my desk lamp and hold it over

him," she said, nodding toward the wriggling brown thing. "Quick."

Christensen pushed his way into the small office, set his briefcase on one of the chairs, and did as he was told. "That's a mouse," he said, peering into her palm.

"Gerbillus perpallidus," Pearson said. "Hand me those fingernail clippers."

The creature was on its back. She was holding it in place with her right thumb, which was wedged firmly against the underside of the gerbil's chin. Its long tail whipped madly at her wrist as its bony feet scrabbled for leverage.

Christensen was nearly dumbstruck, and not just because he hated mice. "Gerbil manicure?" he managed.

Pearson looked up and snorted, the kind of laugh that would embarrass most people. "Yeah, right," she said, and snorted again. "See those?"

She pointed her left index finger at the rodent's yellow front teeth, which jutted over her thumbnail like two half-inch strands of uncooked spaghetti. "If you don't clip 'em, they get so long the poor things can't eat."

"Maura," he said, "it's God's plan. They shouldn't exist in the first place. He's just correcting a mistake."

The oral surgery took only a second, reducing the length of the gerbil's teeth by half. Pearson returned her patient to a mound of cedar chips at the bottom of an aquarium on her bookshelf, then rummaged through her desk's lap drawer. She found a packaged antiseptic wipe, tore it open, and rubbed it between her hands.

"Pet-store food isn't rough enough to wear them down, and chew blocks upset his stomach," she said. "This works fine. You coming to the opening?"

A conversation with Pearson could be as hard to follow as a conversation with one of her demented art students. "The opening?" he said.

She looked exasperated. "The Once-Lost Images exhibit? The Sofa Factory?"

"I'm sorry. Of course. That's *this* week?"

"The calendars just came back from the printer," she said. "Want one?"

Pearson clomped over to a box on her windowsill and pulled a glossy hanging calendar from inside. Its cover read "Once-Lost Images: The Visual Imagery of Alzheimer's Patients"—the latest fundraising premium for the Three Rivers Alzheimer's Association. The calendars were to be sold at the first public exhibit of art produced in Pearson's class at Harmony.

She offered one across her desk. "You've probably seen some of these pieces, but the calendar turned out great."

Christensen fanned the pages. He recognized some of the paintings, but he was struck again by their power. Coupled with the artist's chosen title and description, the images offered eloquent testimony to remembered moments and forgotten feelings. He looked at the painting on the calendar cover: five flowers around a woman's crude self-portrait, with one dark flower off in the upper left corner of the canvas. The artist, now dead, was a mother of five who lost a sixth child at birth. She'd titled the piece *My Beautiful Garden*.

"It's so damned easy to forget the feelings that are still inside them," Christensen said. "All those memories. All that emotion. That's the beauty of what you do, Maura. The art's like a taproot into all that stuff. You give them a way to express some really profound stuff that their brain just won't let them understand. It gives them a voice."

Pearson looked away, typically uncomfortable with his compliment.

"Assume you heard about Floss Underhill," he said, looking for a place to sit. He settled finally on the arm of a chair stacked with boxes of modeling clay.

"Poor thing," Pearson said, "but she's a tough old bird. I'd be surprised if she's out a full week. There's a card going around. You should sign it."

"Where is it?"

"I'll have it for the class to sign later. Do it then."

Christensen eyed the gerbil, whose recovery seemed complete and instantaneous. How high were the sides of that aquarium? Could gerbils jump?

"Actually, I stopped to say hello to her at Mount Mercy on my way here this morning," he said. "You'll be happy to know she was painting when I got there."

"Phillip came through, then."

"Phillip?"

"Doctor friend. I asked him to take her some water-colors, just in case she had something to say. So she got them?"

"Well," he said, "she *had* them."

Pearson peered over the top of her glasses.

Christensen shrugged. "Her husband didn't want her to have any paints. Pretty strange scene, really. The guv— ex-guv I should say, not the future guv—got pretty huffy about it."

"So what, then? He took the paints away?"

He nodded. "He asked me to get rid of them. Thought I was a hospital staffer. Are there problems there I'm not aware of?"

Pearson shook her head. "They pulled her out of the class a couple days ago. With the weather turning nicer, Vincent said he wanted her spending more time in the rehab garden. But they've really supported the program. He's probably just upset about everything. Any idea what she was painting?"

"She was a big equestrienne, right? I mean, years ago."

Pearson nodded.

"There was a horse, like Pegasus, gray with wings. Looked like it had a dark marking on its nose, shaped like a mushroom. The background was one of those weird landscapes they're always doing. A sun with squiggles or letters or something on it. Nothing too decipherable."

"It's always horses with Floss," Pearson said. She picked up one of the calendars and flipped to April, then set it in front of him. "A variation on the theme."

Christensen read the title and credit: *Some Crazy Story about Gray*, by Florence.

"It's not exactly the same, but almost," he said. "Same horse. I think Gray is its name. Same sun thing. Florence is Floss's given name?"

"Nobody calls her that, but yeah." Pearson pulled the calendar back and studied the picture again. "She's done maybe half a dozen like that. She rode jumpers when she was younger. Probably explains the wings."

"Plausible," he said. "She said 'Gray could fly' when she talked about the one at Mount Mercy."

"The sun thing looks almost like a little rebus puzzle, doesn't it? With the interlocking letters, the M and the R?"

Christensen tugged the calendar back across the desk. The printed version was much clearer than the one she'd done at the hospital. "You've spent more time with Floss than I have. How much help would she be in helping us understand things like that?"

"Late second stage. Hard to tell." Pearson swept the gerbil tooth trimmings into her wastebasket. "I just give them the paints and make sure they stay on task. Figuring out why they paint what they do, that's your job."

"Until they pulled her, Floss was pretty regular in class, right?"

"Used to come every day with Selena, her home-care nurse. You've seen Selena at the back of the room, haven't you?"

Christensen conjured a face he'd seen waiting patiently on the fringes of the art class: a dark young woman, lips like sofa cushions, eyes like coals, usually hidden behind one of the tabloids at the back of the art room. She came with Floss, left with Floss. In his two months there he'd never heard her speak. "She's the Hispanic-looking woman?"

"Right. The Hopper picks them up in the morning and takes them home in the afternoon," Pearson said. "The family has always wanted Floss treated just like every-body else. No special privileges.''

''Good PR.''

''It wasn't just that, though. Vincent told me he'd have burned out a long time ago without those breaks in the middle of the day. Take a lesson, though. Just last week, Floss was insisting that Art Rooney Sr. drove her back and forth every day.''

''The old Steelers owner? He's about a hundred and fifty years old, isn't he?''

''Actually, he's dead,'' Pearson said.

''Oh. Sorry. Sports aren't my thing. So what's your point?''

''Trust Floss's explanation of what she paints—her ex-planation of anything, for that matter—at your peril,'' she said. ''She feels it, but she can't articulate it. You'll def-initely need the family to help understand what an image like this might mean.''

Christensen eased himself off the arm of the chair and walked to Pearson's window. In the parking lot below, he spotted the cherry-red titanus that was her beloved 1956 Buick Special. Among the assembled Chevys, Fords, Chryslers, and the occasional Toyota, it stood out like a rhinoceros at high tea. Just the thought of Pearson behind its oversized wheel made him smile. When he turned back, Pearson was pulling off one of her sneakers. She tugged her athletic sock tight and slid the shoe back on, unlaced as always.

''You're sure there aren't some problems there, Maura? I mean, this was sort of a don't-mess-with-me conversa-tion with Vincent Underhill, delivered, of course, in the mannerly style of the well-bred. Just 'No paints. No ci-gars.' Period. End of discussion. I tried to tell him about the nicotine research, but he just stuffed me.''

''I saw him Thursday and everything seemed fine.'' She opened one of her desk drawers and pulled out a photocopy of a newspaper article. ''I think I even showed him the *Press* preview story on the show. He seemed de-lighted.''

The photocopied newspaper story announcing the open-ing of the Once-Lost Images exhibit was headlined "Memories in the Making." Two images accompanied the article, both reprinted in the paper's grainy black-and-white. One was the calendar cover, *My Beautiful Garden*. The other was *Some Crazy Story about Gray*. Christensen nodded toward the article. "How'd they pick the pic-tures?"

Pearson shrugged. "I sent slides of all twelve from the calendar and left the choice up to them. I think the writer really liked Floss's. Personally, I don't think it's one of the best. But he went on and on about it in the story, how it hints at the complicated world inside their heads. Of course, he's got no idea who Florence is.''

"You're sure?"

"First names only. Always.''

"But people here know. It's no big secret who painted the pictures, is it?"

Pearson shook her head. "Not here, I guess. But the writer didn't call. Can't imagine he'd know it was Floss. That's why we went with first names only for the public showing.''

"But if someone wanted to find out who painted a par-ticular one, it wouldn't be that hard, right?" he said.

"Whoa, whoa, whoa, Jimbo. You're missing the point.''

"Which is?"

Pearson spread her hands wide. "It's the images and the stories they tell that are important. As long as we explain the context, why would the name of the artist matter?"

He thought for a moment. "No idea," he conceded.

The copy of the *Press* story was still on the corner of Pearson's desk. In the same motion, Christensen picked it up and looked at his wristwatch. "Aren't you late for class?" he said.

Pearson looked at her own watch and sprang to her feet. She was past him without a word, the faint smell of cedar chips in her wake. "You coming?" she called from down the hall.

"Be right down," he shouted. He glanced at the paper in his hand, noticing the publication date in the top left corner of the page. Christensen looked closer. Thursday, April 26. Two days before Floss went into the ravine.

12

Taylor had fallen asleep with his head jammed in the space between the bedpost and the wall, his legs splayed and uncovered. Christensen extracted, covered, and kissed him, then went to check on Annie. She was buried deep in her comforter with the shredded remains of one of Molly's silk nightgowns clutched to her chest, much as she had slept for the past five years.

Christensen stepped into the hall, leaned against the doorjamb, and closed his eyes. Dinner was grilled cheese and Campbell's Chicken Noodle. Homework had been postponed. Baths had been marginally effective. After some tactical back-scratching, both kids nodded off on the couch while watching a Discovery Channel special on walruses. By any measure, he should be exhausted. But he wasn't.

He creaked down the stairs and into the office, which remained a maze of moving cartons and upended furniture. The considerable chore of unpacking what they'd moved was falling to him, since Brenna was so seldom home, and he wanted to make at least some progress before bed. The nearest carton was labeled DEN BOOK-

SHELVES. He split the packing tape with the letter opener he found in his top right desk drawer. The top item in the box was a picture frame turned facedown. He turned it over and came face-to-face with his father.

Molly had taken the picture one Thanksgiving early in their courtship, but it so perfectly captured the damaged spirit of the man that it had, for Christensen, become a defining image. Edward James Christensen was sitting in his reading chair, a half-full tumbler of Johnnie Walker on the chair's sturdy arm, his nose in a Sidney Sheldon potboiler. At the moment Molly opened her camera's shutter, he recalled, his parents' house was alive with holiday clamor. Half a dozen young cousins kept the decibel level high, competing with the dull roar from a dozen grown-ups watching a televised college bowl game. But the image of his father, the damaged mathematics teacher alone there in that rear den, so typical of his life at home, was a portrait of a functioning alcoholic retreating into himself, to a place where his wife and children were never able to follow.

Christensen folded the frame's rear prop and set the picture on his desk. His father was an angular man in the same way as Christensen, but the years and liquor had softened his face. His salt-and-pepper hair was swept back and anchored by Vitalis in the same reliable way his only son used Paul Mitchell Sculpting Lotion. To this day, Christensen wore the same rimless spectacles his father had preferred in the years before his death. That his parents' marriage had survived his father's emotional retreat was remarkable. That they'd raised two children, Jim and his older sister, was testimony to his mother's will. If their father had found any joy in that, neither Christensen nor his sister could say. He was that much a mystery to his children.

The photograph was buried for years in a family memento file. When Christensen had run across it three years earlier, as he struggled with Melissa's rage in the wake of Molly's death, he'd framed the print to remind himself how damaging an emotionally detached parent can be.

"Where you gonna put him?"

Christensen spun around, more reaction than movement. Brenna was standing at the office door. How long had she been watching?

"Jesus." His heart was pumping pure adrenaline. "When did you get home?"

Brenna laid her suit jacket over the arm of a chair. She crossed the room and wrapped her arms around his waist. She smelled the same as when she left that morning. "Just now. So where does Dad go? Back on the corner of your desk?"

"Always," he said. "Long day for you, huh?"

"Long and strange, and I'm in a deep hole on the Mother-of-the-Year title."

"Taylor's fine, but he does want to see you. He's not over the first-day jitters yet."

"He's awake?" Brenna pulled away and started for the door.

"Finally crashed about thirty minutes ago," he said. "He tried to stay up, but he was one tired soldier. Spent the whole day tight as a drum, compliments of Annie and her new-kid horror stories."

Brenna let the words settle, then dabbed at the corner of her eye with her finger. "Well, shit," she said.

"I talked to her about it."

"No, no, not that. I just needed to be with him today and I wasn't."

Christensen pulled her back to him. "But I was, Bren. It's okay."

She rubbed away a tear that had curled from the outside of one eye. Her attention had shifted over his shoulder, up toward the ceiling. He turned and looked, too. "Does that look like it's bulging?" she said.

"Where?"

She pointed to the spot above his desk where he'd noticed the stain the day before. "That whole section looks like it's bowed out a little. Is that a stain?"

"I told you about it yesterday, the stain I mean. I checked and I think it's old."

"But does it look bowed to you?"

"Hard to tell because it's so white." Christensen looked again. "No."

Brenna kicked off her shoes. In her stocking feet, she was a foot shorter than him. He kissed the top of her head.

"I tried to call you all afternoon. Liisa said she didn't want to interrupt, so I didn't push it."

"It was pretty nuts."

"I wanted to tell you about the hospital."

Brenna seemed to lose her focus for a moment. "I completely forgot you were going," she said. "Right after we talked this morning, I . . . geez. So what happened?"

Christensen looked at his watch, then nodded toward the kitchen. "Want some tea?"

The microwave clock read 11:34. Brenna poured the dregs of her decaf Constant Comment into the sink, rinsed her cup, and opened the dishwasher door. She closed it with the cup still in her right hand, his panicked Post-it note from that morning in her left.

"Kachunk?"

"That was the sound," he said. "It started, then it just stopped. Just one more thing we'll probably have to replace."

Brenna spun the dial to normal cycle. The machine was dead, although everything else in the kitchen was working. "It's on its own circuit. You checked the breaker, right?"

He felt himself suddenly exposed, as if he'd forgotten to check his car's gas tank before replacing its engine. "Of course," he lied.

"Really?"

She had him. He shook his head.

"It's the circuit, Einstein. I'll check it before we go to bed. You're pathetic, you know." She leaned back against the counter and crossed her arms, cradling her breasts beneath the white silk of her blouse. "So what's your best guess about why Vincent doesn't want her to have paints or cigars?"

"No idea." Christensen leaned back in his creaky kitchen chair, grateful for the change of subject.

"And you can't see her ever remembering what happened on the deck?"

"It's just not that simple, Bren. Her memory's like Swiss cheese to begin with. Getting her to remember something specific, even something traumatic, it's a crapshoot. I'd need hours and hours to work with her over weeks or months, with no guarantee that anything she remembered would be accurate."

She smiled. "What good *are* you?"

"Afraid you're on your own on this one," he said.

Brenna twisted a strand of her hair in one hand and studied it a long time.

"What?" he said.

She dropped her hair, but her eyes roamed the kitchen. "Myron."

"The TV guy?"

Brenna nodded. "He's a cagey son of a bitch, but he's good, too."

Christensen's face must have given away his confusion.

"I called him back this morning, just to see what he wanted. Off the record. I've dealt with him before. Pretty straight shooter. Jim, he's up to something on this case."

"He interviewed the witness, right?"

She turned around, swabbed a pool of chicken noodle soup from the tile counter with a dishrag, then turned back. "That, too. Says Chembergo told him more than he told the deputies, and he says the guy didn't sound like somebody with an ax to grind. 'Scared shitless,' was the way he put it, actually. Beyond that, Myron said he's been kicking over the rocks in Ford Underhill's background for more than six months."

Christensen shrugged. "Standard pre-election stuff,

Bren. Levin probably had to get in line behind the Republican National Committee.''

"No, that's not—'' She searched for words. "The thing is, I've done Myron some favors along the way, on other cases. He owes me.''

"So?''

"He said he just wanted me to know why he's so interested in Floss's accident. Jim, he says he's close to breaking something pretty big about the Underhills. 'Little skeleton in the family closet,' is what he said.''

Christensen sat forward again in his chair. "Cue the eerie music.''

"He wouldn't talk about it.'' Brenna waited. "What he did say was pretty weird, though.'' Another pause. "Really out of left field.''

"I'm still with you,'' he said.

"Stays between us?''

He nodded.

"Myron's saying there's gonna be a shitstorm, and I might want to think twice about taking this on. He says what happened to Floss this week might have been somebody trying to keep her quiet.''

Christensen shook his head. "That's pretty far out in left . . . He's a TV reporter, for God's sake. They don't report anything unless it involves smashed cars or picket signs.''

"Myron's different. And he's not a Chicken Little kind of guy, at least off-camera.''

"So you're taking him seriously?''

"There's only one way he gets any points for telling me that, Jim, and that's if he's right. He's knows he'd be screwing up a decent relationship by just blowing smoke.''

Brenna opened her arms to him as he crossed the kitchen. When he held her close, she sighed. "So what do you think?''

"Your call, counselor,'' he said. "When's all this supposed to happen? Before the election?''

She nodded.

"I think that's your answer. Somebody on the other side probably got this guy Myron's ear. To him, it's Watergate. But I'd bet a nickel it's nothing that'll seem the least bit relevant the day after the election."

Brenna ran a hand around his belt and patted the back of his jeans. "Any mail?"

"On the counter. So it's okay to load the dishwasher?" He was pouring an extra measure of Cascade into the soap dispenser when Brenna tapped him on the shoulder.

"What's this?" She was holding the Once-Lost Images calendar he'd set on the counter with the day's stack of catalogs, home-equity loan offers, and credit-card bills.

Christensen took the calendar from her and fanned its pages, stopping at April. "Maura organized a gallery showing of some of the art produced by the patients in her Harmony classes. It's a fund-raiser for the Three Rivers Alzheimer's Association. They're selling calendars and auctioning off the pictures."

He handed the calendar back, open to Floss Underhill's painting. She read the title and artist's name. "Florence?"

"Floss."

Brenna studied the image. "They're horse people, that's for sure." If she found any significance beyond that in the painting, it didn't register on her face. "When's the opening?"

"Later this week, down at the Sofa Factory. I think I need to go."

Brenna flipped half a dozen pages of the calendar, reading the captions beneath each image. "This really *is* interesting stuff."

"There's so much we don't know," he said.

She leveled the same curious gaze at him. "Will Maura be at the opening?"

He nodded.

"Why don't we all go?" she said. "I've *got* to meet this woman. And after the past two days, we should all be ready for a family outing."

"With the kids?"

"Why not? It's on the north side, the Mexican Wars area, right? We can hit that little barbecue place beforehand."

Christensen smiled. For the first time since he'd started his research at Harmony, Brenna finally seemed to share his fascination with Alzheimer's art, or at least with the eccentric Maura Pearson. "Deal," he said, looking again at the microwave clock. "I'm going to bed."

He turned toward the stairs. Brenna turned toward the back door. She flipped on the backyard floodlight, unlocked the deadbolt, and stepped outside in her stocking feet.

"Bren, you coming?" he called through the open door.

"When I find the circuit breakers." Her voice shrank as she moved into the shadows and rounded the corner of the house. "We've got no power, remember?"

13

Christensen had never appreciated modern art—any art, really—the way he wanted to. He envied friends who said it spoke to them, moved them, who reached rare moments of insight by gazing at a given piece. He was genuinely bothered by his stunted sense of wonder and anchored imagination even as he enjoyed the loopiness of the modern stuff and its weird, free-form sense of humor.

"It's made entirely of individual pieces of whole-wheat toast," Brenna read from the wall-mounted plaque beside an installation titled *Jesus, Lightly Browned.*

Both kids were standing remarkably still beside him, staring at the life-size image of the crucified Christ on the facing wall. "Wheat," he repeated. "Interesting medium." He leaned in for a closer look. "How'd they get the crown-of-thorns pattern?"

Brenna socked his arm. He was grateful for the attention. He'd seen so little of her since Sunday, felt her slipping into the gray zone where little else outside a case matters. And with whispered rumors that the crime lab had found someone else's skin beneath Floss's fingernails, the Underhill situation was becoming more than just another case. Would she have come along on this weeknight family outing if it didn't promise some insight into Floss Underhill? Did he really want to know the answer?

"Where do people come up with this stuff?" Brenna said. "A room full of balloons getting blown around by fans? What's with that?"

"This is weird," Annie said. "Let's go."

Christensen squeezed his daughter's shoulder. In the ten minutes they'd been strolling through the Sofa Factory looking for the Once-Lost Images exhibit, only two things had sparked any interest with either Annie or Taylor. The first was *Head-to-Head with Toyota,* a hideously mashed Chevy Chevette—the nameplate still dangled from the hatch lid—that Christensen interpreted as a wry comment about the decline of the American automotive industry. Taylor solemnly pronounced it "cool." Annie was more taken by a dynamic piece called *Bad Environment for Monochrome Paintings*—a sealed room aswarm with houseflies and hung with large white canvases on white walls. An equal number of flies lay dead on the white floor. "Way gross," his daughter said, but he had to pull her away.

Brenna nodded toward a wide door to their left. "I bet it's that way."

The kids shuffled ahead, keeping their distance, whispering whenever they spotted a flash of nudity in one of the works. He took Brenna's hand as they walked.

"What do you mean he was weird about it?" he said.

"Who?"

"The Underhills' security guy."

"I don't know. Just a feeling I got. Staggers talks in vagaries. He says he'll do things and he doesn't. Like the life-insurance stuff. He didn't seem to have a problem the first time I asked for it, but now every time I ask I get the same runaround about how Raskin has those files Downtown, not at the house. 'Temporarily unobtainable,' he said."

"You don't really think that's important, do you?"

Brenna shook her head. "These aren't the kind of people who'd try to rip off a life-insurance company. They own a couple of them, as a matter of fact. If someone did push her, you know that Mercer and Dagnolo are looking at all the obvious motives. And they probably could find *something* that looks suspicious enough to blow out of proportion before the election. But that's not the point. I asked for the information, Staggers agreed to get it, then nothing."

"You said he didn't seem too bright."

"He's working on it."

Christensen laughed, remembering her story about Staggers's earnest and constant pursuit of self-improvement. "Tried dealing with Raskin directly?"

"All tied up on campaign stuff, his secretary said. He hasn't returned my calls."

"Vincent?"

"Him either. I've been trying to get back over there to talk to the gardener and his wife. Staggers was supposed to be setting it up. So why hasn't it happened? They live right there on the property, for God's sake. How complicated could it be?"

From a narrow exhibit space hung with open umbrellas and dangling polyurethane cuts of meat, they followed the children into an open room that was either another incomprehensible artistic statement or undergoing renovation.

Annie turned around. "This is creepy. Can we go?"

Christensen spotted a small Once-Lost Images sign outside a narrow door, through which he could see an apparently clean, well-lighted place. Outside the door, a guest register was open on a small pedestal. He directed the kids toward the door. "Through there, guys. This is where we're going."

"Strange place to have an Alzheimer's fund-raiser," Brenna said. "Who picked it?"

They looked at one another, then mouthed "Maura" at the same time.

Christensen stopped and signed the register, flipping

back to the first page. The opening was an obvious success so far. Seven-and-a-half pages were filled, each with twenty-five names. For all her eccentricities, Maura Pearson was a remarkably magnetic personality. Her sixth sense for people with large checkbooks was legendary around Harmony, and it was the main reason the center's art therapy program was one of the country's best.

He picked up an exhibit catalog, handed it to Brenna, and pushed into the crowd. Annie and Taylor had gravitated toward a gallery employee, a zaftig woman of about twenty-five with a stunning array of piercings and deep, deep cleavage. Christensen counted three studs in her nose alone. She appeared to be answering questions from a young black couple interested in one of the paintings as the children waited patiently, no doubt to quiz the woman about her appearance.

"Number fourteen," Brenna said, reading from the catalog. "That's Floss's."

They began with the painting just to the left of the door, Number 1. The watercolor showed a white sailboat skimming across a blue bay toward some distant harbor. The simple scene was rendered in bold strokes of bright color and titled, *Racing for Cocktails*.

"This piece was painted three years ago by Candace, an early second-stage patient at the time," Brenna read. "She spoke often of family vacations at Lake Chautauqua when she was a teenager. Though her family never had a home there and did not own a boat, relatives say many of Candace's wealthier friends did."

"She died right around the time I started working at Harmony," Christensen said. "Maura talks about her a lot."

The next painting, an acrylic, was an odd family portrait—two people, a man and a woman, standing proudly on either side of a computer terminal as though it were an only child. The background was deep burgundy, the woman green, the man pale yellow, the computer a brackish purple. Artist: Walter. Title: *Talk, Talk, Talk*.

"Walter was a deep second-stage patient when his wife began participating in an online caregiver's support network," Brenna read. "He knew she relied on the terminal for comfort and communication, and at first resented its presence in their home. Eventually, he accepted the computer as an important part of their household."

Christensen studied the picture, so full of bright colors and smiles. "A pilot program run out of Harmony," he said. "They put terminals and Internet connections into homes, thinking the caregivers would use them to talk to doctors about care decisions. They ended up talking among themselves, being there for each other. You should read the postings, Bren. It's the kind of poetry only people on the edge can write."

Three paintings down they passed the kids as they debriefed the human pincushion. She was leaning down to talk to them, and Brenna caught him staring as they circled wide. "Excellent breasts, well displayed," she whispered. "Don't you think?"

"What?"

"She could be your daughter."

"Shhh." Christensen strained to overhear their conversation, wondering what Annie might be talking about so soberly with someone so exotic.

"Where else?" his daughter was saying. "You know what I mean."

They waited to laugh until they were safely out of earshot. Christensen turned and watched as the embarrassed woman urged the two children along. "Curious little thing," he said. "Mind if I move out when she's twelve, Bren? Just for five years or so. Bren?"

She had moved on, toward the only empty spot on the gallery wall. He caught up to her, then realized what had drawn her attention.

"Number 14," he said.

"Where is it?"

The wall plaque described the empty space. Artist: Florence. Title: *Some Crazy Story about Gray*. A laminated copy of the *Press* review with its photograph of the painting hung cockeyed from a pushpin beside the plaque.

Brenna flipped pages of the catalog and read: ''Florence was an avid equestrienne, and she rode a horse named Gray to many victories in competition. She speaks of Gray with great emotion, perhaps because she lost the horse several years ago following a tragic accident.''

They looked at each other. Christensen scanned the walls again to see if any other paintings were missing or not yet hung. But the space in front of them was the only irregularity on the whole perimeter of the gallery. He shrugged.

''Ask somebody,'' Brenna said.

He hadn't yet found Maura in the crowd. A young man dressed all in black was leaning against a nearby wall, ignoring everyone, one black Beatle boot resting flat against the wall. He was wearing the most god-awful set of horn-rimmed glasses Christensen had seen since the early 1960s, a retro-hip victim down to his flattop haircut and Speed Racer belt buckle.

''Are you with the gallery?'' Christensen asked.

He nodded, extending a flaccid hand. ''Can't talk sales, if that's what you mean. Auction's this weekend. They should be back in thirty minutes or so.''

''No, no. I'm not a buyer.'' Christensen nodded toward the spot where Brenna was standing now with both kids, still inspecting the empty wall space. ''I'm just curious about the missing painting over there.''

The young man smirked, an expression that completed the caricature. ''Took it out right before we opened tonight,'' he said. ''We didn't have time to rearrange everything.''

Christensen waited, hoping for some further explanation. ''There was a picture of it in the paper last week, you know, with a write-up about the show. They had a picture of that painting, see, and then when we got here it was gone.''

The young man studied his fingernails.

Christensen wanted to smack him. "We were just curious, see."

The kid shifted the Beatle boot to the floor, then put the other one up against the wall. Conversation seemed to greatly inconvenience him. "Alls I know is they called a couple hours ago and wanted it down. So Evan took it down, like, fast."

"Evan, the gallery director?"

Christensen knew the question was dumb. Everyone knew local iconoclast Evan Garde, the former Corky Chaiken, a man best known for once quipping that he wanted to be Andy Warhol for fifteen minutes. Christensen interpreted the young man's look as one of raw contempt. "You must know a lot of Evans," he said finally.

"Who wanted it down?" Christensen asked. "The Harmony people? The patient's family?"

"Bingo," the kid said.

"Which?"

"Family, I think. The lady from Harmony seemed a little jagged off about it."

With the publication of Floss's painting in both the Once-Lost Images calendar and the *Press* article, its fundraising value no doubt had increased enormously. Christensen couldn't imagine Maura Pearson taking it out of the show, much less off the auction block, without raising some hell.

"So they did take it out, though."

"Uh-huh."

"Because the patient's family wanted it out?"

The young man looked around. "You should talk to Evan."

"So the family said 'Jump' and everybody said, 'How high?' " Christensen said. "Why is that?"

The kid looked around again. Another smirk, this one more conspiratorial than the last. "Slam dunk, man," he said. "They've got *bucks*."

The opening theme of *Eyewitness News* announced the time, but Christensen double-checked it against the Windows clock on his computer. Eleven already? Brenna had planned to be home from her Seventh Ward schmoozefest an hour ago, but he'd been too busy to worry. The evening had slid into that odd dimension between reality and personal computing where time's pace quickens and logic is meaningless.

For two hours, since the kids went to bed, he'd been caught in a swampy tangle of modem connectors, printer cables, and power cords as he tried to set up his computer in their downstairs office. Nothing about it was intuitive, at least not for him. Thank God there were no software problems. Finally it seemed to be working.

The CompuServe Information Manager blinked onto his screen. He sat back as the modem made its digital appeal to the gatekeepers of cyberspace. Above the electronic chatter, he heard the throaty purr of a luxury car's engine outside, slowing, then stopping. He pushed himself away from CompuServe's welcome screen and went to the front door expecting to see Brenna's Legend at the curb, but the only car on either side of the street was something sleek and dark two doors away. Its brake lights went off. Christensen watched for a long time, but when no one got out, he went back to the office. Burglars don't drive cars that nice.

He clicked through the online service's menu until he reached the alphabetized Newspaper Archives list, then scrolled down to *The Pittsburgh Press*. He knew that the paper's electronic database extended back only three years, long after Floss Underhill's career as a champion rider had ended, but he wanted to search the types of stories that Terry Flaherty might have overlooked during his earlier electronic research. He couldn't say exactly what it was about this whole affair that bothered him. Maybe it was cumulative. He was willing to dismiss Myron Levin's dark warning as nothing more than a TV reporter's hyperbole. But ongoing and judicious leaks from the sheriff's department made him think its investigation was far from over, and he'd also begun to wonder about the version of Floss's fall that the family had given Brenna. Why had Ford Underhill, out of the blue, floated the possibility that his exhausted, burned-out father threw his wife into the ravine? He'd presented it to Brenna that first day almost as an option—a perfectly defensible backup story in case the suicide explanation didn't fly. With Brenna's much-publicized passion about the plight of the caregiver, it just seemed a little too convenient.

At the search prompt, he typed FLOSS UNDERHILL and HORSE and waited. A short list of headlines flashed onto the screen. Nearly all were society columns by Alexandra Pogue, the paper's ancient chronicler of the Chanel-and-charity circuit. He scanned three of Pogue's stories, enough to determine that she used the phrase "horsewoman extraordinaire" as the standard prefix for any mention of Floss. The most recent story was four years old, headlined "Pittsburgh's Royal Family Steps into Alzheimer's Charity Spotlight"—an account of one of the Harmony Center's early fund-raisers, he guessed.

He remembered the event, remembered how long ago it was. If that was one of the latest stories about Floss, she'd practically disappeared from the paper's pages following her diagnosis.

In terms of real information, all of Pogue's stories were useless. Christensen tried again, throwing his electronic net wider. He typed UNDERHILL and HORSE.

That search turned up dozens of stories in addition to Pogue's worshipful blather. Several headlines alluded to the Oaks Classic, an annual equestrian event near Latrobe. He called up one of those stories, curious what connection the Underhill family had to that competition, and quickly found a reference to "longtime Oaks organizer Floss Underhill." That seemed to him a logical progression for a woman so deeply involved with horses. When her riding days were over, she must have turned her passion toward staging competitions.

Christensen scanned the other headlines, looking for something, anything, that might shed more light on Floss's apparent fascination with the gray horse. He called up a five-year-old feature called "What It Costs" that listed the Underhill family's Fox Chapel stables among "the most expensive goods, services and extravagances in western Pennsylvania." The story cited in particular the polished oak stall doors and the "computer-controlled air fresheners mounted high above each spotless floor."

The headline "Zoning Board Settles Fox Chapel Horse Dispute" caught his eye, but it turned out to be the resolution of another resident's complaint about "recurrent horse litter" left on public roads crossed by the Underhills' mounts.

A sudden, indistinct thump jolted Christensen from his online browsing. He froze, not sure what to make of the noise, or where it came from. He got up and went to the office door.

"Bren?"

He walked to the bottom of the stairs, listening for the kids. The sound was a lot like the muffled thump they made when they rolled over in their sleep and bumped against the wall. He listened intently to the house's unnerving silence, then tiptoed up the stairs to check both kids' bedrooms. Taylor was restless, as usual, and had probably kicked the wall. Christensen covered him for a third time and tiptoed back downstairs to the office.

The modem connection was still live. Christensen scrolled down the *Press* headlines, back through the years, until he reached one published three years earlier that read, "Underhill Boy Dies in Riding Accident." The story was among the photocopied clippings Brenna got in the mail the day before, but at the time Christensen hadn't given it a second thought. He selected the story and printed it out, reading on-screen even as his laser printer began to purr.

The Pittsburgh Press
(c) Press Publishing. All rts. reserv.
0762261 UNDERHILL BOY DIES IN RIDING ACCIDENT
Edition: FIVE STAR
Section: METRO
Page: B-1
Word Count: 155

TEXT: The young son of industrial heir Ford Underhill died Sunday in what investigators say was a tragic horseback-riding accident on the Underhill family's Fox Chapel estate.

Vincent Underhill III, 3, the only grandson and namesake of the former Pennsylvania governor, was thrown from a horse ridden by his father, police said. The gray gelding, one of the family's champion show horses, apparently balked and reared along a narrow wooded trail, throwing both Underhill and his son, known as Chip. In the confusion that followed, police said the horse apparently kicked the child in the head.

Underhill's wife, Leigh, called paramedics to the

scene just minutes after the accident, but police said the child was dead on arrival at St. Francis Hospital. A coroner's report is pending.

The Underhill family declined comment through its attorney, Philip Raskin, who asked news reporters to respect the family's need for privacy "at this time of profound and unexpected grief."

Christensen plucked the printed version from his output tray and read it again. He remembered the incident, if not the specifics, because of the sudden influx of Underhill money the accident represented to various brain-injury facilities around the city. What were the chances that the horse involved in that accident was named Gray? He returned to the list of *Press* headlines on his computer screen and scrolled back up the chronological list, looking for follow-up stories. He found two, both published in the week after the accident. But when he tried to read the first, his CompuServe screen blinked a message he'd never seen while searching a newspaper's electronic library: "Story unavailable."

He tried the second. "Story unavailable."

Christensen tried the first again with the same result, then logged off. He was too tired to figure it out. He checked his watch. Eleven-thirty. Now he was starting to worry. Brenna had left him and the kids shortly after the Sofa Factory visit, headed to a Seventh Ward fund-raiser. He understood why she had to go. She'd always considered public service a noble calling, never mind the city's unrepentant culture of petty politics and its tolerance of small-minded, self-serving hacks. "We can't just turn government over to incompetents who don't care," she often said. "Then where will we be?" That's why she'd outlasted her contemporaries in the public defender's office, at least until the chance to build a private practice with Flaherty, her longtime friend, proved irresistible. But she'd entered the private sector vowing to continue some civic role, and she'd set her sights on the Pittsburgh city council.

The Seventh Ward was a clubby shark tank of educated liberal Democrats, and for Brenna it seemed a logical political base. If she was going to swim with them, she at least wanted to swim with her kind of sharks. And she did know a lot of the Seventh Ward players. But presenting herself, an outsider, as a potential candidate was a delicate thing. Even with Brenna's qualifications, commitment, and name recognition, there were rings to be kissed.

She should have been back by now.

Christensen sat back in his chair, rubbing his eyes. How could he find out the name of the horse? Could it be that simple? Trauma, whether physical or emotional, tended to etch memories deeply into the brain, but no one really understood why. Even in Alzheimer's patients, traumatic memories seemed the most durable. His own theory was that hormones, nerves, cells, and the more traditional components of memory all worked together to preserve the harshest memories, and together they became sort of an early warning system for the body. What better than a vivid memory of pain or anguish or injury to remind us of danger?

He needed more information. What if one of Floss's favorite horses *was* responsible for her only grandson's death? Wouldn't at least remnants of that anguished memory withstand the ravages of Alzheimer's? The context might erode, the overall significance of the events might be lost, but given the circumstances, he'd be surprised if some sort of horse-related imagery *didn't* find its way into Floss's artwork. Could understanding how Floss's memory cataloged that trauma help him connect with her memories of what happened at the gazebo?

Eleven thirty-five. Christensen turned off his computer and tucked the printed story into his briefcase. It had been a while since he'd worried about anyone being out late. Melissa gave him fits as a high school junior, but when she'd left to spend the last half of her senior year living with a host family and studying French culture, he'd accepted his loss of control over her comings and goings. And he'd never given Brenna's whereabouts a second thought until they moved in together. If he told her he was worried, would she be grateful for his concern, or would the confession brand him forever in her eyes as a pathetic, paternalistic schmuck?

He stared at the ceiling above his desk. The stain was bigger, but still small enough to ignore. *Some Crazy Story about Gray.*

He couldn't wait up any longer. It seemed as if he'd made the kids' cheesy-egg omelets three days ago, not eighteen hours ago. The museum visit, the missing painting, and everything else about the day was a blur, a sure sign he was exhausted. Besides, tomorrow was Floss Underhill's first day back at Harmony for adult day care. They could resume their conversation, or try to, and he could talk to her with more confidence than he had during their brief hospital visit. He had every right to be at Harmony and to work with the patients as part of his research, and he didn't intend to let a mystifying episode with Vincent Underhill undermine that.

The scene in the street hadn't changed. Brenna's usual parking spot in front of the house was still empty. Two doors down, the same car he'd noticed before, a Thunderbird, he guessed, was still along the curb. He squinted into the darkness until he was satisfied that whoever was in it was gone, then flipped on the front-porch light just as a pair of headlights turned the corner onto Howe. He watched until he was sure it was Brenna's Legend, then watched some more as she wedged it into her spot. Something odd caught his eye as he turned to head upstairs. Their front-porch swing was moving ever so slightly from side to side. The day they moved in, he'd set a small clay pot of nasturtiums on a small table beside the swing. Now it was shattered on the porch floor, just a pile of terra cotta shards and a forlorn clump of soil. And something else: A delicate stitch of damp footprints crisscrossed the porch, a man's, he guessed, but from a man walking carefully across the dew-slick concrete porch. The prints closest to the door and front windows were missing a heel print. Who the hell was tiptoeing around their porch at this time of night?

Brenna opened her car door and stepped out, hauling her briefcase and an armload of files. Christensen hurried up the stairs, suddenly uneasy and a little embarrassed that he was behaving more like Brenna's father than her lover.

15

The sign on the door said, "Welcome to The Club. You will be going home on the bus at 3 P.M." Beside it, the bright red hands of a smiling cardboard clock face registered three o'clock. From the other side of the door came music, Sinatra, and a voice that was an improbable mix of Jane Pauley's gentle compassion and Sgt. Vince Carter from *Gomer Pyle, U.S.M.C.* Maura Pearson's morning art class was already underway.

Christensen eased the door open and stepped unnoticed into the art therapy room. Except for the subtle touches—standard-sized furniture and the dozen Alzheimer's patients gathered around the painting table—it could have been an elementary school classroom. The linoleum was a soothing pale blue, a complementary shade to the plastic chairs on which the artists sat. Along the opposite wall, a spinet piano and an organ awaited the next music therapy class. Each donated item bore a gleaming brass plaque crediting the donor. A full-length mirror on wheels was beside the organ. The self-portraits done with the mirror's help were among the most remarkable pieces Christensen had seen since undertaking his study. In it, the artists saw themselves in the most poignant and horrific ways, like the man who sketched himself smiling with a pistol to his head. *No Harm, No Foul*, he'd called it. It hung on the wall, along with other matted and framed examples of the art produced in this room.

In one corner, beside the large-screen TV, were a small lectern and a big overstuffed recliner. Two aluminum-frame walkers were parked next to the chair. Next to them, Jerry the parakeet danced between his swing and his food perch, raining bird seed onto the floor of his cage.

Christensen moved quietly toward the table and took a seat as Sinatra kicked into "I've Got the World on a String." Pearson's students were so accustomed to his comings and goings that no one even acknowledged him. Pearson stood over a woman who looked like a Palm Beach society matron circa 1975—hair done just so, pink Oleg Cassini suit, pearls, perfect nails, attitude. She was stabbing at a thick piece of watercolor paper with a red Mr. Sketch instant watercolor marker. Each new dot released a fresh burst of artificial strawberry scent. Angry red dots pocked the once-white surface.

"You're perseverating again, Emma," Pearson said.

The woman kept up her pace, applying each new dot with greater force. "It's my stormy sky," she said.

"I'll say." Pearson slipped her hand beneath Emma's elbow, gently but firmly blocking the motion of her arm. At the same time, she moved the dotted paper away from the woman, who made several halfhearted lunges with the marker.

"I'm not done," Emma said.

Pearson stood her ground. "I want you to try something else for me."

The dot work was typical of an agitated artist. Pearson always seemed to understand the cue, if not the reason, for Emma's anger. She released the woman's elbow, and Emma shifted the marker to her left hand and turned around in her chair. Her face was all outrage and defiance. She poked the marker at Pearson's white smock, leaving a single red dot where her navel would be. Around the table, all hands stopped moving, all eyes turned to Pearson. The therapist examined the dot as if it were a wound, then snort-laughed. "Well, touché!" she said.

"She got you," said Arthur. "Throw her ass out." The man, maybe seventy, was directly across the table from Emma. As he spoke, he trimmed a Malboro ad from a magazine with blunt-nosed scissors.

"That'll be enough, Mr. Gemmelman," Pearson chided. She stooped down until she was facing Emma and waited until the woman looked her in the eye. "I understand you're angry with me, Emma, and that's okay. But I also want to help you understand your body a little better. May I show you something different?"

Emma nodded, her hostility in check, at least for the moment.

Pearson got busy taping a new piece of watercolor paper on the table in front of Emma. She took the marker from the woman's hand and replaced it with a 2-inch-wide brush. "I want you to start with plain water," she said, moving an unclaimed cup of water to within Emma's easy reach. "Just brush it straight across, back and forth. Get the paper wet, then we'll start with the paints."

The idea, Christensen knew, was to calm Emma down. To convert her agitated stabbing blots of red into slow, flowing strokes of something pale and watery. He marveled again at Pearson's patience and her ability to meet each student's needs just when they needed her most.

"Everyone else set?" Pearson asked, but her charges were too focused on their work to answer. She joined Christensen in the supplies room, where he'd retreated to store his briefcase.

"Emma's daughter was supposed to bring her down this morning, but she had car trouble." Pearson shook her head. "She made her take the Hopper and it's got Emma all discombobulated."

The Harmony Hopper was the center's adult day-care bus which, thanks to a state transportation grant, shuttled day patients without charge from their homes to the center.

"Don't most of them love the Hopper?" Christensen said.

"Most of them do, but Emma—" Pearson straightened her spine and turned up her nose. " 'Public transport?' she says. 'Why can't a driver bring me?' "

Christensen smiled. "Wealthy?"

"Demented. Lives in Aspinwall. I've got no idea where she got the Jackie Kennedy getup. Oh—" Pearson touched his arm, apparently struck by a sudden thought. "I've got something for you."

She squeezed between stacked cases of art supplies and removed the pushpin from a paper on the staff bulletin board. After shoving the pushpin back in, she handed him the paper. "The answer to your little rebus puzzle, I think. Saw it in a magazine Emma brought to class. She's the one who actually noticed it first."

The paper was a photocopy of a page from *Show Circuit* magazine. A single column of type ran down the right side; three advertisements of equal size ran down the left. "The story?" he asked.

Pearson shook her head. "Check out the ad on the bottom."

Christensen read the ad, which detailed the superior rings, trails, and boarding facilities of Muddyross Ranch in Westmoreland County, "home of the annual Oaks Classic." The word "exclusive" appeared three times. Pearson retrieved a nearby copy of the Once-Lost Images calendar. She flipped it open to April and pointed to the odd interlocking letters etched across Floss Underhill's pale sun, then to the logo in the ad. She took a step backward, hands on her wide hips, tapping the toe of one enormous unlaced basketball shoe.

"She's been painting the logo," he said finally.

"Brilliant deduction, Sherlock."

Christensen compared the two images. The Muddyross Ranch logo was a combination of the letters M and R, blended inside a circle like part of an old-fashioned ranch brand. Floss's version still looked like a melted hood ornament, but it was clearly similar.

"Maybe," he said. "She organized this Oaks event for years before she got sick."

"For whatever it's worth," Pearson said. She pointed to the sun in Floss's reprinted painting. "Floss paints the image so often, even Emma noticed the similarity. I'd bet you a beer that's what that is."

Christensen couldn't argue. If Floss hadn't been trying to recreate the image, it was a strange coincidence.

"Even if it is, it still doesn't mean anything to me," Pearson said. "You'll have to sort that out yourself."

"You've worked with her a long time, Maura. You don't have *any* idea what it might be about?"

Pearson shook her head. "She's a horse freak. Beyond that, it could be any of a million things. What's your guess?"

He held both the ad and the calendar at arm's length. "The prominence of it makes me think it's a top-of-the-mind thing. I mean, I doubt some image that didn't mean much to her would have imprinted itself deeply enough to show up over and over like that. She probably associates it with an experience of some sort, maybe even a trauma. She's back today, right?"

With her foot, Pearson maneuvered a heavy box of art supplies on the floor onto the base of a handcart. "She's around somewhere. Came by earlier and picked up a sketch pad, but I don't expect her back today."

"She by herself?"

"Just her home nurse."

Christensen dropped the calendar, then stooped to pick it up. "Selena Chembergo?"

Pearson tilted the handcart backward and angled it toward the door, shrugging and shaking her head as she headed back to her class. "Another girl. Must be Selena's day off."

*   *   *

The Harmony Center's rooftop dining deck was the most extravagant of the facility's many extravagances. Its granite floor was seamless to ease the passage of wheelchairs. A handrail ran the entire perimeter. A computer-controlled water-jet and drainage system kept the deck clean and food-free in spring and summer with a once-a-day 3 A.M. spritzing. Because of the fall rain and winter snow, the deck was impractical for much of the year. On spring days like this, though, with the sun out and the temperature well into the 70s, the staff made sure the patio tables were set up and the bright blue market umbrellas hoisted. The scene could have been some trendy rooftop restaurant if not for the unusually high Plexiglas barrier that prevented demented diners from climbing over the railing and stepping into the parking lot from the building's third story.

Christensen sipped his coffee in the sunlight as the automatic doors hissed shut behind him. With two hours until lunch, only a few tables were filled. In a wheelchair at the far end, facing the forested hills behind the building, Floss Underhill was sketching on a drawing pad on a tray across her knees. The shoulder-to-wrist cast still encased her thin left arm, and she rested the bulky thing on the arm of the wheelchair. A young blond woman sat beside her in a Cape Cod deck chair, reading a paperback through dark Ray-Bans.

Christensen approached slowly, then moved in front of Floss so she wouldn't have to turn around. "Mrs. Underhill?"

Her arm stopped moving and she looked him up and down. The younger woman may have looked up, too, but it was hard to tell.

"Bring any matches this time?" Floss said. "Some man downstairs gave me a fresh Cohiba and I'm gonna smoke it."

"I'm Jim Christensen, Mrs. Underhill. You remember me from Mount Mercy, then?"

The younger woman sat forward in her deck chair. "I'm Paige," she said, extending a hand toward Christensen. As she did, she turned toward her charge. "Don't be a troublemaker, now, Mrs. Underhill. If I let you smoke it, I'll be in deep doo." Paige turned back to Christensen. "She's not allowed to smoke," she repeated.

"Balls!" Floss shook her head. "You *people*."

On her sketch pad was a pencil drawing, another winged horse in the same galloping pose, larger in this picture than in the two other images he'd seen. Floss obviously had had some instruction on form drawing. Even at this stage, the horse's proportions seemed correct and her shading brought out the defining muscles of the animal's body. She'd added a misshapen dark patch on the horse's forehead, right between its eyes, a lopsided mushroom.

"I'm working with Maura Pearson, Paige," Christensen said.

Paige's face crinkled. "Who?"

"Maura Pearson, the art therapist."

The young woman finally nodded, pulling a folded day schedule from between the pages of her paperback. She unfolded the bookmark. "They told me Mrs. Underhill's not in the art class anymore."

"You're new, aren't you?" he said. "I was expecting Selena."

"I remember her," Floss volunteered. "She always had matches. Whatever happened to that girl?"

Christensen, too, wondered what had happened to Selena, especially since the Underhills were stonewalling Brenna's attempts to talk to Selena's husband, the gardener.

"I started yesterday, over at the house," Paige said, "but this is my first day here. We've become fast friends, haven't we Mrs. Underhill?"

"You're not Selena," Floss said, as though noticing Paige for the first time.

Christensen scouted the dining deck, finally motioning toward a table about thirty feet away. "Paige, would you mind giving me a few minutes alone with Mrs. Underhill?

She's part of a study I'm working on, and we have some catching up to do.'' He waited as the aide's eyes moved between him and the old woman, then added, ''Because she's been out for a few days.''

Paige glanced at her Swatch. ''She's got exercise at eleven in the multipurpose room. How long would you be?''

''We'll wrap it up before then,'' he said. ''Promise.''

''Don't like exercise,'' Floss said.

Christensen waited until Paige sat down at the distant table and opened her paperback again, then turned back to Floss. She couldn't possibly have stared at him any harder. ''How's the arm, Mrs. Underhill?'' he asked.

''Which?'' she said.

He pointed to the cast on her left one. ''Any pain?''

She studied the cast. ''This arm looks broken. You a doctor?''

''No, ma'am, a psychologist. I study memory. How'd you break it?''

She pulled a loose strand of white hair away from her face and tucked it behind one ear. ''You know how,'' she said.

''You fell,'' he said, trying to keep the answer vague.

Floss nodded. ''Told Warren he was skittish before my ride. He's always skittish, spooks at his shadow most days, but those seven-footers with the potted daisies confused him. Went right over his head when the balky son-of-a-gun stopped short on me.''

''A horse? You broke your arm in a horse show?''

''Potted daisies spooked him. Every time. Right over the top, and *wham!* I heard it crack. And let me tell you, it's a problem when you get to be my age.''

Christensen took advantage of the opening she left him. ''How old *are* you, anyway?''

Her eyes narrowed. ''Thirty-five next March, if it was any of your business, which it isn't,'' she said. ''Who are you again?''

This wasn't uncommon. Floss's years as a competitive

rider may have been the most exciting and fulfilling period of her life, and memories of times like that are among the most durable. Her brain went looking for a way to explain her broken arm and found a logical scenario, maybe even a real memory of an injury she'd suffered thirty or forty years ago. But if he had any chance of recovering memories of her fall the previous Saturday or its link to some dark family secret, he needed to anchor her, somehow, in the present, and then work backward, like a mountaineer rappelling into the recent past.

"Everybody at Harmony missed you this week, I hear. Maura Pearson says art class has been pretty dull without you."

Floss looked down at her sketch pad, then around the dining deck, saying nothing. He began to talk, referring first to Maura, Emma, Arthur, and some of her former art classmates at Harmony. He told her about the new carpet in the activity room. He asked her if she'd worked at the potting benches in the outdoor rehab garden, whether she'd tried the wheelchair-accessible swimming pool. From there, he moved on to a litany of current events in sports, weather, national politics, sounding at times like an overeager cocktail-party host anxious to stimulate conversation. He mentioned Ford's run for governor twice, her husband's name three times, told her what he knew about where and how she lived. She listened patiently, with an intensity that told Christensen his efforts were having the desired effect. "And I understand you have quite a rose garden," he said.

She nodded, smiling. "Out back. Blooming now, too. So sweet-smelling it'll knock you back."

"So you've seen the gardens since you got back from Mount Mercy?"

Floss closed her eyes. "Vincent took me out there yesterday. Rolled me right along the path." She kept them shut tight, as if the memory might somehow leak out and be gone forever.

"He's glad to have you home, I bet. So you just walked around, or were you going somewhere?"

She didn't answer, her eyes still closed, motionless except for the strand of hair that worked its way from behind her ear again and danced across her face in the light breeze.

"There's a big gazebo or something out back, isn't there?" he pressed. "Were you going there?"

Nothing.

"Do you go there a lot?"

Silence.

"When was the last time you were there?"

Her eyes sprang opened like window shades. She looked at him a few long moments, then down at her sketch pad, then squinted out into the rolling green hills. She picked up the pencil she'd been using to sketch and resumed work on the horse. Only now her lines were bold and thick, the knuckles on her hand white as she pressed graphite to paper, her hand moving like an excited seismograph in what seemed like a classic anxiety reaction. Which meant nothing. Something difficult and painful had happened to her there. That much he knew. She did, too. The question remained: What? But she obviously wasn't ready to go there again.

"Who takes care of all those roses?" he asked, backtracking to safer ground. But he had an idea, a little experiment: If she reacted so strongly to the place where she was hurt, how might she react to the names of the people he knew were on the Fox Chapel property the day she fell? "You don't do it all, do you?"

Floss shook her head, lips tight against her teeth, eyes focused on the pad.

"You have a gardener, don't you? Selena's husband. Enrique's very good, I hear."

She nodded. "He's gone now."

"With Selena?"

"Gone somewhere." Her answers were clipped and stiff, her pencil strokes leaving angry black scars on the faint outline of the horse. "I want to smoke."

Christensen tried to relax her with an easy smile. "Vincent doesn't like your cigars, does he?" he said, trying another name.

"Didn't used to mind. Now he does."

"Your son, Ford. Does he mind?"

She shrugged.

"How about Leigh, his wife?"

Floss's pencil point disintegrated with a splintering snap. Her right hand slowed and finally stopped moving, as if coasting to a stop. When it did stop, she held the pencil up in front of her face and tried to blow the dangling wood shards from the tip. "I need a new one," she said.

"I can get you one, Mrs. Underhill. There's plenty in the art room."

She handed him the shattered pencil. "Go now."

"You don't want to talk anymore?"

"No."

Christensen looked around. Paige was deep into her paperback, apparently content and unconcerned in the morning sun. The closest occupied table was even farther away from them than Paige. He sipped from his lukewarm coffee, then reached into his briefcase.

"I'll get you a new pencil, Mrs. Underhill." He handed her a Once-Lost Images calendar, open to April, knowing there was a good chance Floss wouldn't recognize *Some Crazy Story about Gray* as her own work. "Maura wanted to make sure you got one of these. You're famous."

The old woman studied the image. As she did, her shoulders seemed to relax. Her face, if not serene, lost its tightness. She wasn't smiling, but at least she wasn't grimacing anymore. "I had a gelding like this once, a three-year-old, just like this one," she said, tapping the horse's image. "A jumper like you never saw." She stared some more. "Broke my heart when Warren took him off, I'll tell you. The good ones are funny that way. Haunt your life like shadows, then they're gone."

Christensen waited, resisting the urge to prompt, wondering where the memory might lead her. Mentioning the horse's age—the same age as her grandchild who died after being thrown and kicked by a gray horse—struck Christensen as significant. Maybe she'd never worked her way through the grief surrounding that death. Maybe it was easier for her to grieve the loss of the horse than the death of the child.

"He was three years old?" he asked.

She nodded.

"And he's gone now?"

Floss shut her eyes again, tight this time. A tear squeezed onto her cheek.

"I can tell you miss him a lot," he said.

She nodded, brushing the tear away with her good hand. She sighed deeply, her eyes still shut in the bright morning sun. "Miss 'em all."

16

The western Pennsylvania countryside sliding past the Special's passenger-side· window was spring green and thrilling. Route 30 crisscrossed the Turnpike in a lazy helix all the way across the state, but along here, Jeannette and Greensburg, the turnpike veered south. Route 30 was the fastest way to Latrobe.

Not that Christensen and Pearson were in any hurry. With no real plans until the afternoon class at two, they'd decided on a lark to play hooky. Pearson wanted to know more about his research. The Special's gas tank was full. They'd looked at one another over bran muffins and cups of Harmony's cafeteria coffee and mouthed the words at the same instant: "Road trip."

Christensen was curious about Muddyross Ranch, of course, but his curiosity now was as personal as it was academic. He had a perspective from outside the Underhills' inner circle that Brenna couldn't, and what he'd seen in recent days—felt, actually—was tinged with paranoia. It wasn't just the weirdness—the dark phone call from Myron Levin, the unexplained absence of the gardener and his wife, the late-night footprints on the front porch—

but the nagging sense that Floss Underhill was trying her best to communicate. Exactly what, he couldn't say. But the same scrambled thoughts were surfacing again and again. The Underhills' attitude toward Brenna, the calculation of her hiring, bothered him as well. Brenna's pit-bull reputation notwithstanding, the Underhills had unlimited resources. Why would they recruit a defense attorney they'd never met? The Underhills were savvy people, and savvy people have a reason for everything they do. Plus, in Brenna's business, information is power. The Underhills were withholding information. Why?

The sun already was heating up the immense car's interior. Christensen reached for the knobby art deco handle of the window crank. "Mind?"

From deep in her vinyl-covered driver's seat, Pearson reached forward and patted the pristine metal dashboard. "Before A/C," she said, somehow reading his mind.

He flexed, ready for a struggle, but turning the crank was like cutting warm butter. Forty years old, and the car made his five-year-old Explorer seem leprous by comparison. "So how long did you spend restoring this beast?" he asked over the dull roar of rushing air.

"What do you mean, restoring?" Pearson said. "You take care of your car, it'll take care of you."

Christensen scanned the interior. "Wait. You're the original owner?"

Pearson shook her head. "Mom was. We shared it for years until she passed."

What little he knew of Pearson's life outside Harmony he'd gathered on the day he gave her a lift to work while the Special was in the shop. Everything fit perfectly with her nutty great-aunt image. She'd lived alone since her mother died two years ago, assuming you didn't count the menagerie with which she now shared their house—a burgeoning population of gerbils, a three-legged cat, an ancient Rhodesian Ridgeback with some sort of gland problem, and a grounded crow whose broken wing she'd splinted to no avail. It lived in her fireplace but had free run of the house. On Pearson's extensive menu of eccentricities, her weak spot for irredeemable creatures, including the Special, was by far her most charming.

Christensen rolled the window halfway up to cut down on the wind, then pulled a folded piece of poster paper from the briefcase at his feet. Laid open on his lap, it looked like one of Annie's preschool drawings—a pink bull's-eye at the center surrounded by a manic, scratchy swirl of Magic Marker colors. "What did you call this again?"

"Mandala."

"Like Nelson?"

Pearson nodded. "Different spelling. Means 'magic circle' or 'center' in Sanskrit." Pearson adjusted the car's massive rearview mirror. "You know all about that Jungian crap, right? This is part of that. From time to time we give each artist a piece of paper that's blank except for a circle in the middle. Then we give them paints and markers and watch to see what they do with the circle."

Christensen pointed to the paper in his lap. "And the 'Jungian crap' says this would be a snapshot of Floss Underhill's subconscious, right?"

"As of two weeks ago. I had her do one down in the dayroom. It's just a way to see where their head's at. Don't try to make too much of it. I don't. Just thought you'd like to see."

Christensen looked again at the circle. "Help me here, Maura. Where was her head on this one?"

Pearson leaned over and poked a finger at the pink bull's-eye. "Dead center," she said. "Strong sense of self. That's been consistent in every mandala she's done going back two years. The essential Floss is still in there somewhere, still knows who she is. But you don't need a mandala to figure that out."

"And the squiggles?"

Pearson shrugged. "Something's got her upset. Same with the colors. Bright ones like that usually suggest agitation of some kind, but it could be anything."

Muddyross Ranch promised nothing more concrete, he knew, but it seemed too important to overlook as he inventoried Floss's mind and memories. He and Pearson had gone through all of Floss's available artwork at the center and found variations of the riding club's logo etched somewhere in at least half of them. The place obviously meant something to her, but what? Maybe it was something simple, like her involvement with the Oaks Classic, or maybe it was just her favorite place to ride. But he had a lot of questions, and the family wasn't exactly approachable. Maybe someone at Muddyross could shed some light on Floss's fascination with the place.

"Has Floss ever talked about men when you were around?" Christensen said.

"To me?" Pearson shook her head. "What men?"

"In general. Not her husband or her son or anything, just, you know, men. Or bring up names you didn't recognize?"

Pearson shook her head again. After a half minute of silence, she said, "Well?"

"Just the way she talked when I visited her at Mount Mercy. Just kind of, I don't know, free-spirited maybe?"

Pearson turned toward him, eyeing the road only as needed. "Spill it. This sounds good."

"It's not. I just mean, in general, Alzheimer's patients aren't usually aware if they're saying things that might embarrass their family or friends. We all have warning systems that tell us, you know, not to talk to strangers about our sex lives, that kind of thing. Late second-stagers like Floss have usually lost those warning systems."

"This is sounding better and better."

Christensen refolded the poster paper and put it back in his briefcase. "Clinically speaking, of course. Maura, help me out here. You've been around a lot more of them, and a lot longer, than I have."

Pearson sighed. "Depends on the person. It's the ones who never talked before Alzheimer's who seem to talk the most toward the later stages. It's like their minds open up and the secrets just spill out. But I don't get the impression Floss Underhill was ever one to hold back.''

"Does it ever cause problems, with hurt feelings, that sort of thing?"

"When it does, it's the spouses, usually. Sometimes it's real personal stuff."

"Ever with the Underhills?"

Pearson shook her head. "They're a pretty unflappable bunch.'' She sighed again, deeply and with great purpose. "You're really not gonna tell me what she said, are you?"

He wouldn't, couldn't. What had she said, anyway, during that brief hospital conversation? She'd told one raw joke about men with beards. She'd used a couple of unfamiliar names. "She didn't say anything, Maura, really. It was just *how* she said a couple of things that got me thinking about the whole issue of privacy. I just never thought about how much we all rely on judgment with stuff like that. What happens in a family when you can't trust the people who know your secrets, or when the patient starts sharing his or her own secrets with anybody and everybody? It's just something I'd never thought about before."

A sign flashed past on the right. Pearson steered on, aiming the Special's bulk into the harsh morning sun. "That might have been our turnoff," he said. "Ridge Road goes right to Muddyross Ranch, doesn't it?"

"Oh, hell," Pearson said. She lifted her foot off the accelerator and the Special slowed, as if she'd cut the engines of an ocean liner.

For someplace so exclusive, the riding club seemed not much different from the public stables at North Park. The parking lot was just as rutted and dusty, filled with big Chevy Suburbans and Dodge Rams and trailers of every conceivable design. Bales of hay were stacked ten feet high at the lot's southern edge, protected only by a flimsy sheet of blue plastic draped over the top and staked into the hard dirt. Pearson bounced the Special into an open space between a trailer and an overgrown thicket of weeds and trees, then stomped the brake. Plumes of dust poured into the open windows.

Christensen looked out across the rolling hills beyond the stables. He consulted his mental catalog of Floss Underhill's paintings for any landscape that might have been drawn from this view, but nothing seemed familiar. The stables themselves, directly in front of them, were sturdy and substantial, more stone than wood but modern in all the right places—built to honor tradition, but with the top-end market in mind in matters of convenience, cleanliness, and civility. The one thing he did recognize was painted on every stall door—the Muddyross Ranch logo. It was unavoidable, like a pox, on trailers, storage sheds, even depicted in the well-tended garden of marigolds and trimmed shrubbery in front of what surely was the ranch's administrative offices.

"Must be the place," Pearson said.

He laughed. "Good guess."

"Think it's okay to just wander around?"

"You're asking me, Maura? These aren't *my* people."

They both watched for a few minutes through the Special's elegantly molded windshield. The ranch population seemed to be a society of women—thin, reedy blondes, mostly, with tight jodhpurs and scuffed black riding boots. As they moved about the grounds, each was trailed by an obedient, muscular mount that moved with the grace of a dancer. The few men on the premises seemed to have been bred for work. One, his black, bald head gleaming in the morning sun, lathered and rinsed a skittish white stallion along one side of the stables. Another moved from stall to stall bent beneath an enormous burlap sack labeled "Sweet Feed." They seemed to speak politely to the riders as they passed, but they never looked up.

"What's our story?" Pearson asked. "We don't look like we belong, and someone's bound to ask."

"If someone asks, we tell them the truth," he said. "We're Jehovah's Witnesses."

"Nice try."

"Maura, relax. We're researchers, doing research. People usually bend over backward to help once you tell them what you're doing."

"Truthseekers."

"Exactly."

The stable area covered maybe two acres, smaller than Christensen had imagined. The only riding facilities he'd ever seen were the sprawling public stables in the county's two regional parks. Muddyross Ranch smelled the same, and the dust clung to your clothes and hair the same way, but that's about all it had in common with the North and South Park stables. Muddyross had the unmistakable feel of a private club.

Stablehands seemed to outnumber the horses on the grounds. A few eyed Christensen and Pearson as they strolled from building to building, but no one seemed too concerned that they were there. In five minutes, they had walked through and around every building on Muddyross Ranch except the administration building. Nothing except the ranch logo seemed remotely like the images in Floss Underhill's paintings.

Christensen propped one of his feet on the low rail outside a stall, stroking the nose of a magnificent chestnut mare. "I don't know what I expected."

"By coming here?" Pearson said.

"Other than the horse and the logo, her paintings are pretty abstract, surreal almost. I just thought maybe there'd be something that connected." He shrugged.

"You said she competed here, or ran some horse show, or something? Why don't you ask around. If she's that big a player there's bound to be people who'll talk to you about her. Maybe you can pick up some background. Did you bring any of the paintings?"

Christensen shook his head. Floss's winged-horse image popped into his head, then disappeared. "Don't you have a copy of the calendar with the Gray painting in it?"

She patted her shoulder bag. "Let's show it around like the cops always do."

"Maura, this isn't *America's Most Wanted*."

Christensen took a last look around, then looked at Pearson. In his jeans, Nikes and light silk sports coat, he wasn't exactly dressed to blend in with the town-and-country set. But the longer they hung around, the more likely someone would wonder about Pearson's odd getup. In her voluminous khaki slacks, Reyn Spooner Hawaiian shirt, and huge, unlaced Air Jordans, she looked like the grandmother superior of some preppy-tropical ghetto gang.

"Let's head on back," he said.

Pearson was squinting into the dim light of a nearby stable. "Did you see that?" she asked, her eyes fixed on some distant point.

Christensen swiveled his head and squinted, too. The wide stable doors were about twenty feet away, but inside all he could see were empty stalls and an occasional knot of tack dangling outside the stall doors. "See what?"

"Second stall on the left side."

She walked toward the stall door without another word. He followed, glancing once over his shoulder to see who might be watching them. A young stablehand was rounding the corner of another building, headed in their direction. "Maura?" he called to Pearson's back. But she walked on.

He caught up to her at the door, where she stood with both arms dangling into a stall the size of a decent living room. Sunlight streamed through a row of clerestory windows about twenty feet off the floor, and his eyes followed the dusty shafts of light from the windows down, down, resting finally on a horse's large gray rump. What looked like a length of fire hose dangled between its legs.

"Stallion," Christensen said.

Pearson gave him a look. "Aren't you the sharp one? Actually, it's missing some equipment. I think he's a gelding.'' She leaned into the stall. *''Tchk, tchk.* Pretty horse, come. *Tchk, tchk.''*

The horse raised his head from a food trough and appraised them. He was chewing something crunchy, the sound like someone grinding uncooked popcorn kernels into meal. Apparently satisfied that the pair meant him no harm, the horse buried his head in the trough again.

''You see the marking?'' Pearson said.

''What marking?''

''Between his eyes.'' She pulled the Once-Lost Images calendar from her shoulder bag, fanned the pages to April and stabbed a finger at the winged gray horse in the picture. ''The mushroom.''

Christensen focused on the odd marking between the eyes of the horse in the painting. *''Tchk, tchk,''* he said.

The horse kept eating. Christensen took one step back. The names of the boarded horses were posted outside each stall, and he scanned quickly for the plastic-coated paper thumbtacked to the wall. ''King, L12,'' he said. *''Tchk, tchk.''*

This time the horse stopped eating and looked back at them. Dead-center between its black eyes was a mushroom of dark hair the size of a man's hand.

''C'mere, Gray,'' Pearson called. *''Tchk, tchk.''*

The horse snorted, then turned its massive body around. In three strides it was at the stall door. Pearson patted its jaw with her palm and rubbed its ear. Christensen lifted a hand and the horse nuzzled it. Except for the coarse whiskers, the nose felt like velvet.

''Here's your horse,'' Pearson said.

''Whoa, Maura. We're not sure it's the same one.'' He tapped on the paper nameplate on the stall wall. ''Different name. Besides, they kept it at their stables in Fox Chapel.''

She looked at the sign. ''Buy your breakfast for a week if it's not.''

Christensen rubbed the mushroom, and the horse tossed its head. Interesting possibility, he thought, even if he had no idea how it might fit into the memory puzzle he was trying to piece together. From what he knew, Floss Underhill's Gray was freighted with both triumph and tragedy, a champion show horse, true, but also the horse responsible for the death of Floss's only grandson.

"Exile?" he said.

Pearson shook her head, apparently confused.

"That riding accident I told you about. The newspaper story I read said the horse Ford and his little boy were riding when it happened was gray. I'm sure that's why the gray horse turns up in a lot of her paintings."

Pearson shoved her glasses up the bridge of her nose with her left hand, her right still moving up and down the horse's jawline. "So maybe having him around their own stables was too much of a reminder?"

"Maybe they sold him, or maybe they board him way out here so they don't have to confront those memories all the time," he said. "I can think of a thousand reasons why he'd be here."

For the first time, Christensen felt as if a puzzle piece had fallen into place. It didn't ease his more nagging concerns about the Underhills, but it was a start. He needed good information, though. What he had so far was speculation based on second- and thirdhand sources, certainly not enough to draw any conclusions about the images in Floss's paintings.

At the sound of approaching footsteps, he whirled around, suddenly aware he was tense. Pearson turned, too.

"Shit!" said the startled young stablehand he'd seen earlier. She was maybe eighteen, her dark brown hair pulled into a tight ponytail, the knees of her jeans dirty from honest work. She dropped the bucket in her left hand.

"I didn't know anyone was in here," she said, bending down to scoop spilled oats back into the bucket.

"Sorry to scare you," Christensen said. He waited for the girl to catch her breath. "I'm Jim, this is Maura. We're just visiting. You work here, then?"

"Kathleen," she said. "Input-output technician."

Pearson laughed. The girl smiled. Both correctly interpreted his confused look.

"First she feeds 'em—" Pearson said.

Christensen put his hand up. "Got it. Then you clean the stalls."

"They call us I-Os for short," the girl said. "I haven't seen you here before."

Christensen shook his head. "Just visiting. Looks a lot like a horse we once knew, though. Know anything about him?"

The girl stepped forward and rubbed the horse's nose. "King's a sweetheart. Aren't you, baby?" She reached into a canvas pouch dangling from her western belt and held out a handful of what looked like granola. The horse nibbled obediently from her hand. She waited until her palm was clean before returning her attention to Christensen and Pearson. "You should talk to Mr. Doti. He knows everything."

"King's owner?" Christensen asked.

"Ranch manager," she said, picking up her bucket. "I've never met his owners. But Mr. Doti's in the office. Second building down, with the garden out front." She smiled and walked away, tossing a "Can't miss it" back over her shoulder. She disappeared into a stall three doors down.

Pearson looked at her watch. "We've got plenty of time."

As they got closer, what from a distance had looked like a rustic old ranch house more clearly became a new building expertly designed to look like a rustic old ranch house. The outside walls were rough timber, but the windows were the kind of extravagant double-paned Pellas that Brenna wanted for their new house, the kind with the miniblind installed between the two panes. They pushed through the oak front door into a cool gust of air, the product of the central air-conditioning unit humming on the building's roof.

A small reception area fronted two offices, both with their doors closed. Each of the three desks in the reception area had a personal computer on top, but no one was around.

"Hello?" he called.

Pearson drifted over to a wall map of the ranch property, reading it while shifting from foot to foot with her hands clasped behind her back. "*Le Petite Ponderosa*," she said.

One of the office doors opened, and the Marlboro Man stepped out. He was tall, well over six feet, with the barrel chest of a wrestler and a sprinter's hips. His belt buckle was the size and shape of a cassette tape, with an intricate pattern of turquoise across it that Christensen couldn't decipher. He was wearing jeans and a denim shirt, but his boots weren't the least bit scuffed. If he had to guess the man's age, he'd say about seventy because of the white hair, lines around the eyes, and the distressed-leather look of his skin. Without those clues, he'd have guessed forty-five. Pearson had turned and was all but leering.

"Sorry to bother you," Christensen said, extending his hand. "We were looking for the ranch manager."

The man beamed. "Y'all got him," he said with a soft Texas accent. He grasped Christensen's hand, his palm as rough as a cheese grater. He wasn't wearing a hat, but he tipped the brim of an imaginary one at Pearson and said, "Ma'am."

"I'm Jim Christensen; this is Maura Pearson."

He nodded. "Pleasure. First time to Muddyross?"

"It surely is," Pearson said, a trace of the South suddenly in her voice. "You're Mr. Doti then?"

He nodded. Christensen followed the man's eyes as he absorbed the full impact of Maura Pearson. "Some fancy shoes you got there," he said finally.

Christensen pushed on. "We're doing some research and were wondering about one of your horses here."

"Now if you're looking to buy, we don't sell," the man

said. "You'd have to talk to the owner about that. I could help put you in touch—"

"No, no," Christensen said. "It's a little complicated. Do you have a few minutes?"

After a pause, the man swept a long arm toward his office door. His stomach was as flat as an Oklahoma state road. "Always. Get you folks some coffee? Coke?"

"Thanks," Pearson said, pushing past Christensen and following the man through the door into his office. Christensen brought up the rear. The office looked like some Ronald Reagan cowboy fantasy, complete with a replica of Frederic Remington's *Bronco Buster* on the corner of the desk. A black cowboy hat hung from the bronc's upturned tail.

The office carpet was plush, and as Christensen closed the door, he couldn't miss the door's engraved brass nameplate: Warren Doti.

17

Christensen smelled something warm and familiar as he closed the door behind him, an inviting blast of exotic jungle blend. A sleek black coffeemaker sat on a low oak bureau behind the matching desk, its warming light on. Beside it stood an electric grinder and a vacuum-sealed jar of fresh beans.

The shelves immediately to his right looked like the trophy case of a championship-mad high school, with its stunning collection of silver trays, plaques, and loving cups. They weren't arranged for maximum exposure, but instead were wedged together in chaotic stacks and disorderly groups. Properly displayed, they would have filled the room. The one nearest the door was engraved with Doti's name beneath the words "National Trainer of the Year, 1964."

Christensen didn't need more coffee, but accepting a cup might put Doti more at ease. "That coffee does smell good," he said.

"You take it with anything, Mr. Christensen?"

"Black's fine. And please, it's Jim."

"Two, since it's already made," Pearson said.

Doti plucked two white cups from the stack beside the coffeemaker and turned them right side up on the bureau. "Hope you don't mind it strong. Grew up making it the western way and never lost the taste for it."

Pearson leaned forward, apparently fascinated. "The western way?"

Doti's face crinkled into a smile. "Boil the grounds in a pot, like soup. When it gets dark like you want it, you just take an egg, crack it over the top."

Christensen blanched, looking at the cups Doti was filling. "An egg?"

"Settles the grounds to the bottom. Works great, but it gives you a real kick-ass cup of coffee." He nodded to Pearson. "Pardon my French, ma'am. Got used to it that way, so even with this thing I tend to make it pretty strong."

The taste and texture were just this side of wet grounds. Christensen smiled at Doti, who was waiting like an anxious prom date for an appraisal. "Just right," he said.

Doti seemed to relax as he circled behind his desk and sank into his leather chair. He seemed out of place in that setting, his skin too dark for office work, his collar open too far for doing business, even horse business. A plated chain around his neck hung down into a thatch of white chest hair, anchored there by a glint of something gold. "Now what can I do for you folks?"

"We're truthseekers," Pearson began.

Christensen chided her with a look. Doti maintained the practiced smile of someone accustomed to dealing with the rich and eccentric.

"Beg pardon?" he said.

"She said we're researchers," Christensen said. "From the Harmony Brain Research Center near Pittsburgh. Alzheimer's research, specifically."

Doti smiled on.

"What's happened is there's this patient we deal with from time to time who apparently spent a lot of time here before she got so sick," Pearson said. "I teach an art therapy class, and practically everything she paints has the Muddyross logo in it, that yellowish MR thing that's plastered all over everything outside."

Doti nodded. "It's a special place."

Christensen sat forward, probably too quickly, but he didn't want Pearson steering the conversation. "Special to her, for sure, at least from what we can tell. And we're trying to figure out why, just as a way of understanding how memory works in Alzheimer's patients. I'm focusing on patients who seem to have strong memories about something, trying to understand why some memories stay strong and vivid and why others get lost. There's so much about Alzheimer's we don't understand."

He tried to read Doti's face. Confused? Concerned?

The ranch manager got up and poured himself a cup of coffee, finishing the pot, then sat back down. "So you'll want to look around, I guess?"

Christensen and Pearson looked at one another.

"Actually, we've sort of done that," Christensen said. "Hope you don't mind. Just around the stables here, not out on the trails."

Doti's face clouded. He took a deep swallow from the steaming cup. "I'd have been happy to show you around."

"We should have stopped by here first, I guess," Pearson said.

Doti appraised them over the cup's rim. When he lowered it, the smile was back. "Naw, really, it's no problem. It's just the members, they know us all here. Know each other, too. Unfamiliar faces just kind of stand out, and we always end up hearing about it. Just let us know you're coming next time and we'll walk you around, maybe even saddle up a couple of lesson horses for the grand tour."

The three sat a moment in silence, each sipping from their cup. Now didn't seem the right time to start asking questions about the gray horse, but neither was Christensen ready to leave without bringing it up. He was phrasing and rephrasing an artful segue when Pearson spoke up.

"What do you know about that gray gelding out there?" she said.

Doti slowly turned to face Pearson. "We must have a hundred horses out there, ma'am, probably a dozen of 'em gray. Beyond getting 'em fed and watered every day and making sure the trails are in good shape, I can't say I've got the time to get to know 'em all."

Christensen tried to buffer the comment. "See, in this patient's paintings—"

"King was the name on the stall." Pearson leaned forward. "And there was a number, L12. A gelding."

"Oh, King." Doti shuffled some papers on his desk, straightened his executive desk set so that both the pen and pencil formed perfect 45-degree angles to the base. He stood and slowly walked toward his office window. "That's one of the lesson horses, ma'am. King. Use him for lessons, like I said."

"Had him a while?" Pearson said.

"A while."

"Since when?"

Doti twisted the rod on the miniblind of his window. The room darkened, then lightened again as he twisted it back. Then he did it again.

"Mr. Doti?"

When he turned back, the smile was unchanged. "Ma'am, he's just one of about sixteen or so lesson horses we keep here. He's been here a few years, maybe more. I'd have to check on something like that."

Doti stepped back to his desk, but made no effort to sit down. He set his coffee cup down and leaned on the palms of his hands so far that the chain around his neck fell forward. The gold charm caught briefly on his chest hair, then tumbled free. Perfect smile. "Be more than happy to get hold of you folks if I find anything out," he said, plucking the pen from its holder. "Care to leave a number or some way to get in touch with you?"

The dangling gold figure stopped swinging and hung straight down from Doti's neck. It was small, tasteful in its way, and Christensen knew without a second look what it was: a golden winged horse. If Christensen had had any doubt that Warren Doti was the man Floss Underhill spoke about that day at the hospital, it evaporated once he saw him wearing the same flying horse symbol that turned up in so many of Floss's paintings. Even more than the unexpected presence of the gray horse, Doti's relationship with Floss suddenly seemed critical to understanding the images in her art.

"How long did you work for the Underhill family?" he said.

It was more a reaction than a question. Christensen didn't think before he blurted it, but from Doti's reaction, he was glad he didn't. The coffee cup stopped halfway between Doti's desk and his mouth, and stayed that way an uncomfortably long time. "I'm afraid I don't follow," he said finally. "I still work for them."

"Here? You mean at Muddyross? They own it?"

A nod. "Managed their private stables before this. Why?"

Christensen pushed the gambit. "Mrs. Underhill, Floss, mentioned your name recently, that's all. She says you're quite a horseman."

Doti lowered the coffee cup and sat down lightly on the front edge of his chair like a man who'd just gotten bad news. His eyes were open, but behind them his mind was clearly reeling.

Christensen poker-faced it, but the conversation's unexpected turn had caught them both by surprise. "Something wrong?"

"Been running their stables for a lot of years, Mr. Christensen. Mrs. Underhill, that's the patient you're talking about?"

Christensen and Pearson looked at each other, then back at Doti. Christensen nodded.

"Sorry. It's just—" Doti ran a thumb around the rim of his cup, then looked Christensen in the eye. "How's she doing?"

"When was the last time you saw her?"

"Three years now. I hear it's bad."

Christensen nodded. "Alzheimer's has three stages, the third being terminal. She's late second stage."

"I hear things, just bits and pieces from people." Doti smiled suddenly. "Mrs. Underhill remembers me, though?"

What had she said? Her words bubbled up quickly: *The man knew horses like I don't know what. Women, too.*

"She said you really know horses," Christensen said.

Doti seemed to relax. "Before I got into this, I was a trainer. Mrs. Underhill's trainer when she was competing about two hundred years ago." Doti nodded toward the hardware along the opposite wall. "We did okay."

Christensen turned, his eye fixing on a 2-foot-tall trophy topped by a golden horse and rider leaping a rail jump.

"I'd say better than okay," Pearson said.

"Won our share."

"Show jumping?" Christensen asked.

"Equitation. Hunting and jumping. Mrs. Underhill's got what I call 'touch.' Best hands of any rider I ever saw." Doti's eyes faded again. "Had 'em, I mean. Before we all got old, before she took sick. Such a goddamned waste—" He ran one of his rough hands through his hair and drew a deep, ragged breath. He looked first to Pearson, then to Christensen. "Sorry. Lost my wife this past year. Cancer. Been rough, is all."

"Our questions probably made it rougher," Pearson said. "We're sorry, too."

Christensen nodded his sympathy, but he wasn't finished. "We were wondering about the gray horse. See, Mrs. Underhill sometimes paints a gray horse with markings just like the one out there in the stall, the one you said was a lesson horse. What can you tell us about him?"

Doti shifted in his seat. "I'd have to check his papers. Like I said, we've got a hundred or so boarded here."

"You said he's a lesson horse, though, one of the ones owned by the ranch." Christensen leaned forward and leaned an elbow on Doti's desk. "There's only a handful of those, right?"

Doti nodded, but the muscles in his jaw knotted and rolled.

"Because here's the thing: The Underhills used to own a horse named Gray, see, a jumper." He turned to Pearson. "Maura, do you still have the calendar?" She fished it out of her shoulder bag. Christensen took it, opened it to April, and slid it across the desk.

Doti stared a long time. "*Some Crazy Story about Gray*," he read.

"That horse turns up a lot in her paintings, Mr. Doti, and that's where my research comes in. For some reason she remembers that horse. And she remembers you, and this place. We want to find out why those memories remain so—"

Doti stood up suddenly. The smile was back. "I really wish I could help you folks, 'cause Lord knows I'd do anything for Mr. and Mrs. Underhill. *Decent* people. But we've sorta lost touch, me being out here and all. They stopped coming once she took sick." He checked his watch, made a face. "God's honest truth, I'm running a little scant on time right now. One of the members is expecting me down at the ring, and I shouldn't keep her waiting."

Christensen stayed in his chair. So did Pearson.

"When would be a better time?" Christensen said.

Doti looked from one to the other. If they'd stood, Christensen was sure Doti would start ushering them out the door. Since they hadn't, Doti seemed a little self-conscious. But he didn't sit down.

"Muddyross is a private riding club, Mr. Christensen. Much as I'd like to help you out with your research or whatever, much as I think the world of the Underhills, I don't think the Underhills would much cotton to me talking about club matters with anybody who wanders in. This kind of puts me in a prickly situation, so there's not much point in us talking again. Maybe you should just talk to them."

Christensen felt himself tense.

"No offense," Doti added. "Sure you understand."

The three of them waited in strained silence. The man clearly wanted to end the conversation, making Christensen that much more determined to push on. What did he have to lose? Suddenly, Pearson stood up. She stuck her hand out. "Well, then, Mr. Doti. We sure thank you for your time."

Doti shook it warmly despite the moment's chill, then reached across the desk for Christensen's hand. When they shook, Doti all but pulled Christensen out of his chair.

Christensen retrieved the calendar from the desk and handed it back to Pearson. "Just one more question, Mr. Doti. It's personal, so I can't imagine the Underhills would mind you answering."

Doti's jaw knotted again.

"That pendant around your neck?" Christensen pointed to the winged horse. Doti reached up and tucked the chain back into his shirt. "Does it have any special significance that Floss Underhill might be aware of?"

He waited for Doti to react, but all he got was that stiff smile and an unblinking stare. The ranch manager motioned them toward the door, then walked over and opened it, saying, "You folks drive carefully on your way back to the city."

Pearson revved the Special's engine again, kicking up another whirlwind of dust in the Muddyross parking lot. She insisted on letting the car warm up for three minutes, no less, before putting it in gear. The brown cloud behind the car was thinning, but also drifting across the lot toward the stables and administration building. When Christensen turned around, he saw at least one reedy blonde waving a hand in front of her face to clear the air. The interior was a broiler, but when he'd tried to roll the window down, Pearson stopped him with a lesson about the deceptive delicacy of vinyl upholstery and how important it was to keep it clean.

"Let's just go, Maura. We weren't here that long. It probably hasn't even cooled down."

"Not till you fill me in," she said.

"On what?"

"What was I missing in there?"

Christensen didn't know if his hunch was right, but the unassembled pieces of Floss Underhill's life had started to fit together as he watched Doti's guarded reactions. He again considered Floss's suggestive description of Doti, her apparent fascination with the ranch where he now worked, and the winged horse he wore around his neck, as well as the behavior of a man who acted as if he had a secret.

"A possibility," he said. "Just a theory."

"Spill." She revved the engine again, seemingly oblivious to the heat inside the car. Christensen's shirt already was stuck to his back, and his armpits were damp.

"I'm just thinking back to Vincent Underhill's years as governor. Remember the big deal about Floss staying in Pittsburgh?"

Pearson eased the three-on-the-tree gearshift into reverse and let out the clutch. The mighty Special began to move. It bumped through a rut and rolled into the middle of the dirt lot. "Didn't she hate Harrisburg?"

"He served two terms," Christensen said. "Think about that. Eight years they lived apart." Dust swirled around the car in a billowing cloud as she stopped and shifted into first. Christensen did the subtraction in his head. "She was probably in her late-thirties."

"So?"

"Still competing, from what I can tell."

Pearson looked exasperated. "So?"

If he said it out loud, would it sound ridiculous? "So maybe Warren Doti was the real reason she wanted to stay home."

Pearson leered. "Lovers?"

"Who knows? They were grown-ups. They must have spent a lot of time together training and competing. Things happen." He glanced over to gauge her reaction.

Pearson shrugged as she eased the clutch out. The car groaned forward. "Interesting."

Christensen looked back a last time through the thinning brown cloud, startled to see a tall figure in denim standing at the edge of the parking lot. Warren Doti jotted something on a piece of paper as he watched their car recede. They were half a mile down the road before Pearson gave the clear signal, and they both cranked open their windows and gulped cool air like swimmers too long underwater.

Brenna set the parking brake, lowered the driver's-side window, and turned off the Legend's engine, startled at first by the eerie Fox Chapel silence. She listened more closely, catching only the faint rustle of fresh green oak leaves overhead. Straight ahead, through the car's windshield, the elaborate wrought-iron driveway gate defended the Underhill estate from unwanted visitors.

On her previous visits, she'd found the gate stately and secure, a privacy measure she expected from a family of the Underhills' stature. This time, though, she noticed something she hadn't before. In a maple tree just beyond the gate, about halfway up, a video camera mounted beneath a small, shingled shelter swept back and forth across the mouth of the driveway. Another just like it was hidden behind the antique lantern atop the gate's left brick pillar. It was aimed directly at her, or at any driver who stopped in this particular spot. In her rearview mirror, she saw another mounted in a tree across the street, presumably documenting the license plate of any car that approached. It bordered on Nixonian.

If she didn't approach the intercom, just sat there, how

long would it take for someone on the other side of the cameras to do something about it? Would they simply offer a crackling, amplified greeting through hidden speakers? Or dispatch Alton Staggers or some other emissary to find out what she was doing there? She wanted to wait, just to see. On the other hand, these didn't seem like the kind of people who enjoyed playing games.

Brenna opened her car door and stepped out, smiling at the pillar-mounted camera about five feet above her head. She blew it a kiss, then pressed the glowing button on the intercom. "Hello?"

The answer came immediately. "Welcome back, Ms. Kennedy."

"Good afternoon, Mr. Staggers."

"Thanks for your affectation."

Brenna tilted her head, trying to decipher. After a few seconds of confused silence, he reminded: "The kiss you blew."

"So those cameras aren't just for show?" she said.

Staggers either didn't hear or ignored the question. "Did I somehow faux pas? I don't have you on today's visitor list."

"No." She resisted the urge to speak directly to the maple-mounted camera. "I was out this way and thought I'd stop by. Is the governor in?"

Staggers laughed. "Past or future?"

Before she could answer, the heavy lock on the massive gate buzzed and sprang. In silence, the gate swung slowly open. "Thank you," she said, waving to the pillar-cam as she climbed back into the car.

Brenna had come for one reason, though she intended to disguise her mission among a number of other fact-gathering chores: She wasn't leaving until she talked to Enrique Chembergo. Staggers and the Underhills had thwarted her attempts to interview the man who said he heard Floss Underhill struggling on the gazebo deck just before she fell. "You don't *have* to defend these people,

Bren,'' Jim had said the night before. ''Are you sure they're being straight with you?''

Vincent Underhill met her at the top of the drive, directing her into a parking spot to the right, standing in almost the exact spot where his son, Ford, had greeted her on the first day she was summoned here. The men seemed to think it a courtesy; she thought it a little weird. She parked next to Staggers's Thunderbird and quickly opened her door, just in case the former governor felt the need to do so. When she stepped out, he stepped forward with an outstretched hand.

''I like your brass, Ms. Kennedy,'' he said. His hair glinted like polished silver.

''Sorry for dropping by without notice. I was out this—''

Underhill waved her off. ''No, no. I'm talking about Myron Levin's little sneak attack the other morning. Liked the way you handled that. Very professional. Very savvy.''

The man, elected twice by landslides, was remembered not only for setting the state's standard for personal charisma, but for his skillful manipulation of the media. This was high praise indeed.

''Never let them see you sweat,'' she said.

''Seriously, very nice job. I just wanted you to know how much we appreciate your work with us so far.''

Brenna closed the car door and pressed a button on her key chain. The Legend's door locks snapped shut.

''I think it'll be safe here,'' he said, then winked.

She suddenly felt stupid. The Underhill estate was an electronic fortress in the middle of one of the world's safest communities. There weren't many places in the world where locking your car door seemed downright paranoid, but this was one. ''Habit,'' she said.

Underhill stepped aside to let her pass, motioning her toward the front door. ''Now, to what good fortune do we owe this visit of yours?''

Brenna turned back toward Vincent Underhill, catching

him with his eyes on her butt. He looked up without apparent remorse. "Loose ends," she said.

"Oh?" Underhill seemed to weigh the comment for hidden meaning. "Such as?"

"I need information so we don't get blindsided, and I'm having trouble getting it."

"Oh, my."

He walked toward the house. Brenna fell in beside him. "There's a statement, on the record, and it's going to come back and bite us if we're not careful. Something you know Dagnolo or the Rosemond people are going to use if they can. They don't need much to float a rumor in public, something they think will do at least some damage. Unless we can shoot it down before it flies, it could become a problem this close to an election."

Underhill opened the front door and held it open. Brenna stepped into the rustic foyer. The house seemed bigger and more comfortable each time she walked in.

"Frankly, I'm having a hell of a time getting what I need from your people," she said. "Phil Raskin. Mr. Staggers."

"The life-insurance paperwork," he said. "Phil mentioned that. He hasn't pulled that for you yet?"

"He promised it, but I haven't been able to get hold of him."

Underhill shook his head. "He's traveling with Ford, you know, crisscrossing the state, one last big push. Allentown, Bethlehem, and Easton yesterday. State College, Lewistown, and Altoona today, overnighting in Johnstown." He sighed. "Some things about politics I don't miss at all."

"I've been trying to get in touch with Enrique Chembergo all week as well. Mr. Staggers keeps saying—"

"You've got an interest in public service, Ms. Kennedy, from what I understand." He looked around conspiratorially, then whispered: "I have highly placed sources in the Seventh Ward."

Brenna studied his face. Was this a good thing, or a

bad thing? Should she be happy her ambitions already were humming along the Democratic Party grapevine, or appalled that word of them traveled so far so fast? "I'm exploring some possibilities," she said.

"City council."

She felt herself flush. So much for her private conversation with the ward chairman earlier in the week.

"I've made you uncomfortable," Underhill said. "I'm sorry."

"No, no. I expressed an interest, and I guess I shouldn't be surprised that word got around. I'm a big girl."

Underhill smiled. "Good news travels fast."

He led her down the hall and into a stunning library across the hall from his study, into the rich scent of leather and old books. She set her briefcase next to an antique liquor cart loaded with crystal decanters, then sank into the cushioned embrace of a solid-oak mission chair.

"Are you set on the council?" he asked.

"How do you mean?"

The former governor poured two fingers of something dark and potent into a cut-crystal glass. He held the decanter up, offering to pour her one as well. Brenna shook her head. "Listening to pothole complaints and whining ward heelers gets pretty old after awhile," he said. "Ever considered public service at a higher level?"

Maybe she should have taken that drink. "By 'higher level,' " she said cautiously, "you mean with the city?"

"The state," Underhill said. "Harrisburg."

Brenna met his gaze and held it. He seemed straightforward and sincere. "I'd like working on public policy at that level."

"It's where people with vision can make a difference," he said. "You can have a real impact there, make changes that improve people's lives. That appeals to you, does it?"

She nodded. "Of course. But I'm willing to start local."

Underhill sipped and smiled. "You're playing by the rules, Ms. Kennedy. Rules are for small thinkers. Don't be afraid to rise to the level at which you can be most effective.''

"That's quite a compliment, governor. Thank you."

Underhill swirled the amber liquid and tipped the glass into his mouth, swallowing with a rasp. "My son is building his transition team, Ms. Kennedy. He's going to need people with your kind of energy, your kind of brass. Is that the sort of thing you might be interested in?"

He said it so suddenly, so directly, she wasn't sure she heard him right. "In Harrisburg?"

"Senior staff, and right now it's wide open. Don't get me wrong, Ms. Kennedy, I'm not trying to run my son's show here. I've just been there. I know what Ford'll be up against. He's going to need someone who knows the players in this end of the state, knows the media, understands politics. I can't speak for him, of course, but we've talked generally about your skills. He's very impressed."

"Public policy on that level—" Brenna struggled for words.

"Impact, Ms. Kennedy," he said. "Impact. But I know it's never a simple choice. You have children, I know, and you're, ah, attached? It's Jim, isn't it?"

She nodded, trying to remember how much information about herself she'd divulged during their previous meeting. She didn't remember their conversations ever straying that far into her personal life.

"So the thought of uprooting is probably pretty unsettling." He winked. "Can't say I blame you. Might make for a few interesting dinnertime conversations, though. Like I said, I've been there. But think about it generally, then maybe you and Ford can talk specifics after the election."

Brenna stared. The man had just unearthed ambitions she had only begun to admit to herself. He'd somehow peeked into her soul, chosen one of her unspoken dreams, and presented it to her as a gift.

"Senior staff," she managed, thinking about Jim, the new house, Taylor's dread of the unfamiliar.

"Ford's going to make things happen. I think you'd be a great addition."

Brenna waited, wondering if Underhill's vague offer might get more explicit the longer she kept her mouth shut. But he said nothing. "Something to think about, for sure," she said finally.

Underhill checked the gleaming Rolex on his wrist. "Now, I've promised my wife I'd get all my busy work done while she's at Harmony today. If I'm going to keep that promise, Ms. Kennedy, I need to get moving. Did you have something else?"

Brenna felt her brain engage. "Mr. Chembergo," she said, "the gardener. I still need to talk to him about what he heard and saw out there on the deck the day your wife fell."

Underhill forced a smile.

"So far Mr. Staggers hasn't been able to put me in touch with him," she said. "Since he lives on the property, I stopped out to get that resolved. He made that statement to the investigators, remember, and we need to be ready for whatever Dagnolo throws at us."

Underhill slowly lifted the crystal stopper from the cocktail cart and replaced it in the neck of the decanter. "Anticipating," he said. "I like that. You can never be too ready when you're dealing with a thug like J. D. Dagnolo."

"Exactly."

Underhill picked up the handset of his sleek black desk phone and punched in two numbers. "The library," was all he said before hanging up. Seconds later, Staggers followed his polite knock through the door. He greeted Brenna with a nod.

"Ms. Kennedy, I believe you've met Mr. Staggers," Underhill said. "He's much more on top of the household staff changes than I am, so he's probably the person you need to be speaking with about Mr.—" His eyes shifted to Staggers.

"Chembergo," Staggers volunteered.

"Changes?" Brenna said.

Underhill made a great show of checking his watch again, then moved toward the study door. "If I don't get upstairs, I'm liable to end up getting the Florence Underhill Glare. You *never* want to be on the receiving end of that. It'll melt the elastic in your socks." He turned to Staggers. "You won't mind filling Ms. Kennedy in?"

"Of course not."

"What changes?" Brenna said, but Underhill was already out the door in a flash of silver hair and the silent glide of Italian leather on carpet. She wheeled on the security man. "What changes?"

"An unanticipated transition in the household staff," he said. "It happens."

"The Chembergos?"

Staggers nodded.

Brenna dropped any pretense of civility. "I still need to talk to him."

"Be my guest." Staggers smiled, just enough to infuriate her. "Hope your passport's up to date."

"Meaning? Where is he?"

Staggers twisted his pinkie ring, then examined his fingernails. He checked his wristwatch. "Guatemala City about now, I expect."

The answer was as unexpected as it was implausible. Brenna opened her mouth, but all that came out was, "Where?"

"The sprawling capital city of the war-torn Republic of Guatemala, bordered on the east by the Caribbean, the west by the Pacific Ocean and—"

"Cut the geography lesson."

"Impressive, no? I took this Conversational Knowledge of World Affairs seminar a couple of years ago. Picked up a lot of stuff like that. Ask me about Syria. I know Syria cold."

Brenna picked up her briefcase and opened the study door.

"Okay, okay," Staggers said. "The peculiars is what you want."

"Particulars," she corrected, setting the briefcase back down.

"Whatever."

She waited, arms crossed, one foot telegraphing her impatience.

"INS," he said. "Out of the blue. Wham! Suddenly they're real interested in Enrique and Selena's paperwork." He shook his head. "Political campaigns are nasty, nasty."

"So they weren't legal?"

Staggers nodded. "Who knew? These people trade green cards like baseball cards. The Underhills just assumed they were paying the taxes, and when they found out we had a couple of outlaws on our hands, well, you *know* Ford would have gotten tarred with that sooner or later. Forget it was his parents, not him, who hired them."

Brenna brushed a stray hair away from her face.

"They didn't want it becoming an issue, so they let the INS take them," Staggers said. "Not that the Underhills even thought about defending these people, you know. They were definitely illegitimate."

Brenna studied the man, looking for cracks in his sincerity. "So they're gone already?"

"Immigration people don't mess around," he said, nodding. "Damned misfortunate, too. You *know* good help's hard to find."

19

What bothered her most, Brenna decided, was not that the Chembergos had disappeared, but rather the smarmy way Staggers had told her they were gone. She'd felt an edge there, the unspoken superiority of a man with a secret. What she'd seen in him before was a sort of goofy charm; what she saw now was a man who was gloating.

As they left the library on the way to her car, she noticed Vincent Underhill at his desk in the study, talking on the telephone. She hung back, waiting for Staggers to move ahead into the grand prairie of the house's foyer, then sidestepped through the study door. She smiled when the startled former governor looked up. He smiled back and motioned her to a wing chair across from his desk as he nodded his assent to whoever was on the line. She was sitting down by the time Staggers caught on.

"Something else you need from the governor?" he whispered, stepping between her and Underhill, moving his arms as if he were trying to scoop her out of the room. "I'd be happy to ask him, if you have any other questions."

She shook her head, noticing before it became obvious

that she had a vise grip on the chair's arm. She wasn't moving, wasn't about to let the house dick hustle her out the door without a few more answers. "Some things need to stay between an attorney and her client, Mr. Staggers." She winked. "Thank you, though."

"He's pretty busy. See?"

"Aren't we all?" she whispered. "Where does the time go? I won't take but a minute. Promise."

"I just think you'd be more comfortable waiting out—"

Vincent Underhill excused himself from his conversation and softly replaced the handset of his desk phone, his face apparently untroubled by the intrusion. Staggers whirled and shrugged in the same motion, but Underhill waved him away. He left obediently. If Brenna had to guess from the former governor's expression, Underhill had the look of a man wondering if he was being seduced.

"Ms. Kennedy," he said, suddenly on his feet. "How wonderful you're still with us." He looked at his watch. "Just checking here and, yes! It's time for another drink." He walked to the liquor cart and hoisted a crystal decanter identical to the one in the library. "Brandy?"

"I've got a full afternoon, I'm afraid. Thanks, though."

"Small one?"

"Thanks, but no."

He sighed, measured the liquid gold into a snifter, then toasted her. "Unemployment has its privileges. Now what can I do for you?"

"It's about the Chembergos," she said.

Blank stare. "Enrique and Selena!" he said after a moment. "Of course." Underhill shook his head. "Damned good people. Been with us at least two years. Quiet. Clean. She was so good with Floss."

"But when did these INS questions come up?"

He whirled the brandy, sniffed, and sipped. "What's today? Two days ago maybe?"

"And they've already been deported?"

He laughed. "When did a federal agency ever move

that fast, Ms. Kennedy? No, once we ascertained the validity of the allegations, we acted on our own in helping them comply with the law.''

"*You* sent them back to Guatemala?''

"It's a statewide election, Ms. Kennedy, and you know how these things can get twisted. We're not taking any chances. Of course, we're not unfeeling. There was a reasonable severance.''

Brenna leaned forward. The man couldn't be that stupid.

"Devil's advocate," she said. "May I?''

"Please.''

"Okay. I'm a publicity-mad D.A. with a grudge. Ten days before a statewide election, I have reason to investigate a suspicious accident, an attempted suicide, maybe even a possible attempted homicide, at the home of the leading candidate, of whom I'm not particularly fond. My case hinges on a witness who claims the victim wasn't alone at the time she was injured. You with me?''

Underhill nodded.

"Now, right before the election, the witness disappears. I check it out, and sure enough, the witness is long gone, out of the country, along with his wife, who was very close to the victim. And they've got a fat wad of cash, *your cash*, in their pockets.''

Underhill set the glass down on the edge of his desk. "But we had to respond appropriately," he said. "Legitimate questions were raised.''

"By whom? The INS?''

Underhill sat down in a chair across from her, studied her over his steepled fingers. "Come now, Ms. Kennedy. In the heat of a campaign, reality becomes whatever fits into an attack ad or a last-minute mailer. People we know at INS told us what Dagnolo's people were up to. Do you know what they were doing? Feeding everything they had, such as it was, to the Rosemond campaign. We know this. They didn't need proof. If they'd timed it right, simply raising the question about our little immigration problem would have been enough to smear Ford as an over-privileged lawbreaker. But in this case, they got lucky. There *was* a hole in this couple's paperwork. They weren't about to let that slide. We know that much. So as soon as we knew there was a problem, we acted.''

Brenna sat forward. ''I'm the nosy D.A., remember? I'm looking at more than an election, I'm trying to bump this whole thing up to an attempted homicide charge, and I'm looking for someone in your family to pin it on. Frankly, I see you trying to solve an entirely different problem here.''

Underhill pinched the end of his nose between his up-thrust index fingers. ''You think it looks like a payoff by someone with something to hide.''

''I think,'' she said, ''it looks like hell. In the hands of an opposing candidate, it's an unpleasant handful of mud. In the hands of a D.A. building a criminal case, it's a coverup.''

Underhill leaned back and stretched his long legs, crossing them at the ankles in the space between their chairs. ''You worry too much, Ms. Kennedy.''

''You're paying me to worry,'' she said. ''But at this point, there's not much you can do about it. But I'd like to fly down to interview Enrique Chembergo. There may be big holes in his statement, but we'll never know that unless—''

''Drop it, Ms. Kennedy. Please. What's done is done.'' Underhill picked up the glass and swirled the brandy, then tipped it all the way back. He studied the bottom of the glass as his head cleared. ''One of life's great lessons, Ms. Kennedy: First, make the right choice, then worry about the consequences. We did what was right. That's how this family operates, has always operated.''

Brenna shrugged. ''You're the client. But I don't think someone like Dagnolo—''

''It didn't start with me, of course,'' Underhill said, looser now, lubricated. ''We all carry forward what we're taught. The guiding principles that my father learned from his father, Ford learned from me. We're Underhills, Ms. Kennedy. That still means something.''

Maybe a different tack, she thought. Flattery is the inquisitor's secret weapon. Stroke him. Let his ego do the talking. "So I read in the papers, governor," she said. "I've always known there were principles behind your politics. So often they get lost.''

Underhill straightened in his chair, offered a benevolent smile. "Not with us.''

Brenna decided to push. "Gosh," she said, "there's still so much about your family I don't know.''

By his third brandy, Vincent Underhill already had covered the proud history of three generations since grandfather Andrew. Now, he was deep into his national political aspirations for Ford. Brenna needed only an occasional nod to keep him talking. What Underhill didn't mention, though, was curious. For a man so infatuated with the notion of legacy, of great and righteous Underhillian values passed like a torch from one generation to the next, why hadn't he mentioned the obvious: With the death of his only grandchild three years earlier, the great Underhill lineage might end with Ford.

"Tragedy is the greatest test of character," she said. "I understand you've had your share of it in the past few years.''

Underhill's eyes drifted, but only for a moment. "Alzheimer's doesn't respect much of anything, Ms. Kennedy. Not money, or power, or privilege. Doesn't give a damn about character. But we're quite involved with the Harmony Center, as you probably know. Whenever we've had misfortune, we try to learn from it, to educate others, to inspire.''

She nodded respectfully. It was time to test him. "And of course you and your wife got so involved in brain-injury causes three years ago. I remember that well.''

Underhill shifted in his leather chair, then fixed his gaze

on hers. She waited in silence for a response, finally prompting: "After the accident with Ford's son, I mean."

Brenna couldn't tell exactly what had changed, but something in the man's face softened. His eyes never shifted, but the skin around them seemed to sag, as if gravity had suddenly gotten stronger. The roots of whatever she'd hit went deep.

Underhill unfolded his hands and laid them on the arms of his chair while he traced the pattern of rivets on the front of the right chair arm with one long finger. "Pray, Ms. Kennedy, that you never experience the kind of sadness that the death of a child can bring."

She thought of Taylor, couldn't help it, couldn't stop every mother's nightmare from bobbing up from the unspeakable depths. "I do," she said. "It's the *only* thing I pray for. I know how painful—"

"No." He held one hand toward her, pink palm out. "You can't know, remember?"

"Yes, Mr. Underhill, I can. You don't have to live a tragedy like that to imagine it, and no parent could imagine it *without* knowing the pain."

Underhill squinted, slowly nodding his head. "Well argued, counselor, but I disagree." He drew his legs up until he sat upright behind his desk, proper but not rigid. "How much do you know about what happened?"

"A riding accident," she said.

A sad laugh. A nod. "You never think much about the word 'accident' until something like that happens, until a child dies. Accidents happen. Everybody knows that. You accept it as part of life. But there's a whole world of guilt and what-ifs inside the word 'accident,' Ms. Kennedy. Anybody who's been there carries it like a cross, and for the rest of their lives."

Underhill stood up, moving now as if in slow motion, and measured himself another dose of brandy, smaller this time. "It was a Sunday," he said, offering the decanter again. Brenna shook her head. "We weren't even expecting them, Ford, Leigh, and Chip. They just came rolling up unexpected, out for a drive or something. And Chip—God, he was irrepressible—came bouncing out of the Range Rover like a little tornado, all full of plans.''

''Chip was three?''

He nodded. ''An amazing age. They're pretty sure they're running the world when they're three.''

''So I'm guessing it was his idea to go riding.''

''Exactly.'' Underhill smiled. She felt she'd connected on some level. Then his face sagged again. ''But it was my idea to send them out on Gray.''

''That's the horse?''

''One of Floss's jumpers. Beautiful animal. Strung tight as a banjo string, though. Skittish. Ford's a decent rider, but my gut told me to give them one of the gentle mares, something high-mileage. But there he was, that damned gelding, the only one in the stable saddled up and ready. So Ford climbed on, I handed Chip up to him, and off they went.''

Brenna smoothed her skirt, leaning forward as she did. ''You can't blame yourself.''

Underhill sipped at the brandy. ''Sure I can.''

''As a friend of mine would say, that's your choice.''

He nodded. ''My choice, yes, because I've never shrunk from responsibility, Ms. Kennedy, although I know that's out of fashion. A different horse, who knows?''

''But that sort of second-guessing—''

Underhill set the brandy glass down with an indelicate thump. ''The thing about an 'accident,' see, is that it comes with a lifetime of second-guessing. There's no debate about what happened. It was just one of those things. But you go back and relive the decisions you made that led up to what happened, turn them over and over again, wondering what you might have done differently, how that might have changed things. And you struggle with the questions, like Sisyphus and the rock, but they roll right back. Sometimes they roll over you.''

Brenna recrossed her legs. "What did happen, governor?"

"Out there, while they were riding?"

"The horse reared or something, right?"

Underhill closed his eyes. "Do you know how Fox Chapel got its name, Ms. Kennedy?"

Brenna shook her head.

"Well, actually, neither do I." He opened his eyes again. "But damned if there aren't still foxes running around out there on all this expensive real estate. We haven't yet taken all their habitat, or at least they seem to like what we've done with it. They stuck around. So there are foxes in Fox Chapel."

"Foxes," she repeated.

"Ford said there was something wrong with the one that crossed the trail that afternoon. It was dull red, not like the others we see around here, my son said, with these tired eyes, head hanging low to the ground like it weighed a ton. Sick-looking, maybe rabid. Something wrong, but we may never know exactly what."

"Horses can sense things," she said.

"This wasn't a trail horse in the first place. Lived its whole life in a stable or a ring. So this fox, whatever the problem with it, just spooked the hell out of him. It was a narrow stretch of trail, down in the bottoms behind the house, and Ford said he couldn't control him. When he reared, they all went over backward."

"The horse fell on them?"

Underhill swirled the residue of his brandy and watched the teardrops roll down the sides of the glass. "Ford was able to grab Chip and jump clear. The horse got up, still agitated, wide-eyed, but everybody seemed to be all right. They thought it was over."

Brenna imagined Ford's relief as he realized his young son was safe.

"But the fox was still there, maybe fifteen yards down the trail," Underhill said. "It started coming straight for them, kind of wobbly-legged. Ford said it looked like a mean drunk. That's when they really knew something was wrong with it.''

Brenna closed her eyes now. "The horse had nowhere to go,'' she said.

"He couldn't turn, couldn't go forward. He tried to back up, but Ford and Chip were standing on the trail right behind him.'' Underhill rubbed his elegant hands across his eyes, pointed to his left temple. "The kick—just one—caught Chippy square, knocked him back maybe twenty feet.''

Brenna felt her stomach clench, imagining the sound, the unreal sensation of seeing your child tossed like a rag doll, the one sickening moment when Ford must have understood that it was bad. She didn't need to hear the rest of the story. She was sure from Underhill's deep sigh that he didn't want to tell it. He seemed to force himself to continue.

"Thank God, he probably never even knew what happened. It was that quick. When Ford picked him up—he was limp, lying in a patch of wildflowers at the base of a tree—he looked like he was sleeping. Eyes closed, no expression whatever. Just a little boy taking a nap. But Ford knew.''

Brenna covered her mouth with her hand, a reflex triggered by the urge to cry. She cleared her throat instead. Underhill was gazing at the ceiling, a single tear spilling from one eye and rolling down his patrician cheek.

"It was a mile, at least, up and out of the bottoms and back to the house. A steep climb, too. Ford doesn't even remember running back, but as soon as I saw him coming toward the house, my grandson so slack in his arms—'' Underhill's voice caught. He drew a ragged breath. "Chippy never woke up.''

"There was nothing they could do?'' Brenna managed.

"He died in the ambulance. The paramedics knew, because they usually won't let parents ride along.'' Underhill couldn't stop the tremor in his lower jaw. "They let Ford and Leigh stay with him.''

Why had she forced the conversation again? What was her point in asking this man to relive the pain of that tragedy? Brenna couldn't recall, and suddenly felt as coarse and insensitive as one of those TV reporters who shove their microphones into the faces of a victim's grieving family and asks how they feel.

"Even before we got the news back here, I'd loaded my shotgun and was headed out to find the horse. Believe me, Ms. Kennedy, he'd have died that day, too, if Floss hadn't stopped me. Half a million dollars on the hoof—at least that's what we paid for him when he was a colt—but I'd have done it without a second thought."

"It wouldn't have brought your grandson back."

Underhill nodded. "Of course it was irrational. But a certain closure would have been of some comfort at that point."

"So you still have the horse?"

"Not here. Like I said, call it irrational. But we just couldn't keep him here, seeing him every day, this 1,200-pound reminder of our grandchild's death. Gray was Floss's favorite, even more than the ones she used to ride, and she couldn't bear to sell him."

"You sent him away."

"We have a horse property down in Westmoreland County, so he's there. It was best."

Brenna wanted to say something appropriate, but managed only a tired cliché: "Out of sight, out of mind."

"The horse, yes," Underhill said. "Our grandson?" He shook his head. "Never."

20

Maura Pearson piloted the Special into the Harmony parking lot at a stately speed, drawing an appreciative smile from the shriveled octogenarian in a motorized wheelchair—the one the staff called "the White Raisin"—who was waiting for a pickup near the center's front entrance. She parked in an open spot beside Christensen's Explorer and cut the engine.

"I still think we're on to something significant here," Christensen said. "We know she's reacted with strong emotion to two memories: the disappearance of the gray horse, and Warren Doti. We know she loved the horse; she may have loved Doti. And you can bet the death of her grandson was another powerful memory."

Pearson checked her hair in the rearview mirror. "But what's the connection? Doti and the horse, maybe."

"The kid died while he was riding the horse." He folded his notebook and slid it into the briefcase at his feet. "I'm not saying they're connected, necessarily. They just all happened about the same time."

"That's assuming her memory can be trusted," Pearson said. "Never A-S-S-ume."

She was right. He needed more information. "I think I'll focus on that time frame for now, see what turns up. If nothing else, I can nail down a chronology of things that happened to her during that period. I can always broaden it later."

Pearson checked her watch. "I need to get in for the afternoon class. The aides can get them started, but I should be there. You must have a guess at this point. What do you pinheads call it?"

"A hypothesis."

"That."

He hoisted the briefcase, rested it across his thighs. "I can't help but think this whole thing gets back to the idea of loss. She lost the horse. She lost Doti. She lost the grandson. And it all happened about the same time. There's a reason those three things are all somehow represented in this very weird, very dark image she paints over and over."

Pearson pulled the polished chrome driver's-door handle. The car rocked as the weighty thing swung open. "House of cards," she said.

"I know. It's just a start, but it feels significant to me." And dangerous, he thought, though he still couldn't say why. He opened his door and stepped out. Ripples of heat rose from the Special's roof as he and Pearson faced one another across its metal expanse.

"You sitting in this afternoon?" she said.

"Don't think so." He turned and unlocked the Explorer's door, tossed the briefcase onto the front passenger seat. It crushed Annie's rendition of Earth's geologic layering, rendered in Play-Doh across sturdy cardboard for an Earth Sciences project at her old school a few months back. Her teacher had returned it the day before Annie transferred to Westminster-Stanton, crisp and fractured, and he hadn't yet moved it from car to house. His daughter hadn't seemed particularly fond of it, actually wanted to throw it away, but when he asked if he could put it in the special box where he kept her momentous accomplishments, she'd flushed with pride. Now, this.

"Aw, hell," he said.

Pearson looked up, startled, from her side of the Special. "What?"

"Nothing. Just . . . nothing." He turned back toward her. "Never mind."

"So, you just goofing off this afternoon, or what?" she said.

Christensen shook his head. "I've got some paper-chasing to do."

Christensen passed Oxford Centre, wondering if Brenna was in her office, then turned off sunwashed, red-brick Grant Street and into the urban canyon of Fourth. He cruised slowly through the deep shadows, between the Grant and City-County buildings, past the jail annex, looking for the squat Gothic masterpiece that housed the Allegheny County morgue.

These few blocks, home to the Pittsburgh police department's old Public Safety Building, the county courthouse, the county jail, and the morgue, were the center of Brenna's professional universe. She knew the plots and players on the grand stage of justice in western Pennsylvania in a way he never would. To him, these blocks were unfamiliar territory, far removed from his professional landscape at the University of Pittsburgh. Truth be told, he was awestruck by Brenna's command of her world of cops and criminals and judges.

He had seen the morgue before, marveled at its turn-of-the-century architecture, but the place struck him each time as something a film director might create for a scene requiring profound gloom. Shoehorned onto a concrete lot behind the courthouse and jail complex, its granite walls were a hopeless gray deepened by layers of soot and grime. Beneath the half-dozen window air conditioners on this side of the building, condensation dripped onto the granite blocks and left dark stains that created the impression that something gory was seeping out. Though a grand example of period architecture, here was a building that would never rise above its purpose.

Christensen circled the block, finally finding a parking spot along the curb near the morgue's rear entrance. A driveway extended from the street into an open garage door, where he could hear voices and clattering metal and the sound of a closing car door. A sign posted beside the garage door seemed morbidly cold: Delivery Entrance.

What struck him first as he passed was an overpowering and noxious smell, worse than anything he could recall. It hit him like a fetid fist, knocking him back with a force he wouldn't have thought possible. He covered his nose and mouth, his eyes beginning to tear, and forced himself to peer into the dark garage. Two men in dark-blue jumpsuits and surgical masks were moving around a white coroner's van, behind which stood two gunmetal gray gurneys, each carrying the ominous black lump of a body bag.

"Get the freezer door, just hold it open," one of the men said. "Whew, baby!"

"Who'd we piss off, anyway?"

"Fucking floaters."

Christensen recognized the term. Floaters were an inevitable consequence of living in a river town where the number of reported bridge suicides always seemed to spike each year in the late stages of Pittsburgh's relentless gray winter. He also knew that the local mob used the city's three rivers as a convenient repository for unwanted union bosses, disloyal employees, and debtors who fell too far behind in their payments. But surely two floaters at one time was unusual; he'd have to check tomorrow's *Press*.

Christensen paused near the morgue's front entrance to catch his breath, which he'd held since that first putrid whiff of death. He sniffed tentatively at first, testing to make sure the odor hadn't followed him around the building, then took a dozen deep breaths, one after another, purging his lungs as best he could.

The morgue's front doors opened into a lobby of what could have been an overdecorated house trailer. The off-white marble extended four feet up the walls like a giant splash guard, and the room was trimmed in varying shades of cheerless gray paint. Only touches of the building's once-grand architecture peeked through its sad redecoration. The lobby was dominated by a large, half-moon-shaped reception desk that all but blocked passage to the lobby's three exits. Empty, the desk seemed ridiculously out of scale. Just behind it was an unmarked door leading toward the rear of the building. On the wall just outside the stairway hung two large black-and-white photographs showing the entire morgue building being moved nearly three hundred feet from its previous location along Forbes Avenue, photographs he recognized from a historical documentary about Pittsburgh's colorful past.

Though he'd never been inside the morgue before, it seemed vaguely familiar from that documentary and from Brenna's descriptions. Decades earlier, the morgue had had a macabre feature on the first floor—angled viewing windows that allowed even casual visitors to peer through the floor into the basement room where unidentified bodies in all states of disrepair were displayed like prone department-store mannequins. With a predictable supply of indigents and other nameless unfortunates, the windows had been the county coroner's first crude attempt at victim identification. But because the lobby was open twenty-four hours a day, the viewing windows also became a favorite stop for death freaks, practical jokers, and blind-folded prom dates.

Christensen sniffed tentatively. The place smelled stale, but nothing like what had just cleared his sinuses. The air was almost fresh, artificially fresh, no doubt the product of some heroic odor-masking products retrofitted to the building's ancient ventilation system. Robust and cheery spider plants hung at random intervals around the lobby, but their placement seemed uncoordinated.

To Christensen's right were the low modular walls of what looked like a small corral. This, he knew, was the modern replacement for those old viewing windows, where the coroner's staff allowed a victim's grieving family or friends to review the basement inventory by closed-circuit television without having to confront the chilling realities of death. The fiber-covered cubicle walls apparently were the budget-minded county commission's laughable way of giving them privacy.

Where was the receptionist? He read the stenciled letters on the glass panels of the heavy wooden doors that branched off from the lobby—Histology Lab, Investigator's Office, Photo Lab. An elevator stood open and ready to his left, but a hand-painted sign on the wall of a nearby stairway seemed more promising: Records. He followed the arrow to the second floor, emerging into a nightmare of bureaucratic design. An impossibly thin black man sat behind a counter among what seemed like a disorganized collection of computer terminals, file cabinets, and institutional desks. He looked up from the keyboard of his computer as Christensen set his briefcase on the counter and pulled a business card from his wallet.

"Help you?" he said.

"Thanks." Christensen handed the card across the counter. "This where I'd find death certificates?"

The man stood up and took the card. He was maybe 6-foot-5, head shaved, with thick black Malcolm X specs whose lenses magnified his eyes to an almost comical size. They looked like Grade AA extra-large eggs, hard-boiled, muted only by his heavy, dark eyelids. He smiled suddenly, revealing a prominent overbite that gave his face yet another unfortunate dimension. The name tag on his maroon shirt read Bragg.

"You didn't look like a lawyer or a reporter," he said.

Christensen nodded. "Is that good?"

"Neither way with me. It's just lawyers and the news

people that come in, mostly. I can tell you ain't either of them." He looked at Christensen's card again, put out his hand. "I'm Lemonjello," he said, pronouncing it *le-MON-jello*.

"Jim Christensen." The man's hand felt smooth as talc, his handshake firm. "This is my first time trying to do this, actually, digging out records. Any help you can give me would be great."

"Death certificate's what you're looking for?"

"One. And any other paperwork you might have on the same case. I assume all that's public record."

Bragg slid a form across the counter. "Fill this out, just the top five lines. Name, address, records you want. We got certificates, autopsy reports, all that. What's the name so I can start?"

Christensen tipped his briefcase on its side and snaked a hand in to retrieve a pen and the yellow legal pad he'd been using to take research notes. "Underhill."

Bragg waited. "I'll need the first name."

"Vincent. The third, I think."

Bragg smiled again, less natural than the first time. He put Christensen's card into his shirt pocket. "The Carrie Crusade," he said. "You people sure keeping us busy over here. That one, seems like I copied it already."

Christensen cocked his head. "Sorry, I don't follow."

"You're with Carrie Haygood, right?"

"Who?"

"CDRT?"

Christensen shook his head.

"No?" Bragg squinted through his thick lenses. "What you want that file for?"

"Sorry, you've lost me here. I'm just doing some independent research, looking for information about this one particular case."

"What for?"

Christensen offered a defensive smile. "Research," he said, adding: "They're public records, right?"

Bragg nodded stiffly, gesturing to the records-release

form. "Just fill all this out. Don't forget the address and phone."

When Bragg disappeared through a door labeled "Indexing," Christensen began filling in the requested information, stopping only to scribble "Kerry or Carrie Haygood?" and the acronym "CDRT" on the second page of his notebook. He also added Bragg's name, spelling the first name phonetically. Within a minute, the records clerk was back with a file as thin as the man himself.

"That's it?"

"Everything we've got," Bragg said.

Christensen opened the manila file. He flipped through four documents inside and read the title of each one: Certificate of Death, Autopsy Protocol, Toxicology Report, and Coroner's Investigative Report. None was more than two pages long. He'd expected the bureaucracy of death to be more substantial.

Christensen began with the death certificate. Name: Vincent Charles Underhill III. Date of death: October 6, 1996. Race: Caucasian. Date of birth: July 6, 1993—just over three years old. He scanned past the names of the child's parents, although he jotted down Ford and Leigh Underhill's Sewickley Heights address. Near the bottom, typed in capital letters, under "Cause of Death": SUBDURAL HEMATOMA.

Bragg was back at his computer, pecking at the keyboard like an elegant black crane hunched into a rolling desk chair. Christensen decided not to ask for a definition. He copied the cause of death into his notebook, as well as the name Simon Bostwick, the deputy coroner whose signature was at the bottom.

The toxicology report was a check-off sheet listing dozens of drugs, starting with acetaminophen. They'd tested specimens from the boy's heart, blood, urine, stomach, kidneys, liver, and the fluid from inside his eyeballs. All along the page, the "None" box was checked.

The coroner's investigative report was a short account by another deputy coroner who actually retrieved Chip

Underhill's body from the hospital where paramedics took him after the accident. That deputy's role, it seemed, mostly involved delivering the boy's body to the morgue and tracking the final disposition of his size 4 clothing, the only personal property noted in the report. Nothing useful.

The autopsy protocol began with a brief history of the death, an account of the horseback-riding accident that injured Chip Underhill. It offered little information beyond what Christensen had seen in the newspaper account. He noted, though, that the lines estimating the time of death and the time of the emergency call reporting the incident were left blank. The rest was a narrative catalog of Bostwick's external and internal examination of Chip Underhill's body, and Christensen was struck by the dispassionate language of death science. The deputy coroner described the boy's height, weight, hair color, eye color, and complexion. The pupils were dilated and equal, but he noted retinal bleeding, again in capital letters. The nose, atraumatic and intact. The upper and lower lips appeared unremarkable, as were the mucous membranes of the oral cavity. His teeth were natural and in good repair. His external genitalia were those of a normal male child. No external injuries were noted, save for an abrasion on the boy's left shoulder.

Christensen imagined Ford Underhill's confusion: His son must have lost consciousness at some point after the riding accident, but from this account he also must have appeared uninjured. What would haunt a parent more? Seeing his child injured in some obvious and horrible way? Or watching him die quietly while seemingly asleep?

Bostwick's account of the internal examination—the cardiovascular and respiratory systems, gastrointestinal tract, pancreas, hepatobiliary system, spleen, pituitary, thyroid, and adrenals—was an inventory of the unremarkable, a grim listing of organ weights and fluid measures.

Christensen scanned to the section describing Chip Underhill's head. There were no contusions or hemorrhages in the deep scalp tissues. The cranium and base of the skull were intact and without fractures. The brain weighed an unremarkable 964 grams, but with "severe edema in the cavity"—blood, apparently, from an "intercranial hemorrhage on both the left and right sides." The fall, or the horse's kick, apparently had sent Chip Underhill's brain crashing around the inside of his skull like a doomed ship caught between rocks.

Christensen shuddered. He didn't fully understand the arcane medical terminology describing the injuries, but he understood right away that a brain injury had killed Chip Underhill. He closed the file, pushed it back across the counter, and paid the preoccupied clerk to photocopy each of the documents. As he waited, he thought dark thoughts about Molly, about Annie and Melissa, about Brenna and Taylor and the depressing fragility of life.

22

The house was as quiet as a tomb in the late afternoon. If not for the sound of his computer's fan and the spider-crawl of his fingers across the keyboard, Christensen knew the silence of solitude would overwhelm him.

He'd come straight home from the morgue, forgoing his planned stop at Brenna's office and the chance to pick up the kids early. He was following a bread-crumb trail into Floss Underhill's forgotten recent past, hoping for a break. He checked his notebook for the name that the records clerk had mentioned: Haygood. He typed it in and waited while the computer searched. The screen blinked and, to Christensen's surprise, it announced that it had found one story. It was published in *Pittsburgh Magazine* seven months earlier and was titled "The Worst Job in the World." The headline alone made it worth the $1.50 it cost him to download it and print it out.

Christensen leaned back in his chair, put one foot up on his desk, and read. According to an information line at the top of the six-page printout, the story had run with a full-page photograph of "Carrie Haygood, head of Allegheny County's new Child Death Review Team." The secondary headline read: ''Why ghetto-born Ivy Leaguer Carrie Haygood is taking on the toughest homicides of all.''

The Child Death Review Team was created by the county commission less than a year ago as a logical outgrowth of the child-abuse awareness movement of the 1980s, the story explained. The team's mission was to scrutinize the circumstances surrounding the death of children in Allegheny County for indications of abuse or foul play, and its initial goal was to begin a systematic review of all child death cases in the county during the past ten years.

He scanned the pages, slowing down to absorb the details of Carrie Haygood's biography: Braxton Heights High School honors student; University of Pittsburgh undergrad; Georgetown University Medical School; forensic training at the University of Virginia; a standout forensic specialist during her fourteen years with the Los Angeles County coroner's office. She called the opportunity to return to Pittsburgh to lead the county's Child Death Review Team ''the worst job I can imagine, and an irresistible obligation.''

Christensen stopped reading. If the morgue clerk had made copies of Chip Underhill's file for Haygood and her team, was it just part of that routine records review of cases going back ten years? Or had the case been singled out by someone who suspected the official version of the boy's death? He wasn't finding answers, only more questions.

He checked his watch—fifteen minutes until he had to leave to pick up Annie and Taylor at Kids' Korner. What now? He picked up his notes from the morgue and read through them again, stopping at the name Simon Bostwick, the deputy coroner who signed Chip Underhill's death certificate. He found the phone number of the coroner's office on his receipt for photocopying the documents and dialed.

''Simon Bostwick, please,'' he said to the woman who

answered "Cahnny Corner" in an unmistakable Pittsburgh accent.

After a long pause, she said, "He's no longer with this office. Somebody else I can direct you to?"

Christensen cleared his throat, stalling for time. Allegheny County still elected its coroner even though most of the rest of the country had gone to an appointed medical-examiner system years earlier. There'd been a change in administration the year before—a comically bombastic Democrat named Cyrus Lawrence Walsh was swept into power on his vague promise to "professionalize" the coroner's office—and he'd replaced much of former coroner Nagiv Pungpreechawatn's staff with political patrons. There'd been lawsuits.

"Your office went through a big transition this past year, I guess," he said.

"Well, uh—" the woman said. "Dr. Bostwick retired before that, I think."

Other lines were ringing, and Christensen could hear the impatience in her voice. "I know you're busy, but do you know if he's still in the area?"

"Hold aahn," she said. WDVE was just coming out of a back-to-back Pearl Jam set, but then, what *would* be appropriate hold music for the county morgue?

Christensen checked his watch again, dashing his thoughts about making a salad for dinner before he picked up the kids.

"He's up near Seven Springs somewhere, is alls we know," the woman said. "Sorry I can't help you more. Nobody here knows much abaaht him." The line clicked, and she was gone.

Christensen dialed directory assistance.

"What city?"

The question stumped him. "Somewhere in the Laurel Highlands?" he said.

"Let's try Somerset. Business or residence?"

"Residence."

"Go ahead."

"Simon Bostwick," he said, checking his notes again. "B-O-S-T-W—"

"Here's your number," the operator said, turning the conversation over to a synthesized electronic voice. Christensen copied it down on a bright-yellow Post-it note, stuck it on the top page of his notebook, then checked his watch again. Kids' Korner levied oppressive fines that increased every five minutes that a pickup parent arrived after 6 P.M. Simon Bostwick would have to wait.

23

Vincent Underhill's study was silent, but for how long Brenna wasn't sure. When he'd finished telling the story of his grandson's death, Underhill had closed his eyes and sat perfectly still, so still that Brenna wondered if he'd fallen asleep. The air in the room shifted, subtle affirmation that the giant house's air conditioner had kicked on. She glanced at the Atmos clock on the mantel. Later than she thought.

As soon as she stood up, Underhill opened his eyes.

"I should go," she said.

"It's late. I know you've got kids of your own to worry about."

She nodded. "Evenings can be pretty hectic, and I've still got some work at the office."

"Of course."

In the weight of the moment, Brenna resisted the impulse to apologize. She was doing her job, doing it well, checking the seams of the family's story, exploring all the possibilities that she knew Dagnolo and the investigators intended to explore, possibilities Myron Levin apparently had explored already. The Underhills would commend her thoroughness if things ever got weird, if the D.A. did file charges and tried to prove in court that Floss was shoved off that deck.

"One more thing, governor," she said. "I'd like to go back to something Ford said that first day we talked about what happened to your wife."

Brenna tried to gauge Underhill's reaction by the flutter of his eyelids.

"Mr. Chembergo described the sound he heard that day as a thumping. Now, if you walk across the floor of that gazebo out back, even in hard-soled shoes, it's pretty quiet. A few creaks, maybe, but nothing like thumping. But there's apparently an empty storage room underneath the floor, and if you stomp your feet on the gazebo floor, you get this thumping sound, like a bass drum. The sound really travels."

"Where are you going with this, Ms. Kennedy?"

"If the investigators are as sharp as I think they are, they're going to see Mr. Chembergo's statement about the thumping as credible. The sound would be consistent with a scuffle, and it's not the sort of detail a witness would dream up. He said he was up near the greenhouses when he heard it, right?"

Underhill shrugged. "I don't recall."

Brenna pressed on. "That's what he told the investigators, and we have no reason to doubt him. Combined with a broken railing where Mrs. Underhill apparently fell, and what Mr. Chembergo apparently said about seeing somebody leaving the area—"

"No reason to doubt him?" Underhill said, standing suddenly. His face remained calm. "You don't find reasonable doubt in the statement of a drunk Mexican who's a football field away? Who lied about his standing with the INS? Who was in this country illegally?"

Brenna stood her ground. To back down would seem defensive. "We have nothing to suggest he was drunk."

"Mr. Staggers says he caught him drinking down by the stables at least twice in the past few months. Lottie has complained, too. Just say the word. I'll get you all the statements you want about that."

"He was reprimanded?"

"By Mr. Staggers, yes."

"In writing?"

Underhill smiled, but his gestures were getting sharper. He was tired of being pushed. "We're talking about a gardener, Ms. Kennedy. How many people do you know who keep personnel records on their gardener?"

"It's a question the district attorn—"

"The district attorney, Ms. Kennedy, can kiss my ass." Underhill smiled again. He poured himself another brandy, just a splash, and drank it in one swallow. "If he's got nothing better to do than chase down phantoms who throw old ladies into ravines for no apparent reason, based solely on the word of an unprosecuted felon, then maybe we need a new district attorney. A few well-placed dollars, an effective TV campaign, and practically anyone could crush Dagnolo like a bug in the next election."

"That's two years away," she said. "If something's going to happen with this, it'll happen long before that."

Underhill set the bulb of glass back down on the liquor cart and turned his back to her. "Fact is, Ms. Kennedy, they've got no witness. Am I correct?"

"The sheriff has his statement. Myron Levin has God-knows-what on videotape."

Underhill turned, unrattled, apparently studying his fingernails. "Myron Levin? How far do you really think we're going to let that little loose cannon roll, Ms. Kennedy? Do you know how many seats I control on the board of CapCom Broadcasting?"

The corporate parent of Channel 2. "I admire your confidence," she said.

"Confidence has nothing to do with it. So enough. End of story. Let J. D. Dagnolo play his little games. Let him and Myron Levin ask their questions. It'll all come to nothing, and both you and I know that. *They* know that.

They're desperate little men playing above their ability in a game they don't understand.''

There was no mistaking Underhill's next gesture. He walked to the study door, his footsteps silent on the thick Persian rug. "I know you're anxious to get home," he said. "May I walk you to your car?"

They crossed the foyer without another word. Brenna was a jumble of emotions. The empathy she had felt for Underhill as he retold the story of his grandson's death was now tempered by a gut feeling about Underhill's arrogance. Dagnolo had an obligation to investigate Floss's fall. Political motives aside, he would have been remiss in not doing so. It wasn't a game, and Underhill's tone went way beyond confidence. It was contemptuous.

Brenna unlocked the Legend's door and set her briefcase on the front passenger seat. Underhill stood beside the car door, his face showing no sign of tension as he watched her bend over. When she stood up again, the door between them, their faces were less than two feet apart.

"If you're not taking this seriously," she said, "why do you need me?"

Underhill put his hand on the top of the car door, nearly touching hers. "Because besides being the best criminal-defense attorney in town, Ms. Kennedy, we felt that you could understand and appreciate the added dimension that politics brings to any situation. We're taking no chances this close to Ford's election. Once that's over, we'll probably never hear another word about it. I promise it'll come to nothing." He swept his hand sideways, lightly brushing hers, a horizontal chop that seemed unnecessarily forceful. "Nothing."

The front door opened behind them, and they both turned at the same time. Alton Staggers strode purposefully across the flagstone porch, between the potted geraniums and across the carport. With his hands clasped behind his back, his gait took on the loping quality of an uncoordinated scientist preoccupied by a sudden discovery. He stopped maybe ten feet away, looked straight at Underhill, and held out a cordless phone.

Underhill looked at Brenna, then at Staggers. "I'll be a minute," he said.

"It's Bragg," Staggers said.

The two men stared at one another, their faces blank. But the name was clearly freighted with importance.

"I've already talked to him," Staggers said, "but you may want to be in on this."

Underhill reached across the top of the car door. Brenna shook his offered hand.

"If you'll excuse me, Ms. Kennedy," he said.

"Of course."

"We'll talk soon." Underhill winked and turned toward the house.

As she backed the Legend into the center of the carport and shifted out of reverse, Brenna saw Vincent Underhill at the window of his study with a cordless phone to his ear, listening. Behind him, Alton Staggers was pacing like an anxious shadow.

24

The building Christensen was about to enter looked incredibly out of place. The city had intensively redeveloped Grant Street during the past two decades, starting with the artfully rusted U.S. Steel building at the north end, adding high-gloss modern towers here and there along the way, then, oddly, returning the actual street surface to the same red brick it was at the turn of the century. Opinions varied as to the overall effect. The new Grant Street was either an eclectic masterwork of urban design or a discordant eyesore of graceless development. Smack dab in the middle, the turreted Allegheny County courthouse crouched like a medieval castle.

Christensen checked Brenna's scribbled directions. She'd come home late, made a cryptic midnight call from the downstairs office, come to bed brooding, then left again before the kids woke up for school. She hadn't even asked him why he was coming Downtown as she told him the best place to park and how to navigate the courthouse entrance. Truth was, he wasn't entirely sure why he was here either, beyond a vague sense that this whole thing was more complicated than he or Brenna had ever imagined. He wanted to talk to Carrie Haygood.

He pushed through the revolving brass door, expecting to emerge into a grand entry so typical of Pittsburgh's ancient public buildings. Instead, he stepped into what looked like a catacomb. He'd seen root cellars with more light and less dust. He stepped aside and waited for his eyes to adjust from the morning sun outside. In the darkness, on the leg of an arched pillar, the dim face of a lighted building directory emerged.

He scanned the listed offices—sheriff, judges, commissioners, clerk of courts. The Child Death Review Team wasn't listed, but since it was technically part of the district attorney's office, he started up the marble steps to the third floor, emerging first into a larger and lighter lobby flanked by tile murals titled *Industry* and *Peace,* past a large window overlooking the building's red-brick interior courtyard, then through another arched doorway and up the building's central stairs. A hand-painted wood shingle—"Office of the District Attorney, J. D. Dagnolo"—hung outside a heavy wooden door. Through the door glass, on the facing wall, hung two black-and-white portraits: John F. Kennedy and Harry S. Truman. The receptionist to Christensen's right motioned him in.

"Carrie Haygood's office?" he said, pushing halfway through the door.

"Fifth floor." She checked a sheet of paper taped to her desk. "514."

The corridors outside the third-floor courtrooms were populated with bored and desperate-looking people, silk-suited lawyers, and uniformed bailiffs. Christensen stepped around a man sitting on the floor and took a narrow set of steps two at a time to the fifth floor. Room 514 was near the men's room, its door closed. Christensen twisted the knob and stepped in, startled to find himself not in a reception area, but in a cramped, overstuffed office. Once inside, he was less than five feet away from a sturdy, unflustered black woman behind the desk who was glaring at him over the rims of her black-framed Ben Franklin glasses.

"I should have knocked," he said. "I didn't realize . . . Sorry."

The woman seemed frozen in place among stacks of boxes and piles of documents, a file folder open in her left hand, an elegant ink pen clamped in her right and suspended above a scribble-filled yellow legal pad. The tailored jacket of her gray suit hung over the back of her chair. Her blouse looked silk, and her elegant strand of pearls seemed especially out of place in this setting. Her eyes, nose, and mouth were closely gathered in a way that would have made her face equally interesting upside down. Her hair was cropped short, making her African-primitive earrings seem too big. She did not smile or blink. This was not someone whose time Christensen wanted to waste.

"Yes," she said finally.

Christensen extended his hand. It seemed too intimate a gesture in a space this small. "My name is Jim Christensen," he said as the woman set down her pen. Her grip was wary. "You must be Carrie Haygood."

She nodded, then checked her leather-bound personal organizer. "Did you have an appointment?" Her diction was precise, its earthy richness tinged with a trace of formidable Ivy League snobbery.

"Sorry, no," he said. "I won't take but just a minute of your time now, or I can come back when it's more convenient."

The woman sighed, folding her arms across her substantial bosom. She nodded to a metal chair to his left. Its seat was stacked with thick manila file folders. "Set those off if you want to sit."

Christensen stood for an awkward moment, searching the tiny office for somewhere to move the stack. From the dated labels and bright Post-it notes affixed to some of the boxes, he was sure there was a system at work in the jumble of cartons, cabinets, and loose files, just as he was sure that the woman across the desk was the only person who could possibly understand it.

"The floor's fine," she offered.

He moved the folders and took the chair. "Looks like you've taken on a huge job here."

"What can I do for you, Mr. Christensen?"

So much for chitchat. "I need some forensic advice, and someone at the morgue suggested I talk to you," he said, which wasn't entirely true.

Her smile was patient, but purposeful. "The morgue couldn't offer forensic advice?"

"It's about a child's death, part of some research I'm doing."

She looked suspicious.

"I'm a psychologist. I study memory," he said, realizing as he spoke that it explained nothing. "It's a long story. I won't bore you with it. If I could just get you to help me interpret a death certificate, I'll be out of your way. But I would beg your discretion on this, as far as my interest, I mean."

"Recent case?" she said.

"Three years old."

"Do you have the file with you?"

"Copies." Christensen pulled his notebook from his briefcase. Tucked between the pages were the photocopied documents given him by the morgue clerk the day before. He gestured around the room. "You've apparently got a copy here as well, they said."

"Name?"

"Chip Underhill. It's Vincent the third on the records."

She took the documents he handed across the desk, poker-faced, saying nothing. "It's entirely possible we requested it, but that doesn't mean anything. We're just working our way forward."

"From ten years ago, right?"

She nodded, adjusting her glasses to the end of her nose. The woman radiated a strength Christensen couldn't quite define, the look of someone on a mission. She was also absorbing everything he said, but giving nothing in return.

"This conversation will stay between us?" he said.

"These are public documents," she said without looking up.

"But as far as me bringing them to your attention—"

Carrie Haygood offered a slight smile, which could have been more reassuring. "I'll let you know if you say something important."

The death certificate was on top. Her smile evaporated, either from focusing her attention on the task, or in response to something she'd read. He wished he could be sure. She flipped quickly through the next document, the toxicology report, and scanned what he assumed was the coroner's investigative report. Her face betrayed nothing but intensity as she studied the information before her.

She laid the manila folder down on her desk on top of the file she had been reading when he'd barged in, folded back the cover page of the final document, the autopsy protocol, and started reading at the beginning. When she finished, she closed the folder, stood up, and walked her fingers along a row of hanging folders sitting sideways on the opposite side of her desk. Even from his angle, Christensen could read the file tabs. They were arranged by year, going back ten years. Her fingers stopped at the one she wanted—the one labeled with the year of Chip Underhill's death written on the tab in black Magic Marker. She pulled a thin manila folder from inside. It was labeled "UNDERHILL, Vincent III."

Christensen searched her inscrutable face for clues, finding no information about what had just happened. He looked at the file. Despite the apparent chaos of her organizational system, there was no mistaking its prominent spot on her desk. But why?

"So?" he said.

She studied him. "What's your interest in this case, Mr.—"

"Christensen."

The woman was like a sponge, sopping up his every gesture, expression, and proffered piece of information without a leak. Give a little to get a little, he thought.

"I'm researching the function of memory in Alzheimer's patients, out at the Harmony Brain Research Center. One of the study subjects is this boy's grandmother, and I'm just trying to construct a reliable account of certain events in her past, particularly events that may have been traumatic for her, so I can see how her mind interprets those memories."

"That's it?"

"That's it," he said.

Haygood knitted her fingers together and set her hands on her desk. "Why this woman in particular?"

"I'm following an art therapy group that she's in," he said, resisting the urge to explain more. He'd said all he was going to say unless Haygood gave a little, too.

Haygood waited. He waited. Haygood blinked first. "So she remembers something about how this child died, and you're just trying to corroborate it?"

"Is this an interrogation?" Christensen hoped his smile would temper his agitation.

"Just curious. Your work sounds interesting."

"Thank you."

Haygood unraveled her fingers and reached across her desk. She slid the hanging file rack around until its front face was angled toward him, then waited as he read the front label. "Team Review," it said. The gesture seemed purposeful, but Christensen wasn't sure what it meant.

"Your team is already looking at this boy's file?" he said finally.

"Mr. Christensen, I'm not at liberty to discuss any particular case, especially one that's officially under review." Her tone had shifted, suggesting something not apparent in her words. "But I can answer any general questions you may have about what we do here."

He tried again. "What does it mean if you refer a case for team review?"

She winked. The gesture was as unexpected and welcome as a first kiss.

"The team has fifteen members," she said. "Experts from various fields—a detective, a prosecutor, two sheriff's deputies, a psychiatrist, a social worker, a pediatrician, a violence-prevention expert, and seven others from various agencies."

"And you," he said.

"And me. It's my job right now to do preliminary screening. At least initially, I'm reviewing details of all the child deaths in Allegheny County for the past ten years. In cases where questions arise, I recommend a full team review."

"In cases where questions arise," he repeated.

"That's correct."

They both looked at the hanging files.

"And these are the cases from the past ten years you feel should be reviewed?" he said.

"I've only completed my review of seven of those ten years." She nodded toward the file from which she'd pulled the Underhill folder. "But you're essentially correct."

"And these are cases you're reviewing because you have questions about them?"

"Correct."

The cat-and-mouse game was annoying, but at least Christensen felt like he was making progress. "What sort of things do you consider when you refer a case? I mean, you must have specific things you're looking for."

Carrie Haygood leaned forward, resting her elbows on the desk and folding her thick hands beneath her chin. Her face was serious now. The stakes of the game seemed to rise. "There are indicators we look for, Mr. Christensen, red flags that are typical in cases of this sort. *Inconsistencies*." She paused to let the word's weight settle.

"Between?"

"Cause of death. Physical evidence. Witness statements. Forensic science has come a long way in the last few years, Mr. Christensen. A physical injury tells a story, but not every overworked detective is able to hear it or understand it.''

"You look for red flags," he said.

"Correct."

"And you saw one in this file?"

She shook her head, slowly and deliberately. "I'm not at liberty to discuss any particular case, Mr. Christensen, as I said."

He tried again. "Are there certain causes of death that are suspicious?"

"Not on their face, no," she said. "But some findings are misinterpreted more often than others."

"And when you see one of those, you pay particular attention?"

"Correct."

Christensen shifted forward in his chair. Their faces were maybe three feet from one another, their eyes locked. "I assume you then examine the other information in the file for those inconsistencies you're talking about."

"Yes."

"And when you come across questions you can't answer, you refer that case to the Child Death Review Team for further review."

Haygood nodded toward the hanging files, her eyes never leaving his. "We have twenty-eight so far."

Christensen sat back, the implication settling on his chest with the weight of an X-ray apron. He felt as if he'd kicked over a rock, exposing something wretched and squirming and very dangerous. He looked around the room at the paperwork of tragedy. Only twenty-eight cases stood apart, and Chip Underhill's was one of them.

A question popped into his mind, and he asked it as soon as it did. "What's a subdural hematoma?"

The air around Carrie Haygood seemed to crackle with tension, an almost electrical charge. "It's a brain injury," she said, "but one with very predictable causes."

They had reached a precipice now, and there was no turning back.

"Such as?" Christensen said.

"It's most common in cases where there's a high-velocity impact."

"Like a car crash?"

"Correct."

"Or a horse kick?"

Haygood shrugged. "In my experience, Mr. Christensen—and I'm speaking generally here—only two things cause a subdural hematoma in children. A high-velocity impact, or an assault."

"By an adult?"

Haygood nodded. "We call it shaken baby syndrome. Snaps their little heads back and forth. It explains maybe ten percent of the two thousand child-abuse deaths every year in this country. But subdural hematoma cases are tricky, because there usually aren't classic signs of abuse. No history. No criminal record in the adult. What you have are people, typically boyfriends or fathers, who just lose control for a minute or two. Which is why we try to look at the SH cases more closely than some others."

She had said nothing, really, but the inference hung between them.

"But a horse's kick would be consistent with that, right?" he said.

"Maybe." She pushed his file of photocopies back across the desk. It was still open to the last page of Simon Bostwick's autopsy protocol. Her finger lingered on a paragraph beneath the section describing Chip Underhill's head. "Assuming the physical evidence was consistent with the witness accounts."

Christensen read the paragraph again. No contusions. No fractures. No obvious bleeding except in the boy's brain and retinas. Nothing whatsoever that suggested the impact of a horse's hoof. He looked up. Haygood still hadn't shifted her eyes from his.

"Of course, we'd never proceed on a case without digging out the full file from the morgue,'' she said.

''The full file?''

''These files I've got don't include the autopsy photos, X-rays, that sort of thing,'' she said.

He nodded. Carrie Haygood sat back, her chair groaning as her weight shifted. Neither of them spoke for a long moment.

''Now,'' she said finally, ''if you don't have any other questions, Mr. Christensen, I've got a lot of work here that needs my attention.''

25

The fifth-floor corridor was empty. Christensen pulled the door to room 514 shut and looked up and down the hall, trying to make sense of an illogical feeling he had. He suddenly knew the uneasy feeling of a small deer who blunders into a wide-open meadow during hunting season. The silence was profoundly disturbing.

He passed the elevator and started down the stairs, reviewing his conversation with Carrie Haygood. She'd told him nothing, and everything. At the very least, she'd implied that there was reason to suspect the official version of the death of Chip Underhill, the only child of the man likely to be the state's next governor. She'd used the word "assault," if only in general terms. He couldn't imagine a more explosive allegation in the heat of a high-profile political campaign.

Then again, who was Carrie Haygood? Boil it all down, filter out her Ivy League credentials and her projected air of sanctity and mission, and in the end she was just an investigator who worked for J. D. Dagnolo, one of Underhill's most rabid political opponents. She'd already decided something was amiss with the previous investiga-

tion. Then she'd sketched a vague theory full of
implication to a total stranger who had wandered unin-
vited to her office just days before the primary-election
polls opened. Why?

He needed to talk to Brenna. She knew better than most
how to navigate the Machiavellian swamp that was Grant
Street. He knew only that he was in over his head, clutching for the hand of someone who understood this world
of expedient loyalties and calculated cruelty and the
strange science of judiciously leaked information. As he
swept past the district attorney's offices on the third floor,
Christensen wondered if Haygood was already on the
phone to her boss.

A flash of familiar color, a brilliant copper, caught his
eye as he passed the large window overlooking the brick
courtyard. A second look confirmed his hunch. Two floors
below, Brenna was standing at the center of a small knot
of men gathered near the blue fountain at the courtyard's
center. Two of the men were holding television cameras.
Klieg lights blazed.

He hurried down the remaining stairs and looked for a
way into the building's central plaza. When he found one,
he slowed his pace to a saunter to stay inconspicuous as
he approached the group. He edged as close as he could
and sat down on a low wall, hoping to snag Brenna as
soon as she was done. If she shared any of his nagging
doubts about the Underhills, she showed no hint of it as
she answered the reporters' questions calmly and patiently.

"—don't know where that information is coming from,
Mr. Levin, but we're certainly going to wait until the investigation is complete before responding to anything like
that."

"So, are you saying you were not aware of this supposed eyewitness, or that you're not concerned about his
statements about the struggle?"

"Neither, Myron, and I think you're aware of that. I'm
saying we know of at least one conflicting account of Mrs.

Underhill's fall, and that we hope further investigation will get to the bottom of it. But right now, we don't find that account cause for alarm.''

"No cause for alarm? No cause for *alarm*?" Astonished reactions were a Myron Levin trademark. "You don't find the possibility that the leading gubernatorial candidate's mother might have been shoved off a cliff ten days before the election any cause for alarm?''

Another reporter, a young black woman, interrupted. "Give it a rest, Myron. Brenna, how is Mrs. Underhill *feeling*?''

"She's back home and doing fine. Because of her age, it may take her broken bones longer than usual to heal, but her doctors don't anticipate any long-term physical problems. Thank you for asking, Tawny. Is that it, everybody?''

Myron Levin wouldn't be denied. "The investigator's report says the witness was part of the Underhills' household staff, a Hispanic male," he said. "It says his wife worked for the family, too. True?''

"I've read the same report, Mr. Levin," Brenna said. "Ask the sheriff or the D.A. if it's true. It's their report. If you'll excuse me, then—''

"Have you spoken to the witness, Ms. Kennedy?''

"I won't comment on that.''

Christensen caught Brenna's eye as she pushed her way out of the tight circle. She started to smile, apparently relieved to see a friendly face and be out of the spotlight, but Levin followed her. He dropped his microphone to his waist as they walked away from the group. "Brenna," he said in a stage whisper.

Brenna turned around, clearly annoyed. They were off-camera now, and Brenna had had enough. Christensen was glad he wasn't Myron Levin at that moment.

"You may want to touch base with Dr. Walsh's office," Levin said. "Something's come up, if you know what I mean.''

Brenna froze, her shoulders going slack. Levin stood

with his microphone dangling at his side, looking very much like a slugger who'd just connected. Brenna wheeled and walked back toward him. "Cut the bullshit, Myron. What's that mean—something's come up?"

Levin just smiled. "Just a hunch. Call."

Brenna shifted her briefcase from one hand to the other, never taking her eyes off the TV reporter's. Then, without another word, she turned and walked away. She was coming straight toward him now, but from her stride Christensen could tell she had no intention of stopping. In her wake, the faintest trace of Eternity.

"Whoa, what's with her?" Liisa cocked her head toward Brenna's closed office door. "She didn't even pick up her messages."

"I'll take them in to her," Christensen said.

The secretary shook her head, handing him a stack of pink message slips. "Enter at your own risk."

He knocked lightly and pushed through the door. Brenna was at her desk, the telephone already to her ear, dramatically framed in an angled bank of wide windows. Every time he came to her office, Christensen was impressed by its stunning panorama view that swept from the South Side past PPG's crystal tower, Point State Park, and across to Three Rivers Stadium. She motioned him in, saying "Tommy Hasch, please" into the phone.

"Problems?" he said.

Brenna covered the phone's mouthpiece. "Not sure. Myron's still up to something. I just need to get ahead of the curve." Christensen started to respond, but she held up her free hand. "I'll hold. Thanks."

He was a pretty good judge of her moods, but this one was confounding—not exactly worried, but uneasy. Brenna was the consummate Grant Street insider, and the thought that Myron Levin or any news reporter knew something she didn't probably bugged her more than she'd ever admit.

"Who's Tommy Hasch?" he asked.

"Deputy coroner." She winked. "My mole over there. Find what you needed at the courthouse this morning?"

He thought of Carrie Haygood. "We need to talk about that. Bren, I think we're both behind the curve on this thing—"

"We need to talk about something else, too," she interrupted. "How do you feel about Harrisburg?"

"Nothing a neutron bomb wouldn't fix."

Brenna flinched. Her eyes narrowed. She was pissed, and he didn't care. Right now, it was a welcome distraction.

"Never mind," she said.

"Bren, this woman on the Child Death Review Team—"

"Tommy?" She motioned for silence. "Since when are you actually in the office?"

Her voice was suddenly playful, almost sultry, a carnal whisper in the ear of any man who ever imagined himself with her. He'd heard her use it on cops and prosecutors with devastating effect, and just as effectively in bed. Christensen knew she was just wheedling for information, knew why, but he felt himself suddenly jealous of a deputy coroner named Tommy Hasch.

"Walsh can't replace everybody," she said. "Clerical I can see, but not you guys. Preech hired good people, pros, when he was in office. Walsh wouldn't play patronage with professional staff. He needs you guys to make him look good."

Brenna listened patiently as the deputy coroner apparently continued his litany of ongoing staff changes at the morgue under new coroner Cyrus Walsh. Finally: "If there's anything I can do, write a letter or anything for you, let me know. Not that it would do any good. Walsh seems to have his own agenda, and I don't know him nearly as well as I knew Preech. But you let me know if there's anything—"

She listened again as Tommy Hasch continued, rolling her eyes toward the ceiling in mock exasperation. "Well, he's—'' she tried. Then, oozing sympathy, ''I know. So you let me know if there's anything I can do. You've done me a ton of favors over the years. Me? Nothing much. A little birdie just told me to call. What's new?''

Christensen walked over to the bank of windows, to the side facing the Monongahela River. He pressed his face against the glass, trying to see the morgue in the dark canyon between the courthouse and the Grant Building, but it was lost somewhere in the shadows.

''I read about that, up in the Hill. You handled that one?'' Brenna shook her head. ''Oh, yuck. Where do kids get guns that big?'' She shifted in her seat, getting down to business. ''Anything come up on any of my cases?''

Christensen tried to read her eyes. They were focused now on a blank legal pad on her desk. She plucked the pen from its holder, ready to take notes.

''Nothing?'' Brenna set the pen down. Her shoulders relaxed. ''You're sure?'' The soft leather of her executive chair exhaled, as did Brenna, as she leaned back and ran a hand through her hair. ''Maybe I need a new little birdie.''

When she leaned forward again, though, she picked up her pen and jotted some notes. ''That was yesterday morning? I didn't hear anything about it.''

Christensen crossed back to the chair in front of her desk and sat down, glancing at his watch. Almost lunchtime, but he wasn't hungry. When he looked up, he was startled by the change in Brenna's expression.

''No IDs, though? Any idea how soon you'll have them?'' She was scribbling furiously now. ''Where'd they come up?''

Christensen leaned forward, trying to read her handwriting upside down. McKees Rocks. Neville Island. Other phrases leapt off the page: Hispanic male. Hispanic female. Execution-style. Powder burns. Wadding in tissue. Bruised wrists. His mind raced to a horrifying conclusion.

Brenna noticed him eavesdropping, waved him off, and pulled the pad away.

"You know those currents around the Point, Tommy. Even if they were dumped together, even weighted, they wouldn't stay down long. Any idea where they went in?" Brenna turned her chair to her left, focusing briefly on the brown sliver of Allegheny River that divided Downtown from the North Side. "You can tell all that from the sediment in his pockets?"

Brenna set the pen down and turned the pad over on her desk. "Nothing, probably. I don't know," she said. Her voice shifted again, back to the carnal whisper. "Would you be a sweetheart, though, and let me know when you've got IDs. I won't know if it means anything or not until you've got those."

She reached forward, her finger poised above the phone's disconnect button. "Tommy? It's probably nothing, like I said, but this stays between us, right? Thanks."

Brenna mustered a provocative good-bye and brought her finger down, then looked across the desk. He waited, breathless. The intercom beeped immediately, and Liisa announced a visitor. Brenna studied him a long time, then stood up. "It's probably nothing," she repeated, "but maybe we should talk later."

Annie wanted Flintstones; Taylor wanted Bugs Bunny.
"Come on, guys," Christensen urged. "Jenny'll be here
in five minutes and we need to decide so I can get it on
the stove."

The two children glared at one another.

"Look, it's all just macaroni and cheese," he said.
"They're both orange. Orange food is good for your eyes
or something, isn't it?"

Annie stood with her legs planted slightly apart, arms
folded across her chest. "Flintstones taste better."

"Bugs," Taylor countered.

"Flintstones."

Christensen opened the pantry, put both boxes back on
the shelf and closed the cupboard door with more force
than was necessary. "We'll have something else then,"
he said, his tone calculated to leave no room for discussion. "Go wash your hands. I'll call you when it's
ready."

Annie could barely contain her rage. She took a step
toward the younger and smaller boy, clenching and unclenching her tiny fists. Taylor seemed to shrink as she
approached. "You're dead," Annie said.

Taylor took one step backward. "You're—" He looked to Christensen, as if for help. "You're mean."

"Work it out, you two. Use your words."

Fog rolled out of the freezer as Christensen opened the door. He waited for it to clear, then dug for a package of frozen hot dogs. He put the icy block of Hebrew Nationals on the counter, then wedged a knife point into one of the pink crevasses, separating two hot dogs from the rest. He recognized Taylor's whimper behind him as he put the greasy packet back in the freezer. When he turned, the boy was clutching his stomach, mouth open in pain and outrage, a strangled cry stuck somewhere just south of his tongue. Annie was five feet away.

"Annie? What happened?"

"Nothing." She held both palms toward the ceiling, exasperated by the need to explain.

Christensen put his arm around Taylor, who was struggling to stifle his cry, and confronted his daughter. "Hands are for helping, Annie, not for hurting."

"I *was* helping."

"Really?"

"He just doesn't understand that Flintstones macaroni is better. I was helping him."

Christensen pointed to the stairs. "In your room. You know better than that."

She sauntered off to do her penance. Christensen stooped to Taylor's level. "You okay?"

Taylor sniffed and nodded, his clutching hands marking the spot of some unspoken offense to his belly. "You didn't hit back," Christensen said. "I'm proud of you."

The boy straightened.

"If Annie or anybody tries to hurt you like that, you just walk away and tell me or your mom or your teachers. Okay?"

Taylor nodded again. "Where is my mom?"

"I'm meeting her at a restaurant for dinner," he said. "We just needed a little time to talk."

Boy, did they. For the parents of young kids, the

greatest stressor is not the day-to-day worry of a child falling sick, or even the hectic dinner-bath-homework-bed routine of school nights. It's the inability to complete a task, thought, or conversation without interruption. Since his conversation with Haygood, Christensen had felt as if they were caught in the powerful undertow of a force he didn't understand, a force he worried could drag them both under. Things were happening too fast, and they needed to catch a breath. "Wash your hands now," Christensen said. "Dinner'll be five minutes."

He washed and sliced raw carrots and apples, arranging them on the kids' plates as the microwave defrosted the hot dogs. When it beeped, he punctured the rubbery skins with a fork and put them back in to cook on high for two minutes. He poured two glasses of milk, then hurried to answer the doorbell.

Jenny was the only sitter they knew who was willing to drive to their new neighborhood. The first time they'd used her, Annie talked about little else for days. Tonight, Jenny wore an electric-pink bikini top and old jeans hacked off just below her crotch. Christensen focused on her forehead as he greeted her, close enough to her eyes but safely away from the perfect expanse of sixteen-year-old flesh. "I know, I know," she said. "Bath at eight, bed at nine. What time will you be home?"

He breathed easier as she passed, noticing as she removed her backpack the tiny butterfly tattoo on her left shoulder. He reacted without thinking. "A tattoo?"

The girl turned suddenly and winked. "One of them."

Christensen looked at his watch. He was supposed to meet Brenna at Fiorello's in forty-five minutes. No time to make other arrangements.

"Jen!"

Annie stampeded down the stairs, preceded by her excited greeting. She practically leaped into the arms of the Manson girl she now worshipped.

"Annie! Brought you that CD!"

Taylor hurried from the kitchen and took Jenny by the

hand, Annie apparently forgiven. The threesome disappeared into the living room, headed for the stereo, as the microwave announced that dinner was ready.

"Did you eat, Jenny?" Christensen called.

"I'm fine, thanks."

He put ketchup on the table and broke the safety seal on a new squeeze bottle of mustard. After twisting off the nozzle cap, he sniffed the contents—an old habit. A few baby dills to create the illusion of a green vegetable, and there, another meal done. Tomorrow, he vowed, a real dinner.

"Food's on the table," he shouted, interrupting the frenzied dance party that had erupted in the living room. The woman's voice coming from the stereo speakers was angry and passionate and pitched somewhere between a trumpeting elephant and a chain saw, and she did not much like men, or so the lyrics suggested. Annie held up one hand, her thumb and index finger forming an O, then kept dancing.

Upstairs, Christensen faced his closet. Most of his clothes were finally out of boxes and moving cartons, but most still bore the inevitable wrinkles and dirt smudges of moving. Fiorello's was New York dressy, not at all his kind of place, but a place he knew Brenna worshipped for the dark anchovies in its Caesar salads and calamari she had already requested as a last meal before execution, should it ever come to that. He pulled out a black-and-white herringbone sports jacket and white shirt, some classic black pants, and what he called his lawyer loafers, their leather buffed and black. He pawed through his slim collection of ties for the one the guy at the store said went well with the rest of it.

He was knotting his tie in the dresser mirror when he noticed his notepad in the center of their bed, a bright yellow Post-it note stuck to the top page—Simon Bostwick's phone number. Any other day, the call would have been a priority. Today, it had completely slipped his mind. He checked his watch. Brenna wouldn't be there for another forty minutes, and Fiorello's, on top of Mount Washington, was maybe thirty minutes away. He closed the bedroom door to block out the music downstairs and picked up the portable phone.

The area code was the same as for all of western Pennsylvania, but the exchange was unfamiliar. When the number rang, it sounded distant and rural. The voice that answered sounded gruff and sleepy.

"Sorry to bother you," Christensen said. "I'm looking for a Simon Bostwick." He waited through a long pause.

"Who is?"

"I'm Jim Christensen with the University of Pittsburgh, Mr. Bostwick. I'm doing some research on a case involving an accidental death, and I ran across your name in some morgue records. I hope you don't mind me calling, and I won't take much of your time now. I was just hoping we could schedule a few minutes in the next day or so to talk. I had some questions about—"

"You said Christensen?"

"Right. Jim—"

"I know who you are."

Disoriented, Christensen ran through every conceivable way this total stranger might know him. He came up blank. "Really?" was all he could manage.

"I knew Grady Downing," Bostwick said. "Primenyl."

Of course. Christensen's most recent brush with fame had been three years earlier when Downing, a homicide detective, had suckered him into working on the decade-old Primenyl product-tampering case. He'd worked with the killer's son, plumbing the young man's mind for memories of the killings that Downing was sure the boy had repressed. Downing was right, more or less, and the killer made Downing pay the ultimate price for his intuition. When it was over, when Christensen had helped end the city's ten-year-old nightmare in a horrific and haunting flash of violence, the newspapers went looking for a hero. He was the only one left standing.

"You must have worked with Grady on some of his cases, I guess," he said.

Bostwick cleared his throat. "More than I care to count. What can I do you for?"

Something in the voice bothered Christensen, something thick and deliberate and affected. He thought of his father, how his voice thickened once the first few drinks of the evening kicked in. But he was glad he and Bostwick had found common ground in Downing. It was the first time he'd found a practical use for the unwanted minor celebrity that followed his role in Primenyl.

"This was a case you handled about three years ago, when you were doing coroner's investigations."

"I'm out of that now," Bostwick said.

"I know. But your name was on the investigation report on a case I'm interested in. You handled the autopsy."

"What kind of research? You're a memory expert or something, if memory serves."

This seemed to crack Bostwick up. Christensen laughed along until Bostwick regrouped. "I suppose," he said finally. "It's like saying an astronomer is an expert on extraterrestrial life. 'Expert' sounds so all-knowing, but there's more we don't know than we do know. Right now I'm trying to find out more about how Alzheimer's affects memory."

After a long pause, Bostwick said, "I'm not following you here. Alzheimer's isn't the sort of thing I could have looked for when I opened somebody up."

"No, no. You're right. This is a case where I'm trying to reconcile someone's memory of an accident with what actually happened, to see how traumatic memories like that evolve over time. And I had a couple of questions about it that I couldn't answer from the paperwork. You were the only person who could answer—"

"The coroner's people are giving out my number?" Bostwick's voice suddenly had a hostile edge Christensen hadn't noticed before, an unpredictable shift of mood, a drinker's conceit.

"They told me you were living in the mountains. I just called information."

"When I left that place, I was done with it. I don't even come back to testify unless I'm subpoenaed. I just don't like the idea of them passing out my number."

Christensen checked his watch again. They were clearly on difficult terrain, and he didn't have time to get bogged down in some old grudge between Bostwick and his former employer. He knew how a drinker's anger can gain unmanageable momentum.

"Like I said, the morgue didn't give me your number. I tracked it down on my own, because I have these questions that I don't think anybody can answer but someone who was—"

"What was the case?" Bostwick said.

"The name was Vincent Underhill the third. Happened in—"

"Doesn't ring a bell," Bostwick said.

Christensen waited. "You don't seem to want to help me here," he said finally.

"I'm perfectly happy to help you," Bostwick said, stretching the R sound like a piece of taffy. "Grady said you were a helluva guy, a standup guy. Let me tell you something: I trusted Grady Downing like nobody else in this world, sir. And you can take that as gospel."

"It didn't sound like you even thought about the name. It's a case I think you might rem—"

"Let me tell you something else," Bostwick said. "Eleven years I spent with the coroner's office. Anybody there'll tell you I was one of the best. Handled a helluva lot of cases in those eleven years, a lot of them kids like that—way too many kids for anybody's taste, let me tell you. But names? Nuh-uh. That's just another line on the form. We didn't deal much in names, except for the paperwork, if you see what I'm saying."

"But this name—"

"So you see what I'm saying here? Chances of me remembering a name, it's just a crapshoot. That one doesn't ring a bell, though. Vincent?"

"Vincent Underhill the third. They called him Chip."

"Nope. Real sorry."

Christensen wasn't giving up, but this was going nowhere fast. "Would it help if I faxed you the report you wrote? Maybe that would jog your memory."

"You're welcome to do that, and I'll be happy to look it over. Anything for an old friend of Grady's. But like I said, there were a lot of cases, and I'm out of it nearly three years now."

Christensen took down Bostwick's fax number and promised to send the autopsy report the following morning. "I'll check back with you in the afternoon," he said, ending the conversation.

The portable phone disconnected with an electronic beep. The music was off downstairs, replaced by the sound of Annie and Taylor arguing over who would squeeze the ketchup onto their plates. The digital alarm clock read 6:27. He had to get going if he was going to make Fiorello's by seven, but he sat motionless on the edge of their bed, trying to figure out what so bothered him about the conversation. Finally, without too much effort, he narrowed it down to a nagging question: If Bostwick didn't remember the case, why had he assumed Chip Underhill was a child?

27

Brenna's Legend was parked beside a gleaming Cadillac Eldorado two doors down from Fiorello's front door, in a space the restaurant's valet parkers reserved for favored regulars with status wheels. In the cramped Mount Washington neighborhood of narrow hill houses and unrivaled city views, Christensen's Explorer had been relegated to valet limbo, that nebulous place somewhere around a corner two blocks away where he'd watched his car disappear from sight. Five minutes late, he hurried past the hulking *Goodfellas* extra at the restaurant's door and into a dim, overpowering world of red banquettes and garlic.

The city skyline loomed just ahead, through a wall of floor-to-ceiling windows designed to showcase every possible inch of the Golden Triangle below—the confluence of the three rivers, the stadium on the North Side, Downtown, Point State Park. It was the same view that brought tourists in droves to the dozen other restaurants clinging to the edge of Mount Washington. Fiorello's, though, was strictly for locals of a particular social caste, that being, according to Brenna, the friends and family of numbers king Dominic Coniglio, for whom the restaurant provided a legitimate cover. Brenna's client roster had at various times included several of Coniglio's top lieutenants.

Christensen found her in the bar, her back to him, in animated conversation with a dwarfish man whose thick, black chest hair spilled over the tie knot and cinched collar of his white silk shirt. From TV news footage and newspaper photographs, Christensen recognized the tinted glasses and red rosebud on the lapel of his shiny suit jacket as the trademarks of Salvatore "One Nut" Gianni. Brenna had represented him two years earlier when his stewardship of Coniglio's East Liberty operations had been briefly interrupted by an ill-conceived sting operation. Christensen still marveled at how easily Brenna adapted to the diverse and dangerous worlds into which her professional life often thrust her.

Gianni stiffened as Christensen approached. Brenna turned and smiled, kissing him on the cheek.

"Jim, I'd like you to meet Sal," she said.

Christensen extended his right hand. Gianni removed his right hand from inside his suit jacket, where it apparently moved reflexively when a stranger approached, and offered a wary shake of his multiringed fingers.

Brenna winked, but with the eye Gianni couldn't see. "Sal here was just offering generous campaign support if I decide to go for the council spot. He said I was the only Irish lawyer he'd ever trusted."

Gianni shrugged. "We like Jews, lawyer-wise, but she done me a real favor. I return favors."

Brenna stood up. "I'm starving. Everything okay at home?"

"Fine. Sorry I'm a little late."

Brenna shook Gianni's hand. "Thanks for the drink, Sal. Stay out of trouble."

"You'll hear from me if I don't," he said.

Christensen followed her to a table with a view of forever. Her perfume trail mingled with the aroma rising from tables covered by plates of warm pasta and chilled romaine, an intoxicating combination. Waiters swarmed as soon as they sat down, plucking the Reserved card from the table's center, depositing a basket of warm focaccia, upending their wineglasses, pouring olive oil and balsamic vinegar into a wide saucer with ceremonial grace. The attention seemed ridiculously overdone, like the decor.

"You're pretty venerated around here," he said.

"They take care of their lawyers."

"A business expense, I suppose." He shook his head. "What?"

"I just don't get to see you in your element that often," he said. "You run with a pretty rough crowd sometimes."

"These guys?" Brenna waved him off. "I'll take them any day over the snakes on Grant Street."

Christensen used a piece of focaccia to sop up some vinegar and oil. A waiter brought wine, one of Brenna's favorite black-roostered Chiantis, and set to work on the cork. He poured a taste in Brenna's glass and waited, apparently thrilled by her smiling nod.

"Do you ever worry about it?"

Brenna cocked her head.

"Working with people like Gianni, I mean. You must know a lot of secrets."

"Defense lawyers always do." She turned an imaginary key, locking her lips. "We get paid to keep them."

The comment weighed heavier than Christensen expected. Brenna's eyes drifted to the windows, to the city below, but once they shifted they never seemed to focus. The wineglass rested against her lips, still awaiting her second taste. The crowd of waiters around their table had thinned, the last one depositing a single-page menu in front of each of them before leaving with a bow.

"Nothing from the morgue yet," she said. "No IDs."

"What if it is the Chembergos, Bren?"

She shook her head. "They're not the only Hispanics in Pittsburgh. They're not even still in the country, supposedly."

"Then why are you so worried?"

She finally looked at him. "I'm not worried. I'm curious."

"*I'm* worried," he said. "I need to finish the story I started to tell you."

In her office that morning, he'd wanted to tell her about Chip Underhill and Carrie Haygood and the possible causes of subdural hematoma. He had so much else he wanted to tell, about the Gray horse and Floss Underhill's strange paintings and Warren Doti and Simon Bostwick and the theory that was percolating up through that murky collection of facts. But Liisa had said someone was waiting and they'd agreed on Fiorello's as he left, leaving him to struggle with the burden for the rest of the day.

He leaned forward, trying to keep his voice low. "Bren, this whole thing got weird today. I think we're into something a lot deeper than we thought."

"Your meeting with Haygood?"

He nodded. "That's why I was so curious about her allegiances and Dagnolo and all that. But I didn't get a chance to tell you what we talked about, or about some of the other stuff that's come up about Floss."

"Like I said, Haygood's a cipher to me." Brenna set her wineglass back on the table. "That review team is so new, and it operates outside the normal channels. There's no buzz about it, or her. At all."

Christensen leaned even closer. "I showed her the morgue paperwork on Chip Underhill. She's already looking into it."

Brenna smiled. "That's her job."

"No, Bren, no. The Underhills' story about the horse didn't wash. She all but said that's not how the kid died."

Brenna stared until a passing waiter was out of earshot. "How, then?"

"The $64,000 question. But there's apparently nothing in the coroner's report that supports the story about him getting kicked by a horse. Remember what your pal Levin said about the 'little skeleton' in the Underhill family closet? I'd bet Haygood leaked something to him. And

I'm wondering if what he said about Floss might be right, the thing about somebody trying to keep her quiet.''

Brenna gave him an exasperated look. ''Aren't you the conspiracy theorist? Well, how about this one: Maybe Haygood's doing all this because she works for Dagnolo.''

Christensen stared. Her dismissal was defensive, not just indifferent. ''There's a lot more I haven't told you about, Bren, but it's all starting to make a strange sort of sense. I don't think it's that simple; it's not just politics.''

''Jim, Dagnolo's watching Ford Underhill waltz into the job he wanted, the one the state Democratic committee told him was his until Underhill decided to run. He's pissed off.''

''I don't—''

''So I'm not surprised he'd sic Haygood—''

''Bren, would you *listen* to me?'' At adjoining tables, heads turned. Brenna froze, her wineglass suspended half-way between the table and her lips.

''I'm sorry,'' she said.

''Maybe the world does work the way you think it does, maybe it's a big power game where everybody's just trying to get an edge. I hope it is.'' Why was he so angry? He ratcheted his voice down to a stage whisper. ''But I don't think we can ignore what's happening here. I don't think we can overlook our questions about the Underhills anymore. It's getting too—'' He searched for the right word. ''—plausible. When I put all the pieces together, I wonder if maybe what happened to this kid is at the heart of it.''

''Of what?'' she said.

''Of everything.''

A waiter arrived to take their order, standing impassively while they stared across the table at one another. Brenna handed him her menu. ''You know what I want, Antonio.'' Christensen ordered his favorite pasta.

''You're not making sense,'' Brenna said after they were alone again.

He took a deep, calming breath, then a sip of Chianti. "Just hear me out."

Brenna listened. She sat back while he described the events of the past few days, events that were the building blocks of a disturbing possibility. Now that he said it aloud, the whole thing sounded nearly as paranoid as it did plausible. When he was done, she waited through the waiter's elaborate Caesar salad preparations before reacting.

"All right," she said, refilling her wineglass. "If some specific memories are leaking from Floss's brain, as you say, how can you be sure they're accurate?"

"I can't, Bren. The thing about Alzheimer's is it doesn't usually distort memories so much as it leaves them without context. That's why the images in her paintings are so, so—"

"Bizarre."

"But they're not, really. They seem disjointed, I know, but the common thread is the time frame. The horse, Gray, is the key. He was involved in the boy's death, then he was shipped off to this private ranch out in Westmoreland County about the same time as Warren Doti. She loses a grandson, a favorite horse, and a man I think was her lover all at the same time. When you understand how all that unfolded, her fixation on those images makes perfect sense."

"It does?"

"Because she may remember it all. It just doesn't make sense to her. Maybe because of her disease. Maybe because she was told a version of events that doesn't add up for some reason. Who knows? But think about it, Bren. What if Floss knew how that child really died and kept it quiet to protect somebody. Hell, say she did it or helped cover it up. If the family all of a sudden couldn't control her anymore, don't you think that would make her a fairly dangerous person to have around?"

Brenna nibbled at a forkful of chilled romaine, then put

it down unfinished. "That's a little melodramatic, don't you think?"

He shook his head, leaning closer, speaking again in a whisper. "Until you think about the stakes, Bren. We're not just talking about a statewide election here. We're talking about a political and social legacy that goes back four generations. We're talking about national aspirations. We're talking about a family with everything, but its whole reputation is based on its image as a positive force in this community. If there *is* a dirty little family secret, something as unforgivable as I think it is, something everybody thought was dead and buried, can't you see how the need to control that secret suddenly could be the most important thing in the world?"

Brenna watched Christensen pick a meaty black anchovy out of his salad, then speared it with her fork. "But kill her? I just don't buy it."

"Even with so much at stake?"

"It's too cold-blooded, Jim. They could have shut her off, kept her from contact with the outside world. She could have lived twenty more years in that Fox Chapel house and nobody would have ever known if she was alive or dead. Look at Ronald Reagan. The guy just vanished the day he was diagnosed."

"Which is pretty much the way it was with Floss until last week," he said. "But remember when all this started?"

Brenna counted back on her fingers. "What day did she fall? Last Saturday?"

"No, the context. Remember what happened just before she got hurt?"

She shook her head.

"Maura's art show. One of her horse paintings was going to be in the show, out there for everyone to see."

Brenna shoved her half-eaten salad away. "Those images wouldn't mean anything to anybody."

"Except the people who knew what they meant, or who knew she was struggling to make sense of something. I mean, the *Press* critic singled out her painting and wrote about it in the paper, for God's sake. A couple days later, Floss Underhill is at the bottom of a ravine and the cops are looking for the person who this gardener says may have pushed her. And now the gardener and his wife are gone.''

Christensen could see he'd connected. Brenna didn't object when a waiter took her plate of unfinished salad.

''Or worse,'' he added.

They fell into an uneasy silence, their eyes drifting to the windows, to the city below. It was getting dark now, and Pittsburgh's skyline was emerging in silhouette against the hills of the North Side. Christensen felt suddenly alone, suddenly afraid. When he turned his attention back to Brenna, a plate of *linguini al pomodoro fresco* was in front of him and a heaping plate of calamari in front of her. When had it arrived?

''Bren?''

''Hmm?''

''What if I'm right?''

She slipped a tine of her fork through a rubbery loop of squid and lifted it to her lips. She chewed it thoughtfully, but without much enthusiasm. ''These are my *clients*. I'm obligated to defend them.''

''No matter what?''

Brenna stopped chewing. ''Time for my Socratic questions,'' she said. ''Let's assume someone in that family is guilty of whatever you suspect. Do you think they should have a trial before we execute them?''

''Of course.''

''Should the trial be fair?''

He nodded.

''Should the accused have an attorney?''

''Yes.''

''Should the attorney be competent?''

''Yes.''

''And honorable?''

Christensen felt her logic tightening like a noose. "Yes."

"Even if someone in the family is guilty, shouldn't I, as their attorney, make the investigators and prosecutors prove their case beyond a reasonable doubt?"

He nodded again, unable to argue a single point.

Brenna set her fork down and leaned back in her chair. "Let me do my job then."

"But Bren, what if?"

He waited. Something had changed her. Private practice? Political ambition? He remembered the idealism that had kept her in the public defender's office so much longer than her contemporaries, remembered her longtime commitment to defending the rights of those who couldn't defend themselves. How different she seemed now. The worst-case scenario was chilling: a little boy dead, a cover-up that led to the attempted murder of his grandmother, a cover-up of that attempted murder that may have led to other murders, depending on identification of the two bodies at the morgue. Christensen knew Brenna was calculating the possibilities, too, as she rearranged the food on her plate.

"If you're one hundred percent right—and you're not—I would withdraw from the case," she said.

"You'd withdraw?" he tested. "That's it?"

"This is bullshit."

"But if it's true—"

"It's not."

"You're too sure."

"I think the Underhills deserve a competent defense."

"And I think—" Christensen weighed his words carefully. "Bren, are you telling me everything? You started to say something today about Harrisburg—"

Brenna pushed the full plate of calamari away and stood up. Even in the dim light, he could tell she was pale. She wouldn't look him in the eye. "I'll meet you at home," she said, and then she was gone.

23

Christensen had to wait for the valet to bring his car, so Brenna got home fifteen minutes before he did. When he finally walked in, she seemed lost in thought as she rinsed hot-dog grease from the kids' dinner dishes. Christensen picked up the compact discs scattered across the living-room floor. The kids adored Jenny. Christensen was less enthusiastic. Both times she'd babysat, she left the house looking like the aftermath of a Kansas twister. Christensen flipped on the front light and checked the porch, dead-bolted the front and back doors, then trudged upstairs to join Brenna.

Even before he turned on their bedroom light, he saw a flashing pinpoint of red light on the reading table beside the bed. He walked to the answering machine and poked the Play button. "You have three new messages," it announced.

"Jenny doesn't answer the phone?" he said.

Brenna shrugged. She was working open the buttons of her blouse and didn't look up.

"Hey, Dad. Hey, Bren." Melissa's voice suddenly filled the room. "Greetings from Grenoble."

Christensen sat down on the edge of the bed to slip off his shoes. He'd grown close to his older daughter in the past three years, and hearing her voice from so far away triggered a sudden and overwhelming sense of loss. He missed her, his sadness underscored by the background commotion of her French host family and the knowledge that she'd grown up and away.

"Just thought I'd check in before I throw myself off the clock tower in town."

The hair on Christensen's arms stood up. He froze.

"Kidding, Dad. Lighten up. I haven't talked to you in a couple weeks, that's all. Thanks for the check. Thought you might be working at home today. How's the new house? Can't wait to see it this summer. I've got an eight o'clock French Lit. exam tomorrow, so don't call back. I'll check in this weekend. Give Annie and Taylor a hug, okay? Bye."

The machine's electronic voice announced 3:53 P.M. as the time of the call. Between feeding the kids and his troubling phone call to Simon Bostwick, he must have forgotten to check the machine.

"She sounds fine," Christensen said.

Brenna slid out of her skirt. "That was uncalled-for back there."

"Maybe. It's, I don't know . . . clients or not, I just think we need to know what we're dealing with, Bren."

"And you're jumping to some pretty outrageous conclusions."

He stood up and unbuckled his belt, letting his pants drop to the floor while he waited for the second message.

"Mr. Christensen, this is Carrie Haygood with the district attorney's office." He reached without thinking for the volume control, turned it up high. "We spoke earlier today."

Brenna was suddenly beside him, staring at the machine as if it had begun a conversation and she was expected to answer.

"I'd like to meet privately to further discuss the case

we spoke about this morning. I'll be at my office until seven P.M. today.''

Christensen lunged for a pen as Haygood recited her office telephone number, then scribbled the number on the back of a phone-bill envelope sitting on his dresser. Haygood had called at 5:37. The alarm clock read 9:24. Why hadn't he checked the damned machine?

Brenna crossed the room again. She stopped by the bedroom window and twirled the miniblind control rod, closing the thin louvers, then slipped out of her blouse. ''You gave her our home number?'' she asked.

Christensen shook his head. He put the envelope down when he realized his hand was trembling. ''I should try her tonight, before the weekend, just in case she's still there.''

The third message began with an indistinguishable rustle and the sound of passing traffic. Christensen waited for a voice, and waited. From the corner of his eye, he saw Brenna's movements slow and then stop. She was waiting, too.

Finally, above the sound of a closing car door: ''This is for Jim Christen . . .'' A pause. ''. . . sen.''

Simon Bostwick delivered his words with a thick tongue, deliberate but impaired, different but somehow still the voice of Christensen's father.

''We're talking about life insur . . . nance, is what we're talking about,'' he slurred. ''I got it, yes I do.'' An exaggerated laugh. ''Got what you need.''

''Your deputy coroner?'' Brenna asked.

''Shhh.''

''If they knew—'' Another laugh, this one with an edge. ''—I'm thinking I'd probably look like the one up there in the springhouse. Worse, probably. But I got it covered. Something I learned a long time ago, something your friend Grady Downing taught me: You gotta leave yourself an out. Always. Always, always, always.''

''Sounds perfectly credible to me,'' Brenna said.

Christensen put a finger to his lips.

" 'Cause that's the thing. Once you're in bed with these people, they know how to make sure you stay there. They know the pressure points. But I could hurt them, too, hurt them like they never been hurt before. Some things you just can't deny.''

They were motionless now, both staring at the answering machine, waiting through a long pause. He knew from the burp and roar of a starting motorcycle that Bostwick was still on the line.

"So don't call me at my house again," Bostwick said finally. "And I can't call you from there. We need to talk, though. Insurance policy's no good if there's nobody to file the claim. Something happens, you know, to me, I'd like to make it right. Might get me out of hell a little sooner. Wait a sec. Here's a number.''

Christensen wrote the number on the back of the phone bill, just below Carrie Haygood's.

"Area code's the same as mine," Bostwick said. "Two o'clock tomorrow. I don't hear from you then, then two the next day. Grady trusted you, I know that much. So I'll take a chance.''

Neither of them moved until the machine announced the time of the call: 5:49. Fifteen minutes before he and the kids got home.

"Drunks make lousy witnesses," Brenna said.

"Come on, Bren. The guy's got no ax to grind, and it sounds like he knows something.''

She looked exasperated. "Or he's trying to blackmail the Underhills. The coroner's office is political, too, you know. They swap favors with Dagnolo all the time.''

Christensen picked up the cordless phone and turned it on. "Something was wrong when we first talked, though. I called him cold, you know, but his answers were just too sure. He said he didn't remember the case, but he slipped when he said he handled a lot of cases involving kids. Why would he say that if he didn't know who Chip Underhill was? He was trying to tell me something even then.''

Christensen dialed Haygood's office number, hoping she was working late. He hung up when the line clicked into her voice mail. "I'll try first thing tomorrow."

Brenna picked up her skirt and hung it in the closet. She sat on the edge of the bed to peel off her panty hose. "What did he sound like to you?"

"Bostwick? Drunk, like you said."

"Play it again."

Christensen skipped the first two messages, then sat down beside her as Bostwick's tape-recorded voice filled the bedroom. Despite the stretched vowels and slurred S's, Christensen heard a deliberateness that he'd missed the first time.

"He's talking in code," he said. "Think about it. He let me know he was lying about not recognizing the name, didn't he? He did that without saying so, didn't he?"

Christensen looked at the machine as if it might dissect Bostwick's words for deeper meaning. Brenna took his hand in hers, rested her head on his shoulder. He could feel her warm skin through the open front of her blouse, and her hair cascaded down his chest. They sat for a minute or more in silence before he crossed the room to his briefcase. He took out a blank tape and knelt beside the reading table.

"I'll listen again tomorrow," he said, popping open the machine. He pried the tape free and inserted the blank one, then bent down to put Melissa, Haygood, and Bostwick in his briefcase. When he stood up, Brenna pressed against him from behind, her arms gathered tight around his waist. He turned, struck at once by the intensity in Brenna's eyes. She held on as if she were afraid to let go.

"What?" he said. "Bren?"

"I'm sorry."

"Me, too. This shouldn't be about us, but it's working out that way, isn't it?"

She didn't answer, didn't blink. All she said was, "Make love to me."

29

Great. No jelly. Christensen rolled the cupboard shelf out all the way, hoping to find a forgotten jar among the canned vegetables and tins of tuna. Nothing. "Taylor'll eat peanut butter and honey again, won't he, Bren? Please say yes."

"Not if you give him a choice," she said, leaning over the kitchen table, scanning the election coverage on the front page of the morning *Press*. "If that's all we've got, just make it."

Four slices of whole-wheat bread awaited, two already slathered with Jif Extra Crunchy. "I've got a banana. Peanut butter, banana, and honey it is. We'll hear about it later, I'm sure."

The banana was beyond ripe, so he peeled it gingerly and sliced wheels onto the sandwiches with his sharpest knife. "How come you're still here? You're usually out the door by seven."

Brenna didn't look up. "Appointment. Out this way. No sense going into town first."

Her answer was too clipped. "The Underhills. Bren, you had all weekend and yesterday to tell me that."

"You didn't ask. Ford called yesterday from Scranton or somewhere, from his final campaign sweep, saying he'd be in Pittsburgh today and wanted to meet. I told Liisa not to expect me before two."

Christensen squeezed the plastic honey bear a bit too tight, sending a thick stream, rather than a thin drizzle, onto the open face of one sandwich. He finished the other, cut them into quarters, and packed them into the two lunchboxes before he'd wrung all hints of anxiety from his voice. "Meet about what?"

Brenna pointed to a story at the bottom of the paper's front page. "The *Press* is off on this Enrique Chembergo thing now, too."

Christensen filled her coffee mug and set it on the table. The story's headline read: "Underhill Denies 'Willingly' Hiring Illegals."

"Everybody wants to talk to Chembergo about the INS stuff," she said.

"Not about Floss?"

Brenna shook her head. "One of the political writers wrote this, not anybody on the investigative staff."

"But Ford suddenly wants to see you?"

"He got some uncomfortable questions about hiring illegals during a news conference late Sunday. Ford's convinced Dagnolo is feeding them information. He liked the way I handled the Floss questions, and he wants my thoughts on how to shut it down. Thing is, I'm sure it's not coming from Dagnolo."

He stirred half a spoonful of sugar into her cup. "From where, then?"

"All they've got is Chembergo's name, and that was in the original investigation report. It's public record. But Rosemond and the Republicans started making a big deal of the INS documentation issue, and now we've got reporters with scandal woodies all over town. But I don't think anybody but Myron has made the connection between the INS Chembergos and the Floss Chembergos. That's too complicated. It'd only become a story if Rosemond made it an issue, and he won't. Even he's not dumb enough to step in that one."

Christensen sat in a chair directly opposite her, hoping she'd sit, too. But Brenna casually, too casually, flipped open the paper. "Bren, is it just me and Myron Levin thinking along these lines?"

"What lines?"

"That maybe there's a link to Chip's death? That maybe this all somehow ties together?"

She was focused on the newspaper, but her eyes weren't moving. "Hard to tell." She finally looked up. "Let's not panic here, okay? We still don't know what happened three years ago. We still don't know what happened to the Chembergos. And the more I think about it, the less likely it all seems to wash. Would somebody really try to kill Floss just to keep her quiet? Who in that family would be cold-blooded enough?"

Her face betrayed nothing. No fear, not even concern. As anxious as he felt, as certain as he was about his theory, Christensen found her confidence reassuring. "What time are you meeting him?"

"Noon. At the Fox Chapel house." Brenna noticed her coffee for the first time. "Thanks, but I should get going. I've got a couple of other stops first. I'll put it in a go-cup."

"Let me try to get the kids up before you go. They didn't get to see you at all last night. Taylor wanted to tell you about the rat in their classroom having babies. They all watched." He shuddered. "Like the world needs more rats."

Annie was curled into a corner of her bed, the tattered remains of Molly's old silk nightgown clutched to her chest. She'd slept with it religiously since her mother died. He bent over and kissed her ear. "Breakfast train's leaving, honey," he whispered. "Aaaall aboooard."

She buried her head in the narrow canyon between her pillow and the wall. According to tradition, she wouldn't stir again for another ten minutes, and only then when he offered her a piggyback ride to the table and a heaping bowlful of whatever noxious breakfast confection was in the cupboard. This morning, though, he wanted to hold her, to kiss her damp forehead and feel every one of her sixty-three pounds in his arms. The urge was as irresistible as the moon's pull on the ocean. He snaked a hand up the back of her oversized T-shirt and scratched her back. "Coo-coo for Cocoa Puffs," he said.

Annie sat up. "We're out."

"You sure? You checked way in the back?"

"I want Cinnamon Toast Crunch."

Christensen opened his arms wide and she crawled to him, clutching his neck and resting her head in the hollow just above his collarbone. As he stood up, she wrapped her legs around his waist. "Think Taylor's awake?" he asked.

"Who cares?"

"Annie. Are you two not getting along?"

She shrugged. "He just hangs around with me and my friends at school."

"And how does that make you feel?" He rounded the hall corner and waited for an answer outside Taylor's bedroom door.

"Sometimes I want to pound him," she said.

"But you don't, do you? You know you're supposed to—"

"I know, I know. Use my words. And I did. I told him I was gonna pound him if he didn't stop."

He pushed open Taylor's bedroom door with his foot. "That's not exactly what I meant. But we'll talk about it later."

Taylor was already awake, moving Matchbox cars across a rugged terrain of rumpled bedsheets. His face fell when he looked up. "Where's my mom?"

"Downstairs, dying to see you. Want a ride?"

Taylor scrambled to his feet as Christensen presented his back. With both kids clinging to him, he felt like a mother baboon crossing the savanna. He started down the stairs, sliding his hand along the banister in case he stumbled, then turned toward the kitchen when he reached the creaky hardwood of the ground floor.

"Found two monkeys upstairs," he announced.

Brenna looked up from the newspaper, apparently startled, her face pale and blank. She smiled at Taylor, but it seemed forced and unnatural, a recovery. She closed the paper and wrapped her arms around all three of them.

"What do monkeys eat?" she said.

"Cinnamon Toast Crunch," Annie said.

"Doughnuts," Taylor said. "Chocolate."

Brenna made a face. "Breakfast of champions," she said.

"Only if you eat some fruit first, guys," Christensen said, waiting for the backlash to his menu modification. "Cantaloupe or honeydew?" He stooped enough to let both kids climb down. His back ached when he stood up again.

"We hate those," Annie said.

Brenna kissed them both, brushing a wave of red hair off Taylor's forehead. "Tell you what. You guys can watch TV until we get everything ready. Okay?"

Christensen watched the pair hurry off for a rare morning treat. Brenna had railed against commercial television for as long as he'd known her, even threatened to cancel their cable subscription once after Taylor sang her the *Gilligan's Island* theme song without missing a word. He knew something was wrong.

"What?"

Brenna opened the paper again and pointed to a short story inside the Metro section. "Maura," was all she said.

She was dead. It said so in the first paragraph, and everything Christensen read after that was a blur. He looked up. "I was with her at the horse ranch," he said, as if her being now dead simply wasn't possible. "Jesus."

He read it again, focusing this time, trying to absorb the details. On his third pass, he understood the basics: A neighbor coming home the evening before saw Pearson slumped over the wheel of her idling car, which was parked in front of the house she had shared with her mother. Police were blaming a carbon monoxide leak from her car's faulty exhaust system.

Christensen sat down. "I just saw her at Harmony yesterday morning."

He didn't know when, or how, but suddenly Brenna's arms were around him, holding him tight. What was replaying in his mind, though, was the morning he'd spent in the mighty and immaculate Special, Pearson's eccentricity on wheels. He first thought about how fortunate it was that they rode the entire way with the windows down. Then he remembered the long minutes they spent with the windows up, sweltering in the dusty Muddyross Ranch parking lot to keep dust off the ancient vinyl upholstery, while Pearson warmed up the engine. The car said a lot about her, but more than anything else it spoke of her eye for detail and her fussiness about maintenance. A faulty exhaust system? He couldn't imagine it.

"Something's not right." He peeled Brenna's arms from around his waist and held her away from him. "There was nothing wrong with her car."

"It sounds pretty old," she said.

His mind reeled. "No, no. It was, but it wasn't like that. Long story, but Maura lived her whole life with her mom. This was her mom's car until her mom died a couple years ago. The way Maura keeps it up, it's like, you know, a part of her mother that's still living and healthy, a rolling memorial."

"But a car that old—"

"Bren, forty-eight hours ago I sat in the front seat of that car with the windows rolled up while she warmed up the engine, revving it the whole time. The ranch parking lot is just dirt, and the thing was kicking up this big cloud of dust. She didn't want it all over the car, so she made me keep the windows closed. See what I'm saying?"

"You think she committed suicide?"

The thought hadn't occurred to him. "That doesn't fit

at all. Bren, I think . . . what if somebody did this?'' To have been more explicit, to use the word "kill" or "murder," would have seemed melodramatic, even though it seemed to him a possibility. An idea pinballed through his head, ricocheting off the faces and unfolding truths since this all began. "The Underhills know her from Harmony. What if they thought Floss was telling Maura what she knew? Or that Maura was snooping around trying to figure out the images in her paintings? It was her art show, remember. What if they thought she knew too much, like about the Chembergos?"

Brenna might have dismissed the idea, might have defended her client from his reckless implication. But she didn't. What she said was, "If that's the case, why not you? You're the one asking all the questions, down at the morgue, at the D.A.'s office, out at the horse ranch. Why Maura? She was just along for the ride."

An image flashed in Christensen's mind: a lean, denim-clad figure standing at the edge of a parking lot, a pencil and paper in his hand.

"Doti," he said.

Brenna repeated the name, but nothing else registered on her face.

"If Warren Doti is as close to the Underhill family as I think he is—" He stopped, checking the seams of his theory. "Bren, that day at the ranch, I was the one along for the ride. I think Doti took down Maura's license number. That's why not me. They probably don't know who I am."

Brenna pushed away, turned her back, an abrupt gesture he couldn't interpret. She said something he didn't understand, then turned around when he asked her to repeat it.

"They know," she said. "I don't know how, but they know who you are. Vincent Underhill asked me some questions the other night that made it pretty clear."

"Questions about me?"

"Not specifically. Nothing explicit. But he seemed to

know things—that we're involved, that we live in the Seventh Ward, that we have kids." She swallowed hard. "It made me wonder, but I honestly didn't think much of it at the time. It's not like it's a big secret or anything. I just don't think I ever told him. He just knew."

"And he made it pretty clear that he knew, probably for a reason."

She looked away.

Indiscretions began bubbling up in his mind: his conversation with Floss at Mount Mercy, the one Vincent Underhill short-circuited; their conversation at Harmony with Floss's new aide looking on. On the records-request form at the morgue, hadn't he included his name, home address, and phone number without a second thought? Could he trust Carrie Haygood? The Underhills were not an ordinary family. They were a power vortex, an omniscient force with all the right connections in local and state government. What if they maintained a casual network of spies, say, in the coroner's office, the D.A.'s office, or anywhere else they felt vulnerable? Hell, what if they'd tapped the phones, or if someone was siphoning off the signal from Brenna's cellular phone calls? How hard, really, would it have been to find out who he was?

"Gilligan's a dork and the palm trees are fake," Annie said, pushing past them into the kitchen. "You guys actually *watched* that show when you were kids?"

Christensen wheeled around as Brenna pulled away and went to the sink. His daughter was dressed like a hooker in short cut-offs and a bikini top, ready for school on a warm spring day.

Annie surveyed the empty table. "Hey, where's breakfast?"

"Coming right up," he said. "You said Cinnamon Toast Crunch, right? What's Taylor want?"

"Kix," Taylor said. "Kid tested, mother approved."

The two kids were crunching away, ignoring their cantaloupe slices, when Brenna kissed their foreheads and said good-bye. Christensen, still reeling, caught her in the hall. "Don't go," he said.

"He's my client, Jim."

He stared, his comeback caught in a snarl of fear and confusion and an unfocused sense of dread. Maura was dead now, and that fit too neatly into the puzzle he was piecing together. He felt as if they'd gotten caught in a whirlpool before they could catch a breath, before they understood the danger, and it was taking them down to a dark and dangerous place. Struggle seemed futile. The stakes were clear, to him anyway, but something besides logic was driving Brenna.

"Look, baby," she said as he seethed, "say you're right. Say it all happened just like you think and we're into something weird at this point. To me that means sink or swim." She picked up her briefcase from the front-hall floor. "Ford's expecting me. He made time on election day to meet. If I don't show up, he's pissed off *and* he thinks something's wrong. So I need to go."

"Withdraw as their attorney."

"For what reason? The Bill of Rights doesn't apply to them? Like it or not, Jim, criminal-defense attorneys sometimes have to deal with criminals."

"But this . . . why are you so willing to ignore all this?"

Her eyes accused him. "Why won't you let me do my job?"

"Why are you guys fighting?"

They both turned at once. Taylor and Annie were together at the kitchen door, closer than Christensen had ever seen them stand together. How could he explain a subtext so impossibly complicated?

"We're just talking, trying to understand each other," he said, but even he wasn't convinced. The kids just stared.

"We're using our words," he tried. "You're not wearing that to school, by the way."

"You both sound mad," Annie said.

He turned to Brenna and offered an awkward hug. It was like trying to embrace a mannequin. "Truce?" he whispered, pretending to kiss her ear.

She patted his shoulder and leaned around him. "Everything's fine, guys. Just let us work this out, okay?"

"Use your words," Annie said.

Christensen felt Brenna relax a little. "Deal," she said.

The kids shuffled back to the breakfast table. They were shoveling cereal into their mouths before Brenna spoke again. "So what are your plans?"

"Harmony." Christensen thought of Maura, his sadness suddenly profound and overwhelming. "Oh Jesus," he said, stifling a sob.

Brenna looked over his shoulder—at their kids, the stairs, the jumble of furniture and moving cartons they hadn't had time to arrange and unpack. Christensen wiped his eyes, fighting for composure. "We've been doing evaluations of everyone in the class," he said.

"If you see Floss, are going to talk to her?"

"I don't know. They pulled her from the class, so I don't know if she'll be around. But I have to go in. Maura's students know me a lot better than the administrators, so I should probably help break the news. That way I can reschedule the evaluations and all that. Bren, call it paranoia if you want, but I've got to get some answers. I'm going to talk to Carrie Haygood this morning and Bostwick this afternoon. Maybe Floss, too."

"You do what you've got to do. Just don't try to run *my* life while you're doing it."

He nodded, his eyes never leaving Brenna's. She looked around him again. "Bye, guys," she said. "Love you."

The kids were watching them again. Brenna offered him a stiff embrace, all for show. As she pulled away and stepped through the front door, Christensen felt the disorienting sensation of movement, as if they all were being pulled toward some dark center, spinning faster and faster as they approached the whirlpool's unforgiving funnel.

30

Christensen had hurried Annie and Taylor through the breakfast, tooth-brushing, and shoe-tying routine, then herded them into the Explorer. Hiding his apprehension as best he could, he'd dropped them at the Winchester-Stanton School with a promise to return as soon as he could after classes ended, wishing he had a better option.

Now, as he moved along the Harmony corridors at 8:30 A.M., Christensen felt the pall that hung over the aggressively cheery ground floor. He noticed it first in the parking lot, where someone had left a large arrangement of roses in Maura Pearson's empty parking space. Inside, the receptionist was crying. Staff members and patients sat quietly together in the central lounge, many of them crying as well. The rehabilitation garden, one of the center's most popular areas with its planter boxes and wheelchair-height potting tables, was empty. On one of the outdoor patios, where patients new to wheelchairs practiced getting into and out of the modified passenger compartment of an ancient Lincoln Continental, two patients from the spinal cord unit argued about exhaust systems.

A hand-lettered sign on the door to Maura's art therapy room announced the cancellation of classes, but without explanation. To one side of the door, Pearson's most challenging student sat perfectly upright in her wheelchair, one manicured hand resting in the lap of her familiar pink Chanel suit, the other fingering her single strand of pearls as if they were rosary beads.

"There won't be any class this morning, Emma," Christensen said.

"Service at this club used to be *so* good," she said. "I don't know what's happened."

He knelt on the corridor's linoleum floor, bracing himself on the arm of her chair. "You're at the Harmony Center, Emma, and I'm Jim Christensen. I've been with you many times in Maura Pearson's art classes. But there's been an accident, and Maura can't be with us today. Is there somewhere else you'd like to go this morning?"

The woman's fingers raced even faster from pearl to pearl, their speed a perfect measure of her agitation level.

"We made reservations a week ago, and I've still been waiting an hour for a table," she said. "This is unacceptable, and believe you me, my husband will hear about it."

Christensen patted her hand. Her husband was at least ten years dead.

"I'm going to escort you to the dayroom, Emma. I saw some of the other members of the morning class there with Allison."

Emma stared.

"Allison is one of the art therapists who helps Maura in class," he continued. "She'll know what the schedule is for the morning now that classes are canceled. I don't think we'll be doing evaluations today as we'd planned."

Christensen tested the art therapy room door. It was unlocked. "Why don't you come into the art room with me for a few minutes first? I want to use the phone in Maura's office for just a minute."

He turned her chair around and backed through the door, wheeling her to the spot at the worktable where he knew she felt most comfortable. They both looked around. Even with the riot of color and ongoing projects, the room seemed empty and lifeless without Pearson's dominating presence. "Emma, is there something you'd like to work on for a few minutes while I make a call?"

The woman looked around. "These tables aren't even set," she said. "I want to speak to the manager."

Christensen set a sketch pad and a box of colored markers on the worktable, within her reach but not so close that they might upset her. "In case you feel like drawing," he said. "I'll be in Maura's office, just for a few minutes."

He found Pearson's phone under a large bag of cedar chips, which were bound, he assumed, for the gerbil habitat atop the bookshelf. The squeaking of the exercise wheel was the only sound in the dim space, and it underscored the sad fact that Pearson was gone. Against all odds, Christensen found himself concerned about the welfare of the tiny rodent. Who would trim its teeth now?

After the fourth ring, Carrie Haygood's office phone clicked into voice mail. He hadn't counted on this, assuming she'd be in after 6:30 as her message had said she would be. "Jim Christensen returning your call at 8:45 Tuesday morning," he said. "I'd like to talk as soon as possible, but I'm moving around. I'll call back in thirty minutes or so."

Christensen looked at the crumpled phone-bill envelope. The number Simon Bostwick had left on his answering machine the night before was scribbled just below Haygood's office number. The deputy coroner had said to call him there at two, but Christensen couldn't resist. Even if Bostwick wasn't there, maybe he could find out where he had called from. On the first ring, a woman's voice answered, "Cook's Corner."

Startled, Christensen said, "Simon Bostwick, please."

"We're closed till eleven," she said, and hung up.

Christensen plucked a colored pencil from the quiver of pens and pencils on Maura's desk and wrote "Cook's Corner" beside the number Bostwick had left. He drew a box around the name and number, then put the pencil back in the cup where he'd found it. The squeaking of the gerbil's wheel drew Christensen closer to the aquarium than he ever had been. Through the glass, he watched the tiny brown form running its endless circuit, wondering what would become of it now that its keeper was dead. The cage was clean, the wood chips apparently changed the day before. Without thinking, he checked the water bottle and the pellet feeder. Satisfied that both were nearly full, he picked his way among the boxes of art supplies and half-finished projects and stepped back into the workroom, where Emma was sitting just as he'd left her. She was still mauling her pearls; the sketch pad and markers were untouched.

"Are you the manager?" she asked.

"No, Emma, I'm Jim Christensen and we're at the Harmony Center," he said, trying again to orient her. "The morning art class has been canceled, so I'm going to take you down to the dayroom. Does that sound okay to you?"

"Fine," she said. "This whole dinner has been just appalling."

The dayroom was at the far end of Harmony's central hallway, probably a quarter-mile from the Alzheimer's unit and Maura's art therapy room. Christensen pushed the woman's chair out the door, past a red-eyed, waist-high sensor and onto the ribbon of silky concrete designed for frictionless wheelchair passage. The electronic bracelets on Emma's left ankle and left wrist warned the aide at the monitoring station that someone had wandered outside of the unit, but Christensen waved her off when she looked up.

They rolled in silence past the stroke unit, the head trauma unit, and the spinal cord unit, and everyone they passed along the way—staff, patients, even visitors—seemed to avoid their gaze. He watched their distorted reflections cross the mirrored half-globe mounted to the ceiling at each intersection, but there was no cross traffic. Harmony was as quiet as he'd ever seen it.

What caught his eye first as they passed the cafeteria was the odd sensation that the eating area was suddenly twice as big as before. It was mostly empty, and the longer he looked through the window, the more he realized it was an illusion. The space seemed huge because only a few of the tables had chairs; so many of Harmony's residents and day visitors used wheelchairs and didn't need them. With no one in the cafeteria, it looked cavernous. What caught his eye next made the hair on his arms stand on end.

Floss Underhill was parked against the far wall, head bowed, her broken arm resting on one of her wheelchair's arms. She gripped the chair's other arm with her good hand as if she was afraid of falling, but the rest of her body was relaxed, apparently asleep. Several feet away, seated in the lotus position on top of a table and reading from a paperback, was the same home-care nurse Christensen had met a few days earlier on the center's dining deck. No one else was seated within thirty feet.

On the way to the center that morning, he'd worried about forcing Floss Underhill to directly confront the traumas in her past. Simply asking her what happened that day three years ago when her grandson died, or on the gazebo deck ten days earlier, could nudge her into psychosis. What if those painful memories weren't simply lost in her crossed neurowiring, but repressed? How would she react to something she was unable to consciously confront? Under normal circumstances, he would lead her to the very edge of the pool, but he would never push her in. These weren't normal circumstances.

Christensen moved on, past the chapel, past the occupational therapy rooms, into the crowded dayroom where he spotted Maura's assistant, Allison, sitting quietly with three other students from Pearson's class. Allison offered a weak smile.

"So Emma, you decided to join us?" she said. The old woman continued to work her pearls. Allison looked at Christensen. "Can you believe this?"

He shook his head. "No one called me, so I just know what was in the paper."

Allison reached into the front pocket of her paint-stained smock and pulled out a folded piece of paper. She handed it to him. "We got this notice from administration at shift change this morning," she said. "Nobody seems to know much more."

"Who's telling the students?"

"We're talking to them individually," she said. "In some cases, we're letting family members tell them. Whatever seems most appropriate."

Christensen unfolded the paper. The notice lauded Pearson's contributions to Harmony and Pittsburgh's Alzheimer's community, but contained even less information about how she died than the newspaper account. It did note that Maura's regular classes would resume the following day.

"You're taking over the classes?" Christensen asked.

Allison nodded, then stood up. She motioned him to step away, out of the group's hearing range. "One thing Maura taught me: You have to make sure they have a way to express whatever emotions they're feeling. This would be the worst possible time to take the art away from them. So we'll carry on as best we can."

Her lip trembled, and Christensen put a hand on her shoulder. No words came.

"What about you?" she said, regaining her composure. "What does this do to your research?"

He shrugged. "I'll carry on, too. I'd hate to walk away from something so promising. If you'll still put up with me hanging around, I'd like to continue."

"You're as much a part of the class as they are," Allison said, cocking her head toward the group. "We couldn't handle you leaving, too."

"Well, then," he said, "I'll see you tomorrow morning."

"You're leaving?"

"There's someone I need to talk to down in the cafeteria," he said. He nodded toward the group. "They need you to be strong, but it's okay to talk about it with them. Preferable, really. They need to grieve, too."

Allison bit her lip, then nodded. "Tomorrow morning, then."

The cafeteria was even less crowded than before. Now Floss and her aide were the only people on their side of the room. The old woman's head remained bowed, her chin on her chest, as Christensen crossed the room. A flicker of recognition lit up the aide's face when she looked up from her book.

"Hey," she said. "I remember you."

"Jim Christensen," he said, extending his right hand, fishing for her name.

"Paige Sullivan. Bummer about Maura, huh?"

Floss lifted her head and opened her eyes. She studied them with the stupefied gaze of someone fresh from sleep.

"Good morning, Mrs. Underhill," he said. "I'm Jim Christensen, and we're at the Harmony Center. How are you today?"

"Hungry," she said.

Paige rolled her eyes and patted the old woman's arm. "You've eaten twice already," she said, turning to Christensen as if in appeal. "She just forgot. She's eaten twice already."

"How about a cup of tea, Mrs. Underhill?" he said. "Can I get you some tea? Or coffee?"

She waved him off with her good arm. "How about a Cohiba?"

He laughed. "You can't smoke in here. Sorry."

"Tea, then," she said.

He turned to Paige, then gestured toward the food line. "Would you mind? I was hoping Mrs. Underhill and I might have a few minutes alone to talk, what with everything that's happened today.''

Paige nodded. ''She really liked Maura, I think.''

''Just a few minutes,'' he said.

When Paige was gone, Christensen slid one of the cafeteria's few freestanding chairs in front of Floss and straddled it backward. He didn't have time for chitchat. He needed to plug the old woman as directly as he dared into that traumatic time three years earlier that suddenly seemed so crucial.

''What happened to Gray, Mrs. Underhill?'' he said.

The name seemed to jolt her like an electric shock. ''Gray,'' she repeated.

''Your horse,'' he prodded.

Floss closed her eyes, the barest hint of a smile playing across her lips. ''That horse could fly,'' she said.

''Yes he could.'' Christensen took a chance. ''Like he had wings.''

In his triangulation, her memories of the horse might link directly to Warren Doti, its trainer, possibly her lover. He was encouraged when her smile eased into something thinner, tighter, nearly a leer.

She nodded, her eyes still closed. ''He was special.''

''But what happened to him?''

''Gone. All gone.''

''Did Gray run away? What?''

She shook her head, gripping the arm of her wheelchair with her good hand. No one else was in line, but Paige, bless her, was flirting with the cafeteria cashier.

''They took him,'' Floss said.

''Who, Mrs. Underhill? Who took Gray?''

''In the dark, like a bunch of sneak thieves. Day before the funeral, with everybody so upset already.'' Her eyes shot open and she looked directly at him. ''Can you imagine?''

Every answer raised more questions. ''Someone took Gray at night? Your grandson's funeral?''

''I watched them. Just walked him right into that trailer

and drove off, like they were taking him to show. But not like that. Took all his tack, too. Cleared out his stall, everything in his equipment locker. Took him off in that Muddyross trailer and never brought him back.''

An image flashed through Christensen's mind: The horse trailers he'd seen at the ranch that day, each one with the distinctive MR brand painted dead-center on the side. "Because he'd hurt your grandson, Mrs. Underhill? Is that why they sent Gray away?"

"Happened so fast. I went down to the stables to find Warren, to find out what was happening. Me in the dark, in my nightclothes, everybody asleep, but the trailer was gone before I got there. Like sneak thieves."

"Warren managed your stables and trained Gray, didn't he? He'd have known what was happening, wouldn't he?"

Floss shut her eyes tight, squeezing a tear from one. It rolled into a crease of her sun-weathered skin and followed the connecting lines until it reached her jaw. The tear traced her jawline to her chin and hung there like one of Christensen's unanswered questions. "He was gone, too. And all his things."

"Warren?"

Paige was back. She set a mug of hot water on the table beside Floss, ripped open a packet of orange pekoe and dropped the tea bag into the mug. "They're out of English breakfast," she said. "Hope this is okay."

Christensen waited, hoping a tense silence would shoo the aide away. To be more assertive might make her suspicious, but every interruption, any diversion at all, could make Floss lose the delicate thread of coherent memories she was following. Paige looked from Floss to Christensen and back again.

"I wanted a Cohiba," Floss said.

Paige rolled her eyes. "You can't smoke in here, Mrs. Underhill. This is tea. We'll go outside in a little while so you—"

"Paige, please." Christensen forced a smile, tried to

tune the tension from his voice. "Could you excuse us for just a few more minutes?"

The aide picked up her paperback from the table with a crisp sweep of her hand and pointed to a spot several tables away. "I'll be over there, I guess." Paige sat facing them, watching over the top of her book.

When Christensen turned back to Floss, she was preoccupied with her tea. The tear still hung from her chin, but whatever emotion had triggered it was gone. "Something goes in this," she said.

"Sugar?"

She shook her head.

"Milk? Lemon?"

She shook her head again, agitated this time, frustrated, struggling to recall something as simple as how she took her tea.

"Honey?" he said.

"That!" she said. A small victory.

Christensen knew he had to get her back on track before she lost the memory thread. "Mrs. Underhill, we were talking about the night they took away your horse, Gray, how someone came with a trailer and loaded him up and took him off somewhere. And you were saying how you went down to find the stable manager, Warren Doti, and he was gone, too."

She stared at him for a moment, then looked again at the steaming mug on the table. "You gonna get me some honey?" she said.

"Yes, ma'am. Just as soon as we finish talking about what happened to your horse."

Floss Underhill leaned forward in her wheelchair, studying him with an intense curiosity he couldn't decipher. He could tell from her eyes that she wasn't struggling like she was before, wasn't trying to understand anything beyond the moment. She was taking him in like a stranger on the street, and when she said, "What horse?" he knew he'd lost a rare opportunity, maybe forever.

From Vincent Underhill's study window, Brenna watched two no-nonsense black Suburbans and three nondescript black sedans, all bristling with antennas, move up the estate's driveway like a parade of black beetles. Ford Underhill's campaign entourage was in full pre-election rut. The drivers wheeled in formation into parking spots outside the house, but to her surprise only two people climbed out—the candidate himself, and Phil Raskin, the family's damp and abrasive political advisor whom she'd met at that first meeting with the Underhills. As they walked together, the two men apparently continued a private conversation that had begun inside the Suburban.

"Mr. Ford's here now."

Brenna flinched at the unfamiliar voice. Lottie, Vincent and Floss Underhill's ancient maid, stood at the study door, hands clasped behind the back of her crisp uniform. On her previous visits, Lottie had been a silent, servile creature. This was the first time Brenna had heard her speak.

"He'd be in soon as he could. Him and Mr. Vincent gonna have a meeting."

"That's fine. Thank you."

The maid offered a slight bow and backed out the doorway, then crossed the house's foyer, headed toward the kitchen. At the same time, Brenna heard the front door open. The men's voices trailed off into silence and their footsteps retreated down a hallway toward the opposite end of the house.

Brenna turned back to the window. All five vehicles idled in the driveway, doors closed, tinted windows all the way up, every cell phone, fax, and radio inside no doubt alive with election-day frenzy. Or maybe it was different at this level, where the outcome was never in doubt. Maybe the aides and advisors inside the juggernaut's mobile headquarters were looking beyond the formality of the election, coolly planning the inauguration, building a staff, cutting deals.

Brenna checked her watch—nearly one, an hour later than the appointment Ford had demanded. A billable hour, but still. She'd spent the time worrying. Lottie had ushered her into the study without fanfare, like a job applicant. The house was still, and she couldn't tell if Vincent Underhill was even home. With Floss and her aide apparently at Harmony this time of day, she had the feeling she and Lottie were the only creatures about. But in a house this size, one could never be sure.

Brenna noticed the canvases as she backed away from the window, maybe a dozen or more in varying sizes upright on the floor and leaning against the study's paneled wall in a far corner of the room. They were facing the wall, with only the back of the outermost canvas visible. Unlike the others, that canvas was framed.

She crossed the room, wondering if the paintings might be Floss's. Other than Jim's descriptions and the one reproduced in the Once-Lost Images calendar, she'd never actually seen the coded images he was so sure betrayed the Underhill family's dark secrets. She could taste the adrenaline as she recognized the frame on the outermost canvas. It was the same as those on the paintings she'd seen at the Sofa Factory exhibit. Leaning forward, she saw a hand-lettered identifier, the number 14, affixed to the frame's bottom edge—the exhibit's missing painting. Brenna looked over her shoulder to make sure she was alone.

Even upside-down, she recognized the image from the calendar: the dark sky, the fading yellow sun scored by the interlocking letters of the ranch brand, the gray winged horse at the center of it all. Brenna flipped to the second canvas, a smaller one. It was a variation on the theme. The differences were hard to spot, mostly just gradations in color, but the image was the same. Same with the third canvas. And the fourth, fifth, and sixth, all the way to the final painting. Floss was fixated, no question. And the family obviously had corralled the images. The framed one, she knew, they'd pulled from public display.

There *was* a pattern here, she conceded, not only in the art, but in the family's determined effort to keep Floss's paintings private. But her job was not to unearth the truth of what happened on that gazebo deck, she reminded herself. That job, the burden of proof, fell to Mercer's investigators and to J. D. Dagnolo. Her role was to make sure her client's rights were protected during the investigation and, if it ever went that far, prosecution. Why couldn't Jim understand that?

Somewhere in the house, a heavy door closed. Brenna stepped away from the paintings, startled. Back at the study window, she faced the door and assumed as casual a posture as was possible for someone whose heart was beating like a hummingbird's. Only then did she notice, in the upper corner of the study, at the juncture of two dark-paneled walls, the glowing red eye of a miniature security camera.

Ford Underhill entered without breaking stride. He nodded a greeting and closed the door behind him. When he turned back toward her, his face seemed grim, almost ashen, startling for a man in the full flush of political power.

"Thank you for coming, Ms. Kennedy," he said. "As I'm sure you understand, I don't have much time."

"Of course."

"Did my father explain to you why I wanted to talk?" He gestured for her to sit, and he took the wing chair directly across from her, making no effort at all to look relaxed.

"Only that you're concerned about where the media are getting information about the INS problem."

He waved her off, a gesture of frustration and power. The man clearly was here to talk, not listen. "You can't imagine what it's like out there, Ms. Kennedy. Same goddamn reporters following me into every little burg and hamlet, asking the same goddamned questions at every stop. I'm in New Castle yesterday to announce plans for a downtown redevelopment project, and they're asking me how long this Chembergo fellow worked for my parents, for Chrissakes, whether I knew he was illegal. Like it was any of their goddamned business in the first place. Like it has anything whatsoever to do with public policy in this state. I want to know where that crap's coming from."

"My recollection—"

"Somebody's leaking it, and I'm guessing Dagnolo."

Brenna wouldn't be bullied. "Not necessarily," she said. "Mr. Chembergo's name and statement are in the police reports about your mother's fall. They're public record. Any reporter with any enterprise at all could take that name and run a routine INS check. It's possible someone did, and if they did, they hit pay dirt. My recollection is that Myron Levin broke it first."

"Pain in my ass, that guy," Underhill said. "I can't figure his agenda, but he's poking around in stuff he's got no business poking around in. Know anything about him?"

Brenna thought of Levin's warning to keep away from the Underhill case, from the "impending shitstorm." He was onto something bigger than the standard pre-election muckraking, but what? "No," she said.

"Nothing?"

"He's good. A good reporter, I mean." It was a mechanical response. Even as they spoke, she was replaying her conversations with Levin. Suddenly, from somewhere deep and nearly forgotten, Levin's words bobbed up like a submerged mine: "A little skeleton in the family closet." Brenna felt a chill. Levin *was* acting on the same hunch as Jim. Both saw Floss Underhill's fall as part of a bigger picture linked somehow to Chip Underhill's death. Working independently, both men were seeing the same troubling patterns.

"When you say Levin has been poking around—" Brenna hesitated, feeling as if she were about to step off a ledge, knowing that if she did there would be no turning back. "Mr. Underhill, do you have any reason to believe Myron Levin is investigating the circumstances surrounding your son's death?"

Brenna knew she'd hit a nerve. Underhill flinched. The corners of his eyes drooped and his cheeks seemed to sag, a cartoonist's version of a stunned reaction. She half-expected his jaw to drop to the floor with a clang. From there, his expression blurred into something closer to panic. It wasn't the look of a man overcome with the raw emotion of a painful memory; more the look of cornered prey.

"I—" Underhill's eyes shifted. For a politician, a dead giveaway. The man was rattled.

Underhill abruptly stood and crossed the room, a reaction without purpose. Brenna waited for an answer as Underhill adjusted the pen set on his father's desk, straightened the telephone, aligned the paper in the stationery tray. When he turned back, his face was no less affected.

"We're speaking now in confidence, Ms. Kennedy, is that correct?"

She nodded.

"And what we say here comes under the veil of attorney-client privilege, does it not?"

Brenna swallowed hard. "Of course."

Underhill returned to his chair. His eyes roamed the room, settling on everything before finally meeting hers. He summoned a weak smile and seemed about to speak when a tear at the corner of one eye dropped onto his cheek. Its irregular trail made Brenna realize that Underhill was wearing telegenic makeup that exaggerated everything on his handsome, overlarge face.

Brenna tried to reassure him. "I need to know what's happening, Mr. Underhill. I can't competently represent you or your family unless I understand what's going on."

He nodded. "My son—" he began. "Chip didn't die in a horseback-riding accident."

A wave broke over Brenna, a jolt of cold followed by a sudden lurch in her stomach. She had the unnerving sensation of falling. She thought first of Taylor, her son. She thought of Annie and Jim, especially Jim.

Underhill brushed away the tear. His eyes finally settled on hers and didn't waver, and she suspected that what he was about to say might be the truth. "It *was* an accident, though, Ms. Kennedy, a terrible, terrible accident. You're going to have to trust me on that." Underhill looked down, watching his fingers trace the fabric pattern on the arm of his chair. "Do you trust me?" he said.

"Yes."

"I need that, as much as I need your assurance that this conversation will remain between us."

Brenna glanced up at the camera's glowing red eye. "You have it, but right now you need to tell me what I need to know."

Underhill drew a ragged breath. "I don't come to this disclosure without considerable pain, as I'm sure you can guess. You're a parent. You understand how devastating the loss of a child can be. But the loss of a child by—" Another breath. "An accident, Ms. Kennedy, a flash of anger, a moment of rage, and that was it. Children are so . . . fragile."

Brenna wanted, needed, answers. And she had dozens

of questions. But when she opened her mouth, what came out was, "Oh God." She covered her mouth with her hand.

"One reads about these things happening, but until they happen in your own family, they're unimaginable," he said. "Horrifying. Repulsive. But they do happen."

"What—" she said, still struggling for words. "How?"

Underhill's face was tough to read. Brenna saw genuine distress in his eyes, but his voice was calmer now. Had he ever told this story before, or was she the first to hear it? Underhill's grim face flickered. He offered a sad smile, but his face changed quickly into something uncertain.

"I'm not looking for sympathy, Ms. Kennedy. Not offering excuses. Nothing like that. Believe me, there was damned little of that after it happened."

Brenna couldn't hold back. "After *what* happened?"

Underhill looked away. "This is very difficult for me."

"I'm sorry, but you've left too much unsaid. What happened?"

"It did happen here, at this house. We'd brought Chip over to see his grandparents, just to spend the day." Underhill pinched the bridge of his nose for a long moment, then, collected, folded his hands in his lap. "Mother wasn't wandering the way she does now, see. My father wasn't nearly as overwhelmed as he is these days, trying to keep up with her. She was fraying around the edges, of course. We'd known something was wrong for a few years. Fact is, with Alzheimer's, you're never really sure until the autopsy. But she was more together back then. Definitely. So it was just a rare Sunday with nothing special planned, all of us here."

Brenna nodded.

Underhill studied her. "A hectic time for all of us, three years ago. The airport project, that was Dad's main thing. Mother was still doing some charity work then, still active with the Oaks Classic. Leigh was starting early fundraising for this campaign. We all just had so much going on at the time.''

Underhill stood up suddenly and went to the liquor cart, just as she'd seen his father do when he'd told her about the riding accident—a story she'd found so convincing. The crystal decanter rattled against the rim of his glass as Underhill poured two fingers of brandy. He tossed it back like a man steeling himself for a challenge he could no longer avoid.

''You know about three-year-olds, Ms. Kennedy. You've been there, haven't you, trying to get something done, a simple little thing—read a report, make a call, whatever—and you can't because you can't even get a few goddamned minutes to think? You know what someone so demanding can do to somebody who's got a lot on their mind, don't you?''

Brenna closed her eyes, trying to make sense of Underhill's narrative. Suddenly, an image: her own hand sweeping across her mother's gaunt face, a regrettable impulse to control something that was out of control. She remembered the explosive rage that had come from nowhere the night her mother spilled her water cup for the third time, the stunned silence that followed, her mother already so weak that her sunken eyes weren't even able to tear. What had fueled her anger that night? She'd been terrified enough that it might happen with Taylor that she sometimes trusted Jim with her son more than she trusted herself.

''Who hit him?'' she blurted.

Underhill shook his head. ''No one hit him, Ms. Kennedy. Nothing so primal. With a child that size, just shaking—'' Another deep breath, then he stood up. ''I think you get the idea. That was it, all it took. One moment, one mistake, an instant when reason was lost to impulse, and within minutes our son was dead and nothing would ever be the same again.''

Brenna wanted to say something, but what? She felt as if a bee were caught in her throat. ''I—'' she managed before covering her mouth with both hands, trying to hide the horror she was sure had registered on her face. "Who?"

Underhill stared, his eyes sincere, pleading. "Does it even matter now? Please."

"The riding accident," she said. "The story your father told me—"

Underhill nodded. "Something we told the paramedics, a small lie at first, we thought, just to give us time to think. It happened so fast, and so much was at stake. You have to understand, we were in shock, absolute shock."

She watched him until she couldn't stand the silence. "That's not a small lie."

"No. But my father . . . See, it happened so fast. We knew Chip was dead, knew it right away. It was like flipping off a light switch and hearing the bulb pop and knowing it'll never light again. There was nothing we could do. Nothing. Please believe me when I say saving his life would have taken precedence over everything else, everything, *if* that had been possible. But by the time . . . It wasn't."

"But if it had just happened—"

"Don't go there, Ms. Kennedy. Please. Your second-guessing would serve no purpose."

Brenna moved on, but sure she'd hit on something important. "Your father. You started to say something about your father."

Underhill looked away with a tight smile. "The most practical of men, isn't he? At that point, for him, the issue became damage control. I think you know how a mistake like that could be twisted by our enemies."

Brenna stared long and hard, but Underhill wouldn't look at her. They were his father's words, almost exactly, except his father had used them only to justify an elaborate lie. Somehow that seemed more forgivable than this man using them to justify the "mistake" of his only child's death. "In my neighborhood, we'd call that a cover-up,'' she said. ''And everybody who knew about it we'd call an accessory after the fact.''

Underhill flinched again. She sensed a weakness in him that she had never seen in his father, a misunderstanding of power and how to use it. He nodded his contrition. ''That's fair.''

''At this point, it's also history, isn't it?''

''Meaning?''

''He did a very thorough job. No one's ever questioned the horseback-riding story, have they?''

''Not that I'm aware of.''

''You're sure?'' Brenna baited, thinking first of Myron Levin, then of Jim, then of Maura Pearson. ''Never?''

''No. Why? And let me just say, I'm not sure I like your tone.''

Slow down, she thought. She was losing control, letting feelings overpower her professionalism. ''Because to have someone questioning the official version of what happened would be very damaging, wouldn't it?''

Underhill's eyes narrowed, like closing windows. In an instant, the contrite, emotional man who had just wrung himself out was staring at her with a look that could melt steel. ''I'll trust that's not a threat, Ms. Kennedy.'' His voice was steady now, but Brenna felt suddenly off balance.

''No. I just meant . . . you're very vulnerable, considering your high profile right now. With all the media attention since you announced for governor . . .'' Her voice trailed off. She wished it hadn't, knew it would cause problems, but she needed time to collect her thoughts.

''Meant what?''

''I need to ask you something,'' she said. ''And please understand my reasons for asking: How many people know what happened?''

Underhill studied her. ''Three,'' he said finally. ''My father, my wife, and me. We let Mother believe the story about Gray.''

''No one else? The investigators? The coroner?''

Underhill nodded. "You're wondering if anything contradicts what we told the paramedics and police, correct?"

"I'm guessing not, or there'd have been problems."

"Nothing," he said, shaking his head. "The story held. The sort of injury that killed Chip, this shaken-child thing, there's nothing obvious about it. So life went on. We all went on, doing what we had to do to cope. Me, I went on because my father's a great believer in destiny. He made a great case, too. There was so much he wanted to do during his time in Harrisburg that didn't get done. Good things. Things that would have made life better for people in this state. The rural poor. In the inner cities. Schools. Specific plans for things we're sure can be effective. My job, my destiny, is to finish what he started. Without me where I am now, a lot of good doesn't get done. Without me, the legacy ends."

"So it was best just to let the lie stand?"

Underhill waved her off. "Spare me the sanctimony. Try to imagine our burden since then, Ms. Kennedy. But is it really any different than if Chip had been a passenger in our car? If we'd made a mistake, run a red light, and he'd died when we were broadsided, would that be any different?"

Brenna understood the obliviousness of the guilty. She'd heard rapists blame their victims, even the infants. She'd heard guilty men rationalize atrocities as benign overreactions. Rationalization made it possible for them to live with the reality of what they'd done. But none of those moral gymnastics bothered her the way this did. Few of those other men were educated. None of them portrayed themselves as the moral center of public policy. None of them were about to be elected governor.

"I'm withdrawing as your attorney," she said.

Underhill's face faded for one stunned moment. He had the just-clocked look of a steer at a packinghouse. Then his face flushed bright red. His body shook. The release finally came when he hurled his brandy glass at the fireplace. It shattered with a thin, anticlimactic pop, and he stood there facing the mantel with his back to her. He seemed calmer when he turned around, as if his flash of temper had never happened. The instant mood change was frightening.

"That would be a mistake, Ms. Kennedy," Underhill said. "It solves nothing."

Brenna stood up. Her choice was clear, and she'd made it on instinct. The longer she stayed, the more complicated it would become. "It solves a personal dilemma. Like you said, life goes on. We each do what we have to do. And this is something I have to do, for myself and for you. You need an attorney who can devote his or her full energy to your defense, should it ever come to that."

Underhill crossed the room, closing the distance between them to an intimidating five feet. "I would remind you, Ms. Kennedy, that you represent my family in matters involving the sheriff's misguided investigation of my mother's recent fall. That has nothing to do with a tragedy that happened three years ago. What, exactly, is your dilemma?"

Brenna stood her ground, fighting the urge to back away. "I'll keep my reasons to myself."

"We hired you to represent us," he said. "That doesn't give you the right to judge us."

Brenna kept her eyes on his. "I can recommend other attorneys, if you'd like."

"Oh, *can* you?" he said with a schoolboy's sarcasm.

"If you'd like."

It took every ounce of Brenna's strength to hold her tongue, to keep her revulsion in check, to demonstrate that she would no longer be intimidated, or seduced, by the Underhill power.

"I don't think your recommendation would be of any interest whatsoever," Underhill said.

Brenna picked up her briefcase and turned toward the study door. "I know my way out," she said over her shoulder, then turned back to face Ford Underhill from a more comfortable distance. "My office will be in touch to settle the account."

"I'm sure it will," he said.

She was nearly out the door when Underhill called her name. When she turned around, he was standing right there, even closer than before. The features of his face were hard, a look calculated, she was sure, to scare her. It worked.

"I would only remind you again of the sanctity of attorney-client privilege," he said.

"No reminder needed."

Brenna was several miles away, out of Fox Chapel's hollows and hills, before she pulled the Legend into the gravel parking lot and dialed the Harmony Center from her cell phone. She glanced in her rearview mirror, half expecting to see one of Underhill's black Suburbans, but she was alone.

Busy. The handset shook in her hand as she pressed the redial button again and again.

32

"Carrie Haygood, please." Christensen drummed his fingers on the fake walnut desktop in his sparse Harmony Center office as the county operator searched her directory.

"What department does she work in?"

He was getting the definite impression that Haygood's sense of holy mission with the Child Death Review Team wasn't shared by many others in county government. Hardly anyone even knew she worked there, which suggested two possibilities: Either District Attorney Dagnolo was keeping her work very low-key, or the whole lofty notion of a special child-death investigator was nothing more than a feel-good political gesture intended to show that He Cares.

"The district attorney's office," he said. "Fifth floor. Five-fourteen, I think. Look, if—"

"Found it. Please hold."

Haygood answered on the first ring in a voice Christensen found reassuring, though he didn't know why.

"Hi, it's Jim Christensen returning your call. I'm sorry it took me—"

"Where are you calling from Mr. Christensen?"

"The Harmony Center, out near Fox Chapel," he said.

"Pay phone?"

"No. I've been using an office here during my research. Why?" He heard shuffling papers.

"I'm going to give you another telephone number," Haygood said, dictating a Downtown exchange. He scribbled the number on the back of a patient-evaluation form. "Please find a pay phone and call me back on that number. Give me about two minutes. If you have a cellular phone, please don't use that."

"I'm—"

"Please. Thank you."

He waited until he heard the dial tone, uncertain whether the click he'd heard was the sound of her hanging up. Then he walked down Harmony's bright main corridor to a bank of pay phones, dialed the number Haygood had given him and started to punch in his credit-card number. He stopped halfway through as Haygood's odd request suddenly made sense. She was worried about the security of her own office phone, maybe even Maura's office phone at Harmony. He replaced the handset and fished into his pocket for change. Paranoid or not, cash offered an anonymity that a credit card couldn't.

Haygood answered on the first ring again. He heard an echo in her voice, which was keyed lower than before. Wherever she was, Carrie Haygood was trying hard not to be overheard.

"I'm very sorry about the inconvenience, Mr. Christensen," she said calmly, as slow and smooth as a cello. "Thank you for calling back."

He waited for an explanation. Haygood offered none.

"You called me," he prompted.

"Yes. About the case we discussed. I wanted to follow up on some of the—" She cleared her throat. "—questions that arose regarding the investigation's integrity."

He wasn't being paranoid. The woman was being careful, cagey. He listened hard for the telltale signs of fear in her voice, but was reassured by its confidence. "Your concerns about the cause of death?" he said. "You've developed more information?"

"No, but my attempts to do so were met with unusual resistance. Do you understand what I'm telling you?"

Christensen felt like a Cold War spy. He turned around, wondering who might be watching. Except for a single rehab patient wheeling himself slowly toward the cafeteria, he was alone in the corridor. "Is there some reason we're speaking in code?" he said.

"Yes," Haygood said, "but I'll try to be as clear as I can."

Christensen tasted fear at the back of his throat. He looked around again.

"First, sir, do you have any additional information at this time you feel is relevant regarding the incident itself? Or any information about attempts which may have been made to obscure the actual cause of death?"

Haygood's question, so loaded with implication, struck with unexpected force. Christensen felt his legs go weak. "Yes," he said.

"Can you explain in general terms what that information might be?"

Was it information, really? A vague conversation with Floss Underhill that seemed to confirm the link between Chip Underhill's death, the disappearance of the gray horse, and Warren Doti? His unfocused suspicion that the deputy coroner who investigated the child's death knew more than he was saying? A theory about an impossibly coldhearted effort to stop damaging memories from leaking from Floss Underhill's brain? Maura Pearson's unexplained death?

"I believe—" he began. "Several things have happened that make me think there's an ongoing effort to obscure the cause of death in this case. A very *determined* effort."

He let his words hang. Haygood listened without responding.

"Look," he said finally, "I think we need to be clear. We may be in a very dangerous situation, and at this point confusion or ambiguity could make things worse. I'd like to speak more freely."

Haygood was silent so long that Christensen wondered if she'd hung up. "Hello?" he said.

"Go ahead then," she said finally, "but no names."

Christensen looked around one more time to make sure he was alone. "I'm pretty sure the family is involved in trying to cover up the circumstances of the child's death, for reasons that should be obvious today, of all days," he said.

"I don't understand."

"Election day."

"Go on."

Christensen nodded to a passing occupational therapist and waited until she'd passed out of earshot. "You'd know better than I do what actually may have happened to the boy, but you can imagine how damaging the story might be if it ever got out."

"Please wait." Through the phone, Christensen heard the clip-clop of footsteps along what must have been the courthouse corridor. Haygood waited until they receded before saying, "Go on."

"I think the deputy coroner who handled this case knows more than he's saying, may even have been a part of covering it up. But I also think he's not entirely comfortable with his role. I think one family member may know what happened, or at least suspects something, and may be trying to communicate that to me and to others. That's gotten her family very concerned in the past few weeks. There may have been an effort to keep her quiet, and—" He checked the Harmony hallways again, just to be sure.

"Mr. Christensen?"

"I'm here. It's just, this is going to sound pretty far-fetched, because I have no proof whatsoever. But two people who I think knew about the attempt to keep the family member quiet have disappeared, may even be dead. And there's another person, a woman I work with . . . I think word must have gotten back to the family that she was looking into the whole mess, and now she's dead, too. And I'm looking at all these things, all these isolated events, and the only way it all fits together is if you begin with the scenario you suggested when we first met, that the child's death couldn't have happened the way they said. Does any of that make sense to you?''

"Yes.''

"Can you tell me what you've found on your end?''

Haygood paused, then seemed to laugh. The reaction caught Christensen off guard.

"You don't buy it?'' he said.

"I deal in theories, Mr. Christensen. Because of the nature of what I do, they are my reality. No one ever tells me what really happened. I'm left to sift the details, then reconstruct a story from that which is indisputable. Sometimes what I build looks like a house of cards, but sometimes, *sometimes*, it's solid enough to hold up.''

She stopped. He needed more. "Right now, I need you to be clear,'' he said. "What are you saying?''

"I'm saying I'm in the same position as you on this. Do I have anything solid? No, I do not. But even if we don't know exactly what happened here, I'm getting some interesting official reactions to my questions about this case. Similar stimulus, *unusual* response. Going from our premise, your theory makes sense.''

Christensen thought of Brenna, of how vulnerable she suddenly seemed standing at the center of this quagmire. That she'd stepped into it willingly and ignored his earlier warnings was understandable, if not forgivable. "Please be specific,'' he said. "Other people might be in danger.''

Haygood waited. She was so guarded when they first met, and pushing her made him realize how far she'd already come. Something, maybe his naïveté that first day they met, had earned her trust. He felt a partnership with her, like the unshakable bond between soldiers under fire.

"I've been warned away from pursuing this case any further," she said.

"Warned away? By?"

"It's a complicated situation, political. Word got out that I'd focused on this case, and the response was immediate."

"Dagnolo?"

A long pause. "My boss is a political man, Mr. Christensen, but in this case I believe the pressure is coming from somewhere else. Political pressure from someone who numbers the family in question among his most generous supporters."

"One of the county supervisors?"

"Yes."

It could have been any one of them, Christensen thought. The Underhills were generous donors to anyone who might someday be useful. But it didn't really matter. "What sort of pressure?"

"Let's just say that the issue of funding came up in a conversation with my boss, who passed it along to me."

"Funding for the Child Death Review Team? Someone threatened to pull the plug on it?"

"Precisely. To use their phrase, 'We don't want any witch hunts.' "

Christensen steadied himself against the wall, leaning his full weight against the pay-phone carrel.

"But, how did anyone know? Forgive me for saying so, but you strike me as pretty cagey, not someone who goes around telling people, even your boss, what you're up to."

Another pause. "After we spoke, I made a records request at the morgue. The file I had was incomplete, and I wanted more information. Specifically, I wanted the autopsy photographs and X-rays that should have been in there. They'd tell me right quick what we're looking at, whether what the deputy coroner decided about the cause of death was justified. The compression marks we talked about. Cranial damage. I'm guessing here, but at that point only one person besides you was aware of my interest in this case. He works at the coroner's office."

Christensen flashed on the face of a black man. Its features were indistinct except for the thick horn-rimmed Malcolm X glasses. "The records clerk," he said.

"Has to be," Haygood said. "He's the choke point. I think he's keeping an eye on those files, letting somebody know if anyone comes looking."

Christensen felt sick. He remembered filling out a records-release form the day he asked for the file. How much information had he given? How much was too much?

"You got the files, though, right?"

"I got what's there," she said. "It's what's not there that's got me curious."

It took a few seconds, but Christensen caught on. "The photographs."

"X-rays, too," she said. "Nothing."

From the forbidding signs that had surfaced, phrases from Bostwick's disjointed message burst to mind: *Life insurance. Always leave yourself an out. Some things you can't deny. Got what you need.*

"I think I know who might have copies," Christensen said. "Or at least I know someone who knows something about them. I got a call last night—"

The faint sound of a woman's footsteps stopped him. They were close, somewhere around the corner of Harmony's long main corridor but approaching fast, the distinctive sound of high heels on smooth concrete.

"Mr. Christensen?"

"Guy named Bostwick," he said, keeping his voice low. "The deputy coroner who handled the case three years ago. He was drunk, I think, going on about how he had what we needed, talking about his insurance policy. But it was in the context of this case, because I'd called him about it and asked him some questions. Hold on a sec."

The footsteps were just around the corner, still approaching fast. Something in their rhythm suggested purpose, and they stood out among the shuffling struggles and quiet passage of wheelchairs in the research center's main hallway. Suddenly, Brenna rounded the corner, nearly colliding with him with a startled yelp. What was she doing here? He knew from her eyes, even before she recognized him, that something was wrong. She backed off, regained her composure, then paced back and forth in the corridor. She wouldn't look him in the eye.

"Stay with me," he said into the phone. "Hold on, okay?"

He put his hand over the receiver. "Bren? What is it?"

She mouthed the words, "Who's that?"

"Carrie Haygood."

Brenna rolled her eyes.

"I trust her," he whispered, his hand still covering the mouthpiece. "She's getting pressure—"

"Is something wrong, Mr. Christensen?" Haygood asked.

He removed his hand. "No, no. Just hold on, please."

Brenna waited until he covered the mouthpiece again. "They killed the boy," she said in an urgent whisper. "Ford told me what happened."

Christensen reached for Brenna, impulsively wanting to hold her close, but she backed away. His second impulse was to relay that information to Haygood, but Brenna grabbed his wrist as he uncovered the phone's mouthpiece.

"That's between us," she said.

"She needs to know," he said.

Brenna shook her head, her glare leaving no room for debate.

"She says the photos and X-rays of the child aren't in the coroner's files," he whispered. "Bostwick has them, or copies of them. I'm almost sure of it. She's also getting heavy pressure to stay away from this thing, from people with ties to the family."

"Mr. Christensen? Is everything all right?" Haygood's

voice filled Christensen's head even as the world shrank to himself and Brenna. "Mr. Christensen?"

"I'm here," he said. "I'm fine."

"Anything wrong?"

Christensen kept his eyes on Brenna, holding her gaze, hoping to hold her trust. He uncovered the telephone's mouthpiece. "If the possibilities we've discussed about this case were true, Carrie," he began, "how important would those photographs and X-rays be in proving or disproving what actually happened?"

Brenna was watching him, suspicious, maybe startled that he and Haygood already were talking in such terms. But she didn't interfere.

Haygood considered her answer a long time. "Short of an exhumation order, which I don't think we'd get in this case, they may be the only way to prove it didn't happen the way they say. If they're conclusive, they'd suggest very strongly how it did happen. Having said that, let me just add that it would be very unusual for a deputy coroner to have material like that."

"Unless he was part of it," Christensen said. "Say he was bought off. Say he agreed to support the story, or just agreed to look the other way if any evidence conflicted with the horseback-riding story. He'd want some security. Maybe for his own safety. Maybe to blackmail the people who paid him off. Hell, maybe the guy's just got a conscience—that'd be a nice change of pace. But more than anyone else, he'd know the value of those photos and X-rays, wouldn't he? And just based on the message he left on my answering machine, I think he's got copies."

In the silence that followed, Brenna's glare intensified. Christensen felt like a man in a vise. But everything fit. Bostwick was trying to tell him something with that business about insurance policies and getting himself out of hell a bit sooner.

"Way I see it," Haygood said, "we've got to find out. Word's already out that we're looking into this thing. It's just a matter of time before they shut us down, maybe twenty-four hours. And I can't jeopardize my work here. There's too many other cases that need attention, Mr. Christensen. I can't let them pull the plug on the review team. I just can't.''

Christensen weighed her words, trying to understand. He felt more vulnerable than he had in years, utterly exposed in a way he hadn't been since the Primenyl case. He thought of Maura Pearson, of the Chembergos, of Annie and Taylor and the eggshell that insulated them from this unfolding nightmare. As of now, he was defenseless. They all were.

Brenna's eyes had softened into a look of pure anxiety. He covered the mouthpiece. ''We should get the kids from school,'' he said. ''I want them with one of us.''

She nodded.

To Haygood again, he offered the only help he could: ''I'll try to find Bostwick.''

33

Christensen bounced the Explorer over a curb, nearly sideswiping a white van full of special-needs students that was blocking the Westminster-Stanton School's parking-lot entrance. The shortcut didn't help. The lot was jammed with cars and buses, some of them garishly decorated in streamers and poster paint celebrating the girls' soccer team. A steady stream of parents and students were moving toward the school's small stadium, where he could see a game already underway.

He cut off a minivan, triggering a harsh hand gesture from an otherwise pleasant-looking mom, and bounced over another curb onto the street. A block away, he found a too-small spot in front of a fire hydrant and wedged in. He'd pay a ticket, if it came to that, but right now he wanted, needed, to find Annie and Taylor.

Kids' Korner was the name given to two modular buildings set at a back corner of the school property. Far from the perfect after-school program, it was where the young children of the school's working parents could report between the end of classes at 3 P.M. and the arrival of parents by six. Christensen already was looking for an alternative. The staff was too young, kids themselves, really, probably earning minimum wage to make sure nobody got hurt or misbehaved. But that was about as constructive as the program got. After less than a week, he'd decided the facilities were inadequate, the staff was disorganized and apathetic, the kids bored. Annie was calling it "Kids' Cage" after just two days, but Christensen hadn't yet had time to find something better. He fought his way across campus, suddenly aware of how accessible the modular buildings were to the wide-open playground and public streets that ran along the school's unlocked back fence.

He opened the Kids' Korner door and stepped from bright sunshine into a dim room full of cross-legged preadolescent zombies, their eyes fixed on a glowing television screen to his right. Why weren't they playing outside? The group guffawed at a butt joke that Christensen recognized from *Ace Ventura, Pet Detective*, a movie he'd forbidden Annie and Taylor to watch at home. As his eyes adjusted to the darkness, he vowed to place the kids in another program within a week.

Faces emerged, upturned and lit blue by the television's glow. He recognized some among the thirty or so in the slack-jawed crowd, but didn't see Annie or Taylor. He scanned the group again, just to be sure. Christensen stepped lightly through the crowd of kids toward one of the program's afternoon supervisors at the back of the room. The woman, maybe nineteen and morbidly overweight, was flipping absently through an IKEA catalog and didn't look up.

"I'm looking for Annie Christensen and Taylor Kennedy," he said finally. "Do you know where they are?"

His intrusion only seemed to intensify her concentration as she studied a page of $25 floor lamps.

"Excuse me?" he said, louder.

She scanned the group in front of the TV, then offered a noncommittal shrug. "Checked the other building?"

Christensen squinted as he stepped back outside and

made his way down the ramp to the adjacent building. He opened its door into a riot of fluorescent light, the smell of school glue, and a flash of pride that Annie and Taylor apparently would rather work on art projects than watch mindless videos. But his stomach knotted as he scanned the two dozen faces there. Where were they?

Another fat supervisor was applying a Band-Aid to the forehead of a teary boy whose torn jeans and crumpled shirt suggested he'd recently lost a fight. "Have you seen Annie Christensen or Taylor Kennedy? They're not in either building."

The woman looked up. She was older, maybe twenty-five, but with a world-weary look that made her seem ten years older. "Who?" she said.

Christensen tried, for a moment, to keep his anger in check. He failed. "I wonder if there might be someone here who gives a shit?"

The injured boy's head shot up. The woman glared. She handed the kid an ice pack and stood, snapping off her latex gloves and dropping them into a nearby wastebasket.

"No need to get hostile, sir. What can I do for you?"

"I'm looking for my kids. They're not in either building."

"You checked the playground?"

"No."

"The handball courts?"

Christensen shook his head.

"If they're here, that's where they'd be. What were their names again?"

Like it mattered, Christensen thought. He turned and stalked out, headed for the nearly empty playground. A group of maybe ten kids were scrimmaging with a football. Annie might be among them, Christensen thought, but not Taylor. But he didn't recognize either of them among the players as he drew closer. Three other kids, all boys, all unfamiliar, were taking turns tossing a playground ball toward a netless basketball hoop, playing Pig. The handball courts were empty.

With a flash of daylight, he burst into the dim room where *Ace Ventura* was playing, the door propelled by his angry shove and righteous indignation. Still, most of the kids' eyes never left the screen. The supervisor waddled across the room and met him halfway.

"I'm having a little trouble finding my kids here," he said, struggling for control, "and I'm not getting a hell of a lot of help from your staff."

"You checked the crafts room?"

"And the playground."

Something in the woman's eyes told Christensen everything he needed to know: She had no idea where Annie and Taylor were.

"Let's check the sign-out sheet," she said.

He dutifully signed the clipboard every morning and evening, logging the times he dropped off and picked up the kids each day. Other than occasional reminders to parents that a full signature was required by state law, he had no idea what practical use the Kids' Korner staff found for the logs. No one seemed to notice or care who came and went, but he followed the bovine woman across the room anyway and watched her scan the rows of names and signatures.

"What were their names again?"

"Christensen and Kennedy," he said. "Annie and Taylor."

The woman pointed to a spot in the middle of the top page. "Here's the problem, then. Your wife or somebody else picked them up half an hour ago." She handed him the clipboard with a smug smile.

Christensen snatched it from her hands, looking for familiar handwriting among the blur of scribbles across the page. The names of enrollees were printed in alphabetical order along the left edge of the chart, last names first. He'd signed both of them in that morning at 7:36. His scrawled signature was beside each name, but there also was a signature in the space to sign the kids out. He looked closer, trying to decipher handwriting that definitely wasn't his or Brenna's.

He thrust the clipboard back at the supervisor. "Can you read this name?"

She scissored open two slats of a closed miniblind and squinted into the wedge of daylight. "Somebody named Robbins. Tony, maybe? Tony Robbins?"

Christensen swallowed hard, tried not to think the worst as he grabbed the clipboard back. "Could that be another parent? Maybe they signed on our lines by mistake."

"I don't recognize the name, but we have over fifty kids here," she said.

Christensen didn't find a single Robbins on the list. "Did you see who signed them out?"

The woman shook her head.

"Did you even check to see if this person was authorized to sign them out?"

She looked as if she might cry.

Christensen pushed past her and jabbed the power button on the television. The room went dark, so he reached between the set and the window and yanked the cord of the nearest miniblind. The *Ace Ventura* fans protested as one, shielding their eyes like cave dwellers prodded into daylight.

"Does anybody here know Annie Christensen or Taylor Kennedy?" he demanded.

One boy stood up. " 'Do *not* go in there,' " he said, waving away an imaginary odor, pantomiming one of the movie's sillier bathroom jokes. Peals of laughter.

"I need some help here before I turn it back on," Christensen said. "How about it? Anybody?"

A tiny blond girl with pink-framed eyeglasses raised her hand. "I know Taylor," she said.

Christensen bore in with an intensity that seemed to frighten the girl. He tried without success to keep his voice even. "He left a little while ago. Did you see who he left with?"

The girl shook her head.

"It's okay, thank you," he said, eyeballing the supervisor. "It's not your job, sweetheart. Anybody else?"

"Annie has red hair, right?" asked the boy who stood up earlier.

Christensen shook his head. "Sort of blondish brown."

The kid shrugged. "Never mind."

Christensen couldn't waste any more time. He shoved the door open and ran out onto the playground, toward the pile of kids on the football field. "I'm looking for Annie Christensen or Taylor Kennedy. Do any of you guys know either one of them?"

The players, all boys, untangled themselves and stood up, a riot of denim and grass stains. "Annie was here a while ago," said one freckled ruffian. Christensen recognized him from Howe Street, but didn't know his name. "She left."

"Where'd she go?" he said.

The boy pointed to a gate along the school's back fence. "Over there."

"Do you know why?"

The kid shrugged. "That other kid was talking to some guy through the fence."

"Taylor?"

"I don't know his name. Is it her brother?"

"Are they in trouble?" another kid said.

Christensen ignored the questions, focusing on the kid from their neighborhood. "How long ago?"

"A half-hour, maybe."

"What did the guy look like?"

"Just some guy. Why?"

"How was he dressed? Did he have a car?"

Christensen's tone was sobering up the freckled kid, fast. "A suit, like dark blue or black. White shirt, I think. Black car. He was pretty far away."

"Did it seem like Annie and Taylor knew him?"

"Dunno."

"How long did they talk?"

"A while. We were playing Steelers."

"Did he come onto the playground?"

The boy shuffled his feet. "I think so, but I don't know."

Christensen hesitated before asking the next question, as if speaking the words might make it true. "Did they leave with him?"

The kid looked around, suddenly aware that all eyes were on him. "We were playing Steelers," he said.

"So you didn't see?"

A black-haired boy stepped around his teammate. He wore his untucked shirt like a badge of honor. "I was over playing basketball. They had their packs and lunchboxes and stuff, headed that way." He pointed to the gate again.

Christensen felt sick. Annie and Taylor knew better than to leave with a stranger. But what if the stranger knew their names? Or knew enough about Brenna or him to make a convincing case? He couldn't outrun the possibilities as he sprinted across campus toward his car.

Christensen snatched the fluttering parking ticket from under the Explorer's windshield wiper, opened the door, and tossed it across to the passenger's side. He juggled the car phone and the stick shift in his right hand as he bullied his way out of the tight parking spot, nudging the cars in front and behind, trying to decide whether to call 911 or home.

He dialed his home number as he lurched into traffic. Maybe he'd misunderstood Brenna. Maybe. But no. Even before she answered, he knew. There was no other possible explanation. Someone had taken their kids.

"Bren?"

"Where are you?"

"Tell me you have the kids." He squeezed the steering wheel tighter during the long silence.

"What are you saying?"

"So you don't have them?"

"Don't fuck with me, Jim. This thing is too—"

"Jesus." How to tell her? "Bren, someone signed them out of Kids' Korner. Used a fake name, and apparently they left with him."

"Him?"

Christensen ran a stop sign a block from the school. The crossing guard in his rearview mirror stood defiantly in the middle of the intersection, apparently taking down his license plate number. "Couple of the other kids saw them talking to some suit at the fence about thirty minutes before, then whoever it was signed a fake name and they left. I looked everywhere. The goddamned staff didn't have a clue."

"The kids wouldn't do that, Jim," Brenna said, clinging to a faded possibility. "Taylor wouldn't."

"Bren, I'm pretty sure they did."

Christensen cradled the phone between his shoulder and his ear as he worked the Explorer up through the gears on Penn Avenue. Traffic was mercifully light; rush hour hadn't yet started. "I'm five minutes from the house," he said. "You call the police."

"I don't . . . There's . . . You're sure?"

"They're not there. No one I talked to saw them leave, but *someone* signed them out and I couldn't find them. They're gone, Bren."

A screeching yellow-light left turn onto Fifth. Had she responded? "Bren?"

"I'm here."

"Just call. I'm on Fifth Avenue, so I'll be right there."

He wished he hadn't hung up. Alone in the car, he searched for some trace, any trace, of the optimism that usually sustained him. He wanted to believe it was a misunderstanding, that Annie and Taylor had simply made other arrangements, that some kindly uncle was driving the carpool and simply confused the days. But there were no local relatives, no carpool. What made sense, the only thing that did, was a scenario that could pass for a flop-sweat nightmare: They'd blundered into something bigger than they ever imagined, and now it was too late to back away. On their first try, the Underhills had found the fleshy pink chink in his armor, then shoved to the hilt. Nothing else made sense.

Howe Street was a jumble of cars. He could see their house two blocks away, but had to wait excruciating minutes as two amateurs tried to parallel park, then tried and tried again. Brenna was pacing the front porch, arms folded across her chest, when he wedged the Explorer sideways in the alley entrance. It was probably the only opening for blocks. He left it unlocked with the emergency lights flashing. Brenna watched him take the porch stairs in a single bound, but even from the street he thought he saw muted panic in her eyes. Could she see the anger in his?

Brenna turned and walked back into the house.

"What'd they say?" he said.

She stopped in the front hall, her back to him.

"Bren?"

He expected tears, terror. But when she turned, she had the look of someone well in control.

"We're not calling the police, not right now," she said, refolding her arms. Her voice was defiant, certain, even.

"The hell we aren't. Enough, Bren. You're too close to this. You can't see what I see, and I see your goddamned clients completely out of control."

He knew he'd swung wildly, exorcising the doubts he'd had about the Underhills, and her, since this all began. He respected the role of a criminal-defense attorney, but he could no longer abide Brenna's defense of the indefensible.

Brenna absorbed his words like body blows, not surrendering, but not defending herself either. "They're not my clients now. Look, we can deal with my stupidity later. But we've got some decisions to make right now, and I just think we need to be smarter than calling the cops."

"Because you still don't think the Underhills are capable of this, do you?"

She waited, ignoring the bait.

"And you don't think we should call?" he said.

"No."

If she'd wavered, if he'd heard even the slightest hitch in her voice or seen a flicker of doubt in her eyes, he might have pushed it. But the way she stood, the way she spoke, he knew Brenna was somehow two steps ahead of him.

"You don't trust the police?" he said.

"Do you?"

He thought of Bostwick, of the coroner's odd clerk, of the politicians of both parties whose fealty to the Underhills was unquestioned and unchallenged. Brenna put his thoughts into words.

"Think about it, Jim. This is a family that demands loyalty, even pays for it. If they could buy a deputy coroner, who else could they buy? Cops would be easy, probably cheap. Who else? The sheriff? Even the D.A.? What if their feud with Dagnolo is just a cover?"

"There's nobody down there you could call? Somebody who wouldn't just blow off this whole story as paranoia or fantasy?"

"Maybe, but they'd be starting from zero. We don't have time to start someone at the beginning and bring them up to speed. Are you ready to take the chance they'll buy it and follow up?"

She hugged him, holding on like someone whose fingers had found a rock in roiling white water. He wished he still trusted her instincts.

"What, then, Bren? I'm scared."

"Me, too. But—" She pushed him away.

"But what?"

"What would they accomplish by hurting the kids?" Her voice was analytical, wrung of emotion. "They wouldn't."

"You're pretty damned sure," he said. "I don't get it."

She stared. "They hurt the kids, they've got nothing on us, nothing to keep us quiet. They play that card, they've got no hand. And I think they're smarter than that."

Christensen couldn't stand it. "Bren, this is Annie and Taylor we're talking about. They're not—"

With a brusque sweep of her arm, she cut him off. "Think *logically*, goddamn it. We have to now."

After two weeks in the new house, boxes still littered the front hall. Those that hadn't been unpacked were shoved against walls, out of the way. Brenna knelt beside one labeled B. K. DOWNSTAIRS STUDY and popped the tape that kept it closed, oblivious to the dust she was grinding into the hem of her skirt.

"I've dealt with people like this before," she said. "The Underhills move in a subtler world, but they know the same thing any Blood, Crip, pimp, or mob guy knows: It's all just control. It's like judo. To control someone, you have to know their pressure points."

Brenna pulled a handful of books out of the box and set them on the floor. She probed the remaining contents of the box, refolded the top flaps, then opened another one that was marked the same way.

"They're showing us they know how to control us, but they understand the deal. They lose their advantage the second something happens to the kids. At that point we'd have nothing to lose."

More books. Brenna made a face as she peered into the box.

"I want to believe that, Bren, but I don't think it's that simple. I mean, Maura probably had pressure points. They didn't exactly work those before—"

Brenna waved him off. She sat back on her feet, brushed the dust from her knees with a chop of her hand. He could tell the comment had thrown her off stride. "With us, they're showing what's possible," she said. "That's all. Jim, I believe that. I have to. Otherwise—"

Her eyes drifted, caught suddenly on another box. She moved two small boxes to get to it, then popped the tape that held it closed.

"So, what then? If you're right, Bren, if we play by their rules, they've got us, forever. Say we don't call the police, and the kids come back safe and sound. Can we live with that threat the rest of our lives? Can we live . . .

hell, could we look ourselves in the mirror every morning knowing what these people are capable of?"

Brenna stopped digging through the box, but didn't turn around. "I can," she said.

"You're a lawyer. You're used to it."

She wheeled on him, a familiar gun in her right hand, a small yellow box in the left. Her eyes were like jade-green lasers, searing straight through to the back of his skull. "Look, fuck you. You've never made a mistake? You've never misjudged anybody? Jesus God, Jim, save the sanctimony for sometime when it matters what you think about me. Right now, let's just deal with what's happened and sort the rest out later. Deal?"

Christensen felt sick as she set the box on a nearby plant stand and released the pistol's clip. She opened the box and, one by one, pushed the bullets inside. She must have noticed the color drain from his face. "You just never know," she said.

"I'm not . . . Bren, don't. We need help. We're in over our heads here."

She shoved the loaded gun and the box of bullets into her purse. "We can swim," she said, looking up.

"But we're not the only ones in the water now. They've got the kids."

Neither wanted to linger too long on the thought.

"Right now, the worst thing we could do is panic," Brenna said. "The worst thing. They're going to play this out their way. We just have to let them and assume they won't panic, either. That's all we've got."

Christensen ran a hand through his hair, brushing away the few strands that hung over his forehead. "For now," he said.

"Meaning?"

He closed his eyes, wishing his head were clearer. But from the murky snarl of theories and hypotheticals that defined the Underhill mess from the beginning rose a single, certain truth. "There still may be a trump card out there somewhere," he said.

When he opened his eyes, he knew he had Brenna's full attention.

"The autopsy photos. The X-rays. I think Bostwick has them. Carrie Haygood thinks so, too."

Brenna's eyes narrowed as she considered the possibility. "You don't know that. And even if he does, we're nowhere near getting them."

Christensen shook his head. "I could try."

"If we *did* have something like that—"

He nodded. "Pressure point."

Something crashed behind the closed door of their downstairs office, a thunderous sound preceded by nothing, the sound of sudden and uncontrolled violence. He turned toward the door at the end of the hall, but felt Brenna's firm hand on his arm. She held a finger to her lips, then reached into her purse.

Christensen pulled away, headed down the hall. The sound was too big, too outrageous to be an intruder, even a clumsy one. He opened the office door into a nightmare of ruined electronics and water trickling from a yawning hole in the ceiling above his desk, at the exact spot where he'd noticed the moisture stain. He knew that beneath the pile of soggy plaster his printer would never print again, and that his computer was dead.

"Holy shit," Brenna said, lowering her gun. "The leak."

Christensen turned and urged Brenna back out, then closed the door on a disaster that couldn't have seemed more trivial.

35

"Let me make it real clear what's at stake here."

Christensen was on the road again, wheeling through rush-hour traffic toward the Parkway East, holding his car phone like a lifeline. Bostwick had listened without a word as he sketched the broad outlines of the story, skipping over details that would need longer explanations. If Christensen was right, the man already knew the story. He just needed to know how much more deadly it had become. When he was done, though, all Bostwick had said was, "Told you not to call me at home."

"Look, I don't know you, you don't know me, but I know what you've got." Christensen remembered Bostwick's voice on the rambling phone message, its drunken defiance masking fear. He was sure now it was the voice of a man who no longer wanted to carry the burden he'd shouldered three years before. "You kept those autopsy films. I don't know why, or how, and I don't have time to figure it out. What I need you to understand is what's happening right now, what these people are capable of. It's way beyond just covering up forensic evidence. A woman the Underhills thought was on to them is dead.

Two other people have disappeared and may be dead. When they figured out I'd pieced it all together—'' Christensen's voice caught. ''I think they've just taken my kids.''

Christensen could hear Bostwick breathing, even over the road noise. But Bostwick wasn't denying, wasn't backpedaling. The man was thinking, and Christensen knew then that his strategy had worked. Bostwick had a dirty little secret of his own, and he knew it was out.

''I'm guessing the family bought your cooperation,'' Christensen said. ''I want you to know I'm not judging you. I don't care about that right now. I can't. What I care about is making sure no one else gets hurt, and the only way I know to shut them down is with those films.''

He waited through a long silence. Finally: ''You shouldn't have called this number.''

''Look, Simon, I'm sorry. But the clock's ticking. I'm just getting on the Parkway. I'll take the Turnpike from Monroeville.''

''You're coming here? Now?''

''There's no time. I need your help. Please.''

''Oh, Christ. It's bad enough you called here—''

''What's your address?''

''No fucking way.''

Christensen passed a Corvette on the Parkway entrance ramp, his adrenaline pumping, but at the same time he felt himself go limp. He'd brought Bostwick this far on bluff and confidence, but what would he do if that stopped working? ''Please help me,'' he said suddenly, startled by the raw desperation in his voice.

''Christ,'' Bostwick said. ''You've got no idea.''

''Please,'' Christensen whispered.

He waited, trying to interpret the deputy coroner's silence as the man faced down the truth. Christensen had left no room for doubt; Bostwick knew he knew. Christensen drove on, sensing the man's dilemma, knowing he'd destroyed the rationalizations that had sustained Bostwick during his alliance with the Underhills. Psychologically, Bostwick was exposed without a shield.

"You're maybe ninety minutes away," Bostwick said at last. "There's a little place in Champion, just off 31. Cook's Corner, it's called. Stop there."

Christensen breathed again. He fished into the Explorer's door pocket for his western Pennsylvania map. "Ninety minutes," he repeated. "Cook's Corner. Thank you. That a restaurant, or what?"

The phone clicked, and Bostwick was gone. Ahead, traffic was moving smoothly along the Parkway East toward the Squirrel Hill Tunnel. If his luck held, the inevitable delay at the tunnel would be short. If it didn't, he'd be late. His finger found the phone's speed dial button and he punched in the code for home. He should let Brenna know.

Busy.

"Shit," he said. "Come on, Bren."

He tried again. Still busy. A mile short of the tunnel, taillights glowed red—a mixed blessing. It would slow his trip to the Laurel Highlands and his meeting with Bostwick, but the snarled traffic would give him a few more minutes before passing through the tunnel. After that, his chance of a getting a clear cellular connection to Brenna was pretty slim. He wasn't looking forward to being out of cellular range, thinking about all the possible consequences of what he was about to do. Then he realized he wasn't alone, that the Explorer was crowded with demons—residual rage, insurgent fear, self-doubt, guilt. He was about to spend the next ninety minutes with the carpool from hell.

Annie's face flashed into his mind, giving him one of her full-pout, Machiavelli-in-pigtails glares and demanding to know what the hell was going on and why he wasn't doing something about it. He wondered where she was, wondered how whoever had her would react if she got rude or defiant, which of course she would. He'd known for years she was indomitable; that she was still just eight years old was irrelevant. She'd inherited her mother's strength and, from somewhere, the resolve of a pit bull.

"Poor bastards," he said, thinking of her kidnappers, trying hard to smile at his hopeful little joke.

Busy again. Who could Brenna be talking to? Christensen fell into the obedient line of cars squeezing through Pittsburgh's eastern choke point, waiting, dialing, waiting some more, creeping toward the tunnel entrance and God-knows-what on the other side.

36

Brenna knew she was pacing, trying to keep a step ahead of panic, but her rational façade crumbled as soon as she hung up the phone. She trusted Levin, knew he was as deep into this swamp as they were, but what he'd told her in confidence just now left her no illusions. Enrique Chembergo had seen enough on that gazebo deck ten days earlier to reduce the Underhill name to a cinder.

Why he'd told Levin more than he told the sheriff's investigators was, she guessed, a secret that died with him. But no, the gardener didn't just hear a scuffle and see someone running from the scene after Floss went into the ravine. He saw a struggle, saw the old woman clock her attacker once as he surprised her from behind, saw the man cup his hand over her mouth, press her back against the wooden railing, and boost her into the void as she screamed and clutched and fell from sight. And he'd given Levin the attacker's name: Mr. Staggers.

She passed the stairs again, avoiding what she knew was at the top—Taylor's room. It was too real. For now, she was clinging to abstractions, hoping the thin veneer of emotional distance would protect her from flat-out hysteria. Jim was right. She'd ignored the signs, let the defender's zeal and political ambition blind her to the truth. How could she step into her son's room, see his Batman sheets and his odd collections of boyhood, and at the same time know that he now was in the malevolent hands of people she'd trusted?

And yet, here she was at the top of the stairs, drawn to the bedroom door like a moth to a flame. She felt the danger, knew it wasn't smart, but she pushed it open anyway and stepped in, wishing suddenly she'd spent more time there.

Even at seven, Taylor had arranged his new room with a decorator's attention to detail. He was a neat child, frighteningly so, and nothing was out of place despite the usual morning rush to school. His maple bed was made, the Batman logo on the spread perfectly centered, the sheets turned neatly over the spread's lip. The caped crusader glared from the case of a perfectly plumped pillow. The frothy pink bows and pink front wheels of his Barbie skates, inherited from Annie, peeked from beneath the bed frame. A withered lei she had brought back from Hawaii two years ago hung around one of the short posts of the headboard. Why hadn't she taken Taylor with her?

His brass piggy bank sat on one corner of his desk, no doubt full. Taylor was a conservative child, the antithesis of Jim's Annie. Taylor had coveted the black lacquer pen and pencil set that once sat on her office desk, and she knew the moment she offered it that no Christmas gift she'd ever give him could delight him more. It was placed along the desk's outer edge, the pen and pencil ready for plucking by some efficient junior executive. Other than that, the desk's top surface was clear. It looked like the work space of an honors graduate from a time-management seminar. Sentimental items and other distractions—his geode collection, two model airplanes webbed with Testor's glue, a plastic ant farm filled with industrious workers—were relegated to a shelf across the room. His father, the CPA, would be so proud.

The bookshelf seemed messy, with the spines of varying sizes placed side by side. Tall books next to short books, fat books next to skinny books, paperbacks next to hardcovers, an apparent hodgepodge of volumes until she recognized her son's personality at work. The books weren't arranged by size, but alphabetically, starting with *Aardvark's Ark* and ending with *Where's Waldo*. She smiled.

The walls were bare except for a single photograph taken during his first and only AYSO soccer game. He'd quit after the game, terrified by a coach's gentle reprimand. He'd been picking dandelions on defense, his attention diverted as a swarm of players shuffled past him toward an unlikely goal. In the photo, though, he was all business, crouched and ready for action, his voluminous shorts hanging nearly to the tops of his brand-new spikes, which never quite fit. Geek-boy gets physical.

And suddenly, she was crying, imagining her odd and irreplaceable baby in the hands of a stranger, possibly a killer. Brenna closed the door and leaned against it. She was alone. No one would know. But still she stifled a sob and went straight to the kids' bathroom for a tissue. The face in the mirror startled her. She'd stayed in control, kept it together while Jim was there. But now her eyes were rimmed in red, her hair falling in reckless strands across her forehead. It was as if the past hour had aged her five years.

Brenna wiped her eyes and tucked the stray hair behind her ears. She took a deep breath, then another, then headed back down the hall to their bedroom. She'd told Jim she'd wait by the phone, promised him, in fact. What she hadn't counted on, though, was the oppressive silence of the house, the overwhelming sense of isolation and helplessness. Inaction contradicted everything she understood about the world. She needed to do something.

She cleared her throat and tried to wring the anxiety from her voice, then jabbed the Record Greeting button on the answering machine.

"You have reached the home of Brenna Kennedy and Jim Christensen," she began. "We're not home right now, but you can still reach us by dialing our mobile phones." She enunciated her cell phone number and the number of Jim's car phone, knowing he was probably out of range. "We very much want to talk to you. Please call."

She played back the greeting, distressed by the wavering fear in her voice, at the weak-kneed plea at the end. She recited the Pledge of Allegiance, modulating the tone, projecting control, then recorded the greeting again, skipping the "Please call" at the end. It sounded better, stronger, determined but fearless.

Within minutes, she'd stepped out of her St. John suit and into her jeans and Reeboks. She pulled on one of Jim's dark-blue Pitt sweatshirts and gathered her hair into a tight ponytail. After one last look down the hall toward Taylor's room, she was back down the stairs and looking for her purse.

She found it where she'd left it, on the front-hall table. Its weight didn't surprise her because she knew the gun was inside. What surprised her was her resolve in picking it up and stepping without a second thought out the front door.

37

Cook's Corner Inn was the inevitable intersection of two of the nineties' most onerous trends—a rural gourmet coffee bar frequented by wealthy, urban Harley riders. Christensen was surrounded by men and women his age and older who were sheathed in leather, grasping at lost youth, pretending to be rugged individualists, the type of people who could take a Tuesday afternoon off if they damn well pleased.

None of them were Simon Bostwick.

Christensen drained his third cappuccino. How long should he wait? He'd arrived fifteen minutes late because of the Squirrel Hill Tunnel traffic, but Bostwick would have waited, wouldn't he? After twenty minutes, he'd quizzed a few Cook's Corner patrons about Bostwick. After thirty, he'd pretended to be an old friend and cadged some rough directions to Bostwick's house from a waitress who Christensen was sure had slept with the former deputy coroner. He looked down at the crude map she'd scribbled on the back of a napkin, then at his watch. Nearly an hour late—an hour Christensen didn't have to waste.

He slipped a $20 bill under the sugar bowl and stood up, nearly colliding with the waitress, a vivacious, high-mileage brunette, but no less stunning because of the world-weary lines around her eyes. Maybe more so.

"Where do you know Simon from again?"

"Pittsburgh," he said, flustered. "We've lost touch, though, since he moved up here." Backing away, Christensen knocked a spoon off the table. It clattered to the floor. He bent down to pick it up, and when he stood up she was eyeing him like prey.

"Be an odd time of day for him to be here," she said. "He's a partier. Mostly comes in for a java jolt after the bars, or first thing in the morning if he's been out all night."

"Still a partier, eh?" he bluffed. "That's Simon. Never on time, either."

The wall clock behind her read 7:04. Christensen wanted to find Bostwick's house before dark. He laid the spoon on the table beside the twenty.

"Lemme get you some change," she said.

Christensen shook his head. "It's fine, thanks. If he comes in, tell him I'm headed to his place and I'll wait for him there."

"Straight out Mountain Laurel Road, right at the ranger station," she repeated. "If you pass a tricked-out Sportster on the road between here and there, it's probably him."

Christensen backed toward the door. "Appreciate it."

Mountain Laurel Road ran in a straight line between Champion and the ski resort of Seven Springs, western Pennsylvania's version of Aspen but with hills instead of mountains. It billed itself in recreational brochures as a "year-round resort community," an effort, Christensen suspected, to attract the region's upscale second-home investors without stressing too heavily winter's often undependable snowfall. This time of year, its leafy trails and silent ski lifts were given over to mountain bikers. Every car Christensen passed had at least one bike on the roof rack.

He checked the napkin, then hit the brakes hard as he passed a ranger station on the left. The Explorer's speedometer plummeted from eighty-five to zero as it skidded to a stop. His heart was pounding, fueled by adrenaline and caffeine, as he jammed the transmission into reverse and backed up to the turn. In the dim, dusky light, he checked the napkin again. The waitress hadn't given the road a name, and now he could see why. It was hardly a road at all, but a narrow, unpaved tunnel of parallel tire tracks disappearing into the woods. A decent rain would turn it into a bog, but at the moment it seemed dry and passable. Still, he was glad he had four-wheel drive. She'd said to follow it all the way to the end.

Christensen turned on his headlights, trying to imagine Bostwick navigating the rutted road on a motorcycle. He passed an A-frame on his left, apparently unoccupied, and an identical one on the right. Every hundred yards or so, a For Sale sign designated another undeveloped lot. Maybe half a mile in, through a brace of birch trees just around a bend, he saw the pale glow of a window light. At the same moment, his headlights caught the rear reflectors of a car sitting squarely in the middle of the road, well away from what he now could see was another A-frame.

He turned off his headlights and killed the Explorer's engine with a vague something's-wrong-with-this-picture feeling. From the waitress's directions and the way it sat at the end of the road, he knew the far house was Bostwick's. He assumed Bostwick had a car as well as the motorcycle, but what would it be doing there, so far from the house and blocking the road?

Christensen stepped out, taking care to close the Explorer's door quietly. He was maybe a quarter-mile from the house, but the forest was silent and unforgiving. Something about the skewed scene still bothered him. Stealth couldn't hurt.

The car itself was a puzzle, a standard black Thunderbird with its engine still ticking. Three antennas of varying styles and lengths rose like stiff whiskers from the roof. Through the tinted driver's-side window, the car was alive with electronics—at least two telephones, a headset, a laptop computer, indecipherable black boxes. All along and underneath the dashboard, tiny red indicator lights blinked. Unfamiliar dials glowed pale green. It looked like a communications satellite on radial tires. Christensen wanted to lean closer, to press his face against the glass for a better look, but the car reeked of paranoia. Surely it was alarmed.

He walked in the right tire track toward the house, slower now, listening. The cabin sat at the road's dead end, sunk into a level spot of an otherwise hilly lot that reached up into thick woods. The lot had only two other structures, a separate garage to the left of the main house and a small, squat building no bigger than a child's playhouse on the hillside behind it. Inside, Christensen guessed, a single lamp was on.

Suddenly, the cabin's angled ceiling flooded with light. Someone inside had turned on the track lights that studded the roof beams. From where he stood, still downhill looking up, all Christensen could see was the ceiling and what appeared to be the railing of a loft. The sudden light was followed almost immediately by a crash, as if someone inside had upended a heavy piece of furniture. Then the sound of breaking glass.

He circled to the right, up a small hill that offered a view into the cabin's wide-open front windows. The ground was dry, but the climb was steep. Stepping from rock to root, he moved as quickly as he could in his slippery leather-soled loafers. Hooking one arm around a tree to hold himself steady, he tried to see across maybe fifty yards and over the front porch railing into the cabin's ground-floor living area. From there, though, the view was blocked by stacked firewood along the bottom of the windows. Christensen skidded down the loamy hillside and moved closer, climbing farther up another hill that was closer to the house and less steep.

A man inside was moving. Christensen squinted, trying to make out details. He had no idea what Bostwick looked like, but his first impression was that the man was older than Bostwick, and overdressed. A dark suit hung neatly over his stocky frame, its fine lines holding even as the man heaved cushions from the living-room couch. He tossed them across the room, then pulled open the frame of a sofa bed, stripped its sheets, tipped the mattress off the frame, then upended the entire couch and let it fall upside down, shattering a glass coffee table. Christensen thought, unexpectedly, of his father, of the one time alcohol had loosed his rage as his family cowered in a corner of their normally quiet house.

This was different. The man was too controlled. He pulled open the lap drawer of a desk, rifled the contents, then upended the drawer onto the floor. He repeated the procedure with each of the desk's other drawers, chuckling and talking to himself or to someone elsewhere in the cabin as he did. A two-drawer file cabinet beside the desk was next. The man walked his fingers across the tabs of the top drawer, occasionally pulling a file, opening it, then letting the contents drop to the floor like falling leaves. He bent down, out of sight, and presumably did the same with the bottom drawer. When he stood up, he casually tipped the filing cabinet onto its side.

Christensen looked away. He was breathing hard. The air tasted like chilled champagne, but that wasn't why he felt suddenly dizzy. He shook his head to clear the cobwebs, knowing instinctively he needed to think clearly.

It wasn't Bostwick. It couldn't be. Raging alcoholics sometimes ransack their own homes, but never systematically and with the patience this man showed. No, the man in the suit was looking for something, Christensen decided, and suddenly he understood. The scene blinked into focus like a high-speed Polaroid: The car. The dark suit. The search. This was the man in the dark suit who had been talking to the kids outside Kids' Korner four hours earlier. He worked for the Underhills. He was looking for the same thing Christensen was—the films from Chip Underhill's autopsy.

Who else could he be?

Where the hell were the kids?

A three-quarters moon was cresting the hill behind Bostwick's house. Its pale glow lit the thin white trunks of the birch trees, which surrounded Christensen like anorexic ghosts. For the moment, he had the advantage of being able to see what was happening inside the cabin without anyone seeing out. He looked for somewhere closer to the windows where he might perch unseen for a while, wondered if he could climb high enough in the maple tree to the left of the cabin's front porch to get a better view.

He sidestepped down the hill and into the cabin's carport, then hurried across to the base of the maple. Ten yards away, wooden steps led up to the front porch. They looked creaky and forbidding, too brightly lit by the lights from inside to give him the cover he needed. He tried the footing along the maple tree's trunk, but his shoes slid off as if the soles were icy. He slipped them off and tried again, grabbing the maple's lowest branch and swinging one leg up and over. Within minutes, he was where he needed to be, wedged in the crotch of two high branches, looking through a gap in the leaves into a part of the room he couldn't see from the hillside.

A second man was sitting on the floor, his hands behind his back, his flannel shirt open and askew. A web of blood covered the left side of his face, but he seemed conscious and alert. He answered whenever the other man spoke to him, but otherwise he watched the sacking in silence. At one point, he shifted positions and Christensen saw a glint of chrome at his wrists. If Christensen was right, Simon Bostwick was handcuffed to the railing at the bottom of the loft stairs.

Christensen could hear the roar of blood in his ears,

pumped by a heart in overdrive. The man in the suit was in the loft now. He hoisted a twin-bed mattress and leaned it against the angled ceiling. He did the same with another, then reached into his pants pocket. With a flick of his wrist, he snapped open a blade and traced an X across the face of one of the upended mattresses. Peeling away the ticking, he peered into the opening like a surgeon, then stepped to the next mattress and opened it the same way. Finding nothing there, he heaved both over the loft rail. The mattresses landed with a crash on the accumulated plates scattered across Bostwick's narrow plank dining table. The man disemboweled the box springs in the exact same way, but left them leaning against the loft ceiling when he was done. But as he walked back down the stairs, the open knife still in his hand, he seemed more agitated than before.

Christensen felt a prickly wave of dread in the hair on his neck as the man dragged the point of the blade along the wall toward the bottom of the stairs. The whole scene had a dreamy feel to it. When the man stopped in front of Bostwick, Christensen resisted the urge to look away. He breathed again when the man folded the blade into the knife's handle and put it back in his pocket.

But just as quickly, the man, still talking, reached into his suit coat, stooped down, and pressed the barrel of a gun against the side of Bostwick's head. Bostwick nodded, and the other man stood up. He circled slowly around and started up the loft steps again. About halfway up, he turned around and sat. Bostwick tried to turn, to keep the gun in sight, trying to see behind him. But his eyes were full of fear. The other man talked on, the conversation one-sided, and even without hearing the words, even from a distance, Christensen felt the man's cruelty. Bostwick was helpless, aware of the threat behind him but unable to face it down. The man wasn't just in danger; he was emasculated.

"Just give him what he wants," Christensen said out loud, resisting the urge to look away.

He wished he had.

With a muffled pop, Bostwick's head snapped, thrust backward by a jet of gore from the exit wound. His face transformed in an instant, like that of a startled child. When Bostwick slumped forward again, a crimson geyser suddenly rose straight up from the entry wound at the back of his head. His body went limp.

"Oh, Jesus," Christensen said.

He'd seen an execution only once—on black-and-white film, that unforgettable horror from the streets of Saigon—but there was no mistaking this. The man behind Bostwick moved up another step, casually putting more distance between himself and the shrinking fountain of blood. He put the gun back inside his suit coat, then took off one shoe and wiped its toe on the carpeted stair.

Christensen retched twice, as quietly as he could. It tasted like coffee grounds.

Steadying himself against the maple's branches, he forced himself to look back through the window. The killer was moving again, stepping carefully around the flannel heap and the widening pool beside it. Christensen wouldn't—couldn't—let his eyes stop there. Still, his stomach lurched again.

The killer disappeared behind the stairs, into what looked like the cabin's kitchen. Maybe with his final nod and a gun to his head, Bostwick had finally told where he hid the films. Even so, would the killer shoot Bostwick before he actually found them? The man in the suit crossed the opening between the stairs and the left wall. There, he opened every cupboard door and swept the contents—cans, jars, bags of rice and sugar—onto the floor, more agitated than before.

Still looking.

Suddenly the killer was outside, appearing on the cabin's front deck from a walkway that ran down the right side toward what must have been a back door. Maybe thirty feet away, he tucked the gun back into his suit jacket and headed for the stairs to ground level.

Christensen looked down, thinking first of the vomit that had landed at the base of the tree. Would the killer notice the smell as he passed on the way to his car? What caught Christensen's eye instead were his own shoes, two brown loafers side by side beneath the maple's lowest branch. It was dark, and they blended with the dirt and leaves. But they were too out of place, too unexpected. If the man saw them, he'd know. Christensen held his breath and prayed.

Time slowed, then stopped, as the man coasted to a stop just below. In that frozen moment, with a killer staring at the stranded shoes, instinct took over. As soon as the man's right hand moved inside his lapel, Christensen swung silently off his perch and into a fifteen-foot freefall, landing his socks on the man's shoulders and unleashing a primal scream just as the man looked up. He heard the unmistakable snap of bone as something heavy skittered into the brush.

Christensen landed on his feet, then lurched forward and fell. He rolled and stood, surprised that the impact hadn't been more painful. The killer was struggling up to all fours with an unknowable smile, shaking his head like a punch-drunk boxer. When he looked up at Christensen, he lost his balance and fell onto his right side. His jacket yawned open, and against his white shirt Christensen could see that the shoulder holster was empty. The way the guy was struggling for breath, Christensen figured he'd broken his collarbone.

The gun was somewhere close. Christensen charged, and when the man reached his left arm up to shield his face, he kicked him hard in the ribs. Even through the dark suit jacket, Christensen's foot connected with a dull thud, another soggy crack, and the grunt of emptying lungs. The only other sound was Christensen's own scream as pain shot up his right leg. He backed off and kicked again, his injury numbed by adrenaline and fear. The man crawled forward and collapsed as Christensen limped away, cursing a pain that felt like hot knitting needles jammed point-first between his toes.

The man wasn't moving. Ten seconds. Twenty. "I saw everything, you son of a bitch," Christensen said to the dark heap, looking away only to steal quick glances for the gun. "I already called the cops." He took a sharp breath. "From my car phone, before I even knew what you were doing." Another breath. "They're coming, so don't try anything."

He circled closer, wary, convinced the man was bluffing, too. When he was close enough to see the closed eyes and empty hands, Christensen nudged the limp form with his left foot. The man's face rolled in the dirt until it settled back into place. Christensen knelt on the back of the slack left hand, easing his full weight down to make sure it was immobile, then pulled the limp right arm back and turned it palm up. The man groaned, but didn't move. Pinning that arm in the middle of his back with his right hand, Christensen started searching the bastard's pants pockets with his left. He might never find the gun, but at least he wanted the knife.

The keys were a bonus. Somewhere on the ring that Christensen pulled from the killer's pocket was a handcuff key, he was sure, but it was too dark to find it outside. He shuddered at the prospect of going in, of confronting the horror at the base of the loft stairs. But he didn't want this guy up and around.

Slipping the switchblade into his own pants pocket, he limped up the deck stairs and followed the walkway around to the open back door. He was still out of breath and squinting as he stepped into the track-lit disaster of Bostwick's cabin. The fallen mattresses blocked his view of what lay just beyond, but there was no denying it. The far corner of one mattress was turning red, soaked with blood.

He stepped quickly but carefully in his stocking feet, picking a path toward the dead man, his need for the handcuffs outweighing the need to preserve the crime scene. No telling how long before the killer came to. Was this really happening?

The answer came too quickly. Bostwick was slumped forward, his chin on his chest, a matted flap of dark hair at the back of his head. Christensen stepped wide of the crimson pool and onto the loft stairs, busying himself with the key ring, focusing on something other than Bostwick's body. He found the small handcuff key quickly, but he felt for a pulse before unlocking the dead man's wrists from the stair railing. Nothing, of course. How could there be?

Bostwick fell forward as soon as Christensen turned the key, then moaned as the motion forced trapped air from his lungs. The sound split the cabin's silence, followed by the crack of the dead man's skull as it hit the plank floor.

"Sorry," he said, an instinctive reaction.

Bostwick lay facedown in his blood, his silence underscoring the absurdity of the apology. Christensen stretched forward and unlocked the second cuff. Bostwick's freed arm fell forward, coming to rest awkwardly, palm up, beside his torso. For a moment, Christensen felt the need to see Bostwick's face, to know what the man looked like. But he hesitated, unprepared to carry that image with him for the rest of his life. He moved quickly across the room, stopping only to peer through the cabin's front window to make sure the dark heap was still at the base of the maple tree.

Outside, Christensen nudged again with his foot. The killer stirred, still unconscious but struggling back to the surface. He grabbed the man's starched shirt collar and pulled, dragging him maybe ten feet to the base of the tree, then tugged the bulk until it was sitting upright. He leaned him against the foot-thick trunk and cuffed one wrist, then pulled the left arm around the tree and reached for the man's right. He closed the second cuff with a reassuring snap, anchoring the killer, then fell backward into the dirt. He landed on the gun.

Christensen never seriously considered pulling the trigger, but as he sat face-to-face with the man he'd seen kill so casually, the gun's barrel wedged solidly between the killer's teeth, he had to admit the urge was there. He'd released the safety once he'd found it, and felt his finger tighten when he thought of Annie and Taylor, of where they might be and what might have happened since they disappeared.

He tensed again when the eyelids fluttered, at once frightened and relieved that the man's brain was functioning again after ten minutes of unconsciousness. The head rocked from side to side, and Christensen felt the man's tongue pushing against the cold steel. He gave no quarter, shoving the barrel even deeper. The man gagged and his eyes opened all the way, but it took him at least a minute to fully grasp his circumstance.

"Can you hear me now?" Christensen asked when their eyes finally met.

A nod.

"And you understand what I'm saying?"

Another nod.

"That's good. Let's start with the easy stuff." Christensen withdrew the gun and put the barrel in the center of the man's forehead. "What's your name?"

"Tony."

Christensen counted to ten. Anything less and he might have lost control. "Tony Robbins?" he said finally.

"Uh-huh."

Christensen moved the gun's barrel from the man's forehead and teased it into one of his nostrils. "Like the personal power guy in the infomercials? That Tony Robbins?"

"You know him, too?" The man seemed sincere, weirdly so, as if they'd discovered a mutual friend.

Christensen shoved the barrel as far up the man's nose as it would go. "Let's start over, you lying sack of shit. What's your name?"

After half a minute of silence, Christensen withdrew the gun, thinking maybe the man couldn't talk, or worse, maybe his attempt at intimidation made him sound like a cheesy Hollywood mobster. Either way, all he got was stony silence and that same strange, grotesque smile he'd seen as the killer went down. What now? Christensen backed off and sat down cross-legged about five feet away, leveling the gun at the man's chest. He needed another tactic, an exposed nerve he could manipulate. He'd probably get nowhere trying to bully the guy. He needed to get into his head.

"Then let me tell *you* some things," he said. "You work for the Underhill family."

No reaction. Just that smile.

"Part of your job, maybe all of your job, is making sure the family secrets stay secrets. I'm guessing from that suit that you're paid pretty well, so you must be good at what you do. Loyal, too. These people treat you well, don't they?"

A modest shrug. The smile broadened into a grin. A clue.

Christensen lowered the gun. "Loyalty is a great thing. Really. Very commendable."

The man nodded. " 'Devotation is the hallmark of the committed.' "

"Devotion," Christensen said, nodding. "So true. You made that up?"

He shook his head. "Maya Baba Mankar."

Christensen smiled, imagining the phrase highlighted in yellow marker in the man's copy of that tinhorn mystic's bestseller, *The Prophesies of Q*. Here was another of the New Age's misguided spiritual seekers; here was someone whose buttons he could push. "Wise man," Christensen said. "You've read his book?"

The man shook his head. "Tapes."

Of course. " 'The nobility of the follower,' " Christensen said. "He really hit the nail on the head, didn't he?"

" 'The joy of selfless service!' "

"Yes!" Christensen pretended to marvel at the wisdom of the idea. "Service is *such* a noble calling."

An appreciative nod.

"Okay. The thing is, it's over." Christensen waited a beat. "The secret's out. I'm not the only one who knows about Chip Underhill. And you killing the guy inside, or my friend Maura, or anybody else who knows, that doesn't stop the ship from going down. So it's your choice: You can help me out here, or you can go down with it like some faithful family dog.''

The man said nothing, but his eyes strayed to the gun.

"Loyalty's a great thing, a noble thing," Christensen said. "And you tried your best. But, fact is, you still couldn't keep the secret. *I'd* never fault you for that, but your bosses, well, you know, they'll have to blame somebody. People like that don't make mistakes, you know, they hire people like you to make mistakes for them. Because they'd never make a bad decision, would they? And they'd never, ever get their own hands dirty. Not people like that. Hey, you a gambler?''

The smile was gone. The man shook his head.

" 'Cause I'll make you a bet: How loyal do you think the Underhills will be when they find out you let them down?''

"I didn't," he said.

"They needed your help, expected it. But now everybody knows. That family's going down, and it's your fault. You failed.''

"Go to hell.''

"It's true. Everybody knows, and it was your sloppy work that did it. The dead gardener had Fox Chapel silt in his pockets when they found him downriver, so they know where he went in. And I just saw you kill Simon Bostwick. You got cocky. You didn't even close the blinds.''

"Fuck you.''

"You think the Underhills are going to admit all this was *their* idea? Even if they did, who'd ever believe them? I guess what I'm saying here, sport, is maybe you should check to see if the people you were following are still out in front. I think when you look up, when you understand what's happened here, you'll see there's nobody left to follow. Know why? Because they're all hiding behind you. You're propped up in front, all alone. You're the tackling dummy.''

"Bite my pipe.''

Christensen squinted down the gun's barrel, as if drawing a bead on the man's head. "Where are my kids?''

The sick smile became a grin. But no answer. Enough with the mind games. Time to speak the man's language.

The gunshot echoed once and stopped, muffled by the surrounding forest. The sound startled them both, and the killer pressed his right ear against his right shoulder in obvious pain. Christensen breathed easier when the man looked up, the ear intact. No blood.

"Let's try that again,'' he said. "Where are my kids?''

"They're fine.''

"Answer the question.''

"I don't know, but they're fine.''

"Where'd you take them after you left the school?''

"They're fine, I said. Nobody's gonna maltreat 'em.''

Christensen edged closer, out of kicking range but close enough to put the gun's barrel just inches from one of the man's tasseled loafers. He looked him in the eyes. "Tell me now.''

The killer's eyes shifted between Christensen's eyes and his own foot. "Now. Later. What difference does it make?''

Christensen studied his face. "Explain.''

A shrug. "They served their purpose this time. You already got the message.''

He tapped the man's foot with the gun, lightly, to make sure he understood. "I'm a little slow, and I'm not playing games. What's the message?''

"You don't get it yet?''

"I'm slow. Say it.''

That smile. It infuriated Christensen even before the man answered. Then he spoke: "We can find 'em anytime we want.''

The second gunshot was lost in a scream. Christensen didn't look away as the man thrashed helplessly against the tree, cursing, twitching, his body convulsing from the pain. The shoe came off and Christensen picked it up. The tassel was gone; there was only a hole where it used to be.

"Where are my kids?"

The man threw his head back against the tree, his face contorted into something grotesque. His leg was moving by shattered reflex, a living thing whose spastic movements he couldn't control. It was bleeding, but not much. "Fuck you," he screamed.

Christensen shifted to his right, the man's left. This time he drew a bead on the knee of his other leg, startled by his own sadistic will. When he was sure the man understood his intention, he asked again: "Where are my kids?"

"Fuck your mother!"

"I'm going to count to three."

"They're safe, I said!"

"One."

"Cocksucker!"

"Two."

"Just kill me!"

"Three."

Suddenly, Christensen was standing, the gun aimed into the dirt, looking down on a fetal form whose legs were drawn up tight to his chest. He'd heard an explosion, sharp, final, but it was lost in the howl of an anguished animal, a howl that rose from Christensen's chest and died in the surrounding woods. Jesus. What had he done? He waited, remorse overtaking him with each passing second.

Finally, the man's wounded foot twitched. He unfolded slowly, opened his eyes, and looked down at the knee. Christensen looked, too, surprised it wasn't a gory mulch. Had he lost the stomach for it, or did he just miss? Their eyes met again, and the man whispered something.

"Speak up," Christensen said, still rattled by the power of his rage.

"Kill me."

Christensen turned his back, breathing as hard as he might after a long run. The man was a killer, cold and efficient, but this was wrong. He thought of the kids again. Even that wasn't enough to provoke him. When he turned around, the man closed his eyes. Waiting.

"No," Christensen said. He slid the gun's safety back on.

"Please."

The man's eyes were still closed as Christensen turned away, headed for the car.

39

If he'd followed his first impulse, Christensen might not
have noticed the tape. If he'd twisted the Explorer's ignition key, jammed it into reverse, and backed down the
rutted dirt road and away from this nightmare, he might
not have spent minutes panting behind the wheel, trying
to collect himself, surrounded by the ghostly birch trees
and the silence of the woods, remembering why he came.

Bostwick had the autopsy films, and he'd died because
of it. Christensen was sure of that. But if the killer's
search hadn't turned them up, where were they? His
leather briefcase had spilled onto the passenger-side floor
during the rough ride to Bostwick's cabin, and the
answering-machine tape was among its scattered contents.
He turned the key without starting the engine, then slipped
the tape into the player and rewound it for several seconds. Bostwick's had been the last of the three messages.

Carrie Haygood's voice filled the car. "... case we
spoke about this morning. I'll be at my office until seven
P.M. today."

He waited through the low white noise until Bostwick's

message began with an indistinguishable rustle and the thrum of passing traffic. A closing car door. Where had he called from? Suddenly, the dead man's voice filled the car. "This is for Jim Christen . . . sen."

He tried to conjure an image of the man inside the cabin, wishing now he'd looked into his face, wanting to put the voice to something human, something alive. With his eyes closed, though, all Christensen saw was the damp snarl of hair at the base of a skull and the collar of a flannel shirt soaked through with blood.

"We're talking about life insur . . . nance, is what we're talking about," the voice slurred. "I got it, yes I do." An exaggerated laugh. "Got what you need. If they knew—" Another laugh. "—I'm thinking I'd probably look like the one up there in the springhouse. Worse, probably. But I got it covered. Something I learned a long time ago, something your friend Grady Downing taught me: You gotta leave yourself an out. Always. Always, always, always. 'Cause that's the thing. Once you're in bed with these people, they know how to make sure you stay there. They know the pressure points. But I could hurt them, too, hurt them like they never been hurt before. Some things you just can't deny."

In the background, a sound Christensen had heard again and again just an hour before, the roar of a starting Harley. And then he knew: Bostwick was calling from Cook's Corner.

"So don't call me at my house again. And I can't call you from there. We need to talk, though. Insurance policy's no good if there's nobody to file the claim. Something happens, you know, to me, I'd like to make it right. Might get me out of hell a little sooner. Wait a sec. Here's a number."

Christensen rewound the tape again. What struck him at first was Bostwick's fatalism. He wanted someone to know before it was too late, someone who could piece together a story perhaps only he and the Underhills fully understood. Thinking of the clue Bostwick left in the written records—the unflinching reference to the subdural hematoma that ultimately killed Chip Underhill—Christensen wondered if the man's conscience had bedeviled him from the moment he was co-opted. To someone who knew enough and who read the coroner's file closely, someone like Carrie Haygood, that conclusion would be as obvious as if he'd stamped HOMICIDE across the file folder.

"If they knew," the voice said again, "I'm thinking I'd probably look like the one up there in the springhouse. Worse, probably."

Stop. Rewind.

". . . knew, I'm thinking I'd probably look like the one up there in the springhouse. Worse, probably."

In a message full of vagaries and abstractions, that one specific reference stood out. But Christensen had no idea what it meant. He played it again—". . . up there in the springhouse."

Did Bostwick own a second home? No, people who bought in these mountains owned summer homes or winter homes or weekend places, not springhouses. So what was a springhouse? He closed his eyes, conjuring what little he knew about Bostwick. It meant something, but what?

Christensen grabbed Annie's Big Bird flashlight from the glove compartment, surprised that the batteries were still good, if weak. He opened the Explorer's door and stepped back out. Pain from his injured ligaments shot up his leg, and he suddenly realized he was still in his stocking feet. He passed the Thunderbird, again giving it space, and approached the cabin.

The track lights inside were still on, casting a pale glow into the enfolding woods. He stopped to survey the property from about thirty yards short of the maple tree and the motionless dark form at its base. The cabin had been thoroughly searched, which left two possibilities among the structures on Bostwick's property. The garage to the left was closed and dark. Maybe that's where the killer was headed when he came out of the house. But if Bost-

wick kept the films in the garage, wouldn't he have used
that word? Plus, he'd said "up there in the springhouse."
In relation to the cabin, the garage was down.

He'd barely noticed the other structure, the playhouse-
sized outbuilding on the slope behind the cabin, but suddenly it loomed very large. City boy that he was, he still
knew that western Pennsylvania's forests were nourished
by countless cold-water springs that bubbled from aqui-
fers to the surface, sometimes in the most inconvenient
places. Many became streams. On developed properties,
they were corralled into drainage systems and diverted,
sometimes using pipes and pumps to manage the flow. A
building the size of the one behind Bostwick's cabin was
useless, except maybe for small-equipment storage . . . or
to disguise a system that diverted springwater away from
the house.

Christensen limped past the killer without a word, but
he felt the malice in the man's eyes as he watched him
pass. His head was back against the tree, but he tracked
Christensen's passing with a smile that conveyed something between contempt and intense pain. The man was
motionless except for his own injured foot, a snarl of damaged nerves that continued to twitch.

The garage was padlocked, and so probably hadn't been
searched. If need be, he'd get inside somehow and look
there. But by the time he passed into the rectangular
shadow to the left of the cabin, Christensen was following
a strong hunch up the slope toward the smaller structure.
As he neared the small outbuilding, his socks suddenly
soaked through. That's when he knew this was the place
Bostwick had chosen. The springhouse.

He found the latch to its tiny door, which was just large
enough to allow someone to crawl inside. Small spaces
bothered him. Small spaces where rodents or woodland
creatures might hide bothered him even more. But he followed the flashlight's pale beam through the door, relieved to find himself alone amid an inelegant knot of
pipes and damp aromas but disappointed that the space

contained nothing that looked like a packet of photographs. Now what? He started to back out, but then swept the light once into the structure's upper corners. Once was enough. There it was, a cellophane-wrapped manila envelope duct-taped to the plank underside of the roof.

Christensen squeezed himself inside, hooked an arm around one of the cold plastic pipes, and peeled the envelope from the planks. There, using Big Bird's golden beam in the cramped privacy of Simon Bostwick's springhouse, he inspected the contents—two contact sheets of autopsy photographs, one strip of 35-mm negatives in a plastic sleeve, and four X-rays of a child's skull.

His hands were trembling as he slid the films inside, then backed out the tiny door. By the time he waved the envelope at the helpless killer and retrieved his shoes from near the maple tree, Christensen was crying.

40

The Explorer fishtailed onto blacktop, its headlights sweeping the tunnel of trees that bordered the road. Even in the dark, Christensen felt as if he were driving in plain view of the Underhills. How big was their network of spies? He thought of the electronic surveillance hive inside the killer's Thunderbird and wondered if they somehow already knew what had happened, if they might even be watching him now. He leaned down and tucked the manila envelope deeper beneath his seat. The carpool from hell had a new passenger: paranoia.

He tensed with each car that passed. Even in the dark stretches where there was no traffic, he imagined them watching from some omniscient aerial view, as a spider might watch a fly's futile attempt at escape. Right now, he felt as alone and vulnerable as ever, desperate to find someone he could trust with what he knew, with what he could now prove. But a question perched on his shoulder like a nagging crow: Who?

Brenna would know. He picked up the car phone, but stopped, wishing he'd paid more attention to the alarmists who warned about cellular's lack of security. Could someone monitoring the signal triangulate his exact location, or Brenna's? He imagined the call registering on a computer somewhere in the Underhills' web, sounding like a sonar signal echoing off a lost submarine. He replaced the handset in its holder.

On the near horizon, he recognized the glow of an isolated Arco gas station. As he slowed, he checked the bay for cars and the convenience mart for customers. The only vehicle outside was a ridiculously large motor home, its owner draining the pump into its gas tank. Besides the clerk, the only people inside were two teenagers. Christensen parked next to the pay phone, locking the door as he stepped out because . . . just because.

Brenna's voice filled his head, their home answering machine. "Bren, pick up," he said at the beep. "It's me, Bren. Please?"

She was supposed to be waiting for the kidnapper's call. Where could she be?

"I'm—" How much should he say? "I'm okay. But I need to talk to you. Don't try to call me on the car phone. I'll call back." Before he hung up: "I love you."

In the open, beneath the station's buzzing fluorescence, Christensen felt exposed, like a deer washed in onrushing headlights. He could stand dumbstruck on the center line, or he could move. Every instinct told him to move, but he resisted.

Who could he turn to now?

A logical name came to mind, a name weighted with bad memories. The irony struck him immediately, that in this most desperate hour he'd turn to someone who'd once tried to destroy him, who'd tried to twist the simple act of mercy he'd shown toward the woman he loved into something criminal, who would have sent him to jail for ending what remained of Molly's life.

The directory-assistance operator asked what city.

"Pittsburgh. The Allegheny County District Attorney's office."

He closed his eyes, memorizing the number. It was nearly 8:30 P.M. What were the chances he'd still be in?

"J. D. Dagnolo, please," Christensen said.

The voice was tired, male, clearly not a regular receptionist. "It's election night. The office is closed."

"Please, wait. If he's in, I need to talk to him. I have information—"

"Who's calling?"

He hesitated. What twisted god of fate could have brought him to this point? "My name is Jim Christensen," he said. "I'm sure he remembers me."

"What's the information?"

Christensen held his breath. The risk was calculated. Dagnolo was scum, but Brenna said he wasn't intimidated by the Underhill family, either. "Tell him . . . just tell him it involves the Underhills."

The teenagers, two girls, stepped out of the convenience mart with Snapples and microwaved burritos and swept past him in a cloud of lemon perfume and synthetic chili, headed for a battered Honda Civic parked at the side of the station. Christensen curled around the phone, avoiding their eyes. After they'd passed, he scanned the rest of the service bay to make sure no one was watching. The motor-home owner was still pumping. Christensen realized after several minutes that the hold music was an instrumental version of "My Favorite Things."

"Mr. Christensen, this is J. D. Dagnolo."

The voice made him jump, like screeching brakes. "Thank you for taking the call," he sputtered. "Look, I don't know if you remember me. We never actually met, but my wife, Molly—"

"Yes, of course."

"She was in an accident a few years ago. You—"

"Mr. Christensen, I'm due at a function. What can I help you with this evening?"

"Okay." Where to start? "It's a long story."

"Involving anyone in particular?" Dagnolo baited.

That's why he'd taken the call. To a Democratic political maverick like Dagnolo, Christensen had said the magic word.

"The Underhills." He waited through a long silence.

"You're not being very specific, Mr. Christensen, and I'm afraid I'm due—"

"Chip Underhill."

This time, the silence was different. Less expectant than genuinely startled. "Not Ford?"

"Are you familiar with the case?"

"Ford's son," Dagnolo said. "The riding accident."

"Three years ago, out on the family's Fox Chapel estate."

"He was riding *with* Ford, though, if I recall."

"Yes," Christensen said. "No! That's what they said, but I'm pretty sure his head injuries weren't caused the way they said. I think someone shook him, an adult, someone in the house that day, and when he died they covered it with the horseback-riding story."

Dagnolo said nothing.

"And the cover-up, it's still going on. I'm sure of it. I've worked with Floss Underhill, out at the Harmony Center. When she fell ten days ago, I think that was part of it, too. And some other stuff, deaths, disappearances, may be part of a pattern."

He'd probably said just enough to qualify as a fringe conspiracy theorist. Dagnolo's office probably got dozens of calls like that every day.

"It's primary election night, Mr. Christensen," Dagnolo sighed. "Three blocks from here, at the Grant Hotel, there's a goddamned coronation going on. Come next fall, Ford Underhill will be the next governor of Pennsylvania, and you're stepping forward now, of all times, saying he's part of a conspiracy to protect his own son's killer?"

Christensen wanted to say what he knew, that Ford Underhill had already undercut the official explanation of the boy's death, that what he'd said might even be a confession, but he couldn't betray Brenna's confidence. Instead, he just said, "Yes."

Dagnolo laughed.

"You don't believe me?"

"I don't believe your timing."

"I have evidence," Christensen said.

"A signed confession, I hope. Anything less—"

"The name Simon Bostwick mean anything to you?"

Dagnolo wasn't laughing anymore. "Former deputy coroner," he said.

"He did the autopsy on Chip Underhill three years ago," Christensen said. "Left the coroner's office not long after."

"What about him?"

Christensen took a deep breath, an image of crumpled and bloody flannel swimming into his mind. "He's dead. Shot in the head about an hour ago by someone I'm sure works for the Underhills. I saw it happen."

Dagnolo waited. Finally: "Where are you calling from, Mr. Christensen?"

Christensen felt a change in tone, felt himself suddenly in the spotlight. "I'd rather not say."

"Interesting," Dagnolo said. "You've just witnessed a murder, and you'd rather not say where it happened?"

"That's not what you asked. It happened at Bostwick's house."

"Easy enough for the Westmoreland County sheriff to check. Answer me this, though, Mr. Christensen: How come so many people wind up dead when you're around?"

"Like I said, long story."

"How many people know it?"

Two, he thought, Brenna and Carrie Haygood. "A few."

"I'd love to hear it," Dagnolo said. "And this evidence you're talking about? Can you give me even a little hint?"

The conversation arrived, finally, at the issue of trust. The man he'd loathed for five years, the man who'd wanted to send him to prison for ending Molly's life, who might even suspect him in Simon Bostwick's death, was asking for the trump card in a deadly high-stakes game. Christensen wasn't about to turn it over, at least not without a witness.

"I'd like to meet with you in ninety minutes, at your office," he said. "And I want Carrie Haygood there as well."

"Carrie Haygood?"

"I want your word on it."

He imagined Dagnolo calculating: If he'd just witnessed Bostwick's murder and was still ninety minutes away, surely the D.A. had figured out he was calling from somewhere in the Laurel Highlands. If Dagnolo ran his license plates, how long would it be before some Westmoreland County sheriff or state trooper pulled him over during the drive back into the city? Then what?

"One other thing," he said. "Anybody tries to interfere with me before I get there, I take what I know to someone else, maybe state or federal. Is that clear?"

"Very clear."

"Say it."

He waited while Dagnolo chose his words. "We'll meet here in ninety minutes. I'll arrange for Ms. Haygood to be here as well. At that point you'll tell me everything you know about this situation—and I mean *everything*, Mr. Christensen—and deliver whatever evidence you have that supports it."

"And?"

"I'll wait an hour and a half before, ah, before notifying anyone."

"Whoa, whoa," Christensen said. "What's that supposed to mean?"

"Mr. Christensen, if what you say is true, you've just left a crime scene."

"Meaning?"

"Meaning, sir, that for the moment you're a suspect in the murder of Simon Bostwick. That's information the Westmoreland County sheriff needs to know. And based

on our conversation just now, there might even be suffi-
cient cause to issue a warrant.''

Christensen felt suddenly dizzy. Dagnolo had just
played a trump card of his own.

''Do we understand each other?'' the D.A. said.

Christensen was alone now. The teenagers were gone.
The motor home's taillights were shrinking to a red pinpoint down the road. Inside the convenience store, the
clerk was watching a small black-and-white television. In
that moment, Christensen stepped into the void and felt
the first empty rush of a long, long fall.

''Ninety minutes,'' he said, and hung up the phone.

"And you really think the family was involved in all of this?"

Dagnolo's words, delivered with a piano-key smile, hung like a challenge in the dead air of the district attorney's imperial office, above the Persian rugs, the antiques, the hammered-brass lamps; above the studded leather couch and heavy curtains drawn across floor-to-ceiling windows; above the tuxedoed man now extending a long arm toward the silent television to the right of his polished walnut desk. Dagnolo stabbed a button on the TV's remote control, and the black screen blinked on, filling the room with a scene of red, white, and blue bunting and the sound of election-night revelry. He pressed another button, muting a brass-band celebration.

Christensen glared. "Sounds like you don't."

Dagnolo set the remote down on the desk and adjusted the cant of his red silk bow tie. At 6-foot-2, he would have been intimidating even without the black hair that swept straight back from his perpetually tanned forehead. Slender and well-conditioned, he used his size and regal bearing as a weapon. If his stature didn't overwhelm, he relied on his ice-blue eyes.

"It's not that I don't want to, Mr. Christensen. You probably know with your—" A conspiratorial wink. "—*connections* along Grant Street that there's no love lost between the Underhill family and myself. But you have to admit, the scenario you've just described—"

"Unbelievable, I know. But it can't have happened any other way. The pieces all fit."

Dagnolo's smile was no less infuriating than the one on the thug in the mountains. "You've never presented a case to a grand jury, I'm assuming, is that correct, Mr. Christensen? Do you have any idea, any idea whatsoever, how skeptical that group can be? Let me be the first to tell you, they do not act decisively on *theories*, especially ones woven from coincidence and psychobabble."

Christensen stood up, his every suspicion about Dagnolo confirmed. He'd risked everything on the misguided illusion that the truth somehow mattered, that it could rise above murky politics and personal animosities, that it could raise a long-dead child and give him a voice. He'd followed vague clues into Floss Underhill's diseased mind, knowing only that the truth lay somewhere within that labyrinth. He'd pieced together from wisps of memory and threads of logic the damning evidence that proved that even the most civilized among us are capable of killing and conspiracy.

But for the first time since the Underhills' dirty secret began to unravel, his hunch had been wrong. If Annie and Taylor ended up paying for it, he knew then and there he would lay the blame at the Gucci-clad feet of the condescending bastard behind the desk. And he would find a way to make him pay.

He stood up. "My mistake. Maybe it's the state attorney general who has the spine."

Dagnolo's face turned the color of his tie. "Look at that television, Mr. Christensen," Dagnolo said finally, his voice restrained. A commentator was standing in front of a massive black-and-white portrait of Ford Underhill, the apparent backdrop for the podium at Democratic Party headquarters. "These are not insubstantial people you're talking about. These are people with resources, people with the will to use them to whatever end necessary, without remorse. Think about it, Mr. Christensen: Ford Underhill will be the next governor of this state. Remember who appoints the attorney general? You think whoever gets that job after this election is going to turn around and piss all over their patron?"

Dagnolo stood up, too. Their faces were just two feet apart, but they stared across a gulf Christensen knew was impossibly wide.

"The FBI, then. I'll take what I have to them."

"Look," Dagnolo said, "what I'm asking is, are you sure you're ready for what these people are going to throw up against you? Forget for a moment that these deaths you say are part of a cover-up would be a capital crime. Say you were just accusing the Underhills of shoplifting. To step forward now with any allegations . . . I'm sure you understand how easy it would be for them to dismiss the whole thing as just so much election-year mudslinging. The timing's wrong."

Christensen leaned forward, his hands on the D.A.'s desk, his voice even despite his rage. "Let me be very clear here: Even without Maura Pearson or Simon Bostwick, even without the fact that the Chembergos and my own two kids have disappeared, somebody in that family killed a child three years ago. Together, they invented a story to cover it up, a story so implausible that even *my* snooping around blew it out of the water. And for three years, nobody—nobody?—in this office figured it out?"

"And let me be very clear, too." The district attorney leaned forward, practically whispering. He could smell Dagnolo's minty-fresh breath. "In life, as in politics, Mr. Christensen, illusion becomes reality. What this looks like is less important than what it may be. And this, especially if it comes from me, looks like a petty election-year smear. I'm not saying there's nothing here. I'm saying—"

"Three people are dead. Three more are missing. All

this bluster about the bad blood between you and the Underhills. It's just a cover, isn't it?''

"Be careful, Mr. Christensen.''

"Hell, they've bought off everybody else for three years. Why *not* you?''

"Gentlemen?''

Both men wheeled. Carrie Haygood was at the inner office door, her glasses pushed up onto her forehead, a lab apron covering what Christensen assumed was her off-duty wardrobe—a dark-blue University of Pittsburgh sweatsuit. She'd taken the manila envelope of films from Christensen as soon as he burst into Dagnolo's office a half-hour before, then disappeared. When she fanned a series of eight-by-ten black-and-white prints across Dagnolo's desk, it was clear she'd taken the autopsy negatives to a photo lab somewhere in the courthouse. She held the X-rays up to the light one at a time.

"This boy's telling us his story, sirs, and babies don't lie.'' She handed the X-rays to Dagnolo. He stared at them as if she'd just handed him a turd. One by one, he lifted them to the light from the chandelier.

"No cranial fractures on these, like we thought,'' Haygood said. "But these—'' She tapped the prints on the desk, then pulled the corner of one so it bloomed into full view. The boy, blond and perfect, looked like he was sleeping. "No trauma or compression marks anywhere on the scalp.'' She folded her arms across her bosom and stood up to her full five feet, making sure she had both men's attention. "Horse didn't kick this boy in the head.''

Dagnolo lowered the X-rays, but held them away from Christensen with a slight, confusing smile. "And so we're back where we started, aren't we?''

"Sir?'' Haygood said.

"Now that we know what didn't happen, tell me what *did* happen.''

Haygood shook her head. "I can't do that, not from these. But the subdural hematoma, what that suggests—''

Dagnolo raised a hand, stopping her. "Suggests," he said, turning away, walking toward one of his massive office windows. He spread the curtains with two fingers and peeked out into the night. "A difficult word, 'suggests.' Because we're at the point now, I'm sure you both understand, where we have to answer an altogether different question. What does that finding *prove*?"

"That somebody lied," Haygood said.

"Yes, of course. It's a way of life in that family. But then, who killed the boy?"

Haygood looked down, and Christensen knew she'd done as much as she could. "I don't know."

Dagnolo turned, but kept his distance. "Mr. Christensen, who killed the boy? Give me the proof."

"You know I can't," he said, seething. "But I can give you the truth. Floss Underhill knows that something happened that day, something terrible. She may not know exactly what, but she knows it's something a lot more complicated and confusing than the version Vincent and Ford told the cops. And her confusion about that, trying to square her memories of that day with the story they told, became these uncontrollable images. They started leaking into her art, and I think that's the key to what really happened here."

Dagnolo clasped his hands behind his back, listening. "Go on."

Haygood's glance was reassuring.

"A lot of this started after her art went on public display, after people started to pay attention to it," Christensen said. "Think about that. Is that a coincidence? You want to talk about *timing*? One painting is picked for an art show. The *Press* prints a picture of it. Hell, they print her first name with it. Was it a coincidence that the family pulled that painting out of Maura's show? Suddenly, Floss is looking like a liability just as her son is stepping into the public spotlight for the first time. This fall she had a couple days later—another coincidence? Maybe. Only she doesn't die like she's supposed to—the damned gardener

wasn't supposed to see or hear anything, but he does—
so to cover that up, the family floats these theories about
caregiver burnout and suicide. They even hire an attorney
who's known for defending caregivers in those situations,
hoping to spin the whole thing into a sympathy vote for
Ford.''

Dagnolo was as still as a statue.

"A couple more things," Christensen said. "All the
people the Underhills think might know the real story suddenly end up dead or missing. And when they realize what
I'm up to, my kids go missing. All coincidences?''

Christensen swept an arm toward the television, where
the bloated, smiling face of the Democratic Party chairman filled the screen. "Literally," he said, "what's wrong
with this picture?''

Dagnolo turned away again. The chirping telephone on
his desk interrupted a long and uncomfortable silence. The
district attorney didn't look at either of them as he returned to pick it up.

"Good evening," he said, then listened, nodding occasionally. Finally: "All right. Keep me posted.''

When he hung up, Dagnolo's gaze shifted to Christensen's eyes and locked. "Westmoreland County sheriff.
Quite a little scene you left behind up there in the mountains.''

A prickly feeling swept up Christensen's spine. "You
called them already?''

"It's a murder scene, Mr. Christensen. Evidence de-
grades. They needed to know as soon as possible, but they
don't yet know you're involved. You should understand,
though, they've already concluded that *someone* else
was.''

"You told them.''

Dagnolo shook his head. "Simple logic. Simon Bostwick is dead in the cabin. The gentleman with the bad
foot is handcuffed to a tree outside. There had to be someone else involved, you see, and at this point they consider
that person their prime suspect.''

"You know what happened, though."

"I know what you've told me. If what you've told me is true—and what they've just said does fit with your version—I assume the physical evidence will bear you out."

Christensen's mind was racing. "That's it, then. Now the Underhills have to explain why their security guy was at the scene. The story starts to unravel."

"Does it?" Dagnolo said, his gaze intense and steady. "He's not talking."

"But he works for them."

"We'll try our best to prove that, of course, but these are not stupid people, Mr. Christensen." Dagnolo leaned forward, his large, elegant hands palms-down on his desk, his voice calm. "You might consider contacting an attorney before this goes too much further. It'll be out of my hands before long."

Christensen flushed. "Not a bad idea," he said. "She knows the whole story. Knows a lot of reporters, too. It'll all get out, one way or the other."

"Look—" Dagnolo glanced at Haygood, then back at Christensen. He sounded like a man who was done playing games. "What I say here stays in this room. Understood?"

Haygood nodded. Christensen stared.

"Mr. Christensen, do I have your word?"

Something in Dagnolo's tone was different. Christensen finally nodded.

The D.A. tapped his perfectly manicured fingertips on the desk, as if reconsidering what he was about to say. Then: "You're not the only one who figured out that Bostwick was bought off. You're not the only one who thought there was a lot more to that story three years ago. You may think we're just a bunch of hacks down here, Mr. Christensen, but we've been gathering string, looking for an opening. And we got it the day Mrs. Underhill went over that railing. Frankly, sir, you blundered into the middle of an investigation that had just gotten new life."

Christensen flashed on Brenna, on her confusion about the Allegheny County sheriff's persistence in investigating Floss's fall. "Sherm the Worm," he said without thinking.

Dagnolo nodded. "Sheriff Mercer's involved, yes." The D.A. looked at Haygood again. "Please understand, Carrie, we'd have brought you in on this eventually."

"And you didn't do anything?" Christensen said. "What about Maura?"

Dagnolo was forcing his words now, sharing information Christensen knew he shouldn't share. "Possibly connected. But if it is, there's no hard evidence. Whoever did it was a pro."

"The Chembergos?"

The D.A. shook his head. "Bodies turned up in the Ohio River, about four miles north of the Point. Shot in the back of the head before they went in—same MO as Bostwick—but the sediment in their pockets was from along the Allegheny. Coroner guesses they went in about ten miles upriver."

"How close to Fox Chapel?"

Dagnolo shrugged. "You could make a case with the right jury."

Christensen suddenly felt sick. "Our kids?"

Dagnolo shook his head. "I just know what you've told me; you somehow neglected to report it to the police. But it's not something we want to wait on. We all know what we're dealing with here."

Christensen tried to process what he was hearing, but felt as if he'd stumbled into thick fog. "I, uh . . . What can you do? About the kids, I mean."

Dagnolo seemed to savor the reaction. "I'll alert Mercer. But where would we start looking? We'd need a search warrant for the estate, if we could even get one with what we have, but they're probably smarter than to take them there. I'm guessing they're smart enough not to hurt them, either."

The room spun. Christensen grabbed the leather arm of a barrel-backed leather chair and sat down.

Dagnolo slid open the lap drawer of his desk, picked up a photocopy of something Christensen hadn't seen before, and laid it faceup between them, angled so Christensen could read it. The top page of several stapled pages was a fax cover sheet from the Westmoreland County Sheriff's Department. The time stamp was from seven hours earlier, 3:11 P.M.

"We're all on the knife edge here," Dagnolo said. His voice was almost conspiratorial. "We're not the only ones who know more than we're supposed to know."

Christensen couldn't hide his anxiety. "What is it?"

Dagnolo smiled. "Your salvation."

Confused, Christensen looked at Haygood. She shrugged. Dagnolo pushed it across the desk. "The original's still at the sheriff's office in Latrobe."

The paper shook in Christensen's hand as he picked it up. "Per this afternoon's phone conversation," the handwritten fax cover note began. "Suicide note to follow."

Haygood moved quietly to Christensen's side and read along.

"The handwriting isn't easy to read," Dagnolo said, "but you'll get the idea."

Christensen flipped to the last of what looked like about ten pages. The signature was clear enough: Warren Doti. He looked up. "Oh, Christ. Dead, too?"

"Shotgun, out in one of the horse stalls. Self-inflicted, they're pretty sure. Still checking it. The note was beside him. Definitely not something the Underhills would plant. Read it."

"But you knew about him?"

Dagnolo nodded. "We took his statement the day Chip Underhill died, but at the time he was supporting their version of the accident. Tried like hell to shake his story back then." He shook his head, then gestured to the fax. "Read it."

The handwriting was uneven, barely legible, the lan-

guage plain and familiar. Christensen had no doubt it was
written by Doti.

> To who it may concern: I want to put something right
> now because it's time. I had not said so before when it
> happened because too many people had been hurt al-
> ready and saying something would have made it worse.
> But I see things going on and I know something is
> wrong and I want to put it right. I want everybody to
> understand certain facts as I know them, and whatever
> happens happens.

Christensen looked up. Dagnolo was back at the massive window, his back turned, peeking through the curtains again.

> My feelings for Mrs. Underhill go back to 1964 to when
> Mr. Vincent was governor. We were training for the
> national trials. We were together alot, traveling together
> to competitions, and it just happened, and it was always
> respectful and never once felt dirty or wrong. It's fair
> that this be known, but it has nothing to do with things
> as I'll explain them. So I won't say more than that in
> respect for my wife, who died last year and never knew.
> The truth is me and Mrs. Underhill stopped our meet-
> ings when Mr. Vincent came back home and never saw
> each other that way ever since. It was the right thing
> because I'd never do anything against the Underhills
> that gave me a life for so long.

"You knew?" Christensen said.
"No idea," Dagnolo said without turning around.
"You did?"
"I wondered."
"You were ahead of us there, then."
Haygood moved across the room, removing the shade
from a floor lamp. When she was done, she held the X-
rays against its harsh light and set her eyeglasses up high

on her nose, which wrinkled as she squinted at the shadow images on the murky blue skull. Christensen felt oddly alone holding the copy of Warren Doti's suicide note.

We stayed friends. That never changed even after the Alzheimer's started and she stopped remembering. But that's what scared me so much, her remembering. She talked alot about things she knew, secrets she was supposed to keep. I knew she hadn't forgot about us and she might say something to Mr. Vincent. That would of killed me, him being so good to me and Suzanne for so long and me having turned on him while he was away. Even with my wife so sick at the time, I'd of quit and moved off without any medical benefits before I let that happen.

Christensen sat down in the chair across from Dagnolo's desk. Across the room, the televised scene from Republican headquarters looked like a wake. Even without the sound, the body language and general lethargy of the people crossing the screen conveyed abject defeat. Even the bunting looked wilted.

If to this day Mr. Vincent knows, he's never said a word to me. The last conversation we had was the day after little Chip died, but he's a gentleman and honorable in every way, and I doubt that he would of ever called me out. But I've come to understand that last conversation better now than I did at the time, and I cannot think of an explanation for the facts I'm about to give except one that I do not want to believe. But it's facts that I feel should be known.

Mr. Vincent came to me that day, the day after the boy got hurt so bad, and offered me this job running their operation up here at Muddyross. (If handling horses is your business, believe me, this is the job you want. Doubled my salary and guaranteed me work and Suzanne medical benefits for the rest of our lives.)

Never said why, but said they were moving Gray and some others off the Fox Chapel property out here and wanted me in charge. I think he wanted me to go, too, because I knew where that horse was the day before.

I can't say I know what happened to the boy, because I don't. I wasn't there. Neither was Mrs. Underhill (Florence). What I do know is that we had trailered Gray down to Westmoreland for a show the day before, and we'd decided to rest him the day it happened. Gray never left his stall the day they say he threw Mr. Ford and his boy.

I did not think the worst, even when he asked me to lie to the sheriff. I just figured they had their reasons and I respected that. But a few days ago two people, a man and a woman, came here asking questions about Mrs. Underhill and that horse in particular, and I felt Mr. Underhill should know about it. So I called him with their names and the license number of the old car the lady was driving, never thinking I'd be reading about her turning up dead. That's when I put things together, when I knew something was wrong.

With Suzanne gone and the kids grown and gone, it's just me now. I've told what I know, these facts, as truthfully as I could, making my peace. So this is my decision.

Christensen traced the signature, which was strong and certain. Something so grim shouldn't make him feel so good, but it did. He looked up, certain now that he was holding the final piece of the puzzle. Let the bastards deny it now. Christensen stood up. "Carrie, look at this." He crossed the room and handed Doti's letter to her. "They weren't riding the horse that day."

She laid the letter on a table without reading it and resumed her study of the X-rays. "I knew that."

"But it's proof!"

"No," she said, nodding toward the table. "That's a bunch of papers." She cocked her head back toward the

X-rays she was holding at arm's length. "These are proof."

Christensen wheeled, his mind racing, surprised to see Dagnolo still at the window with his back turned. "So everybody who knew was bought off. Doti, Bostwick. You should check out the desk clerk at the morgue, the black guy. He was really curious why I wanted the files. I bet they paid him to keep an eye on things, just in case anybody got curious. What about Mercer? His people did the investigation."

"Sherm's clean," Dagnolo said. "His reputation for sucking up notwithstanding, he wanted this one as bad as I did. We just never had enough."

Christensen clapped his hands. "Until now!"

The hollow report echoed in the sepulchral office. Dagnolo turned slowly, his face waxy and grim, and buttoned his tuxedo jacket. "Mr. Christensen—" He clasped his hands behind his back, opening a diamond-shaped gap in the front of his jacket. The district attorney's eyes were everywhere but on his. "Let me be the first to say that this new information is important, and will add substantially to what we know about this case."

Suddenly formal and sincere, like an undertaker.

Dagnolo shrugged into his topcoat. "You may be right, though. It's information that may be better served in the hands of state or federal—"

"You're not going to do anything, are you?"

Dagnolo nodded toward the television. On the screen, a wide shot of the riotous lobby of the Grant Hotel three blocks away. The crowd looked restless, waiting for the campaign's inevitable crescendo, waiting for Ford Underhill.

"These are powerful people," the D.A. said. "From me, this is just a smear. Let's not give them that. Let's turn it over to an authority that—"

"You son of a bitch."

Haygood dropped the X-rays.

"Stop right there, Mr. Christensen," Dagnolo said.

"You want me to start over with the FBI. You want them to do the dirty work for you."

"With what you have, they'll move swiftly," Dagnolo said. "I can put you in touch—"

"You *bastard*! My kids are gone seven hours already. You've got what you need. *Do* something."

"Do *what*? What have we proven here tonight? That Chip Underhill did not die in a horseback-riding accident. That perhaps someone killed him instead."

"That the family covered it up!" Christensen shouted. "Maybe the boy's death was unintentional. But the others, the cover-up, that's the evil here."

Dagnolo pointed an elegant finger directly at him. "Go back to my original question, damn it, the only one that matters right now: Who killed that child?"

"Somebody in the house that day!" He turned to Haygood, who nodded reassurance.

"But who?" Dagnolo said.

Without thinking, Christensen swept his arm toward the television: "If I had to guess, it was your next governor."

The D.A. crossed his arms in silence as Haygood, the X-rays back in hand, walked toward him and waited.

"You know this?" she said.

It was reckless speculation, he knew, but as far as he was concerned the rules were suspended the moment the kids disappeared. Christensen shook his head, and turned toward Haygood. "It's a guess. But didn't you tell me it's usually the father in cases like this?"

Dagnolo waited.

Christensen left no room for misinterpretation: "I think Ford Underhill killed his son."

The district attorney unfolded his arms, looking first at Haygood, finally at Christensen. A tight smile. "*Prove* it," he hissed.

In that moment, even as Dagnolo's words dangled like a schoolyard challenge, Christensen spun toward the office door. Just before stepping into the corridor, he stopped and looked back. "You pathetic coward."

And then he was running despite the pain in his right foot, across the hall and down the marble steps, across the courthouse lobby and into the street-level catacombs, ignoring Haygood's frantic shouts from far behind as he raged toward the Grant Street exit.

The entire block outside the Grant Hotel looked like a frat party out of control. Throngs of giddy, mostly drunken Democratic faithful celebrated beneath an enormous banner draped across the building's marble façade: "Underhill—A Legacy of Progress!" Most wore Styrofoam boaters. Two halves of a costumed donkey wandered the sidewalk independently, the head dancing on blue-jeaned legs, the woman wearing the back legs and tail sipping white wine from a plastic cup beneath a Grant Street crossing signal.

Christensen shoved past a knot of revelers and into the hotel's revolving brass doors, which were in constant motion as the party moved indoors for Ford Underhill's victory speech. Three of the faithful squeezed in with him, the tiny, triangular space filling immediately with the smell of booze and fizzy optimism. The door jammed briefly but soon revolved into a dense wall of Underhill campaign workers trying to make their way across the marble entrance and down the half-dozen steps on either side that led to the main lobby. Above it all hung a comically ornate chandelier the size of a Volkswagen Beetle.

The muffled voice of a warm-up speaker was talking about integrity and progress and the promise of a renaissance for all of Pennsylvania, not just Pittsburgh. His final, resounding applause line triggered a brass-band rendition of "Happy Days Are Here Again" and a crowd convulsion that might have been a spirited attempt at dancing. Moving across the room was like trying to run underwater, only slower. Christensen felt a hand on his ass, found it attached to a smiling blonde with smeared lipstick. An Underhill campaign button was pinned strategically to her dress just beneath a deep gorge of cleavage.

"This a great country, or what?" she shouted.

He pulled away, threading himself into the gap that suddenly opened between a stalled TV camera crew and an enormous potted palm. Things were a little better on the stairs, with some discernible movement toward the rally below. "Your next governor will be down in a few minutes," began a fresh speaker, a woman, but Christensen lost her next words in the dull roar they triggered.

The speaker tried again but was interrupted by another round of "Happy Days," the band seemingly caught on an endless loop. As soon as Christensen turned the corner into the main lobby, he recognized the speaker's face as that of Allegheny County's lone female county commissioner, a woman who had chaired Ford Underhill's western Pennsylvania campaign. She was hard to miss, her waxy smile and sturdy hairdo dominating the room from the twenty-foot Jumbotron screen just behind the podium where she stood.

A squat mushroom of a man in a blue blazer leaned against a nearby wall, his Grant Hotel Security name tag identifying him as Kurt. Christensen worked his way toward him, leaned as close as he could, and shouted above the din, "Kurt, where's Ford Underhill now?"

"Still upstairs," Kurt shouted back. "Fifteen minutes."

"Which room?"

Kurt studied him. "Who are you?"

"I need to talk to him."

Kurt nodded toward a bank of brass elevator doors, each one blocked by a behemoth with suspicious eyes. The Underhill campaign's private version of the Secret Service. "Good luck," he said.

Christensen felt a hand at the small of his back, a gentle, insistent touch, and turned expecting to find the blonde again. Instead, Carrie Haygood, out of breath and sweating, grabbed his sleeve and said, "Come."

They moved away from the crowd. "He's upstairs!" he shouted.

Haygood led on, down another flight of steps. "Penthouse," she said. She was a foot shorter than most in the crowd, but wider; Christensen found himself at times following little more than a depression in the sea of shoulders and heads, knowing only that Haygood was down there somewhere. They passed a sign at the base of the stairs: Laundry Services.

The crowd thinned and Christensen caught up. "He's upstairs, I said."

"I know."

"Carrie—"

"Just follow."

Past the men's and women's rest rooms. Past the Pittsburgh Room and its mounted collection of historical photographs. The rally was directly above them now, the band still blatting its mindless tune, as they moved deeper into the hotel's basement. Haygood opened an unmarked door and they were met by a wave of damp heat and the smell of powerful detergent. From the dim hallway they burst into a fluorescent room alive with industrial washers and rumbling, tumbling dryers. Haygood led him across a floor piled with mountains of monogrammed hotel towels and bed linens.

"My mother's domain," Haygood said over her shoulder, her voice clear and strong above the roar of machines.

"Thirty-three years down here, never more than $6 an hour. How she managed me and my sister and paid for my medical school—" She shook her head. "I worked here weekends and summers, housekeeping, but still."

"So you know where you're going?"

A look.

"I mean, you must know every inch of this place."

They rounded a corner and Haygood stopped in front of a nondescript elevator door. "Express," she said. "Take us right to the penthouse."

He wanted to hug her. "You're sure they're there?"

"Election nights, they always are." She grinned. "Personally short-sheeted George Wallace there in sixty-seven." Her grin faded fast. "You're sure you want to do this?"

He nodded. Haygood nodded back and poked the elevator call button. The door opened with startling speed.

"There's a long hall," she said. "Main elevators are at the far end. That's where they'll be watching people coming and going. This one opens in a little hallway off to the side, right near the suite. Get off and turn right. Don't stop. You stop, they'll be on you, hustling you out. The penthouse door'll be open, I expect, so you just walk right in like you belong. Understand?"

"Don't stop," he repeated.

Christensen followed Haygood onto the elevator, seeing his stark reflection in the mirror that filled its back wall. His clothes were filthy from the fight in the mountains. Pine needles and small twigs clung to his hair. Somehow, in all that had happened in the last twelve hours, he'd acquired a deep red scratch just beneath his left eye. He looked like a man coming off a nasty bender.

Haygood stabbed the button marked 17 and turned toward him, eyes alive behind her Ben Franklin specs. "Remember now what my momma always said." Waiting until she had his full attention.

"How's that?" he said. For the first time, he noticed the manila envelope in her hands.

Haygood held up the packet of X-rays and photographs as the elevator started to move: "He who hesitates is lost."

43

Brenna swept the flashlight's beam across the top of the brick wall, looking for security cameras. If there was going to be a blind spot anywhere on the Underhills' sprawling Fox Chapel property, she figured, it would be at this low corner of the estate, well off the main road. She'd parked her car maybe two hundred yards from the gate, followed a small stream into a stand of oak trees, and walked until she found the place where the estate's wall ended. To her right, the ground dropped suddenly into the gorge in which Floss Underhill might have died. She turned and scanned the trees behind her, satisfied that the area was unmonitored.

She turned off the light and waited for her eyes to adjust to the darkness. The kids were here. She knew that as surely as she knew they were okay. Not that she hadn't imagined the worst; she had. But after fifteen years dealing daily with the criminal mind, she couldn't make any other scenario fit with the known facts and her mother's intuition. Simply, Taylor and Annie were somewhere behind this wall. She believed that. Or, at the moment, maybe she just needed to believe *something*.

The flashlight rattled against the gun as she shoved it into the pouch of Jim's Pitt sweatshirt. Once over the wall, she'd leave the light off while she looked around. Why advertise her movements to the security creeps watching the monitors?

The lowest spot of the wall was maybe six feet high. She rolled a large rock to the wall's base and stood on top of it, and with one good jump was able to hoist herself over—finally, a practical payoff for all those noontime Centre Club workouts. She dropped through the dark and into the hedge that rimmed the estate's rear gardens, her landing announced by the noisy crackling of branches and her own muttered *"Shit!"* Did the Underhills have dogs? Trying to remember.

The main house and the massive garage loomed just up the hill, silhouetted against a bright three-quarters moon. Only one window on the house's second story was lit, a wan yellow beacon among the dozen or so backside windows in the great gabled roof. From where Brenna stood, downhill and looking up at its wide rear veranda, she couldn't tell if any of the ground-floor rooms were occupied. From the faint glow, she guessed at least some were.

The path was wide and clear, so she followed it into the center of the gardens, her hands groping for cold-steel reassurance in the sweatshirt pouch. To her right, the massive gazebo rose like a state capitol dome in the moonlight—the place where, for her, this nightmare had begun ten days earlier. How had it come to this in so short a time? How could illusions die so quickly?

The dirt path turned to gravel as it approached the house. Stepping carefully, she moved toward the wide stone steps that rose from the garden to the veranda, where she had first heard Ford Underhill's pained version of his mother's difficult slide into Alzheimer's and his father's noble struggle to manage her care. Now that version sounded so contrived. What had happened to her instincts?

The steps were slick with dew. She moved slowly, keeping close to the rough wall, rising into the covered patio area where she'd first met with the Underhills. Through the French doors, downstairs lights defined the empty rooms—the foyer with its hammered-iron chandelier, the massive kitchen with its targeted track lights, a rear living room with its rustic antique lamps. All subtle, but bright enough to expose her if she was careless, because someone was definitely inside. From the scratchy electronic voices and wavering light from a window at the far end of the house, she knew a television was on. And music? She strained to hear. "Happy days are here again . . ."

Brenna moved along the back wall, her right hand on the gun, ducking below other windows as she went and wondering just how this might play in court if something went wrong: The Underhills' former defense attorney caught stalking the family estate with a gun on the night Ford Underhill rose to political prominence. Pittsburgh's own Squeaky Fromme.

The television volume was loud enough that she could hear it through the leaded-glass window that overlooked a less formal living room than the one she just passed. It was more of a den with a casual Western theme, mission furniture and Navajo blankets. Peeking over the window's bottom ledge, through the wavering glass panes, she saw two people with their backs to her. They seemed riveted by the televised election coverage: Floss Underhill, her tiny fist clutching the stem of an empty champagne glass resting on her wheelchair's arm; to her right, a younger woman leaned forward with her elbows on her knees, watching the anointing of Ford Underhill as the Democratic candidate for governor. From time to time, the younger woman rolled a champagne bottle in a silver ice bucket, rubbing its neck between her palms to keep it chilled. Floss said something as she gestured toward the TV, and both she and the other woman laughed out loud.

Nothing about the quiet celebration suggested the perverse scenario she'd seen unfold in the past ten days. It was disorienting because it seemed so normal. She'd come filled with righteous rage, expecting a blackhearted cabal of killers. Or kidnappers. What she'd found was a scene of gentle celebration and camaraderie between an old woman and, apparently, her home-care nurse.

Brenna forced herself away from the window, wondering if there was any way Jim could be wrong. She retraced her path across the back of the house, then retreated down the stone stairs to the garden. Her hands shook, her legs felt weak. She took a deep breath, realized she was crying. Suddenly, the puzzle that had fit together so neatly when she arrived had an extra piece. Where did this scene belong in the picture of corruption, intimidation, and murder that had seemed so plausible just an hour ago? Or was her mind playing tricks, letting that inconsequential snapshot of calm overshadow the truth Jim had fought so hard to uncover? How could something so simple throw her so completely off stride?

Moonlight bathed the garden path to the gazebo, the path she'd walked that day with Alton Staggers to see where Floss tumbled into the ravine. The man's damp face floated into her mind. He'd been here every time she came, hovering around the family like a territorial bird. She knew he monitored the security cameras, but from where? Where was he now? She'd seen him come out the side door of the estate's immense garage once, reading a computer printout as he walked. Maybe the security operation was there.

Brenna moved, pulled toward the garage by the resolve that had brought her. If Taylor and Annie weren't here, she at least wanted to leave knowing she'd looked in all the logical places.

A rustle of shrubbery stopped her as she neared the corner of the house. And voices, indistinct but harried, coming from around the corner, near the garage she still couldn't see. Pressing herself against the back wall of the house, Brenna felt for the gun's grip and hoped whoever it was couldn't hear her ragged breathing.

The elevator door opened almost without a sound into the dim service corridor. It seemed strangely quiet compared to the noise in the hotel lobby, though Christensen heard voices and the crackle of a walkie-talkie somewhere down the hall.

"Go right," Haygood whispered. "Now."

The penthouse door was twenty feet away, open at the end of the floor's main hallway, as Haygood had predicted. The walkie-talkie crackled again at the opposite end, probably near the main elevators. Christensen was running on pure adrenaline now, filled with purpose and anger and a coppery fear he could taste at the back of his throat. Suddenly, they were in, that easy, exposed like startled cockroaches in front of a half-dozen strangers, including the new Democratic nominee for governor. Ford Underhill looked up, unmistakable in his rolled-up shirt-sleeves, as did his father and another man in a dark suit seated with him around an elegant glass conference table littered with three-by-five note cards. Beyond them, scenes of the growing mayhem downstairs filled the screen of a large television. Beyond that, a wall of sliding glass opened onto a roof deck facing the Oliver Building across Underhill Square, seventeen floors below.

A clinking glass to his left diverted Christensen's attention to a perfectly coifed woman he recognized from campaign commercials as the candidate's wife. Leigh Underhill was frozen in midpour at the suite's bar, her mouth open, a bottle of Veuve Clicquot suspended above an empty champagne glass. Beside her stood a beefy, well-dressed man.

Christensen looked back at the conference table, and in that moment, though he didn't see how, the man from the bar covered half the distance to the doorway where he and Haygood stood. The man, dark, a Pacific Islander maybe, had drawn a gun and held it discreetly at his side. He'd use it without a second thought, Christensen was sure, ready to protect his man from what must have seemed like two disheveled and possibly deranged intruders. Christensen stepped in front of Haygood, ready for whatever happened.

"Wait." A familiar voice.

The man with the gun stopped. Ford Underhill stood up, his handsome, oversized head already made up and ready for prime time. A telegenic red tie was knotted just so against his brilliant white shirt, and he wore a relaxed, unflustered smile. "I wouldn't want our guests to get the wrong idea," he said. "Mr. Samala, please."

The man retreated, laid the gun down on the bar without hesitation, and stepped away, obediently clasping his hands behind his broad back, his eyes scanning Christensen's body for signs of a weapon. Underhill stepped into the center of the room.

"What can we do for you, Mr.—" A shrug.

"Christensen. We've never met, but I'm guessing you've met my daughter and Brenna's son."

Brenna's name seemed to connect. Christensen imagined Underhill rewinding his private conversation with Brenna, wondering if his attorney had betrayed him. His smile suddenly was less practiced than forced, the look of a man calculating his next move. Ford turned back toward the table. Vincent Underhill was standing now, anxious, his eyes shifting back and forth between his son and his daughter-in-law.

"Gentlemen, this is actually less unexpected than it might seem," Ford said. He glanced at his wristwatch and turned to the conference table, to the damp older man seated across from his father. The man casually spit an ice cube back into his half-full highball glass. "We're pretty much wrapped up here, Phil. If you'll all excuse us, we'd like a moment alone with these folks. We still have a few minutes before we're scheduled to go downstairs for the speech."

No one moved.

"Really," Underhill said. "It's fine. Mr. Samala, you, too."

The man at the table stood up, his glass still in hand. "You know what you're doing, right, Ford?"

"Phil, please."

The security man moved toward the door, leading an apparently reluctant Phil around Christensen and Haygood. "We'll be right outside, of course," Phil said as they moved through the door.

"Of course. A few minutes is all."

When the door closed, Underhill smiled as if greeting old friends. "I'm sure you understand the security concerns of a campaign like this. Now what can we do for you, Mr. Christensen?"

"Talk. Answer some questions. We've been doing some investigating, and we know what's been going on."

Underhill dropped the pretense and twisted his face into mock surprise. "Now which are you? Frank or Joe Hardy?" He nodded at Haygood. "Nancy Drew?"

Christensen bit his lower lip. He'd never seen raw power on this scale, but he now understood not to underestimate the Underhill family's willingness to use it. "This is Carrie Haygood," he said, "with the county's Child Death Review Team."

Something changed in Ford Underhill's eyes. They narrowed, shifted once to his wife across the room, then back again to Christensen. For the first time Christensen could recall from the dozens of television interviews and speeches where he'd seen Underhill perform, that giant face registered a genuine emotion. If he had to guess, it was a mix of shock and confusion.

"Now I'm afraid you've lost me," Underhill said. "This is about Chip?"

The reaction seemed real, not contrived. Christensen lost himself for a moment, sensing a father's pain despite the circumstances.

"You lost a son, Mr. Underhill, every parent's nightmare. Never mind what happened, I'm sure you felt that loss as deeply as anyone else." The moment had arrived, the confrontation he'd imagined since the truth became clear. "But—" Why was he having so much trouble taking the next step? "We know it wasn't a horseback-riding accident."

Haygood stepped forward and held up the manila envelope. "Autopsy X-rays and photographs," she said. "There are things we know, and things we don't know, sir. What we know now is that somebody shook this child. That's how he died."

"So you were there? When it happened, I mean?"

Haygood patted the envelope. "Didn't have to be, now that we've found these."

Underhill shook his head as he rolled the cuff of one white sleeve down and buttoned it. "I'm afraid the coroner's office disagrees with you on that."

"Simon Bostwick gave them to us," Christensen said. "Right before he died."

Underhill didn't pause as he rolled the other sleeve down, but behind him, Vincent Underhill blanched. "Who?" Ford said.

"Spare us the bullshit," Christensen said.

That got him. Ford Underhill stared him down. "What I'm wondering at this point, Mr. Christensen, is if the bar association might be interested to know about Ms. Kennedy's casual approach to attorney-client privilege.''

"You ass."

Underhill squared his shoulders. "Excuse me?"

"Hide behind that if you want," Christensen said. "What about everything else, though? Your son's not the only victim here. Bostwick's dead. The Chembergos are dead. Maura Pearson's dead. Warren Doti's dead. Now you've got our kids. Where does it stop?"

Underhill glared, clenching and unclenching his fists. Then something registered on his face, a look of revelation tempered by suspicion. Slowly, he turned toward the suite's bar, to the woman who now stood with the gun trained on Christensen and Haygood.

"Leigh?"

Ford Underhill turned back to his famous father, who quietly buried his face in his hands.

"Dad?"

Leigh Underhill moved across the room, the gun held straight out in the two-handed grip of someone who'd had pistol training. Christensen tried to absorb the scene, to shape it into coherent narrative. Suddenly, the truth exploded like a buried mine: It was her.

"I'll take those," she said, pointing the gun at the envelope in Haygood's hands. "Slide them across the floor."

Christensen felt sick. He thought of Simon Bostwick, of what he'd sacrificed for those films. He tried to imagine this whole circumstantial house of cards standing without them, and couldn't. They'd gambled against the most powerful family in the state. As Haygood tossed the envelope onto the carpet toward Leigh Underhill, he knew they'd lost.

"Somebody mind telling me what the *hell* is going on?" Ford demanded. He started toward his wife, stopping short when she pointed the gun at him.

"Just shut up," she said, backing toward the bar again. "Let me think."

Vincent Underhill stood up suddenly, his handsome face still pale. He stepped around the conference table and moved into the space between his son and his daughter-in-law. "Leigh—" he began.

"Shut up. Both of you."

Vincent Underhill held out his hand, asking silently for the gun. "It's over," he said.

"I just need time."

"It's gone too far, Leigh."

"Shut up!" she screamed.

No one moved. Ford Underhill was a picture of dumb-struck impotence. He looked like a man who'd just been hit in the forehead by a two-by-four, standing with his mouth open and his brow furrowed. His father, his hand still extended, looked flash-frozen. The only sign of life was the agitated movement of Leigh Underhill's gun hand as it twitched between her husband, her father-in-law, and the intruders.

Finally, the woman nodded toward the penthouse door. "Lock that," she said to Haygood.

The deadbolt's click was followed by a desperate knock. "Vincent?"

"It's okay, Phil," the former governor said, raising his voice. "A few more minutes, please."

"I don't think so," Ford said suddenly. He moved toward the conference table, reaching for the handset of the hotel phone. "I'm not about to go down there until I get some answers." He started to dial, nodding toward the continuing celebration playing quietly on the penthouse television. "This can wait."

"Get a goddamned clue, Ford," his wife said. "You just keep smiling and go downstairs and do your thing. We'll deal with it, just like always."

Ford hung up the phone, suddenly less cowed than confident. "How the hell *have* you been dealing with it?"

"Listen to you," she said. "Like you could have handled this? Like you could have managed something this complicated? I'm the one who took a fourth-generation heir without an ounce of ambition and pushed you this far, molded you like your father wanted. And now that it's happening, now that we're on our way, you suddenly want to know details?''

Ford Underhill flushed again. He pointed at the TV. "So this is all about you?''

"It's about destiny." She glanced at Vincent Underhill, defiant, then back at her husband. "You've never understood that, Ford. We did. We knew you couldn't handle the pressure."

The moment Vincent Underhill turned away from his son's accusing gaze, Christensen understood. The full story unfolded in body language and gestures that couldn't be faked: Ford Underhill knew nothing of the cover-up, blissfully ignorant of the ruin carried out on his behalf. He was trembling now, facing down the truth of his betrayal.

"Pressure?" Ford said. "After what happened, you're telling me I'm the one who can't handle pressure?''

Leigh Underhill's mouth twisted into a pained smile. "Don't ruin it, Ford.''

"You're the one who shook him like a rag doll that day.''

"Shut up.''

"Shook him until he convulsed, then shook him some more. Then waited so long before telling anybody it was too late.''

"Shut up! I couldn't undo what was done," she screamed. "I couldn't bring him back. But the lie, Ford, the horse story kept the dream alive, spun the whole thing into something forgivable. Tragedy forges character, right? Says so in your campaign brochures. For you, Ford. All for you." She nodded toward the television. "Don't you see? The dream's still alive.''

Ford looked again toward his father. "But whose dream?''

Vincent Underhill cleared his throat. "I—'' He swept

a trembling hand across his mouth and tried again. "Ford, your mother—"

"The weakest link," Leigh Underhill interrupted. "The paintings. They were in the paper, for God's sake."

"She knew the horse wasn't out that day," Christensen said. "So did Warren Doti."

Leigh Underhill glared at him, then shook her head. "She only knew what didn't happen—just enough to blow it. We had to do something." She turned back toward her husband. "It would have been fine except for goddamned Enrique."

If Ford Underhill had any illusions left, he framed them all in a single question. He directed it to his father. "You did this?"

Vincent Underhill opened his mouth, but said nothing. His face crumpled and he sobbed, still unable to look his son in the eye. "No," he said. "But I went along. There was just, oh Jesus, so damned little of her left, so much at stake. I—"

Ford cut him off, his face a mask of horror and disbelief. "Mother?"

"Others, too," Christensen said, bolder now, sensing an ally. "Ask them about the ones who weren't so lucky, Mr. Underhill. People died, people who knew just enough to make them dangerous to this dream they were pushing."

"That's enough," Leigh Underhill said.

"A damned fine art therapist at Harmony, someone your mother loved. The Chembergos, who just wanted to help. They bought the deputy coroner's silence, even had someone purge stories about it from the *Press*'s electronic library, the ones that would have listed details about the actual cause of your son's death. They weren't about to let someone who knew it was all a lie go on living. Then Warren Doti figured it out. Now he's dead."

"Enough!" Leigh Underhill screamed.

"We were figuring it out, too, and they knew that. Ask them about my kids, Mr. Underhill. Ask them where they are. Ask them how many more people have to die to keep their dream alive.''

Ford Underhill directed his full attention to his wife.

''Open your goddamned eyes, Ford,'' she said. ''You think any of this would have stayed quiet with you in public office? With assassins like Dagnolo out there? With jackals like the Channel 2 guy looking everywhere for dirt? We did the work we did because you had a mission, Ford, destined for generations, to fulfill the promise of our family name—''

''*My* family name,'' Ford said, the life suddenly back in his voice.

The woman looked as if she'd been slapped. She pointed the gun at the television, where the camera panned across an undulating sea of red, white, and blue Underhill campaign placards. With her other hand, she stabbed the volume button on the remote control on the bar. A rhythmic chant filled the room: ''We want Ford! We want Ford!''

''You're going to be the state's next governor, and that's just the start,'' she said. ''But you never understood the idea of destiny. Never. But I do. Vincent does. Your name? *Your* name? You think you'd be anything but a shiftless trust-fund baby without me?''

Time stopped, the players frozen as if in tableau. At the center of it all stood a man stripped of all dignity, pathetic and exposed, betrayed by the people he trusted most, his father, his wife. Christensen stifled his instinct to reach out to him, to somehow ease the trauma of revelation. Finally, Ford Underhill turned toward the conference table. He searched once more for his father's eyes, but was denied even that honor. Vincent wouldn't look at him.

Almost casually, Ford lifted his suit jacket from the back of his chair and slid it on. ''I'm going downstairs,'' he said.

Leigh Underhill's shoulders relaxed. She lowered the gun a little, but pointed it again at Christensen and Haygood. A smile, warmer now. "Don't deny our destiny. Seize it, Ford. Let us take care of everything else."

Ford Underhill straightened his tie and started across the room. He swept past Christensen and Haygood in a wave of subtle cologne and hair spray, unlocked the penthouse door, and stepped into the hall. Christensen turned in time to see a covey of aides and security people behind Underhill scramble into action near the elevator doors, about thirty feet away. The one named Samala raised a walkie-talkie. "Penthouse elevator coming down," he said. "Cue the band. Repeat: He's coming down."

Leigh Underhill waved the gun, backing Christensen and Haygood away from the door, then walked across the room and stood sideways in the door's frame. Samala's bronzed jaw dropped. "If they wonder where I am," she said to her husband's back, "just tell them I'm home taking care of your mother. That'll play."

The elevator doors yawned open. Ford Underhill stepped inside, turned around, and pressed a button on the control panel. His face was calm. "I'm going downstairs, Leigh, to decline the nomination."

The first bullet sent Underhill staggering to the back of the elevator, a tiny red bloom on his crisp white shirt just above his belt. As his hands moved toward the pain, the second shot apparently crashed into his groin, crumpling him. Underhill grabbed the elevator handrail, trying to keep his balance, his still-calm eyes fixed on the woman with the gun.

"No!" Vincent Underhill screamed. He started toward the door, frantic, knocking two chairs over as he scrabbled to help his son. Ford Underhill was doubled over, clutching the handrail, but with his head up.

The third bullet found its mark before anyone else could react. Underhill's thick neck snapped back, his head crashing into the elevator's back-panel mirror in a delicate spray of blood. The legs went limp, but his eyes were still open as he dropped to the floor in a shapeless dark-wool pile. Leigh Underhill pivoted with the gun just in time to stop her father-in-law's advance.

"Do you people think this is a *game*?"

She stepped into the room, closed the door behind her, twisted the deadbolt. In the stunned silence, Christensen heard the ancient elevator door rumble shut.

45

They watched it happen, live, along with anyone else tuned to KDKA's televised election coverage. The news anchor's bubbly announcement that the victory speech was about to get underway. Her enthusiasm trailing off into confusion. The producer's decision to cut without warning to a mobile camera as it jostled through a crowd toward a gilded hotel elevator. The gasps as a panicked campaign worker rolled Ford Underhill onto his back and saw the web of blood across his face, those vacant eyes. The stunned silence. The screams.

"Turn it off," Leigh Underhill ordered.

No one moved until Christensen stepped forward. Anything could happen now. The unimaginable already had. Seeing the result of her violence could only complicate the situation. The woman was unstable. She had a gun, locked in a room with the people who had made her face her past, who knew everything. This wasn't over.

He pushed the television's power button, obliterating the scene downstairs, leaving the room in eerie silence. Leigh Underhill was chewing her lower lip, the gun wavering in her right hand, focused on the city-lights view through the sliding doors. Vincent Underhill sat with his face in his hands, elbows on the conference table. The heave of his powerful shoulders gave away his tears.

"They'll be here soon," Christensen said, nodding toward the locked door.

Leigh Underhill nodded. "I know."

He held out his hand, but stayed where he was, nonthreatening, maybe fifteen feet away. "Please give me the gun."

"I'm not done with it."

She lowered it and moved across the carpet toward the glass doors. Carrying the weapon almost casually, the manila envelope clutched to her chest and her back to him and the others, she slid open the center door and stepped outside. Christensen followed, his feet moving on pure instinct.

"I wouldn't," Haygood said.

He stopped at the glass door and looked back. "As long as she's got the gun—"

"Somebody'll be here directly. I wouldn't."

The first knock was gentle, not the battering-ram approach Christensen expected, but Leigh Underhill flinched at the sound. "Police," a voice said. "Open the door." He heard shuffling feet in the hallway outside, imagined a skittish herd of men with their own guns drawn, looking for a killer, unaware of the details. On the deck, Leigh Underhill leaned stiffly against the wall rimming the patio, her gun hand resting like a bird on the waist-high railing, eyes unnervingly even and locked on Christensen.

"We're in here," Haygood called toward the door.

"Okay. How many people?"

"Four."

Christensen couldn't tell if Leigh Underhill could hear. If she did, she wasn't reacting.

"How many guns?" the cop said.

"One."

"Where is it?"

"Outside. There's a porch."

Christensen turned, mouthing a single word to Haygood: "Stall."

She nodded.

"Please open the door," the voice said again.

"We can't do that right now."

"We need you to open the door."

"We need *you* to stay put," Haygood said.

Christensen stepped outside. Leigh Underhill hadn't moved, but the wind at this height had loosened a strand of hair from the French twist at the back of her head. It danced around her face in the evening breeze, the only thing moving as she stared him down. He did not hate easily; it wasn't his nature. It felt odd.

"My children," he said. "Where are they?"

Her answer was a sad smile.

"Please."

"You must know about three-year-olds," she said, clutching the envelope tighter. He nodded, trying not to look at the gun. "They don't care how busy you are, who you're talking to on the phone, how important the work is, the need to get things done. The planets revolve around them. They're at the center of the universe and can't be budged."

"Is that so bad?"

Another smile, but coy, almost seductive. "Sometimes."

"Like the day it happened?"

She didn't flinch. "You're a parent. You've been there, too, I bet, seen the edge and thought you might go over. Too many things to think about. Too much going on. And a three-year-old who won't be denied."

"We've all been there."

She waved the gun toward the penthouse, toward Vincent Underhill. "The rich really aren't so different. We have the same problems as everyone else. We just get less sympathy," she said. "Not that I'm looking for it. Believe me, there was damned little of that after it happened. No excuses. Nothing like that. It happened, is all. It happened.''

"Your son pushed you too far. You reacted."

Leigh Underhill took a deep breath, seemed to savor the breeze. She looked up at the bright moon, ignoring the wail of emergency vehicles seventeen floors below and the dull roar of panic from the crowd spilling into Underhill Square. Somewhere in the distance, a faint but familiar thrum.

"My son had this thing, this purple dinosaur thing. When you pressed its belly, it made this awful sound, this, I don't know, screeching. *SCREEEE!* The kind of sound . . . it drives you nuts. Makes it impossible to think of anything else. Just utterly . . ." She looked up again. "I still hear it sometimes."

"He was making the noise, what, while you were trying to do something, something important?" he prodded.

She shook her head. "That makes it sound so benign. This phone call I was on . . . very important. Critical. A coalition Phil and I had been trying to pull together for months, laying the groundwork for all this."

"The governor's race?"

She nodded. "Ford's parents had gone missing. Lottie was nowhere around. It was just me and Chip with my files spread out over their dining-room table and the biggest soft-money guy in the state on the phone and the goddamned dinosaur screeching over and over even though I'd interrupted the call twice already to ask Chip to stop or take it in another room or just leave me alone for just a few goddamned minutes."

Christensen imagined what happened next, understood the rage that can explode from nowhere at moments of maximum stress. Yes, he'd seen the edge, too, been terrified by the possibilities.

"I reacted, that's all," she said. "I swear, that's all it was, a reaction. As soon as I hung up, I knocked the, the dinosaur thing out of his hands and grabbed his arm to get his attention, to tell him I needed a few minutes. That was all, I swear. But I shook him hard, and just like that he was . . . just—''

Leigh Underhill choked off the words, but with a sigh, not a sob. Christensen felt sick.

"One moment, one mistake, and my son was dying on the dining-room floor and nothing was ever the same again.''

Christensen wanted to say something, but what? "I—" he managed.

"Don't think me a monster," she said.

"But everything else? The cover-up wasn't a mistake.''

She shook her head. "We made a choice, made it that very day. The horse story seemed right to Ford. He *was* part of that; it was his idea, typically brilliant. But the story was so full of holes, somebody had to button it up. Once it was out, though, we had to see it through.''

"We?''

A sharp laugh. "Vincent. Me. The only people who understood the stakes. We knew something like that could derail all the good that might have come from our return to public life.''

"All the damage control, Bostwick, Maura Pearson, the Chembergos, Floss. You're saying Ford never knew about it?''

Leigh Underhill's eyes narrowed. "This was his moment. He knew that, knew without it he'd end up forever as a footnote to his father. So let's just say he didn't ask a lot of questions when things started to unravel. He's used to letting other people handle the details. And we did, Vincent and me. We'd come too far for me to end up as some charity chairwoman pushing the disease-of-the-week to the Chanel-for-lunch crowd. That's not me, not where I was headed.''

"So you just let your husband take the blame and made sure nobody looked too close at the mess you made.''

"He took the blame for an *accident*," she said, looking away. She said something else, but her words faded in the wind.

"Sorry?"

" 'Tolerant, true, tested and ready,' " she said, quoting her husband's campaign slogan. "A man of destiny, yes, but tested? Depth? Texture? Character? No. Not like some one-legged Kennedy kid, or Al Gore with the dead sister. Vincent knows what'll play, and what could be more character-building than suffering through the accidental death of a child? We all agreed it was the best way. But Ford wasn't even at the house when it happened."

"Vincent was?"

"Out in the stables with Floss. He found us twenty minutes later, me half out of my mind, Chip all blue and not breathing."

"They were with the horse. Doti, too. So Floss knew—"

"—the horse wasn't out. But she was starting to slip then."

"She knew something was wrong," Christensen said.

The woman's eyes narrowed. She was still thinking, shading the story, protecting herself. "How much else she put together after that, I don't know. You never know with her. But she was still outside when Vincent found us. By then I was so frantic . . . not thinking at all. And Vincent's saying, 'The future is what matters, Leigh. There's nothing we can do for Chip now.' "

"Wait," Christensen said, a reaction. "Before, you said your son was 'dying.' "

She looked away, ignored the comment, and he knew she was lying less to him than to herself. All his questions were answered except one, and he knew she wasn't going to help him find the kids. Now they stood outside a door into the darkest chamber of her soul, a door he doubted even she had opened. Should he force it and make her confront the truth, hoping to break her down and get the gun? Or should he back off, knowing the confrontation could destroy her? Did he care?

Christensen stepped forward; she stepped back. "Who called for help?"

Leigh Underhill pressed herself against the railing. She nodded through the glass doors, toward Vincent Underhill.

"I begged him."

"You were alone in the house with a telephone. Why didn't you?"

"I did. There's a tape of the call."

"How long after it happened?"

"It was too late."

Christensen zeroed in, wondering how far he could push her. "Chip was still alive, wasn't he? You waited until you and Vincent got the story straight."

"No."

"Maybe he wasn't breathing, maybe he *was* beyond help, but your son was still alive on that dining-room floor. You knew it. How long did you wait?"

The woman lifted the gun, aimed it at his chest. She was trembling now, her hand unsteady, her eyes those of a trapped animal. The thrum was louder now, more distinct, the unmistakable chop of a helicopter. "I said it was too late!" she cried. "He wasn't breathing."

"But he wasn't dead."

"We needed time to think!"

"You needed time to come up with a story."

"You're wrong!"

"If paramedics had saved him, he might have told somebody what happened. How long did you wait?"

His words hit their mark. She turned her back, her defenses ruined, dropping the manila envelope at her feet. The gun clanged on the metal railing as she gripped it with desperate force.

"What was done was done!" Screaming now over the noise of the police helicopter hovering several hundred feet above them, Leigh Underhill stretched her arms wide, as if embracing the city and the night, then turned back toward him. The downdraft was as powerful as falling water, a baptism, and she strained to make herself heard.

"There's no changing the past! But the future, the future we can change! It does matter!"

The helicopter's spotlight blinked on, washing her in its harsh, obscene light just as she raised the gun to her temple. She smiled a smile he knew would haunt him.

"*Did* matter," she shouted.

Christensen saw her tense, but turned his head. The pop was immediate, sharp, definite. He steeled himself for another unthinkable scene, but when he looked back, Leigh Underhill was gone.

46

She'd never held a gun anywhere but the pistol range where she'd learned to shoot. The emphasis there had been on safety.

Brenna focused on her breathing, trying to calm herself, listening to the agitated voices coming from just around the corner of the house. Something snapped, a branch maybe? She tried to remember what was there, knew only that Alton Staggers kept an apartment above the Underhill estate's garage.

Think. Her advantage was surprise, assuming Staggers hadn't been watching her the whole time on the security monitors. Then again, maybe he was out looking for her. When her breathing was steady and the blood roaring in her ears had slowed, she closed her eyes and listened for clues.

"Tommy's a boy." A familiar voice.

"So."

"So, I'm Tommy. You have to be the pink ranger."

"No way."

"Way."

Brenna lowered the gun and edged toward the corner

of the house, stunned. She leaned forward and peeked just to make sure she was right.

Taylor was maybe forty feet away, snared in a bush just below one of the garage's second-story windows. Even in the dark, even as he thrashed to free himself from the tangled branches, Brenna recognized the hooded white sweatshirt her son had worn to school that morning. Annie was about ten feet above him, inching down a knotted rope of bedclothes, curtains, towels, and blue jeans, hissing: "Could you make any *more* noise?"

Brenna stepped around the corner into plain view. "Guys!" she said.

Annie dropped to the ground and fell backward, but stood immediately in a rough approximation of an *Action Rangers* karate stance, panting and ready for action. She squinted and finally focused on Brenna, who raised a finger to her lips and waved them over, realizing too late the gun was still in her hand. Annie's smile lit up the night as she pulled Taylor from the bush.

Her son ran into her arms, crying, with Annie close behind. Brenna hugged them both against the corner of the house, held them until Annie pulled away.

"Can I hold the gun?" she asked.

Brenna shoved it into her sweatshirt pouch. "You're both okay?" she whispered.

They nodded. "Mr. Robbins said he'd take us home, but he brought us here," Annie said. "Then he said he'd be right back, but he never came. And he locked us in."

"So you were up there the whole time?"

"Plus, he wears too much cologne or something. Gag."

Taylor wiped his eyes. "But he's got really cool stuff in his car. He showed us."

Brenna looked back at the garage, at the makeshift rope. "That was a really great idea."

Annie shrugged, rolled her eyes. "Indian Princesses? My fire-safety badge? Like, duh."

Brenna hugged them again. Then she said, "Let's go." They moved quietly through the gardens, away from the house and toward the low corner of the walled property where she'd first come in. She looked back just as the pale glow from the rear den disappeared. Somebody inside had turned off the TV.

Fox Chapel's hills turned a deep green this time of year. The sun seldom broke through the canopy of branches, leaving bridle trails, lawns, and roads perpetually damp. Everything seemed to hang in precarious balance between renewal and rot.

Through the Explorer's open window, Christensen could smell both. He steered along Fox Chapel Road, straining to hear the dialogue between Annie and Taylor in the backseat, enjoying the tortured logic of their discussion about earthworms. They'd watched a documentary about composting last night, alternately fascinated and horrified, and by this morning had decided there was big money in worm farming. The ecological advantages of composting were lost already. They were far more interesting in opening Shadyside's only live-bait shop.

"You're not talking," Brenna said.

"I'm listening."

"You're avoiding."

"Think you could be happy filling bait cups? They'll only be open after school."

She rolled her eyes and turned away, watching the passing landscape. Developers were turning Fox Chapel's peripheral property into just another bedroom community with a high-status mailing address. The grand estates remained, scattered and isolated, but each construction season brought more backhoes, more foundations, more custom homes. Fake Tudor country manors and suspiciously ancient Tuscan villas were sprouting like mushrooms.

"Good God, look at that one," he tried. "Are skylights and a basketball court pretty standard in a French Provincial?"

Brenna ignored him. She was right. He wasn't talking to her, at least not about anything important. An old habit, one he was trying to break, but it was too soon, too raw, too scary. Combining their families had been a new beginning for both of them, and neither had taken that step casually. For five years he'd seen her through a lover's eyes, accepting her career and ambition as a strength rather than a weakness. Now, he wasn't sure. The defense attorney plays a critical role in the justice system; he understood and appreciated that. But he understood, too, that defense attorneys can choose who they will and will not defend. As the Underhill nightmare unfolded, Brenna had made selfish choices, choices that might have come at an unthinkable price.

"Bren?"

"Hmm?" Still looking out the window.

"I just need time to sort it out, that's all."

"I know."

She was angry at herself; she'd said as much. For letting flattery blind her. For overlooking the Underhills' calculation in hiring a well-known caregiver advocate as their defense attorney. For not anticipating that they might use her own child at the end.

"Staggers is talking," she said suddenly. "Or so I've heard."

"About?"

"Leigh Underhill, mostly. He's copped to the cover-up

killings—Maura, Bostwick, and the Chembergos—and to shoving Floss over the rail. Not much else he could do once the cops found his skin under her fingernails and that scratch on his forearm. But he's saying Leigh pulled all the strings.''

"Convenient."

"Not unusual, though. Whenever these guys talk, surprise! The mastermind is usually a corpse.''

Christensen flashed on a scene, looking down from seventeen stories up onto the patterned concrete walkways and spotlit fountains of Underhill Square. Leigh Underhill had landed on the overhanging roof of the hotel's rear entrance. The helicopter's beam had tracked her all the way down. *Real TV* was having a field day with it.

"And Vincent?" he said.

"Good old Staggers." Brenna shook her head. "Loyal to the end. Vincent didn't know a thing.''

"Think he'll get away with that?"

She shrugged, still not looking at him. "Maybe. It's the O. J. problem: How could someone so famous and likable do such a thing? Not sure jurors would ever buy the former governor consenting to a hit on his wife.''

"They'd need to understand Alzheimer's," he said, "how little of a person it can leave behind.''

He eased the Explorer onto Silver Spur Road, crossing an old stone bridge, looking for an address.

"What about Raskin?"

"No idea. They're working it to see how much he knew. I'm guessing a lot. He and Leigh are charter members of the Machiavelli Fan Club.'' She waved him on. "About a half-mile, straight. When you see the stone pillars and a gate on the right, pull in. Know what else Staggers is saying?'' She turned and cocked her head toward the backseat, where the debate had moved on to the miracles of an earthworm's digestive tract. "Taking them was totally his idea.''

"Staggers?"

"Strange guy."

"You get that with psychopaths."

"I mean, he told the cops this long story about this seminar he's been taking. Effective Decision-Making, or something. To help develop leadership skills. He had this assignment: Identify a problem, find a solution, and take the initiative."

Christensen took his foot off the gas, wincing at the twinge in his damaged ligaments. The car slowed. This was bizarre. "So taking the kids—"

She nodded. "Just a guy trying to show a little initiative at work. Cops don't think he had time to even tell anybody. Just dropped them out here and headed off to find Bostwick in the mountains."

Christensen rewound the scene in the penthouse, recalling the blank looks he got from the Underhills each time he asked about the kids. "I think I believe him," he said.

"Here." Brenna pointed to a short drive leading to an enormous iron gate. Beyond it, a driveway curved up and into a property that seemed obsessively private. "Roll down your window and wait."

"How will they know we're here?"

"They'll know." Brenna pointed out the cameras on top of the pillars, in the trees.

They waited. Thirty seconds. A minute.

"When Mr. Robbins brought us here the gate just opened," Annie said.

"He let me push the button," Taylor said.

"No."

"Uh-huh."

"Did not."

"Did too."

"There's a call button over there on that pillar," Christensen said. "I don't think anybody's watching." He stepped out, crossed in front of the Explorer and pressed the glowing red button. An amplified voice burst through the speaker.

"Who's calling?" A woman. One of Floss's aides, he guessed.

"Is this Paige?"

"Hi. Who's this?"

"Jim Christensen. We brought something for Mrs. Underhill."

Long silence. What were the chances she remembered meeting him at Harmony, or his name? Or would she recognize his name from Myron Levin's overwrought, overhyped Channel 2 news exclusives of the past three days?

"I suppose we could leave it at the gate, if you'd prefer. But I was hoping—"

Without a sound, the gate began to move. He climbed back into the driver's seat as it yawned open. "Not sure what this means," he said, "but here we go."

He felt as if he were moving into the pages of a shelter magazine. The driveway wound through a copse of trees, over a wooden bridge, through an expanse of carefully cultivated meadow. Just past that, at the edge of a commanding view of forever, the house. He parked in the empty spot near the garage. His was the only car in sight.

"You guys climbed out of there?" he said, pointing to one of the garage's second-story windows.

"Easy," Annie said.

"My idea," Taylor said.

"Was not."

"Was too."

"Guys," Christensen said, turning around, "that was very brave. You used your imaginations. Very cool."

"We're really proud of you," Brenna added.

Both kids beamed. "My idea," Taylor said.

"My knots."

"I helped."

Christensen cut off the debate with a wave of his hand. "Wait here."

He stepped out and opened the Explorer's rear gate. From inside, he grabbed the handle of the aluminum case they'd bought that morning and pulled it out. Brenna joined him, and the house's front door opened just as they closed the tailgate. Twenty yards away, Paige wheeled Floss's chair onto the stone landing. In the old woman's good arm, a cigar the size of a baby's arm.

"Thanks for letting us come up," Christensen said.

Paige shrugged. "It's just us now, except for the lawyers and the relief nurse who does nights. Don't tell anybody I let you in, okay?"

"Why did you?" Christensen asked.

The nurse nodded toward Floss.

"You're the man from Harmony," the old woman said suddenly, tapping an inch of ash from the tip of her stogie. It fell onto the flagstones. "I remember you."

The nicotine was working its strange magic on Floss Underhill's faulty synapses, but he knew it was temporary. Hope, even false hope, wasn't a luxury that Alzheimer's allowed for long. He bent down so they were face-to-face. "Hell of a cigar you've got there, Mrs. Underhill."

"Havana," she said, and took a long puff. The three of them watched her savor it until the silence grew awkward.

"We brought you this," Christensen said, setting the case in her lap. Floss stared at it, at the heavy buckles that kept it shut. She'd need both hands to open it, and neither one was available. "May I?" he asked.

She nodded.

The buckles snapped open, but he left the top closed, stepped back and took Brenna's hand. She squeezed. After a confused glance, Floss stuck the cigar between her teeth and lifted the case's top with her uninjured hand. Tubes of watercolor paint lay in neat rows, arranged by color in shades stretching from one end of the spectrum to the other. In the front compartment, a dozen new brushes of varying lengths and widths lay crosshatched and ready. A sketch pad fit neatly into the underside of the lid.

Floss scanned it all, her eyes growing wide, then scanned the watercolor set again. Suddenly that face, normally so unreadable, transformed. The old woman snatched the Cuban from her mouth and flat-out grinned.